HER OUTCAST SCOT

THE HIGHLAND WARRIOR CHRONICLES

CHRISTINA PHILLIPS

PHOENIX 18 PUBLISHING

Edited by Amanda Ashby
Cover Art by Kim Killion Publishing
12/2023

ISBN: 978-0-6456305-6-5

For the offspring,
Who grew up when I wasn't looking.
Victoria, Charlotte & Oliver
This one's for you.
With all my love

CHAPTER ONE

THE KINGDOM OF FIB, PICTLAND. LATE SPRING, 844

Orabel, Princess Annag of Fib, glanced at the young noblewomen who dutifully gathered behind the waist-high stone wall that surrounded the forbidden section of her cherished garden. The five girls, aged between eleven and fourteen, wore expressions of earnest concentration, and were doubtless intrigued by the deadly selection of plants that flourished there, but she wasn't fooled.

The hours they spent with her were nothing more to them than another necessary facet of their education. They saw only how a plant might be used in everyday life or in an emergency, and Orabel knew imparting that knowledge was all that was required of her.

But it wasn't enough. Tenderly, she glided her fingers in the air above the large palm shaped leaves of the powerful wolfsbane, that she had painstakingly grown from seeds bartered from a merchant, when she had been little more than a child.

A faint tingling sensation, so familiar to her, warmed her blood, as the potent magic within the herb interflowed with her senses. It was wrong of her to wish that at least one of her charges might share her awe when it came to the power that nestled within every blade of grass, for it wasn't their fault.

No matter how diligent the young women were, none of them were blessed by the sacred breath of the great goddess, Bride. Orabel could ensure they became esteemed healers, proficient in using plants that were not generally grown in every stronghold's medicinal garden, but she couldn't teach them something that was a part of the very fabric of her being.

"My lady."

She tore her ruminating thoughts back to the present and glanced at her friend, who had clearly just received a message from a servant who stood nearby.

"Yes, Saoirse?"

"The queen requests the princess' presence in her sanctum."

Orabel's cocoon of peace shattered, and she left the protected garden through its sturdy gate, before inhaling a calming breath. Not that it worked. Her sister, whose husband had ascended to the throne of Fib upon their father's murder a year ago, always had this effect on her.

She wasn't going to think of their father's brutal betrayal. It did no good and there was nothing she could do about it, yet the ache in her heart burned for vengeance.

But if, goddess willing, vengeance came, it would not be by her hand. She knew what Bride demanded from her, and it was not to meddle in the politics of mere men.

She had walked that path once. Against her will, perhaps, but nevertheless, the outcome would haunt her for all time.

A shiver skated along her arms as memories of her late husband clawed through the barriers in her mind. She and Edwin, Prince of Ayr, had wed to appease their kings and strengthen their forces against the barbarous Scots. But their marriage had been disastrous and the alliance between Fib and Northumbria scarcely worth the blood spilled onto the contract of their union.

She and Saoirse made their way along the path that wound through the herb garden, the young ladies following at a respectful distance. The sun was low in the sky and the aromatic scent of rosemary and lavender drifted on the breeze, easing her anxiety at her sister's summons.

There was no cause for worry, even if most of the time Etain preferred to ignore her existence.

"Perhaps the queen wishes to ask your advice on delicate matters." Saoirse gave her sideways glance. It was clear her friend thought the idea as unlikely as she did herself. Etain had her own healer Aisling, whom she kept close, and had yet to ask Orabel's advice on anything, let alone something as momentous as her current, longed-for pregnancy.

"It's possible," she conceded. "But only if Aisling has passed through the veil."

"Which I doubt has transpired. I'm certain that wise one will live until she has witnessed one hundred winters."

"I believe you're right. But that reminds me. We should call upon Lady Daracha in a day or two. I wish to ensure all is well with her."

Saoirse inclined her head. "I shall ensure a messenger is sent to inform Lady Daracha of our arrival."

Although by Orabel's calculations the child wasn't due for another five weeks, during the last few years Daracha had endured the loss of seven babes. She and Daracha had been close childhood friends, and the messengers informing her of the sad news, while she'd been trapped in Northumbria, had deeply grieved her.

Daracha's current pregnancy was the first one Orabel had been in Fib to oversee. She was dedicated to ensuring that, this time, the young woman's dearest wish of a happy delivery would come true.

They entered the palace and Orabel stifled a sigh as Saoirse fussed over her, straightening her gown, and smoothing her hair.

"There." Saoirse stood back and frowned as she scrutinized her handiwork. "Now you're presentable."

Orabel flashed her a mocking smile as they made their way across the great hall. She lowered her voice so the young noblewomen couldn't hear her reply to her dearest friend. "The day our queen finds me presentable will be one of great astonishment, and I may not survive the honor."

A warrior who stood guard outside the queen's private chambers bowed his head before opening the door. The young noblewomen remained in the chamber and she and Saoirse continued into the inner sanctum and closed the door behind them.

Etain sat behind the great desk, flanked by four of her ladies, and a pang shot through Orabel as a memory of her father in this very same chamber flashed through her mind. She quashed the recollection before it consumed her and dropped a respectful curtsey. "My lady Etain."

Etain ran a critical eye over her but thankfully it seemed Saoirse's ministrations met her sister's approval. "Orabel." She glanced at Saoirse. "My lady."

The dowager queen, her mamma, came forward and took her hand.

"Come," her mamma said, and led them to the chairs before the desk and they sat, her mamma's ladies and Saoirse standing behind them. "We are eager to hear your news, Etain." There was the slightest tinge of frost in her mamma's tone. Clearly, she had as little clue as Orabel as to why they had been summoned.

Etain brushed her fingers over her belly, a protective gesture and Orabel reined in her impatience at her sister's need to always ensure her elevated status was recognized. Etain's son was now seven years old, but she had not yet been blessed with a second child. Instead, the goddess had taken three babes to her realm long before they had been strong enough to draw their first breath.

The grief clung to her sister like a dark shroud. Perhaps, if her babes had lived, she would not have turned her back on Bride, nor encouraged their people to embrace the new religion that crept with insidious intent across the land.

An uneasy whisper slithered through the shadows of her mind. Perhaps those terrible losses were Bride's price, for Etain's loss of faith.

But she didn't want to think that. And even if it were true, surely the goddess would not claim this babe, too, when it had survived so much longer than the previous three?

Guilt ate through her. She had been happy for Etain's news, of course, but she should have done more. She would beseech Bride this very night to protect her sister for the next four moons. Indeed, it was—

"Prince Raedwulf of Northumbria wishes to offer an alliance with the royal house of Fib," Etain said.

Her contrite thoughts collided inside her mind, splintered, and turned to ash as her heart thudded painfully against her chest. Surely Etain was not suggesting… she could not possibly mean…

"An alliance?" Their mamma's voice was cool. "What does this minor prince of Northumbria possess that could possibly entice our royal house into such an alliance against his king, Aethelred?"

Etain's smile didn't reach her eyes. "How dramatic you are, Mamma. The alliance would not be against the king of Northumbria. We must protect our borders any way we can, and Raedwulf extended a hand of friendship."

She could not contain herself. "Raedwulf cannot be trusted, Etain. If he's approached Fib for an alliance without the knowledge of his king, then his motives are most suspect."

Etain gave a tight smile. "I know you did not think highly of him during your marriage to his cousin, but he has been most flattering about you, sister."

Her stomach churned with distaste. And something more.

Fear.

She gripped her fingers together on her lap and strived for calm. How could she have been so unaware of these plans brewing under her very nose? "How long have you been in correspondence with the prince?"

"We haven't been in correspondence at all." A touch of irritation heated Etain's voice, and Orabel released a relieved breath. She hadn't been unforgivably oblivious to political machinations unfolding within the royal court. "His messenger arrived only this day and waits for our response."

All was not yet lost, then. Before she could respond, her mamma intervened.

"What manner of alliance is he proposing?"

Etain gave an impatient sigh. "What other alliance could he offer but marriage to Orabel, of course."

"Which we cannot accept." The words burst from her, untactful, but she couldn't help herself as the horrifying vision of a lifetime shackled to the Northumbrian warlord seared her senses.

Marriage to Edwin had been hard but at least he hadn't been an attentive husband in the bedchamber once the novelty of a new bride had worn off.

Raedwulf was a different matter entirely. Fifteen years younger than his cousin, he had never tried to hide his interest in possessing her and her refusal to entertain a clandestine affair had merely inflamed his determination. A determination that had only magnified during the final year of her marriage after his sweet, utterly submissive wife had died in childbirth.

But it had never occurred to her that he would continue his obsession once she left Northumbria. "Etain, you can't entertain this notion. I beg you."

Etain flattened her hands on the desk and drew in a deep breath. "You are a princess of Fib, Orabel. It's your duty to do everything within your power to protect our interests."

The accusation stung. "I put Fib and our people before all else when I wed Edwin. But you know my true calling is to dedicate my life to the great goddess."

"Oh, please." Etain did not quite roll her eyes, since she considered such behavior beneath her, but her intent was plain. "Do not call upon the memories of ancient myths to excuse your reluctance to undertake the obligations of your bloodline. In truth, it is remarkable Raedwulf should want you for wife, since your first marriage produced no heir."

Orabel sucked in a shocked breath at her sister's words. It was one thing to quietly encourage the worship of a new god. But to slander the ancient ones was not only foolish.

It was dangerous.

"Etain." The dowager queen didn't raise her voice, but the power she had once wielded in the land throbbed in her voice. "One should refrain from casting such shadows. The lack most likely rests with Prince Edwin."

Her mother briefly clasped her hand, and heat burned Orabel's cheeks. She had taken issue with Etain's slight against the goddess, and completely missed the jibe arrowed at her fertility—or, rather, lack of.

It was best to remain silent. For although it was a woman's own business as to whether she wished to fall pregnant or not, it was certainly assumed a new bride embarking upon a political alliance would do her best to produce an offspring to seal the deal in blood.

Not do everything within her power to prevent it. It was not as though Edwin lacked heirs. His three children from two previous marriages were almost full grown before she had wed their father. Even so, she was thankful only Saoirse was aware of her subterfuge that had prevented any pregnancy, and her friend would never break her confidence.

"It's true the fault may have lain with Edwin," Etain conceded. "But we know that is not the way the men of Northumbria think.

And besides, he had already proved his virility before accepting Orabel's hand."

"A man's virility may be impaired by many things. Prince Edwin was not, after all, a young man when Orabel wed him."

Good goddess, the last thing she wished to talk about was the state of her marriage or the performance of her late husband. Especially with her mother.

Especially when she knew the truth of the matter.

"This discussion is irrelevant. I refuse to wed Raedwulf. He treated his first wife most cruelly."

She had tried to befriend the timid young girl, but Raedwulf had kept her virtually imprisoned in his stronghold, determined to breed many sons with her despite the frailty of her constitution.

With an effort, she unclenched her fists. Raedwulf's unfettered lust had killed his wife as surely as if he had plunged a dagger through her womb. Nothing would convince her otherwise.

And nothing would convince her to wed such a creature.

"That is a poor recommendation for any man." Her mother sniffed her disapproval. "However, with your royal lineage and connections such a fate would never be yours."

Her mouth dried as the possible implication of her mamma's words settled like a stone in her chest. Surely her mother, unlike her sister, was not contemplating sacrificing her to yet another barbarous Northumbrian? Especially when eight years ago she had been tacitly against the alliance with Edwin. "Indeed, you are correct," she said, hoping her voice didn't betray her rising panic. "I shall never marry again."

I should never have married at all.

Silence fell across the chamber. Was it her imagination that the air seemed heavy with menace?

Perhaps. But she did not imagine the glance Etain shared with their mother, not the unspoken message that passed between them.

"You may not have a choice, Orabel." For the first time, reluctance threaded through her sister's voice. "Would you rather an alliance with the Northumbrians, whose ways we at least have some understanding of, or a coerced union with a favorite of MacAlpin?"

The breath lodged in her throat as Etain's words thundered through her mind. Was her sister *threatening* her?

"You would consider an alliance with the *Scots?*" She could scarcely push the words out and surged to her feet as agitation gnawed deep into her breast. "After the way they betrayed and murdered our father scarcely more than a year ago?"

Etain kept her gaze focused on the desk. "I'm only considering the political winds that have shaped Pictland this last year. Surely even you are aware of the upstart's strategy."

It was a rebuke, but it was unfair. Of course she knew how MacAlpin was ensnaring the princesses of Pictland since he had brutally annexed the High Kingdom of Fortriu for his own.

After he had callously murdered any royal born Pict who had a legitimate claim to the throne and might have contested his presumptuous assertion.

Including her beloved father.

Except, foolishly, until this moment, she hadn't considered she might also fall beneath the Dal Riadan king's rapacious eye.

She had the mortifying urge to collapse back onto the chair, but that would only prove to Etain that her veiled accusation of Orabel's grasp on the political upheavals blighting Pictland were correct. She stiffened her spine and hoped to goddess her alarm didn't show on her face. And not for the first time, voiced something that had been close to her heart since she was a girl of ten.

"Our ancestors had holy enclaves where the chosen ones of the ancients could follow their calling, without being subject to the whims of kings." Curses, that was the wrong thing to say now, even though her feelings on the matter were scarcely news to anyone in her family. For although Etain's husband was the King of Fib, in every way that mattered it was her sister who ruled the land of their birth. She hastened to correct her error. "I merely feel a spiritual sanctuary, outside of the political sphere, can only be of benefit to all."

"It was a different time, daughter." Her mother sounded wistful. "The great goddess turned her eye from her faithful for so long, many of the old ways were abandoned. It is, after all, only this generation that has seen her once again bless a favored few."

"Be that as it may." Impatience threaded Etain's voice. "It's clear the new religion from Rome gains momentum. Do you truly believe, Orabel, that the Scots would honor what they would see only as a pagan sanctuary? Because I do not."

In truth, she agreed with her sister. The Scots were uncivilized savages, on a par with the Viking devils. But equally, and personally, she knew the Northumbrians, and their ambition to regain the lands they had lost to the Picts one hundred and sixty years ago burned deep within their souls.

There was little to chose between any of their enemies but it was the Scots who had extended the hand of friendship, and then unforgivably assassinated her father.

She exhaled a shaky breath. She could not wed Raedwulf. But what if MacAlpin set his sights on her? Would marriage to the southern warlord be a preferable fate to a duplicitous Scots warrior?

No. Her destiny was to dedicate her life to Bride, using the goddess' blessed touch to heal her people when they were in need. The visions of her future had remained unchanged since she was a child.

Her marriage to Edwin had been a wretched aberration and the mighty goddess had not allowed her to forget it. Not even the desired peace between their lands had come to fruition. Which only reinforced her conviction that her path lay in a different direction to that of her two sisters, both of whom had wed advantageously for Fib, and her unfortunate cousins who had been ensnared within MacAlpin's web.

"It grieves me that you cannot follow your calling, Orabel." Her mamma sighed and briefly closed her eyes. "I always hoped one day you could dedicate your life to the goddess. But alas, your sister speaks the truth. I fear MacAlpin will do all in his power to encroach into Fib through an alliance with you, and I cannot imagine a worse fate."

Etain shot their mother a frosty glare before returning her attention to Orabel. "You understand our dilemma. We cannot afford to offend the Northumbrian and reject his request to pay his respects in person. We shall invite him, and you must look to your conscience for guidance in this matter."

Perhaps the barb was unintentional, but Orabel doubted it. Etain knew she lived her life according to her goddess' wishes, which had little, if anything, to do with her conscience. But this time she held her tongue, for she couldn't trust she would not say something that resulted in Etain issuing a royal command to obey.

The way her father had, eight years ago, when she'd recoiled at the prospect of tying the knot with Edwin.

But inside, injustice burned. Etain might no longer believe in the old ways, but Orabel knew the truth. The power of the ancients flowed through her blood, Bride herself honored her with sacred insights, and despite how Pictland was plagued on all sides by her enemies, she knew, ultimately, her people would prevail.

She was not an eighteen-year-old maid anymore. If Etain issued an ultimatum, she would rather be banished from the palace than obey an order to be given to another barbarous warlord. A foolish pang burned through her chest at the thought of, once again, abandoning her beloved garden but if that was the path her goddess chose for her, all would be well.

She trusted Bride. And as soon as her sister ended this torturous confrontation, she would offer sacrifice at the hallowed standing stones, and beg for guidance. Even during the most terrible times in Ayr, when she had feared her goddess might forsake her, Bride had always bestowed her benevolence in the bright light of day.

The safety of Fib was paramount. But it would come from the blessing of the ancient ones, not a bloodied union crafted by man.

CHAPTER TWO

THE KINGDOM OF DAL RIADA

oss MacIntosh strode from the great hall of his family's stronghold, Dunmor, into the courtyard, where a contingent of warriors from the king, MacAlpin, were dismounting. He nodded in acknowledgement as his childhood friend, Rourke MacConall, marched his way, his usual scowl firmly in place.

"How goes it?" Rourke briefly gripped Ross' shoulder, before handing the reins of his horse to a stable lad.

"Well enough." Understatement of the year. It had been three weeks since his older brother's accident. Three weeks since his life had irrevocably turned inside out.

Rourke grunted, as if he could read Ross' mind. "Aye. I know you were never close to your brother, but it must still be a shock." His gaze roved over the stronghold and Ross clenched his jaw. "Dunmor is yours now, whether you like it or not."

Dunmor would never be his but that was something he couldn't share even with Rourke. Just another secret he kept locked inside, along with all the other sordid secrets he'd hidden all his life.

From the corner of his eye, he saw MacAllister, the king's

right-hand man, strolling his way. God damn it. He knew this wasn't a social visit but the presence of MacAllister could mean only one thing. MacAlpin had another scheme in play.

"Condolences on the untimely loss of your brother," MacAllister said. "I trust your lady mother is bearing up."

"As well as can be expected under the circumstances." It was all the information MacAllister would get from him concerning his mother. Ross sometimes feared his lady mother didn't understand what had happened to Gordon, for she had yet to mourn his loss.

But then, she understood so little these days.

Brutally, he shoved the thought to the back of his mind. It did no good to dwell on things that couldn't be changed. And even though it was good advice, offered to him from more than one source over the years, it didn't help ease the pain.

Or the guilt.

But now his brother was gone, there was one thing he could do. Ensure his mother's remaining years were filled with every comfort he could provide.

"Yet our king sees no reason why that should prevent you from embarking on yet another diplomatic quest." Rourke's tone was dry with undercurrents of contempt, and MacAllister shot his son a dark glare before returning his attention to Ross.

"Word has reached us that the Kingdom of Fib may be looking across their southern border at an alliance with the Northumbrians. Naturally, we need to confirm this is nothing more than a distasteful rumor."

Ross frowned. "An alliance with Northumbria would leave Fib in a precarious situation with Dal Riada. And why would they risk alienating the rest of Pictland?"

"Indeed," MacAllister said. "Yet for all its small size, Fib's strategic position has long given their kings a strong political hand. We cannot allow a treaty between Fib and the southern barbarians to occur."

"What are our orders, should we discover such a treaty in place?" Rourke exchanged a glance with Ross. The same thought had crossed his mind.

"To eliminate the threat, by any means possible." MacAllister returned his attention to Ross. "We leave at first light. The king personally requests you lead the contingent to Fib-eviot to pay respects to the royal house, and officially deliver an invitation to attend the coronation in Fortriu and assure them of Dal Riada's continued support."

That wouldn't go well, considering the bloodied outcome of the last official invitation MacAlpin had extended to the kings of Pictland. He'd be lucky if the Fib king didn't have him thrown from the great hall for such impertinence.

But it wasn't as if he was being given a choice. Besides, there was something else of interest in MacAllister's comment. "You are not accompanying us?"

MacAllister smiled but, as usual, it didn't reach his eyes. "I shall accompany you as far as the stronghold of Lord Finn and the Princess of Fortriu. There are matters to discuss regarding the king's coronation. You will continue onwards with the men. Be certain to assure the Fib king of Dal Riada's continued support."

Ross gave a brusque nod but held his tongue. It had been some time since he'd led his men. MacAllister outranked him, and the older man had been an unwelcome fixture commanding Ross' contingent during the last year.

"I shall ensure a chamber is made ready for you."

"There's no need to disrupt your household, MacIntosh. We should not wish to distress the ladies. The men and I will make camp."

With that, he marched back to the men, and Rourke gave a disgruntled snort. "Is there an unwed princess of Fib our esteemed king wishes to ensnare? You'd best beware, Ross. I'd wager MacAlpin's set his sights on you to capture her, if so."

"I don't possess royal blood." His voice was grim. For surely, if he did, the events of the past year would have revealed such a sordid truth. "I'm certain no princess of Pictland would be coerced to wed the likes of me."

"Don't be so sure." Rourke eyed his father, who was issuing orders to the men. "Connor MacKenzie hasn't a drop of royal blood in his veins, and there was no obstacle to him wedding the Princess of Ce."

"Aye." It was true their friend had married the princess. But Rourke had been at sea during the time when Connor had fallen for the widowed Lady Aila and hadn't witnessed the madness that had gripped the other man. A madness that might have cost him his head, had MacAlpin not decided to bless the union between his warrior and his most prized of hostages. "But I am not Connor."

Rourke was silent for a moment. Then he cast Ross a dark glance. "You'd be safe from such machinations were you already wed."

Ross exhaled a long breath. It had been many years since this subject had been broached, even obliquely, and he didn't pretend to misunderstand what Rourke was really saying. Hell, how could he, when ten years ago it had been Rourke who had hauled him back from the brink of destruction?

"Gordon has been dead for only three weeks. I couldn't in good conscience approach Lady Una with such a proposition when she is in deep mourning."

Rourke grunted, apparently unmoved by Una's state of mourning. "Lady Una has no son for protection. She'd consider your proposition, now you're the master of Dunmor. A betrothal between you might keep MacAlpin's claws from your back."

The words were blunt, even for Rourke, but how could he find fault with them when he spoke only the truth? Una might well accept his hand, now. And he was too weary of his king's tactics to defend his honor when, deep inside, he agreed with

Rourke's sentiments. Even if he doubted he was the one in MacAlpin's sights.

He offered Rourke a humorless smile. "Lady Una has my protection as the widow of my brother, and her daughters are my responsibility. I won't use her as a shield against our king's ambition."

Ten years ago, a betrothal with Una was all he had wanted. But he was no longer a raw seventeen-year-old who imagined himself in love.

It wasn't my imagination.

No. He hadn't imagined it. But he'd certainly fabricated illusions surrounding the beautiful girl who had stolen his heart the year he'd turned sixteen.

But no one knew the real truth of why Una had chosen his brother over him. Even after she had ground his heart into the mud, he'd retained a sliver of self-preservation. Some deeply buried fragment of pride.

He hadn't confided the real reason behind Una's betrayal to anyone. Not even Rourke.

She had rejected him because he'd told her the truth. That he was a bastard, the product of a brutal rape, who had no claim to Gordan's father's name. The past was a place he never wished to visit again. And Una was his past. The reason he would never open his heart again.

Some things could never be healed.

The journey was uneventful. The weather was fine, and at night they camped under the stars, as they trekked from Dal Riada into the Kingdom of Fotla and across the border to the smallest Kingdom in Pictland, Fib.

The stronghold, only half a day's ride over the border, was a mighty structure, strategically located on a hill that gave uninterrupted views across the nearby village and surrounding land. An impressive legacy indeed, left to Braeson's wife by her first husband.

Finn Braeson—although, since MacAlpin had acknowledged him last year his correct address was Lord Finn, Prince of the House of Alpin— and his bride, the Princess of Fortriu, greeted them warmly and insisted the entire contingent stay the night for a great feast. Rourke accompanied Ross as they led their horses to the stables.

"Braeson looks well content with his lot." Skepticism laced every word Rourke growled under his breath. "Although who can blame him? The princess is a vision, to be sure."

"A trait all the princesses of Pictland appear to possess."

Rourke gave a mock bow. "I have met but two and must agree. Still, it was a match made to further MacAlpin's agenda, nothing more. Although I'm glad if it pleases Braeson. He deserves this recognition from his sire."

Ross glanced over his shoulder to ensure no one could over-hear. Speaking against their king was, after all, tantamount to treason. "I confess the princess' welcome surprised me, after the way her heritage was snatched from her when MacAlpin annexed the Kingdom of Fortriu. Yet she also appears content in this marriage."

"Aye." Rourke flashed a rare grin as he paused in grooming his horse. "And no one can say Braeson is a vision to look at, can they?"

"True enough." Ross returned the grin, but said nothing more as fellow warriors entered the stable. He knew all the men, some better than others, but these were topics he would never discuss in front of them.

He may have considered Finn Braeson a friend when they were growing up. But Braeson's bloodline had been acknowl-edged and no one, if they knew what was good for them, said anything negative about MacAlpin's kin, even in jest.

Spies were, after all, everywhere.

LATER THAT NIGHT, after the feast had ended and the musicians were tuning their instruments, he caught up with Finn as they filled their goblets at one of the tables that had been pushed back to the wall.

"Congratulations, my lord." How strange it sounded to call Finn that. "Your bride is exquisite."

"Aye, she is." Pride thrummed through every word, and the glance he sent the princess' way, where she was speaking to MacAllister and Rourke on the other side of the great hall, was filled with warmth. It was oddly disconcerting, and Ross swallowed a mouthful of wine in an effort to clear his head. Then Finn rounded on him. "And if you call me my lord again, I'll have no option but to break your fucking head."

He choked on the wine, and Finn smirked, clearly pleased by his reaction. "Noted," Ross said. "I'm happy for you, regardless."

"I accept and thank you for your congratulations." Finn briefly grasped his arm in a gesture of friendship, and Ross understood. He could well imagine how many warriors now courted Finn's favor, warriors who, as boys, had made the fatherless Braeson's life a misery. Finn indicated they should walk, and in silence they made their way through the great hall and outside, where several of his compatriots and ladies of the princess' court were taking the evening air.

When there was no chance of them being overheard, Finn turned to him once again. "Tell me. Do you know the real reason why you travel to Fib-eviot?"

Ross' senses went on full alert. "A reason besides ensuring the royal house of Fib knows of the coronation and offering them MacAlpin's respects?"

He knew there was more to it than that. He was to uncover

any plans the King of Fib might have to align with the Northumbrians. But he wasn't at liberty to repeat that, not even with MacAlpin's recently acknowledged son.

Finn's smile contained no mirth. "You and I both know the depth of MacAlpin's respect. I am tolerated in Fib because of Lady Mae's royal bloodline, but I work hard to gain the respect of her people on my own account. The rumors that sent you here are likely true, Ross. The royal house of Fib holds no love for Dal Riada."

Ross grunted. Finn told him nothing he did not already know. "Yet we are ordered into Fib-eviot to report back to our king. If it's true the King of Fib is seeking a treaty with Northumbria, they're risking the alliance between Dal Riada and Pictland."

"The queen," Finn said. "Don't make the mistake it's the king who holds power in Fib. Even before he was held hostage in Dunadd it was the queen who ruled, and nothing has changed with his return."

Ross frowned. He knew, of course, the political dynamics of Pictland were different to Dal Riada. The queens of the seven kingdoms were not merely chattels of their kings. But certainly, to his knowledge, the final word lay with the king.

Except, it seemed, in Fib.

"That's useful," he acknowledged. It would save unintended insult to the queen by expecting to be received by her king.

"Lady Mae believes there is an ulterior motive to this visit." Finn's voice was dry. "What do you know of that business?"

God Almighty. First Rourke, and now Finn. "I'm not privy to such machinations. And I have no undisclosed royal blood that MacAlpin can use to his advantage."

Finn's lips twitched as though he found something amusing in the comment. "I was thinking of Stuart MacGregor. His great-grandmother was half-sister to MacAlpin's grandfather, even if it's not publicly acknowledged." He paused for a heartbeat. "Yet."

MacGregor? Ross considered that. He had nothing against the man but somehow couldn't see him as a royal consort.

"This speculation is all very well. But is there an unwed princess of Fib?"

"There is a widowed princess." Finn's amusement vanished. "What other alliance with Northumbria would the Queen of Fib be contemplating, if not one through marriage? I fear MacGregor's carefree days will soon be over if MacAlpin gets his way."

Which of course, he would. Although Ross had no clue how his king expected such a thing to come to pass without intervention. And since MacAllister, who during the last year had spearheaded the king's plans throughout Pictland, was remaining at Finn's stronghold, the whole scheme appeared faulty.

But that wasn't his concern. His mission was to observe and report back. And by God, that was all he planned on doing. He had no intention of second guessing MacAlpin when it came to eliminating the threat of a treaty between Fib and Northumbria. Unless the southern barbarians attacked his contingent, Ross wanted nothing to do with his king's hidden agenda.

It had been a long, bloodied twenty hours, but finally, as dusk fell, Lady Daracha was safely delivered of her son. The babe was two weeks early by Orabel's reckoning but, thank the goddess, was healthy and strong.

"Thank you." Daracha's voice was hoarse as she gazed upon the face of her son. "So many times I feared this moment would never happen. If you hadn't been in Fib these last months, I would have lost this one, too."

Orabel traced a gentle finger over the babe's soft hair. "Do not thank me," she whispered. "I'm merely the conduit for our beloved goddess. She guides me in all ways."

"I'm thankful for Bride's benevolence." Daracha tore her

besotted gaze from her son and looked at Orabel. "But you have my deepest gratitude, regardless."

Daracha's husband strode into the chamber, his face ashen, and Orabel stepped back. "Daracha." He went to the bed and cradled his wife's face. "You are well, my jewel?"

Orabel paused in the task of repacking her precious herbs and potions into her medicine casket. During her years in Northumbria, it had been considered scandalous for a princess of royal blood to attend the birthing chamber of a woman who was not an immediate family member. Indeed, it was the same in Pictland, but she had ignored such protocols as a young girl, and she most certainly hadn't abided by those rules when married to Edwin.

She had delivered many babes. But how few and far between were the husbands who gazed so lovingly at their wives in the moments after delivering a longed-for child. Especially, in the case of Northumbrian men, a son. Invariably, it was the infant they examined first, to ensure all was well, before they turned their attention to the woman who had risked everything to bring forth new life.

Warmth glowed in her chest as she secured the casket and glanced at her friend. All Daracha had ever wanted, ever since they were girls together, was to be a mother. She had achieved her wish. And found a good husband, too.

Orabel would take it as a sign that, however grim the odds seemed, she would one day soon achieve her own.

THAT NIGHT, Bride came to Orabel once again.

Chills rippled through her, even though she was asleep, and yet she wasn't asleep. She was in the realm of the ancients and there was no escape unless Bride allowed it.

The sun-filled glen darkened as storm clouds rolled across the sky. Panic clawed her throat as the yew trees swayed, the dark silhouette of their spiky leaves reminding her of the wickedly sharp talons of carrion birds.

She had not been plagued with such terror since returning to Fib-eviot after Edwin's death twelve months ago. But how often had she suffered these nighttime warnings throughout her marriage. Manifestations of the great goddess' displeasure that Orabel had not obeyed her command.

It didn't matter that her own father, the king, had commanded her to wed. It went against Bride's design. And Orabel had paid the price, night after night, for seven long years.

She tried to fall to her knees, beg for mercy, but was frozen in place as the sound of distant battle cries rent the shadow strewn realm. The air thickened, compressing her lungs, and the river that ran through the glen glittered with noxious, crimson blood.

The blood of my people.

The lives of all those who would die if she failed to fulfil her destiny.

But I have returned. The plea echoed around her mind, desperate that her goddess might hear her. Yet there was no answering whisper of comfort, of understanding, or acceptance that finally Orabel was on the right path.

Instead, a wintry gale whipped through the glen, elusive glints of blue and green sparkling through the stormy chaos, and tentacles of ice wrapped around her heart. And in the midst of the howling wind, an implacable warning lacerated her soul.

Do not stray from the path again. You must heal...

With a strangled gasp, she was thrust from the realm of the immortals, and was back in the bed she shared with Saoirse, in the stronghold of Daracha's husband. But no sense of relief assailed her. Her heart pounded, an erratic counterpoint to how her breath floundered in her breast, as though she were drowning.

Bride had never spoken to her in such an icily direct way

before. Not when she was a maid, when the goddess' wishes had been conveyed through an ethereal melding of sensation, nor when she had left her girlhood behind, and the great goddess had shown her the hidden magic embedded deep in every root and stem of her wondrous domain.

Not even in any of the dread visions while she'd lived in Ayr.

The command was terrifying. Implacable. Her duty was to heal her people with the sacred knowledge Bride had entrusted to her, but she had always known this. Yet the goddess was telling her more was required.

The holy sanctuary?

Orabel had always harbored the dream of creating such a refuge, but how could she turn it into a reality without the support of the royal house of Fib?

It wasn't cold, but she shivered, nevertheless. Because the answer was plain, whether she wanted to face it or not.

Her destiny was to forge that sanctuary herself.

CHAPTER THREE

oss and his men had made good time after leaving Finn's stronghold two days ago and, all being well, were on track to arrive at Fib-eviot shortly after noon.

Although he was sure rumors of their intentions had reached the royal stronghold already, he'd sent a messenger on ahead to announce their arrival. As far as he was aware, no formal notice had been given to the royal house that a contingent of Scots were descending upon them and while MacAlpin might like the idea of surprise, Ross didn't relish the undoubted hostility such an act would entail.

Their reception would likely be frosty enough without adding any more insult.

Rourke rode up alongside him and slung him a disgruntled glare. "Goddamn, but MacGregor keeps his brain in his cock. I pity the princess if, indeed, she is destined to be shackled to him."

As his second-in-command, he'd told Rourke of the conversation with Finn. It wasn't as though MacAlpin had confided his plans and sworn him to silence. And besides, however likely the plan sounded, it was still nothing more than speculation.

"MacGregor has a big mouth and loose tongue. Half the time

his conquests are nothing more than fantasy."

"Thank fuck for that. Otherwise, there was scarcely a Pictish noblewoman of the court of the Princess of Fortriu with whom he hadn't tumbled on the one night we stayed there."

"What of you?" Ross gave him a mocking glance. "Lady Struana appeared captivated by your attentions. God knows why, you're such a miserable bastard most of the time."

Rourke flashed a grin. "Aye, Lady Struana was enchanting. I would have knocked MacGregor from his horse had he slandered her name."

"Jesting aside. If MacGregor is to be presented as a potential contender for the Princess of Fib's hand, he'll need to keep his cock leashed. It won't go in MacAlpin's favor if Stuart attempts to bed every female in sight."

"I don't envy you the task of keeping Stuart MacGregor celibate for more than two nights." Rourke paused. "Unless you plan on confiding our conjectures with him?"

"And have him spread rumors before we even set foot in Fibeviot?" Ross exhaled an impatient breath. "I doubt that would serve our king's purpose, either."

The rode on in silence, only the sound of snorting horses drifting in the air. He frowned, uncertain why unease scraped along his spine, and glanced around. The last village they'd passed through had vanished into the glen behind them, a great forest was some distance to the right, and to their left, a wide river.

Nothing appeared amiss. And yet...

"What is it?" Rourke's voice was low, his expression wary.

"Something's wrong." His voice was tense, and he raised his arm, a warning to his men. An unnatural glint from the forest caught his eye and his senses sharpened. "Ambush."

An arrow shot by, grazing his brow, and as one, he and his men charged. A group of mounted men emerged from the shadow of the trees, swords drawn. At first glance he assumed they were bandits, wearing not much more than rags. But the bright metal of their weapons, as they glinted in the sun, told a different story. As did the fine condition of the horses.

The attackers surged forwards to greet them, and the deadly clash of metal against metal shattered the air.

Ross gripped his bridle as one of them swung his weapon in a wide arc, leaving his neck exposed. Fool. He plunged his sword through the throat of his assailant, and the man tumbled from his horse. Panting, Ross swung about, as another took his place.

He'd got lucky when the first man had made a tactical error but, bandits or not, they were well trained. Blood trickled from his brow into his eye, blurring his vision, but he gritted his teeth. It was too close to use his sword this time and he slammed his shoulder into his opponent, unseating him.

The other man grabbed him, and they crashed onto the ground, rolling as one to avoid the hoofs of their horses. Panting, Ross smashed his fist into the man's face, dragged his sword from the ground and readied a killing blow. But the enemy was too swift, and his blade missed its mark, instead embedding into the man's biceps.

"Ross." Rourke's harsh yell whipped through the haze of crimson in his mind, clearing his focus as he wrenched his sword free, and for a heartbeat he took in the carnage about him. Unmoving bodies lay scattered across the ground. Bandits?

His own men?

Were they really bandits? Or Pictish warriors sent to assassinate them?

Fire burned his blood and scorched his mind. The fighting had stopped. The enemy was dead. It wouldn't take him long to dispatch this one, too. He raised his voice above the roar that filled his head. "Get to Fib-eviot. I'll follow."

The rumble of horses as his men obeyed his order shuddered through his bones as he struggled to once again raise his sword.

Too late. The bandit rolled out of reach, and they staggered to their feet, facing each other. Fog swirled across the land, and he narrowed his eyes, but it was so damn hard to concentrate.

What the fuck was wrong with him?

He wrapped both hands around the hilt, and ignored the alarming sensation that, in truth, he held nothing but air between his slick fingers.

It shouldn't be this hard. The other man was bleeding, his damaged arm hanging uselessly by his side, whereas he'd suffered scarcely a scratch. Yet nausea roiled his stomach, and he could barely keep his balance.

The man lunged, and Ross smashed the sword from his hand. Darkness encroached, like black, odorless smoke, swallowing up the landscape and swirling around the looming form of his enemy. God damn it, he could scarcely keep his eyes open, but he would not succumb without taking this bastard with him.

A guttural roar seared his throat, echoed in his ears, as he drove his blade into exposed flesh, before falling beneath the weight of the man as he collapsed onto the ground.

And blessed oblivion sucked him into its greedy embrace.

Rough hands grasped him and rolled him onto his back. Black clouds obscured his vision of the man who loomed over him, a relentless blanket paralyzing his limbs and he could not find the will to fight it. If this was his end, it was an ignoble one, but perhaps death would put an end to the agony eating his gut.

"This one is alive, my lady." The man spoke in Pictish. Another enemy. He hoped to God Rourke and the rest of his men had escaped in time.

Another figure approached and crouched beside him. As gentle fingertips traced his cheek the clouds rolled back, revealing the sun. A blinding, white-hot, light, surrounding the woman's face like a halo of fire.

His tortured breath tangled in his throat as she came into focus. Her raven-black hair tumbled over her shoulders, the sunlight catching glimpses of indigo in her midnight tresses. Mesmerized, he gazed into her flawless violet eyes and the truth hit him.

God help him. He had died, and this vision belonged in the realms of heaven.

ORABEL PUSHED BACK the warrior's dark blond hair from his brow and ignored the alarming sensation that stabbed through her breast at the sight of his piercing blue eyes. She had seen blue eyes aplenty. There was nothing different about these, except for one mighty fact.

They belonged to the enemy of her people.

She pressed her lips together, willed her erratic heartbeat to settle, and dragged her gaze from his to focus on his wound. It was but a scratch on his temple, and a cursory inspection of his sprawled form, before she had looked upon his face, didn't show any blood-soaked injury that would warrant his current state.

Of course, his injury might be internal. And yet…

She frowned, and leaned in closer to examine the scratch. From an arrowhead, perhaps?

"My lady." Saoirse crouched beside her. "Is this seemly? The man is a Scot."

"That is unfortunate," she conceded. "But we cannot leave him here to die."

"Who would know, my lady?" The rough voice of Neilan, one of the warriors who had accompanied them to assist Daracha, cut through the air. "He's more dead than alive. My lady can't save all who cross her path."

"We should return to the palace." Anxiety wove through Saoirse's words. "It's not safe here."

"His own men left him to perish," Neilan said, contempt dripping from each word. "But what else can be expected of Scots? They possess no honor."

"Were no other Scots injured?"

"No, my lady. They butchered the bandits and then fled."

It struck her as an odd picture to paint, when the Scots had clearly vanquished the bandits. Why leave one of their own behind, when they were the victors?

She glanced at the lifeless bodies that lay scattered across the trampled grasses. Their attire was rough, as though they lived their lives in the woods or on the run. There was no way of telling who they were except for the thread of foreboding that snaked through her.

In Ayr she had seen such men before and once had inadvertently overheard careless words. While nothing had ever been confirmed, she'd guessed the truth. They had undertaken covert missions for Edwin's cousin, Raedwulf.

Days ago, rumors had reached the royal house that MacAlpin intended to send a contingent to Fib-eviot. It was inevitable that news had also traveled beyond the border to the Northumbrian warlords.

Bandits were everywhere. But were these bandits sent by a prince of Northumbria to dispose of the visiting Scots?

Would Raedwulf risk enraging the king of Dal Riada?

But why should Northumbria care about that? They, after all, were not part of this bloodied alliance between Pict and Scot.

The Scots had shown their true colors last spring. They couldn't be trusted. They could not even be trusted to help one of their own fallen men. No one would blame her if she determined this Scots warrior couldn't be saved. Especially if her suspicion of his injury proved correct.

Except she, unlike many healers, was blessed by Bride and possessed the gift that could give him the chance of survival.

But does he deserve to survive?

Indecision warred as, with reluctance, she gazed into his aristocratic face. His dark lashes flickered, and her breath caught as she once again lost her senses in the mesmeric blue of his eyes. This was madness. She could not allow her actions to be dictated simply because she found his eyes so foolishly compelling. For all she knew, this warrior may have been the one who had so callously murdered her own beloved father in the massacre at Dunadd.

No one would blame her if she turned her back. And yet she couldn't do it. Even if she should.

You must heal...

An eerie shiver crawled along her arms as the words whispered through her mind. Surely, this was not what Bride had meant in the vision. Why would the great goddess wish to save a Scot, whose people had long ago forsaken the old ways in favor of a new deity?

But then, Bride herself had blessed her with the gift of healing. If, in her heart, she knew she couldn't leave the Scot to die in this blood splattered meadow, it was reasonable to conclude she was merely following her goddess' decree.

It was not her place to question Bride's reasons. Or probe too deeply into her own.

She looked over her shoulder at Neilan. "Find the arrow that shot this man."

"My lady, I am tasked with protecting you. The queen would not have you put in danger for the sake of tending our enemy. We must make haste and return to Fib-eviot."

She straightened her spine and cast a regal glare in his direction. "The great goddess led us here for a reason."

Consternation flickered over Neilan's face as though he couldn't decide whether his ultimate duty lay with his queen, or the ancient one. After a heartbeat, he bowed his head and marched off.

She let out a shaky breath. She could only hope she was,

indeed, doing Bride's will and hadn't been temporarily blinded to her duty by a pair of startling blue eyes.

"Shall I instruct our warriors to ready him?" Saoirse gave the Scot a disdainful glance. "My lady can tend to him back at the palace."

"We don't have time for that." Even if an arrow wasn't found, she was certain of her diagnosis. "Fetch me my casket."

As Saoirse did her bidding, Orabel pulled off her riding gloves and loosened the Scot's shirt. His skin was cool to the touch, and he muttered unintelligible words as she pressed her palm against his chest and closed her eyes.

The world faded as the irregular thud of his heart filled her mind, and the rush of his blood sank into her senses. The poison throbbed, dark and deadly, spreading like a spider's web, the confirmation she needed.

Wolfsbane.

Saoirse placed her casket by her side, and she opened her eyes as one of the warriors handed her an arrow.

"Pict made." His voice was grim.

She cast her gaze over the goose fletching and unease coiled deep inside. "Yes. But not, perhaps, used by Picts."

"An assassination attempt?" Saoirse's whisper was for her ears only. "Who is this Scot, I wonder, to be singled out for such a fate?"

Who, indeed. While she was fairly certain this attack had not been at the command of the royal house of Fib, she wasn't prepared to take any chances. She gave Neilan, her faithful warrior, a telling glance and his brusque nod told her he understood. Without another word, he took one of his men and they searched the fallen assailants.

Orabel opened her casket and found the poison that would counteract the one polluting the Scot's blood. It was a risky endeavor, and not one she taught her charges, for without the guiding hand of the great goddess, success was but a hope in the wind.

She pulled on the gloves she used for such dangerous tasks and prepared the poultice. There was no time to waste, for once the poison captured the heart, even Bride's power might not be enough to halt the inevitable.

As Saoirse held the Scot's head steady, she pressed the poultice against the wound and bound his temple, before pulling off the gloves and placing the mystical crystals on his chest in the powerful five-pointed star alignment, to protect his heart. She spread her fingers above his chest and face, and the potent energy deep within the crystals flared in recognition.

She closed her eyes, her breathing ragged, as her life-force entwined with the sacred energy of the crystals. The world became an iridescent spectrum of violet and crimson, ethereal ribbons of elemental power flowing through her from the goddess and binding with the unknowable spirit of the crystals.

To work in harmony with the potentially deadly, yet life-preserving poultice.

Time held no meaning in the healing realm, as she fought to keep the threads from unraveling. In the far distance, harsh voices filtered through, disturbing the balance. She shuddered, chills wracking the very marrow of her bones as she strived to hold on, but it was no good.

The connection collapsed and she rolled back on her knees, head reeling. Saoirse took her hand and helped her to her feet and as she pulled her scattered wits together, she saw they were no longer alone.

Five mounted Scots warriors had arrived, and the leader leaped from his horse and marched towards them, apparently unmindful of how her own warriors had drawn their swords in readiness for an attack.

He raised his hands. "I come in peace," he said, in deeply accented Pictish. "We were ambushed on the way to Fib-eviot, and our commander ordered us to continue. We were unaware he had fallen."

So, they didn't leave their compatriots behind, after all. She glanced at her patient and released a silent sigh. His face was no longer the color of ashes, which could only mean the wolfsbane in his blood had been neutralized.

"Stand back." Neilan's voice was harsh. "You will not approach my lady."

Goddess, what a mess. She hadn't wanted the Scots in Fib, and she certainly hadn't wanted to confront them, especially on a battlefield. But there was no option. In the absence of her queen, it was her duty to shoulder the diplomatic mantle and explain, in the hopes of averting further bloodshed.

"Neilan." She didn't raise her voice and with clear reluctance, he and the other warriors stepped back so she faced the Scot. He bowed before casting a concerned glance at his commander.

"My lady. My name is Rourke MacConall. I thank you for tending to our commander, Ross MacIntosh."

Ross MacIntosh. The name echoed around her mind, strangely enticing and altogether too foreign. She froze the thoughts before they bedazzled her, and slammed them into a corner.

She inclined her head at MacConall. "Your commander was poisoned with wolfsbane from an arrow. The bandits, to my knowledge, are not Picts."

It was true the only evidence they possessed—the arrow—pointed to the bandits absolutely being Pictish. But she wasn't convinced, and if smudging the truth a little gave the royal house of Fib breathing space to investigate the truth of the matter, then her conscience was clear.

"God." The word spilled from him, laced with horror, and she understood. To be shot with a poisoned arrow was, after all, a death sentence.

"He will live." She stepped back, so MacConall could inspect Ross.

Not Ross. MacIntosh.

MacConall crouched and prodded a tentative finger at Ross' face.

MacIntosh's face. Why did her mind insist on referring to him by his first name? It was far too familiar. Since she couldn't appear to drag her fascinated gaze from Ross MacIntosh without intervention, she swung about, took her riding gloves from Saoirse, and made a great fuss of pulling them on.

"He is recovering?" There was a note of awe in MacConall's question.

"He is." Without meaning to, she cast a furtive glance at her erstwhile patient. Curses. Her precious crystals were still upon his chest. Since no one but she could touch them, for fear of disrupting their energy, there was no help for it but to once again kneel by his side and gather the crystals. MacConall eyed her, as though he'd never witnessed such a thing before.

He likely hadn't.

She closed their leather pouch and handed it to Saoirse, who replaced it into her casket. Standing, she resisted the urge to brush her hands together to counteract the odd tingle assailing her fingers. It surely had nothing to do with touching MacIntosh's chest. Not when she was still wearing her gloves.

What was she thinking? It should make no difference whether she was wearing gloves or not. Good goddess. Her senses were befuddled, and it had nothing to do with the man and everything to do with how the crystals always sapped her energy when she called upon their power.

Concentrate. The honor, and quite possibly the safety, of Fib rested upon her ability to handle this situation. She took a deep breath. "MacConall, have your men bring Ross MacIntosh to the palace. I shall oversee his recovery myself."

CHAPTER FOUR

Christ, he was parched. Groggily, Ross forced open his eyes and an unfamiliar chamber swam into focus. The last thing he remembered was fighting a bandit, before falling to the ground.

No. Wait.

The fog in his mind billowed, revealing glimpses of raven-black hair, breathtaking violet eyes, and a halo of fire.

A hallucination, for sure. But one thing was certain. He was not yet dead.

He struggled to sit up. It was harder than it should have been, and he remained on his back, sucking in frustrated lungfuls of air. Then again, everything since they'd been ambushed had been harder than it should have been. What the fuck had happened? His head throbbed, but apart from that, and feeling as though he'd been trampled by a dozen horses, he couldn't locate any injury that would've robbed him of his senses.

Gingerly, he rolled onto his side, grimacing as his stomach roiled from the effort. And then he froze, his heart slamming against his ribs. Sitting beside the bed, leaning against the wall with her eyes closed, sat the raven-haired creature from his vision.

She had been no vision. He raked his gaze over the delicate structure of her face, her long black eyelashes and high cheek-bones, lingering for a long moment on her tempting lips. Her deep blue gown, with intricate, golden embroidery across the square cut bodice, clung to her curves like a loving embrace. He swallowed, mouth dry, and despite his battered state, lust stirred deep in his loins.

Who the hell was she? She was no village wench. So how had she come across him by the forest?

And where the fuck am I?

She sighed and jerked awake, straightening from the wall as though it burned. Fascinated, he couldn't tear his gaze away as her eyes met his.

It hadn't been a figment of his imagination. Her eyes truly were violet. For the first time in his life, he was speechless in the presence of a beautiful woman.

"Ah." She smoothed her gown, before offering him a tight smile. "You are awake. That's a good sign. I feared you had slipped into an endless sleep."

How long had he been unconscious? It was an important question and yet it faded to insignificance beneath the desire to know who this enchanting woman with the beguiling Gaelic accent was.

"My lady." His voice rasped, scraping his throat but at least, thank God, he had managed to speak. "Who are you?"

Damn it, had he said that aloud? His brain was still addled with whatever had caused him to lose consciousness. Before he could trawl through his mind to find the words to apologize for his breach of etiquette, she inclined her head.

"We came upon you in the meadow. The bandits were slain, and your countrymen had departed to Fib-eviot. You were near death."

He had no recollection of sustaining an injury. And yet… he touched his temple. It was bandaged, and a hazy memory surfaced of an arrow barely missing his eye as the battle had begun.

"The arrow was poisoned." The revelation shuddered through him, as things fell into place. How he had been lightheaded. Unable to focus. And why he had fallen at the end.

But one rarely recovered from a poisoned arrow.

"Wolfsbane."

She confirmed his worst fears. And yet, he had not died.

"Are you certain?" The words were out before he could contain them. "There's no cure for wolfsbane poisoning."

"Yet with the great goddess' benevolence, here you still are." There was only the faintest trace of censure in her tone, and he couldn't blame her. She had clearly saved his life, even if he found the notion inconceivable. And it belatedly occurred to him that she hadn't shared her name.

"My lady." The gruff voice from across the chamber jolted him and he tensed as a Pict warrior appeared by the lady's side. He hadn't been aware anyone else was in the chamber, which just went to reinforce how utterly defenseless he was.

Where in God's name was Rourke? The rest of his men? Had they reached Fib-eviot safely?

"It is quite all right, Neilan," she said. "I will summon you should I require your assistance."

Neilan grunted, clearly unimpressed, but without another word he retreated to whichever corner he had emerged from.

With a monumental effort, Ross pushed himself upright and leaned back against the wall, willing his heart to slow its erratic tempo. He'd rip out his tongue before admitting how much of an effort that simple maneuver had taken, but it was better than lying on the bed while an unnamed healer and her warrior watched over him.

"I thank you for saving my life." He bowed his head and it felt like a boulder was attached to his shoulders. Gritting his teeth, he straightened his neck and once again rested his head against the wall. "I am in your debt, my lady."

"I am but the conduit through which my goddess works. If you must thank anyone, it is Bride herself."

He knew of the heathen goddess that so many of the Picts worshipped, but that didn't mean he believed in those old, pagan ways. But it would be churlish to say such a thing to this remarkable healer.

"Nevertheless, you have my eternal gratitude. I've never met anyone who has survived the sting of wolfsbane."

He wasn't convinced of her diagnosis but she had certainly saved him from something. And he hadn't lied to her. He was undeniably grateful.

"It's true the cure is often associated with death itself. But with the guidance of Bride, it's possible to extract a remedy. No plant is truly all good or evil."

He'd never considered such a thing before. Then again, he'd never conversed with a healer before. The physician who had tended to his dying brother had relied on the renowned dependability of leeches rather than deadly plants.

"Do you mean to tell me there is good to be found even in wolfsbane?" Holy God, was he flirting with this delectable healer? When he was barely even able to sit up without the support of the wall behind him?

"Indeed. But I wouldn't recommend anyone administering it unless they were fully skilled in such an undertaking." She picked up a cup from a table and after a moment's hesitation, handed it to him. "Here. You must drink. And I need to examine your wound."

He took the cup and the cold, spiced, tea soothed his raw throat. The healer took a bottle from a casket and shook a few drops onto her hands. The pungent smell of astringent filled the air and he watched, intrigued, as she rubbed her fingers together.

She gave him an oddly furtive glance as she came to his side and unwrapped the bandage around his head. Entangled beneath the astringent he caught an elusive hint of heather. The fragrance of the healer.

Involuntarily, he tightened his grip on the cup, as the alluring fantasy of wrapping his arms around her and burying his face in her beautiful hair assailed him.

Had the poison warped his reason? Why was he even thinking such things when there were far more important issues he needed to address? Mainly, the wellbeing of his men.

As her gentle fingers stroked his temple he struggled to focus, but the temptation to simply close his eyes and allow the subtle pleasure she evoked with her touch to claim him was inexorable.

He took another gulp of the spiced tea in the hope it might break the spell this healer unknowingly wove around him.

It didn't work. Tendrils of warmth from where her fingertips massaged his temple sank into his blood and flowed through his mind like a seductive serpent. He was losing the battle to hang onto his wits, and the worst of it was, he scarcely cared.

"The wound is clean." Quiet satisfaction threaded through her voice and his eyes snapped open. He'd almost gone under. Again. "You should rest a day or two, to gather your strength, but I foresee no lasting impairment."

She stepped back, and poured some of the astringent into a small bowl, before dipping the bandage into the liquid. It was oddly compelling, watching her every movement. How easy to be lulled into a cocoon of serenity. But he couldn't allow himself that luxury.

He drew in a ragged breath and attempted to whip his lethargic mind into some semblance of order.

"My lady." He waited until she looked at him. Was it his imagination that she seemed reluctant to do so? Aye, it most likely was. In his current state, he couldn't fathom his own responses, never mind anyone else's. "I must contact my men at Fib-eviot, to ensure their safe arrival."

Belatedly, something she'd said when he'd first regained consciousness occurred to him. *Your countrymen had departed to Fib-eviot.* How would she know that was their destination, unless she had been told of it?

"Your men arrived safely and have made camp within our ramparts. You are the only casualty of the encounter with the bandits."

He released a relieved breath. His men were safe. And from her words, it appeared he, too, was within the ramparts of Fib-eviot. She wrung out the bandage, tipped the liquid into a chamber pot, and closed her casket. Was she preparing to leave?

It was likely. Now he was on the road to recovery, why should she stay? A healer as skilled as she would be in high demand. Maybe she was healer to the queen herself.

But he didn't want her to go. Not yet. He might never have the chance to speak with her again. "It was a stroke of luck your party found me."

She paused and looked at him, and her eyes held him captive. "We were returning to the palace by our usual route, but a fallen tree blocked our path. That's why we ended up beside the forest and saw the carnage."

"The bandits were foolhardy to attack a contingent of warriors." Now his mind was clearing, the stranger it seemed. "They must have known their chances of victory were remote."

"I cannot say." She dropped her gaze, and regret flared through him. He never spoke of battles when in the presence of a lady and yet he hadn't thought twice before sharing his thoughts with her. After all, she was a healer and knew of bloodied things.

But that wasn't why he'd spoken out of turn. It was because he hadn't been able to help himself.

"Forgive me." He reached out his hand before he realized what he was doing, and for an eternal second time stopped, before his arm dropped back onto the bed. "I should not trouble you with such unfitting sentiments."

This time her glance showed an unmistakable glimmer of amusement. "Why? Because I'm a delicate female who cannot withstand the realities involved with discussing deadly skirmishes?"

"It's not a topic of conversation I'd normally embark upon in the presence of a lady."

"I can assure you I'm not easily offended, nor inclined to swoon over matters a Scot might find unsuitable for the ears of a lady."

He grinned, entranced. "I'm glad to hear it. Nevertheless, I should have kept my opinions to myself."

"Perhaps you should. One should never be too free with one's opinions when faced with the enemy."

"Are you my enemy?" The question was out before he could prevent it. He was not usually so incautious, especially when dealing with Picts. Even beautiful ones. Because the bleak truth was—they were enemies.

Even if he wished otherwise.

She sighed. "You are a Scot. We can never be anything but enemies."

"Then I'm doubly grateful you chose to save my life. Whatever you may believe, I shall never forget that."

"You forget I'm a healer. I had no choice but to save you."

He considered her for a heartbeat. To hell with it. He would say what was on his mind. "I think you did. In the end, there's always a choice, my lady."

Her startled gaze caught his as though his words were a revelation. And then she spoke and shattered his delusions. "Not always."

Before he could respond, there was a loud banging on the door before it burst open and Rourke marched in, followed by a clearly infuriated Pict warrior. And while he was relieved to see his friend was unharmed, he couldn't suppress the irritation that blazed through him at the interruption.

"Ross." Rourke tossed him a glare before bowing his head at the healer and steadfastly ignoring Neilan who had once again emerged from the shadows to glower at them both. "Thank God you're awake."

"Thanks to this healer." He glanced at her, but she pressed her lips together and shut the lid on her casket. Why did he want her to admit she had chosen to save him, rather than she had done it merely through a sense of duty? It made little sense since the outcome for himself was the same.

"Aye. My lady's assistance is most appreciated." There was an odd inflexion in Rourke's voice which Ross couldn't place.

"I shall go," the healer said, as Neilan picked up her casket. "If you require my presence, let one of the warriors know and a message will be conveyed."

He knew what she meant. But what if he requested her presence merely so they might see each other again?

She swept from the chamber and the two warriors followed her. Rourke slammed the door behind them before coming to his side and scrutinizing his temple.

"I'll live," Ross said. "Was the arrow found that hit me?"

"When we realized you'd fallen, I sent half our men onto the royal stronghold for reinforcements, and the rest of us returned to you. The Picts were already there. And we found no arrow, although we searched."

"You think the Picts have it?"

"Who else? None of the bandits escaped. You took down two of them even after you'd been poisoned."

Last winter, there had been an attempted assassination by a Northumbrian of MacAlpin's son, Constantine, while they had been in the Kingdom of Fotla. And although Ross was no king's son, if he'd been assassinated in the Kingdom of Fib, it would still have shaken the alliance between Scot and Pict, given the rumors that were currently linking the royal house of Fib with Northumbrian warlords.

He grasped Rourke's arm. "Do you think this is connected to what happened in Fotla?"

"There's no proof. But aye. How can it not?"

Fuck. It was true there was no physical proof. But was this enough to confirm MacAlpin's suspicion that the royal house of Fib was in league with the Northumbrians?

"Did you ask if the arrow had been found?"

Rourke's face tightened. "I did. I fear I don't possess your diplomacy, Ross."

"Send our men to scour the area. It's possible the Picts didn't find it."

"We spent most of yesterday combing every blade of grass between the forest and the riverbank. We searched the bandits, too, before disposing of their bodies. There was nothing to identify them."

His head reeled. He'd assumed the attack had happened earlier this day. "Yesterday?"

"You were unconscious for a day and a night. I sent a messenger to inform MacAllister of events. But the princess would allow none of us near you, after you were brought to the stronghold."

"The princess?" Did Rourke refer to the *healer*?

"Aye. She may look as fragile as a thistledown but there was no swaying her. She reminded me we were within the borders of Fib and if we wanted you to survive, we had to put your life in her hands and obey her rules."

"The Princess of Fib is a healer?" The Picts had strange customs, to be sure, but this revelation was astounding. "She is permitted to wander the countryside, aiding foreign warriors?"

Rourke grunted and flung himself onto the stool where the princess had recently sat. "It would appear so. The Queen of Fib didn't attempt to dissuade her when I was taken to her sanctum.

It's a strange, thing, Ross." Rourke frowned. "To be confronted by the queen, the dowager, and the princess. There was no sign of the king while these decisions were made."

"Finn was right, then." Ross shifted on the bed, trying to find a less uncomfortable position. "Did you find time to convey the respects of our king?" He wasn't sure he managed to conceal the sardonic undertones in his voice. Not that it mattered, when Rourke was the only one in the chamber.

"Fortunately, not. It's clear the queen wishes us gone from Fib as soon as possible. You can woo them with pretty words when you're recovered."

That was something to look forward to. And now, because of the attack on his men, he could no longer simply observe and report back to MacAlpin as had been his original intention. He was committed to uncover whatever connection between Fib-eviot and Northumbria that he could. "We can't leave until we discover if the royal house was behind that ambush."

"It will be hard to prove."

"Aye. My gut feeling is the attack wasn't a direct order from the king—or queen. The real question is, did they know about it and give tacit approval?"

"If they did, they'll never admit to it."

That was true enough, but it wouldn't stop him investigating.

His head throbbed. There was nothing he could do until his strength fully returned and considering how weary he'd felt when he'd first awoken, compared to now, that shouldn't be long. Which was another reason why it was hard to accept the princess' diagnosis. Maybe Rourke had some insight.

"The princess believes I was poisoned with wolfsbane. Seems unlikely."

"It wouldn't surprise me." Rourke's voice was grim, and Ross shot him a sharp look. He'd been certain his friend would agree how improbable the diagnosis was. "I thought you were dead when I saw you. I don't know how she did it, but she brought you back. It's as near to witchcraft as I ever want to be."

Unease shivered along his arms. There were no such things as witches, of course, and yet the possibility of them lingered on the peripheral of civilized society. Who was to say that here in Pictland, a land which, for most of his life, he'd been led to believe were peopled by savages, such ancient creatures didn't still exist in the shadows?

Whatever the truth of it, one thing was certain, the woman who had saved him wasn't from the shadows. "The princess is no witch."

Rourke shrugged. "I'm not casting shade on her methods. They worked."

Aye, they had worked. And if the royal house of Fib was behind the attack in the first place, had this outcome been the plan all along?

Maybe the princess had been right when she'd told him she'd had no choice but to heal him. It shouldn't cast a pall over the situation, since it was grim enough, and yet it did. Especially since, regardless of the truth, he owed her his life. "And unless we can prove the Picts were behind this attack, I'm in debt to the royal house of Fib."

CHAPTER FIVE

"You should sleep, my lady. You've had no rest since leaving Lady Daracha." There was quiet outrage in Saoirse's voice as they made their way across the great hall, and Orabel gave a faint smile. Saoirse had been quietly outraged from the moment they had come upon the aftermath of the ambush. "The queen will understand."

They both knew she wouldn't. "I must obey her summons, and then I shall sleep."

"Then I should have stayed with you, while you tended the Scot, so you might have rested there more easily between your ministrations."

It had been a battle to make her friend return to the bedchamber in the early hours of the morning. But Saoirse was not blessed by the great goddess, and there had been no need for her to remain when she could scarcely keep her eyes open. "I did not give you the choice," she reminded her. "There is no harm done. This isn't the first time I have gone without sleep."

"Indeed, but there is a difference between discomforting oneself for one's own people, and for those of our enemy."

Ross MacIntosh's piercing blue eyes invaded her mind and

she foolishly shook her head in an effort to dislodge the memory. She hadn't saved him because he had inadvertently bedazzled her.

She had saved him because it was her duty. And nothing would ever induce her to say otherwise.

Saoirse remained in the outer sanctum with the queen and dowager queen's ladies, and Orabel entered the inner sanctum where Etain and their mother waited, but this time her brother-through-marriage, Dugald, King of Fib, was also present. When she'd returned to the palace the previous day he had been on an overnight hunting trip and judging from his disheveled appearance, he had not long returned from it.

"My lady." He bowed his head as she dipped a respectful curtsey. She had known Dugald since before her marriage to Edwin, and he was not an unkind man. "This is a bad business. We are told the Scot will live?"

"He will, sire. He is already on the path to recovery."

"Thanks to you." Her mamma gave her a strained smile.

Etain expelled an impatient breath and with an imperious gesture, ordered Orabel to sit. "How fortunate the Dal Riadan upstart will be unable to accuse us of murdering one of his dogs."

Orabel sat, and smoothed her gown as she quashed the flicker of irritation that flared at her sister's words. Yet the truth was plain and most unwelcome. She was affronted by Etain's summary dismissal of MacIntosh's worth.

But there was no point in arguing over something that, up until she had come upon the Scot by the forest, she would have entirely agreed with. "There is no doubt the arrow is Pict made?"

"None." Dugald's voice was grim. "You did well to conceal it from our enemies. MacAlpin would use the knowledge to further crush Fib into submission."

She had to ask, even though it risked offending. "The royal house is not behind this?"

"Nothing would give me greater pleasure than to slaughter

every last Scot that infests our beloved land." Etain drew in a deep breath and shot Dugald a concerned glance before continuing. "But no, Orabel. Alas, diplomacy must prevail. It was most fortuitous your journey back enabled you to save him. We will not bend the knee to the upstart, but neither can we give him just cause to invade our borders."

She had to voice her suspicions. And not simply because she'd do anything to avoid another marriage to a southern warlord.

"It's possible Northumbria is behind this. After all, they attempted to assassinate MacAlpin's son in the winter by using a similar trick."

"We may never know." Etain thrummed her fingers on the arm of her chair. "But if this was a political ploy, rather than a random attack by bandits, it has failed in its objective."

"We are still awaiting the reason as to why the Scots are here," Dugald said. "It appears only their injured leader can speak for them."

Etain gave a disagreeable sniff. "MacConall can scarcely speak at all. He communicates in a series of growls and glares. How long before Ross MacIntosh is on his feet so we may eject them from our kingdom?"

"Tomorrow, or perhaps the following day. I'll monitor his progress and keep you informed."

"Indeed." Etain gave her a probing look and for a dreadful instant, Orabel had the unsettling certainty her sister saw more than a simple concern for her patient in her remark. Even though there was nothing more to see. How could there be? She gripped her fingers together on her lap and strived for calm. What in the name of the goddess was wrong with her?

"Well." Thankfully, Etain finally broke the impasse by offering her a wintry smile. "We will receive him tomorrow, Orabel. We are not, after all, a refuge for wounded foreigners. Let his own countrymen deal with his convalescence."

~

IT WAS LATE that afternoon when Orabel, accompanied by Saoirse, once again visited the Scot. After the audience with her sister, she had retired to her bedchamber and the sleep had been most reviving. Not least because no dark visions had haunted her dreams.

Perhaps the vision on the night she'd delivered Daracha's babe had merely been a warning from Bride of the visiting Scots? It was a comforting thought. A pity she couldn't quite believe it.

Stop. She would not dwell on things she couldn't control. Whatever the reason for the return of that nighttime terror would be revealed to her when the goddess saw fit.

It was hard not to see a link with Ross MacIntosh, though.

She gave a silent groan at her apparent inability to take her own good advice and inclined her head at the Pict warrior stationed outside the Scot's chamber. He threw open the door and Neilan, who had escorted them, strode inside, and announced her as though she were a delegation arriving to negotiate a peace treaty. "The Princess of Fib."

MacIntosh was standing by the narrow window, and he turned to face her as she entered the chamber, his blue eyes more startling than they had any right to be. He was barefoot, his shirt unlaced, and why the glimpse of his naked chest caused the breath to lodge in her throat was beyond her.

She had already seen his chest. Goddess, she had pressed her hand against his heart during the course of her examination. Alas, the memory did nothing but cause her own heart to ricochet wildly within her breast.

It was most irregular. She had treated many men. Indeed, she had healed men who had worn far fewer garments that MacIntosh and not once had the sight of exposed flesh discomposed her so.

"My lady." He bowed, before coming towards her, and her

mouth dried. They were in his sick chamber, he was her patient, yet she was behaving like a young maid of thirteen in the presence of a—

A what? Even at thirteen, the sight of a handsome warrior had never affected her so.

"I was unaware my savior was the Princess of Fib." He flashed her a smile that caused knots to twist in her stomach. If that wasn't disgraceful enough, he extended his hand, and a thousand butterflies cascaded through her chest.

To refuse would be discourteous. But how she wished she could.

Lies. She wished no such thing.

She froze her errant thoughts and offered her hand. To be sure, it was a little unconventional, but nothing about this Scot's arrival at Fib-eviot had been conventional. If a feast had been given in honor of their visit, it was likely a greeting such as this would have passed between them. It meant nothing more than common courtesy, and wasn't that the only reason why she had returned to see him, as a courtesy to ensure he was recovering well?

His fingers wrapped around hers, warm and strong, and his thumb skimmed her flesh in a brief caress. Liquid tremors assailed her vitals, and she had the mortifying urge to press her thighs together in an effort to stem the unruly ribbons of lust.

His lips brushed her knuckles, his breath an unspoken whisper against her skin. Her eyes fixed in fascination on his dark blond hair, no longer a tangled mass, but pulled back by a length of black velvet.

He raised his head and their gazes meshed. Against all etiquette, he did not release her hand. Indeed, his grip tightened, or was that only her fervid imagination playing tricks?

She had to respond, lest he think her a fool. But how hard it was to calm her erratic thoughts. "Since you were insensible when we came across you, introductions seemed pointless."

"I'm honored by your attentiveness."

"My calling takes precedence in such matters."

"I'm intrigued that a princess of royal blood is such a remarkable healer. Your skills are beyond anything I'm aware of in Dal Riada."

"One should never turn one's back on the ancient ways. I fear for those who have."

With apparent reluctance he released her hand and bowed to Saoirse. "My lady."

Saoirse inclined her head, but did not offer her hand for the Scot to kiss. After a heartbeat, he turned back to her.

"I must also thank you for accommodating my men. This was not how we envisaged entering Fib-eviot."

"You may thank my queen in the morning, when you explain why you entered the Kingdom of Fib without prior warning."

"Aye, my lady. Your queen has been most gracious in allowing me to recover in this chamber."

She had the absurd urge to tell him that the only reason her sister had allowed him refuge within the palace walls was because Orabel had insisted upon it. That, and the fact none of them wanted the Scots to suspect the ambush was anything other than a random attack. Although it was true the Scots might believe the Northumbrians were behind it, it was equally possible they might not.

Far better not to take the chance.

And so she smiled and kept her counsel. She was, after all, here in her capacity as a healer, nothing more. Which reminded her why she had visited him in the first place.

"I must examine your wound."

His fingers skimmed his temple. "It's fully healed, thanks to your skill."

She was used to men waving aside her assistance, once the danger had passed, and since she did not tolerate such behavior from Picts, she certainly wouldn't from a Scot. With a regal wave, she indicated he should sit on the bed, and Saoirse placed her casket on the stool.

"That's good to know," she said. "However, I need to confirm this myself before discharging you from my ministrations."

For a moment, she thought he was going to argue before he appeared to reconsider his position. "Forgive me. I'm not used to such attentive aftercare when the wounded are once more on their feet."

"A failing I cannot admire. Simply because one can stand, doesn't mean they are recovered."

She caught Saoirse's sharp glance but refused to acknowledge it. It was a passion of hers, although the queen considered it more of an obsession, that she ensured her patients were more than merely functional before discharging them from her care.

"I don't disagree." He sounded fascinated, as though her view was remarkable rather than plain common sense. "But such luxury is rarely afforded to warriors on the battlefield."

"What a pity. Perhaps such a policy might result in fewer casualties."

"An intriguing notion."

He sat on the bed and she concentrated on inspecting his temple, and not allowing the enticing vision of his smile to distract her. Or the fact that he had clearly cleansed more than his hair during her absence, and a faint scent of summer forests emanated from him, making her inexcusably lightheaded.

She drew in a steadying breath, which only served to heighten the surreal sense of giddiness that assailed her. It was most improper, and not simply because she had treated him.

It was because he was a Scot.

The injury had healed to little more than a graze, and there were no indications of any residual noxious elements. There was nothing to prevent MacIntosh from having an audience with the queen in the morning, when Etain would send their unwelcome guests on their way.

Orabel straightened, but the scent of summer forests lingered in the air. Or perhaps it was only in her mind, which was far worse. The sooner Etain bid the Scots to leave her kingdom, the better. MacIntosh was far too much of a distraction when she needed to set her mind to founding her cherished sanctuary and escaping the clutches of Raedwulf.

"All is well," she said. "Although a few days of rest is ideal, I'm certain you wouldn't heed my advice so I shall not offer it."

He laughed and she blinked, taken aback that he'd found humor in her comment when, in truth, she had meant to condemn him. Obviously, she needed to work on her insults.

"My lady's advice is sound. Far from dismissing your wise words, I shall heed your counsel and delay our departure from Fib-eviot for another week, if your queen will grant it."

CHAPTER SIX

The following morning Ross, accompanied by Rourke, entered the royal sanctum. A dozen advisers gathered there, which he'd expected, but not only was the king present but so too were the queen, the dowager—and the princess.

It was, as Rourke had remarked the previous day, somewhat disconcerting. In Dal Riada Ross doubted the queen had ever set foot in MacAlpin's inner sanctum, never mind attended an assembly with foreign delegates.

He bowed, and the image of the princess, as she stood beside the dowager in a vibrant green gown with silver thread, imprinted behind his eyes. God, it was hot in here, and his heart thudded uncomfortably against his ribs, as if a sliver of wolfsbane still lingered in his blood.

"We welcome you to Fib-eviot." There was more than a touch of frost in the king's voice as Ross and Rourke straightened. It was an effort not to glance at the princess, but he couldn't afford such a breach in etiquette when circumstances were so fragile between their people.

"We trust you are fully recovered, MacIntosh," the queen

added, her voice as icy as her king's. "We regret the injury you sustained within our borders."

"Thank you, sire. Madam." He had no idea if here, in Fib, he should have addressed the queen first, but since her expression of disdain didn't flicker, he took that as a positive sign. "I am fortunate the poisoned arrow did not accomplish its objective, thanks to the skill of the princess."

This time he couldn't help himself, and his gaze caught hers. Her eyes were as stunning as he recalled and, unlike most Pictish women he had encountered, her hair wasn't braided. Instead, long raven-black locks tumbled over her shoulder and the flickering glow from the lamps highlighted the intriguing indigo glimpses within each curl.

It wasn't the time and it sure as hell wasn't the place, but that didn't stop a bolt of lust from ripping through his loins. Hastily, he bowed his head before she saw the raw need in his eyes.

"Indeed," the queen said, her inflexion indicating her true thoughts were entirely the opposite to his remark. "We are mindful that you owe your life to the Princess of Fib and trust you will convey such to your king upon your return to Dal Riada."

The possibility that the royal house of Fib was behind the attack for the very purpose of then saving his life for this outcome, loomed heavy in his mind. It all seemed too... convenient.

Yet he couldn't accuse when he possessed no evidence.

"Certainly, madam. My king wishes for nothing more than peace between our kingdoms."

The king gave a derisory snort and Ross glanced at him. There was a glower on his face that could rival Rourke on a bad day. But the king did not break the fraught silence that screamed within the small chamber and caused the hair on the back of Ross' neck to rise with foreboding.

Instead, it was the princess herself who spoke.

"Peace is all any of us wish, MacIntosh. How comforting to know your king is in agreement with this."

Once again, he caught her steady gaze. There was nothing to indicate she was anything but sincere in her words, but he'd lived through the last year when MacAlpin had systematically laid claim to four of the seven Kingdoms of Pictland.

Not through war. A tentative peace shrouded the land. But there had been bloodshed in Dunadd when MacAlpin had begun his crusade, and there was no reason on God's earth why the royal house of Fib should trust the Scots' king.

But he was in Fib on the orders of his king and he had no choice but to carry them out. Especially when the safety of his men had been compromised.

"Aye, my lady. Our alliance is the strongest force we possess to combat the advance of the Norse and the Northumbrians into our lands."

"An alliance that favors Dal Riada." The queen smiled but her eyes were cold and meaning plain. He couldn't even disagree, but he was here to uphold the honor of his king, not wrestle with his own conscience.

"Madam, my king sent me into Fib for the sole purpose of assuring the royal house that Dal Riada stands with Pictland against our common enemies. And to formally extend a warm invitation to King Kenneth MacAlpin's coronation in Fortriu."

He bowed and held out the official document. A member of the king's entourage took it from him but neither king nor queen appeared inclined to accept it.

Unease prickled along his spine as he straightened. Icy hostility spiked from every Pict in the chamber. But he had not been thrown through the door, and so he took a deep breath and made his request.

"While I recuperate from the attack, as directed by the princess as my esteemed healer, I request leave for myself and my men to remain within the ramparts of Fib-eviot."

~

I_{T WAS} a relief to leave the confines of the stronghold where antagonism pulsed from the very walls themselves, and Ross sucked in a great breath as he and Rourke made their way to where their men had camped.

"That went well." Rourke's tone suggested he was merely astonished they'd left the inner sanctum still alive.

"It could have been worse if the queen had refused my request." At least with her approval to stay within the ramparts, they were somewhat protected. Although that didn't mean anything, if the threat came from the royal house itself. "Ensure our men are on alert at all times and keep the camp under guard during the nights."

"It seems the princess hadn't informed her queen of her recommendation."

He was inclined to agree, if the poisonous glance the queen had sent the princess was any indication. "It's given us a week to discover all we can, Rourke. I'm not optimistic, but we might uncover a clue as to the bandits' origin. We'll expand the search you began yesterday into the forest itself."

"Aye." Rourke paused, a frown slashing his forehead. "Although you'd best remain in the camp. The princess was right. You need to rest."

"The hell I do." They entered the camp, and he acknowledged his men as he and Rourke made their way to his tent. "We have the queen's permission to stay. I don't need to indulge in a masquerade of recuperation."

Rourke swung about and gripped his arm. "It's not a masquerade. You nearly fucking died, Ross. I'm not saying you need bed rest, but you're no good to me if you fall ill during the search."

It was galling that Rourke was right. He'd rip out his tongue before admitting it, but the confrontation with the royal house of Fib had taken its toll.

"Very well." He ground the words between his teeth before exhaling a frustrated breath. "Let's hope something of use will be discovered in the forest."

Not that he held out much hope of it.

THIS ENFORCED idleness would drive him out of his mind.

Standing outside his tent Ross stretched and stifled a groan. He'd tended to his horse, his sword, his dagger, and even his boots, but it was not yet even noon. There were dried rations in his pack, but he wasn't hungry.

Just restless.

In the distance the stronghold of Fib-eviot stood, proud and mighty, with unparalleled views of the surrounding countryside and, on its southern horizon, the border with Northumbria.

How easy to surmise what close ties the two kingdoms might share.

He would uncover nothing of interest while he remained in the camp. It was a comfortable stroll to the nearest village, and one never knew what gossip might be overheard in a local tavern.

The spring breeze was warm, and he breathed in deep, savoring the fresh scent of grass and earth. A Christian church nestled beside a stream, and he eyed the ancient stones that formed a partial circle not far from the sacred site. Did the Picts still conduct pagan rituals here, within the shadow of the church?

As he drew near to the village the familiar sounds of livestock, the clatter of cartwheels and the high-pitched voices of children filled the air. It reminded him of the village under the protection of Dunmor, except those Scots' villagers never regarded him with sideway glances of distrust and barely concealed loathing the way these Picts did.

His expectations of discovering anything useful, already low, sank further. It merely reinforced what he already knew.

The people of Fib held as little esteem for Scots as did their royal house.

A commotion ahead caught his attention, where a crowd had gathered outside the blacksmith's. Ross crossed the village square then stopped dead as the Princess of Fib emerged from a side alley. She was clearly in a hurry, and the crowd parted before her, as she disappeared within the dwelling.

While it was common in Dal Riada—and, he presumed, in Pictland—for the lady of the stronghold to maintain a connection with her lord's village, he was damn sure it didn't involve visiting side alleys or blacksmiths. And in his limited experience, princesses of royal blood most certainly didn't mingle with villagers in such a manner.

But then, neither did they tend to foreign warriors.

He shouldered his way through the unwilling crowd and peered through the open door. She was on her knees on the dirt floor, administering aid to a distressed, gasping, youth, who was being restrained by two older men.

"You must keep your head still," she said, as she leaned over the lad's face. "I need clean water."

She addressed her command without looking up, and he pulled his waterbag from his belt and crouched beside her. "Here, my lady."

Her startled gaze caught his, and for a heartbeat he lost himself in the depths of her remarkable eyes. Then she drew in a sharp breath and the illusion shattered.

"Thank you." She took his waterbag and drizzled the contents into the lad's inflamed eye. His agonized groans scraped along Ross' bones, and he winced in sympathy. He was certain there wasn't a blacksmith—or apprentice—alive who didn't bear scars of their trade, but it was bad luck indeed when the victim stood to lose an eye over an accident.

She took a small dark bottle from her casket. "Do not blink," she said softly. "This will help greatly, and with the goddess' blessing you will retain your sight." With that, she administered a single drop of colorless liquid to the lad's eye.

A strange, sweet aroma drifted on the air. He'd never smelled anything like it before.

After carefully returning the bottle to her casket, she placed a small pad over the injured eye before wrapping a bandage around the lad's head, to keep it in place. The lad shuddered but no longer groaned in pain, and when she made to rise, Ross offered his hand to assist.

For a moment he thought she was going to ignore him. Then she accepted, and he wrapped his fingers around hers as they stood. It was such a small, everyday action. Yet it felt as if he'd never done such a thing before.

"He must remain still for the rest of the day," she told the blacksmith, who looked less than happy at the directive. "I shall pray to the great goddess for her benevolence and return in the morning to examine his eye."

"My lady." The blacksmith bowed his head.

She turned to face him, and belatedly he realized he still held her hand. With more reluctance than he'd ever admit, he released her and offered a half bow.

"Allow me to escort you, my lady."

"My lady has no need of your presence," growled the warrior who had been with her the other day. He snatched up a basket and handed the casket to the princess' lady, before shooting Ross a poisonous glare. "We have no need of any Scot within the borders of Fib."

They went outside, where the crowd had dispersed, and made their way across the village square.

"We must make the best of it, Neilan," the princess said. "And since Ross MacIntosh is here, it saves us the need of requesting his presence at the palace so I might monitor his health."

He thought she had discharged him, but he wasn't about to

remind her of it. "My lady has the advantage. Alas, I am not privy to the Princess of Fib's given name."

"You've no right to know it." Hostility radiated from the warrior like a furnace. At least it clarified that this Pict would as soon plunge a dagger in his back than offer a sliver of trust between their people.

"It is no great secret. My name is Orabel."

Orabel. The name echoed in his mind, foreign and enchanting.

Just like the lady herself.

"Lady Orabel." Her name sounded even better on his tongue. "I'm honored to make your formal acquaintance."

Her lips twitched, as though she strived not to smile. "I believe we long passed any such formalities, MacIntosh." Then she came to a halt. "Why did you not go with your countrymen this morning? Are you suffering from any light-headedness? Blurred vision?"

"I am not. But since the queen graciously allowed us to remain while I recovered, we thought it prudent for me to forego the ride today."

"Hmm." The glance she bestowed his way suggested she hadn't forgiven him for repeating her words to the queen.

He leaned in close. Far closer than etiquette allowed but she didn't pull back with affront. "Forgive me if I spoke out of turn to your queen. I wrongly presumed you had found time to share your considered recommendation for my health with her."

"There's no harm done. My sister understands my ways. Although if you wish to keep your head, I suggest you step back, before Neilan relieves you of it."

He grinned, before doing as she suggested. "That would be most inconvenient."

"I should imagine so." This time, a smile broke free, although she smothered it instantly and disappointment shot through him. He wanted to make her smile. And he didn't want her to regret it.

Most of all, he didn't want this encounter to end.

"Do you often come to the village and heal the inhabitants?" It was a poor village indeed that didn't possess at least one resident healer. And he still couldn't wrap his head around the fact that Lady Orabel, healer or not, was a princess of royal blood and as such should not have been in the village in the first place.

"The tavernkeeper's wife had a difficult labor overnight, and word was sent to the palace this morning. In truth, I should have been sent for earlier."

"Uh, I see." Heat washed through him. God, the last topic he wished to discuss was of a woman's labor. Before he could change the subject, she continued.

"I explained to all concerned last month that there might be difficulties and to alert Lady Saoirse and myself as soon as the contractions commenced." There was more than concern in her voice now. She sounded exasperated. "But sometimes being of royal blood and ensconced in a palace is more of a hindrance than anything else."

Women's problems, which most certainly included childbirth, were not the provenance of men and were never spoken about. Unless the woman concerned was one's wife but even then he could scarcely imagine it. Yet Orabel spoke of it as though it was as natural as discussing a broken bone or bloodied leg.

Fascination warred with his natural inclination to avoid all such discussion like leprosy, and he couldn't tear his gaze from her as they left the village. Fascination won. "Are there no healers in the village who might have helped?"

"Of course. Our village is blessed with our healers, but this babe needed additional assistance."

"They are blessed to have you, Lady Orabel. I cannot imagine many ladies would attend the birth of their villagers."

She sighed. "In truth, it is not conventional. But should I only use the goddess' healing gift with those who share my bloodlines?"

He couldn't answer that. In Dal Riada, if royalty or nobles needed specialized treatment, they summoned a physician. Never a woman, no matter how knowledgeable she may have been.

"I trust the outcome was happy." It was as close as he could manage to ask whether the mother and child had survived their ordeal.

This time she smiled and didn't attempt to hide it. "Indeed. It was the happiest of outcomes, thank the goddess. But it is not always so. For such a natural rite, the perils are great."

He supposed they were. He had never really considered it, not even when his brother's wife, Una, had been delivered of her two daughters. It was, as Lady Orabel had said, a natural rite and one that women endured without question.

They walked for a while in silence, away from the village but not, it appeared, directly back to the stronghold of Fib-eviot. Instead, they headed towards a copse where a stream flowed. Not that he minded if the princess wished to take a detour. It gave him the excuse he needed to prolong this intriguing encounter.

Orabel paused and glanced at Lady Saoirse. An unspoken message seemed to pass between them, one that, by the expression on the other lady's face, did not meet with her approval.

The princess returned her attention to him. "Since we didn't know how long we might be, we brought provisions. If you haven't yet eaten, you are welcome to join our picnic."

Neilan gave an audible sniff of disapproval, but it didn't tarnish the moment. He had danced and flirted with other princesses of Pictland, but he had never been invited to share a picnic with one before now.

"I should be delighted."

"Good."

Without a word, but a sour glare that spoke volumes, Neilan thumped the basket onto the ground before Lady Saoirse proceeded to spread a blanket on the grass. Orabel and Saoirse sat, and Neilan loomed with palpable menace as though daring Ross to take up the princess' offer.

"Do sit, MacIntosh." Lady Orabel cast a glance at her warrior that scarcely disguised her affection for the hulking Pict before returning her attention to him. "Alas, Neilan is far too dignified to partake of our repast, but since you are so lately my patient, it's my duty to ensure you are suitably nourished."

He was certain it breached a dozen royal protocols. Commoners in Dal Riada didn't share picnics with princesses and he doubted it was different in Pictland. Yet to refuse would cause offense which was the last thing he wanted to do. After all, this interlude with Orabel could hardly be viewed as a diplomatic mission.

He sat at the edge of the blanket but even that small act of gallantry didn't ensure there was much more than a hairsbreadth between them. Her subtle scent of heather drifted on the breeze, and the exquisite torture of being so close, yet unable to touch her, would surely be worth it.

"Your concern is gratifying, my lady."

"Pray do not be unduly gratified. It would be most unfortunate should a Scot expire while on Fib land."

Was this all an extension of an elaborate plan by the royal house? The more he considered it, the less feasible he found it. Not least because they couldn't have known he'd meet Orabel in the village this day. And using wolfsbane to incapacitate him, merely so Scots might be appreciative of the Picts medical skill, was risky. What if Orabel hadn't managed to save his life?

"It would not bode well for the alliance between our people," he said, since there was little point in deflecting her remark when they both knew the truth of it. "It's a mystery where the arrow is that injured me. I'm told it vanished from the scene."

She inclined her head, and accepted a dish from Saoirse who was unpacking the basket. "The world is full of mysteries, and we cannot know the answer to them all."

He wouldn't dishonor her by asking outright if she knew the whereabouts of the arrow, but if Rourke didn't find it today, there was but one conclusion. The Picts had taken it.

But that did not mean Orabel was aware of it.

"Alas, there is not a spare platter for MacIntosh," Lady Saoirse said.

"Then you must share mine." Orabel placed her dish between them.

"Thank you, my lady." He took a slice of venison pie and his stomach growled in appreciation as he bit into it. He hadn't realized just how hungry he was. "This is most excellent."

"I'll be sure to pass on your compliments to our cook." There was a thread of amusement in her tone, and he smiled at her. How easy it would be to forget he had to stay on his guard while in the Kingdom of Fib. But, maybe, he didn't need to be alert for danger while in the presence of Orabel.

"Are you going to the village again in the morning?" It was scarcely subtle, but what did it matter if she knew he wanted to see her again? They were only in Fib for a week and the queen had made it plain there would be no welcome feast or entertainment for the Scots when he'd have the chance to dance with the princess.

And possibly enjoy a pleasurable liaison.

His cock stirred and he stifled a groan. Best not to imagine such things when an inadvertent glance might betray his salacious thoughts.

"Indeed. I must ensure both mother and babe are thriving, and change the dressing on young Jeb's eye."

"I hope his eye is healed." Saoirse sounded concerned. "That was the last of the sacred elixir, my lady."

"I know." Similar concern threaded through Orabel's words. "There are other elixirs I can prepare, but nothing as potent. It's a great pity we cannot access another coconut."

"A coconut?" Ross had never heard the word before and

couldn't make sense of it even when he mentally translated it into Gaelic. But it was possible his Pictish was at fault. "What is that?"

"A most marvelous gift from the great goddess." There was a reverential note in Orabel's voice. "When I lived in Ayr, merchants arrived who had traded with foreigners from far across the sea. When I touched this strange, hairy, fruit, I knew I had to purchase it, whatever the cost."

"The cost was high," Saoirse said.

"It was more than worth the jewels it cost to secure its possession. The merchants told fantastical tales of its magic, doubtless to increase its price, but it wasn't their words that bewitched me. It was the possibilities Bride allowed me to glimpse of its potency."

By rights, he should be unnerved by how easily she spoke of her heathen goddess and the magic that pagan deity reputedly bestowed upon her misguided followers. But he wasn't. Because Orabel's unabashed awe over this exotic fruit, a fruit he couldn't even imagine, was utterly compelling.

"It has the power to heal eyes?"

"Goddess willing," she responded, and disappointment flared through him. How many times had he heard monks intone *God willing* when faced with the mortality of man? Even the physician who had tended his brother had said Gordon's fate was in God's hands.

But everyone knew that was a fundamental truth. Physicians and healers could do only so much, and most of the time it wasn't enough. If Ross' experience of seeing the aftermath of injuries to the eye was anything to go on, the unfortunate lad was destined to lose his sight, if not his eye itself. All Orabel and her elixir had done, if the lad were lucky, was relieve the pain.

Yet I survived the wolfsbane poison.

And everyone knew that was a death sentence, however fervently one prayed.

He should remain silent. He was no monk or healer, but the

need to know burned deep. "Is it your goddess who heals? Or the elixir?"

The low growl that emanated from Neilan proved he had overstepped, but the princess didn't stiffen in affront. Instead, she smiled, as though she understood his confusion and pitied him for it.

"The two are not separate but entwined. Many can learn the healing arts, MacIntosh, but only a chosen few are granted access to the goddess' greater insights. I pass on my knowledge as best I can, but there are some things…" she hesitated as though trying to find the right words. Or maybe simply words he'd understand. "There are some things I cannot explain. Only feel."

There were things he couldn't explain, either. Such as this fascination with Orabel and her heathen, magical beliefs. He hoped her elixir had worked. And not just because it would save Jeb's eye.

But because it would prove she was, indeed, an extraordinary healer, and there had been no trickery involved when she'd diagnosed him with wolfsbane poisoning.

CHAPTER SEVEN

It was late afternoon when Rourke and his men returned to camp. They brought with them a catch of small game, which would make a welcome change from dry rations, but no news on the elusive arrow.

Ross built a fire, while the men plucked and skinned their catch. Rourke dropped an armload of firewood beside him, and sat on the ground, a brooding expression on his face.

"We must assume the Picts took the arrow," Ross said.

"Aye. And there's only one reason why they'd do that."

"If the bandits were rebels, it makes sense the royal house of Fib wishes to distance themselves from any fallout. I'm not willing to accuse the king—or the queen—of being behind the attack."

Rourke grunted. "The Picts are still our enemy, no matter how many damn alliances MacAlpin tries to forge."

They were surrounded by enemies and had been from the time their ancestors had first claimed Dal Riada so many generations ago.

It wasn't a heartening thought.

"I fear our land will be torn apart should the Norse and

Northumbrians suspect how fragile this alliance truly is. I hope to God those rumors of a treaty between Fib and the southerners has no substance."

"Did you have any luck unearthing anything of value today?" Rourke's voice suggested he doubted it.

"Only more evidence that the princess is an esteemed healer. The villagers summon her to tend their ills."

"I've no need of more evidence. I saw her skill with my own eyes."

The flames caught, and Ross rolled back on his knees to regard his friend. "On your travels last year did you encounter a coconut?"

"A what?"

There was his answer. "It's a powerful, exotic fruit the princess uses as a sacred elixir. It originates from far across the sea."

"I encountered many exotic things. Maybe it went by a different name."

It was possible. And in truth, he wasn't sure why he had even asked Rourke about it. It wasn't as though either of them could manage to summon up this foreign delicacy and present it to Orabel as a token of his gratitude for saving his life.

Gratitude. Aye, sure. It had nothing to do with wanting to give her something that would make her astonishing eyes glow with pleasure, did it?

It was dark, cool, and quiet in Orabel's private apothecary, as she checked on the progress of the wine and healing herbs that were distilling on a bench. She had claimed this small chamber adjacent to the kitchens when she had been but nine years old and her mamma had ensured it would no longer be used as an additional larder.

At thirteen, she achieved her dearly held wish of a sturdy lock on the door, and so had begun her expansion into learning the dangerous secrets of forbidden plants.

"The red gold is all but gone, my lady." Saoirse sighed as she replaced a small, dark, glass bottle onto a shelf. Saoirse was the only one she trusted with a key to the apothecary since Orabel knew she would never touch the hazardous elements.

"It pains me to admit that I miss living in Ayr for any reason, but we certainly saw more merchants there than we do now in Fib." Merchants who had traveled far and traded with others of their ilk who had discovered treasures from unimaginable places in the mystical east. "It's been more than eight moons since I put in a request for saffron. Before I wed, we had far more foreign trade in our ports."

"I should like to blame the Scots, but I fear that would be unreasonable." Saoirse gave her a knowing glance and Orabel shook her head. She too could guess the reason why their ports were not as busy as they had once been, and it had nothing to do with the Dal Riadans.

It was the Northumbrians, steering merchants into their own ports with promises of greater rewards.

"We must trust the goddess in this matter. In the meantime, we need another elixir for the blacksmith's apprentice."

Once again, silence spun between them as they worked on their tasks, a comforting silence born of their years of friendship. And it was such a relief to escape her sister's company, whose derision at the presumptuous invitation to MacAlpin's coronation had been most vocal.

Not that she disagreed. The last time MacAlpin had issued an invitation to the royal house of Fib, to celebrate the marriage of the Princess of Ce with one of his relatives, they had been unforgivably betrayed. MacAlpin had then annexed the Kingdom of Fortriu, dispossessing her dear cousin, Lady Mairi, and now he had the absolute nerve to expect the six remaining kingdoms of Pictland to attend his sham of a coronation?

It would never happen.

She drew in a calming breath and forced her mind from the vexations of political intrigues. The familiar routine as she cleansed the small, dark, bottles was soothing, and unbidden, an image of Ross MacIntosh floated into her mind.

She expelled an impatient breath before casting a furtive glance at Saoirse. Thankfully, her friend remained unaware of the path Orabel's thoughts had traveled. Because there was no excuse to think of MacIntosh unless he stood directly in front of her.

It was sound advice, but her mind refused to obey. His blue eyes glittered with admiration and his magnificent biceps belonged to the realms of dreams. She gave a silent groan at her foolishness. MacIntosh was a Scot and therefore adept at deception when it came to inveigling himself in his adversary's good favor. Although she had to admit, his interest in her calling appeared genuine.

No. She would not allow him to claim her thoughts when she should be working. It was disgraceful enough that he captured her good sense whenever they met.

What had possessed her to invite him to join their picnic? Except the question was redundant when she knew full well why she had.

Because his company enthralled her.

Because he makes me feel things I've never felt before.

Heat swept through her, singeing her skin and causing pleasurable sparks of flame to ignite between her thighs. How could a Scot, of all people, affect her so?

When the Scots were responsible for the death of her beloved father?

It was a shameful secret to lust for her despised enemy, and one she would keep to her dying breath.

"My lady." Saoirse's voice interrupted her tangled thoughts. Thank the goddess for that. "Do you think MacIntosh suspects we have the arrow that injured him?"

She threw her friend a startled glance. It was as though Saoirse had read her illicit imaginings of the irresistible Scot. But no. Wait. The arrow?

Guilt scorched through her, melding with the remnants of lust. While she fantasized about MacIntosh's fine masculine attributes, Saoirse considered only the political implications.

With more difficulty than she liked, she forced her thoughts from their indulgent interlude.

"MacIntosh may suspect whatever he pleases. But he can prove nothing, and that is all that matters." Even as she said the words, regret ate through her. He was no friend to Fib, but she didn't like keeping the truth from him. Even if hiding that truth was essential in keeping the peace between their people.

Even if, in a tiny corner of her soul, she was certain he would believe the royal house wasn't behind the attack, the same could not be said of his king. Who knew what MacAlpin would do, if he smelled even the hint of betrayal in the wind?

It was early afternoon the following day before Orabel left Grizel, the tavernkeeper's wife. As she and Saoirse emerged into the spring sunshine, she let out an exasperated sigh. "These complications could have been avoided had we been called as soon as labor began."

"My lady." The bone-tingling Gaelic accent cut through her thoughts, and she spun around, to see MacIntosh and the taciturn MacConall standing not a horse length from her. Considering a mere three days ago MacIntosh had hovered perilously close to the veil, his robust vitality as he took up far too much space in the narrow alley than he had any right to, was nothing short of breathtaking.

And why did he smile so beguilingly? It was most distracting and annoying. Yes, annoying. It made her forget all the things she needed to remember. She quashed the illicit flares of pleasure that persisted in igniting every time she saw him and offered him a chilly smile in response.

"If I possessed a suspicious nature, I should wonder if you were following me, MacIntosh." The accusation was out before she could think better of it, and inwardly she winced. She wasn't in the habit of direct confrontation, unless it applied to the care of her patients, but it was all the defense she had against his foreign charm.

"Not following," he said, and he didn't sound offended by her barb which was a relief, although it shouldn't be. All she should care about was that he found no fault with Fib, not whether he enjoyed her company or not. Goddess help her. Her mangled thoughts would drive her mad. "But I confess I did hope we might see you in the village. Is that unforgiveable of me?"

She very much wanted to tell him it was. Except his confession was too enchanting. Besides, hadn't she secretly hoped she might see him again today? And since the queen planned no entertainment for their Dal Riadan visitors, they would never have the chance to speak in the more conventional environs of the palace.

And, after all, he would be leaving their kingdom in six days.

The reminder sent a prickle of regret through her, which was beyond irksome. "It's most unforgiveable," she told him. Not that he appeared affected by her rebuke if the warm gleam in his blue eyes was any indication. With difficulty, she tore her mesmerized gaze from his cursed eyes and focused on his nose instead. Alas, it was a very fine nose, indeed. "What, pray, are you doing in the village?"

"We sampled the tavernkeeper's fine ale and an interesting pie."

Her lips twitched, although she tried hard to prevent it. "How interesting was the pie?"

"I have suspicions we deprived the dogs of their meal."

"That is a most grievous accusation." Although she could well believe the tavernkeeper had fed the Scots food taken from his dogs. Bitterness against the Dal Riadans ran deep throughout Fib. "Alas, I have no picnic to share with you today."

And if she did, would she have offered to share it with him?

How exasperating to know she most likely would have.

"That's very kind of you but rest assured, the reason I hoped to see you again today wasn't so that I could share your food."

Behind her, Neilan gave a low growl of warning and inwardly she sighed. What might she and MacIntosh talk about if it was just the two of them alone?

It would never happen. She didn't know why she'd even thought of such an outrageous circumstance. The last thing she wanted was to be alone with him.

A pity she did not believe her own lie.

"Must I ask why you hoped to see me again?" She raised her eyebrows, daring him to respond. Hoping he would.

If only he were not a Scot. Then, perhaps, she could enjoy these extraordinary interactions without the constant specter of guilt hanging over her.

"Forgive me." His smile had surely been gifted by ancient gods and who could resist the lure of immortal bestowed largesse? "I wanted to ask after the health of the tavernkeeper's wife and the blacksmith's apprentice."

He wanted to ask after the health… of her patients?

She inclined her head, so he wouldn't see the confusion in her eyes. Confusion that had no right existing in the first place. What had she expected him to say? That he had come to the village for the sole purpose of seeing her again?

Her good sense was entirely addled when it came to Ross MacIntosh.

After all, she was a princess of royal blood, and he wasn't just a commoner. Despite the charade of the alliance between Pict and Scot, in truth he was the enemy of her people.

Nothing could change that.

Of course he hadn't come to the village merely because he wished to see her. The enticing imaginings that tormented her had likely never occurred to him. If he wanted an illicit assignation with a Pictish noblewoman there were several at court who would be only too eager for such an adventure, and without risking a political scandal. It wouldn't take a great deal of subterfuge to waylay a willing lady, judging by some of the whispered conversations she had overheard among the queen's entourage.

It was imperative MacIntosh didn't guess how badly she had misjudged his interest. The last thing she needed was for him to mistakenly think she found him… intriguing.

"Thankfully, the babe is strong and despite the damage caused before my late arrival yesterday, I'm quietly hopeful Grizel will recover from her ordeal." Why were they still down this side alley? It was a small concern, yet it vexed her greatly.

With an imperious glance in his direction, she made her way from the alley and towards the village square. MacIntosh fell into step beside her, as though he had every right in the world to do so. But it wasn't because he found her or her work fascinating. It was because he wanted to judge her on her healing expertise.

"That's good." Was it her imagination or did he sound uncomfortable by her frank admission? She couldn't think why. He was the one who had asked the question.

"Yes, it is." Her voice was sharper than she'd intended, and even though this conversation should cease at once, she couldn't seem to stop herself. "Had the sanctuary been available, this could have been avoided."

"Sanctuary?" he echoed as though he'd never come across the concept before. But then, he was a savage Scot and quite likely hadn't. Unfortunately, her disparagement of his character didn't make her feel any better. "How is the church not available for those in need of its protection?"

What in the name of the goddess was he talking about?

"The church outside the village," on ancient, hallowed ground, but she wasn't going to start a discussion about that particular affront with him, "is, I am certain, open to its misguided believers but that has *nothing* to do with this."

He cocked his head in evident bafflement, and it was far too endearing. "In Dal Riada, the church offers sanctuary to those fleeing persecution."

"Then I'm sure your churches must be overflowing."

"You could be right." The ghost of a smile touched his lips. She told herself she hadn't noticed.

"I speak of a haven for women in need or distress. And a place of healing for any who arrive at the door."

"The village has this haven?" Now he sounded captivated by the notion. How infuriating that a Scot, of all people, should find her cherished dream to be of such interest, when her own sister, who possessed the means to make it happen, found it anything but.

"It does not." Were it not too undignified, she would have stamped across the square to the blacksmiths. Instead, she compromised and sent MacIntosh a withering glance. Which he didn't appear to notice. Since he had clearly missed her point, she added, "*That* is the problem."

Before he could question her further, she and Saoirse entered the blacksmiths. Jed had been moved to a dark corner and she was relieved that his master hadn't forced him back to work as soon as she'd left the previous day. Sometimes, her royal blood had its uses.

A thorough examination of his eye confirmed he had not lost

his sight. As Saoirse handed him a small pot of salve, Orabel gave the lad a comforting smile. "You must use the salve morn and eve, and keep your eye covered for five days. If any problems arise, send word for us at the palace."

"Yes, milady. Thank ye kindly, milady." Jed bowed as she and Saoirse left him. Her glow at having saved not only the lad's sight but also his future livelihood sputtered when she saw MacIntosh gazing at Jed with a quizzical frown creasing his brow.

If she'd been in any doubt earlier, there was none now. MacIntosh had accosted her simply so he could witness the outcome for Jed for himself.

"Satisfied?" Dear goddess, had she said that aloud? She pressed her lips together before she could disgrace herself further. Alas, her tongue failed to receive the message. "Or do you need more proof of my calling?"

When he tore his gaze from Jed, admiration glowed in his eyes and a despicable curl of flame warmed her deep inside. As if *she* cared what MacIntosh thought of her, or her skill.

Yet clearly, a tiny, depraved part of her did.

"My lady, I did not mean to offend you." His accent infused his words with far more sincerity than he surely deserved. Perhaps in the future she would converse with him in his own language, where she wouldn't be distracted by such inane frivolities. "Your powers of healing surpass anything I've seen before. It's painfully apparent that in these matters, Dal Riada could learn much from you."

Marginally appeased, she inclined her head. "Perhaps I should not have judged you so harshly. It's scarcely your fault that your people turned their back on the ancient ways so many generations ago. It's inevitable your healers lost much knowledge in the process."

And with it, any chance of the great goddess blessing a chosen one with her sacred insights.

"I cannot speak to that. I can only compare this to what I've seen with my own eyes. Please forgive me for doubting you, my lady."

She really shouldn't. But the knot in her chest, caused by his disbelief, was dissolving like snow beneath the first breath of spring. There was no point denying it. His readiness to accept his prejudice was entrancing.

"Not many fierce warriors would admit to being in the wrong. I can admire you for that, at least."

"Fierce or not, a warrior is ruled by honor. I would not have you think badly of me simply because I refused to see what was in front of me."

"Goddess. How different you are from Northumbrians."

His smile was questioning. "I should hope so, although I'm not certain what you mean."

She ignored the warning glance from Saoirse, even though she should keep her peace. What harm was there in sharing just a small sliver of her previous life with this engaging Scot?

It was not, after all, a great secret that Edwin had openly despised her insistence on not limiting her healing abilities to those he considered worthy of them, nor hidden his disbelief that she could prevail when his own physicians failed.

"I do not mean anything by it. Merely that my late husband had his opinions, and nothing would sway him from them."

A strange expression flashed across MacIntosh's face. It was almost as though the fact she'd once possessed a husband stunned him.

"Your late husband was a Northumbrian?"

"Indeed. Edwin, Prince of Ayr. We were wed for six years." She kept a small smile on her face, a façade she was used to wearing when it came to speaking of her late husband.

When recalling his death.

Do not think of it. His ignoble end wasn't her fault.

Keep telling yourself that.

"My lady." MacIntosh's voice was uncharacteristically stilted and pulled her from the dark corners in her mind. "I'm sorry for your loss."

Her senses sharpened, although she could not think why. But something in MacIntosh's manner struck her as off kilter.

It wasn't polite regret that emanated from him. It was…

She frowned, uncomprehending, for it made no sense. Why would the knowledge she was widowed engender such horror?

CHAPTER EIGHT

Ross gazed into Orabel's concerned eyes as denial pounded through his brain. He'd been so fixated on her astonishing healing powers, on the unsavory possibility the attack and his miraculous recovery were part of a royal conspiracy, that he'd completely overlooked the obvious.

Orabel was the princess that Finn suspected MacAlpin wanted to ensnare in his web.

The princess his king wanted to be Stuart MacGregor's bride.

His gut clenched in distaste. Orabel deserved a better fate than that. A better husband than the loose-tongued MacGregor.

God damn it. It was all pure speculation and yet now he knew who the widowed princess was, the prospect took on an ominous shroud of inevitability.

"MacIntosh," she said, wrenching him from his unpalatable visions of her being wed to his subordinate. "Is something—"

A horse galloped into the village square, and Orabel swung about as a messenger leaped from the saddle and bowed before her. "My lady, the queen requests the princess' presence as a matter of urgency."

"Very well. We shall return at once. Inform the queen we shall arrive shortly."

The messenger cast a hostile glance at Ross before returning his attention to the princess. "My lady must take my horse. The queen was most insistent."

"I see." There was a touch of frost in Orabel's voice as though she didn't take kindly to the queen's command. "Lady Saoirse, we shall ride together. Neilan, ask the farrier if he has a mount for you."

As Neilan marched off, Ross accompanied the princess to the horse. "I trust all is well at the palace," he said.

She sighed. "As do I." She hesitated, as though weighing up her words, before adding, "It was good to see you again, MacIntosh. I'm glad we had the opportunity for this talk."

Despite his black suspicions of her fate, he grinned. "So I had the opportunity to admit I was wrong about the magnitude of your skill, you mean? I'm glad of it, too."

"Yes, that's exactly what I mean." She smiled up at him and a strange pain twisted through his chest. It wasn't that he thought Stuart would mistreat Orabel. The man was scarcely deep, but he wasn't a fool. He'd likely treat the princess like spun glass, something rare and precious, as he damn well should.

But it didn't sit right with him. And neither did the prospect that he might never have the chance to speak with her again.

He lowered his voice so no one else might overhear. "I hope we have another opportunity like this before we leave Fib."

"That would be quite agreeable. Lady Saoirse and I will be visiting Grizel for the next several days should you happen to be in the village. Or if you care to taste another of the tavernkeeper's pies, perhaps you will once again have need of my healing skills."

He laughed, couldn't help himself. "A tempting prospect. I hoped for something less damaging to my health."

"You may rest assured that your constitution is well able to withstand the occasional interesting pie. The goddess favors you, and that cannot be in any doubt."

"It is you she favors, my lady."

"Ah. So you believe in her now, do you?"

"I believe in you, and that's all I shall commit myself on."

Her warrior returned, leading a horse, and before Ross could assist, Orabel swung herself into the saddle, before Lady Saoirse followed her mistress. Unlike Scotswomen, both ladies sat astride. And although he knew of this practice, from the time he'd spent in other Pict kingdoms during the last year, nothing had prepared him for this provocative sight of Orabel.

He swallowed and bowed his head in farewell before she spurred her horse on.

By his side, Rourke grunted.

"What?" he said, without taking his eyes from Orabel's progress.

"Don't get involved, man."

That got his attention. And raised his ire. "What the fuck are you talking about? I've no intention of getting involved."

"She's not a woman to have a fleeting liaison with."

Now he was just fucking outraged. "I don't harbor any such base intent for the princess."

"If you say so." Rourke's dour response did nothing to improve his temper, but it did manage to ignite a spark of caution.

Christ. He *was* interested in Orabel. Had circumstances been different there was no doubt he would have flirted with the intention of an enjoyable dalliance.

But he knew there was no chance of that happening. Not when Scots had been relegated to camping in the fields and not invited to share even one meal as a perfunctory show of alliance between their people. It was likely the queen herself had forbidden the ladies in her court to fraternize with the enemy. Unlike certain other Pict kingdoms, where he'd gained the strongest suspicion that the assignations between his men and the noblewomen of the court had received tacit royal approval.

"I do fucking say so." Shit, if that wasn't tantamount to an admission of guilt, he didn't know what was. He followed up his unwary retort with a glare, that Rourke, damn him, ignored.

"It's not me you need to convince," Rourke said as they tramped from the village back to their base. "The Pict who guards her wants to tear you limb from limb and the villagers have eyes—and tongues in their heads to spread rumors."

Ross halted and turned to his friend. "Nothing's happened between us, Rourke. And nothing will. This isn't the Kingdom of Ce before the massacre at Dunadd, when Pictish noblewomen were eager to share their charms with us. Lady Orabel has stated plainly how she despises our race."

"I wasn't in Ce. But I saw well enough when Ewan and I were stationed in Fotla that the political situation is easily put aside when lust prevails."

"I don't allow lust to cloud my judgement."

"I'm aware."

Ross gritted his teeth. Rourke's meaning was clear, even if it was unwelcome. What was more, his insinuation was baseless.

Aye, he desired Lady Orabel but that was all. And desire could be contained. "I've enjoyed my share of illicit assignations with Pictish noblewomen this last year. But I would never put our alliance at risk."

"Not to mention," Rourke continued, obviously intending to mention whatever else plagued his good sense, "if we're right about MacAlpin's plans, Lady Orabel is to be sacrificed to MacGregor."

"You—" Ross bit off his retort and clenched his fists. He was used to Rourke, but sometimes the other man's bluntness was hard to take. He exhaled a long breath, but it didn't help. "We have no orders to see that through. As far as I'm concerned, when we leave Fib, Stuart MacGregor will not be in possession of a bride."

~

AFTER THEY ARRIVED at the palace, Orabel and Saoirse went to her chambers to secure her casket, and she reined in her impatience as her friend combed her hair and straightened her veil. It was irrational to be so irked by her sister's summons, but there was no denying she'd been enjoying Ross MacIntosh's company and hadn't wished to cut their conversation short.

"I cannot believe the Scot had the audacity to question my lady's skill." Saoirse's eyes flashed with anger. "And after you had saved his worthless life, too."

"At least he apologized." And what a difference that had made. She shouldn't allow a few careless words to so affect her judgement but couldn't help it. "That is something."

Saoirse sniffed. Clearly, she did not agree. "If one can call that an apology."

Orabel smiled, as the memory of MacIntosh's compelling blue eyes once again stole her senses. "In my experience, warriors do not readily admit to being in the wrong, even when they most certainly are."

Saoirse hesitated before taking a deep breath. "My lady, forgive me. But I fear the Scot has dishonorable designs upon you."

If only.

The thought drifted through her mind. Utterly scandalous, of course, and yet how spellbinding the notion was. She shook her head, although she couldn't tell whether it was for Saoirse's benefit or her own.

But whatever the truth, she couldn't allow anyone, even her dearest friend, to guess how secretly the idea enthralled her.

"Alas, the Scots have shown they cannot be trusted. We must

always be vigilant. Come, we had best not keep the queen waiting any longer."

Her sister was in their mother's private chambers, which was a surprise. Since their father's death, whenever Etain summoned her, she invariably received her in the royal inner sanctum.

She and Saoirse dropped respectful curtseys, before Saoirse took her place with the other noblewomen. Etain stood in the center of the chamber, one hand protectively cradling her belly, their mother standing beside her.

"Orabel," her sister said. "We have received word that Raedwulf will arrive in Fib-eviot by noon on the morrow."

Ice speared her chest. It had been nearly four weeks since they had last spoken of the Northumbrians, and she'd pushed the distasteful conversation to the back of her mind. Moreover, she had even managed to convince herself Raedwulf had changed his mind about pursuing her.

How foolish of her. She knew better than to imagine problems happily vanished, simply because they were abhorrent. And worse, she hadn't even put in motion any plans to secure her own sanctuary.

A sanctuary that wouldn't only help those in need. But somewhere she could escape from the duties expected of a princess.

Yet deep in her heart she knew her sister was right. The Northumbrians would never acknowledge the sanctity of such a place. She needed to find an unassailable reason, and fast, that would prevent Raedwulf from demanding she became his bride.

Her mamma took her hand. "Orabel, do you need to sit?"

Sit, while the queen stood? It was unthinkable, and Etain would not forget the slight.

"I am quite well," she assured her mamma, even though her heart hammered, and it hurt to breathe. There was little point voicing her objections again. Even her mother had sided with Etain, in the end.

"It is most vexing the Scots are still in our kingdom." Etain expelled an impatient breath. "It will cause friction, there is no doubt."

"Perhaps it will serve as a timely reminder to the Northumbrians that Pictland is allied with Dal Riada." Good goddess, what was she saying? She despised that alliance for its bloodied cost. But that didn't make her retort any less true.

Etain narrowed her eyes and contemplated her in a manner that caused an uneasy shudder along her spine. What new plan was her sister concocting?

"And we should use that to our advantage."

"What are you saying, Etain?" There was a sharp note in their mother's voice.

"That Orabel is correct. If Raedwulf is serious in his intentions, then it is to Fib's advantage if he believes we have… options."

Options? Orabel stared at her sister, aghast. "You would sell me off to the highest bidder?"

"Etain, this is quite unacceptable. We cannot even contemplate such a union after the way the Scots betrayed your dear papa."

"You misunderstand, Mamma." Impatience threaded through Etain's voice. "It is merely a ploy, to raise Orabel's desirability. We need say nothing, for the very fact the Scots are here will say everything we wish to convey."

Pain squeezed Orabel's heart at how ruthlessly her sister meant to use her. They had never been close, but they were of the same blood, after all. "You think Raedwulf wouldn't see through this scheme? He's not a fool, Etain. And he won't take kindly if you attempt to manipulate him in this game."

"There will be no manipulation." Her sister's small smile belied her words. "If you are to be the wife of Raedwulf, he will pay dearly for the honor and, as such, be obligated to treat you in a manner as befits a princess of Fib."

Was that supposed to make her feel better? A carelessly tossed breadcrumb in a swirling storm of treachery?

"Therefore," Etain continued, "as a sign of your elevated status, we shall assign the five noblewomen who are completing their education in Fib-eviot as your personal entourage."

"But that is not their purpose," she protested. She had only ever had Saoirse, and her friend was all she needed. How could she tend to her patients if she was always surrounded by a cluster of young, sheltered, girls?

"That is of no account. Their parents will be delighted by their elevation to serve a future queen of Northumbria."

A future queen of Northumbria. Her stomach twisted and she fought for a calm that slipped further out of reach with every frantic beat of her heart.

"I presume a great feast will be laid on for the Northumbrians arrival," their mamma said.

"Indeed. May I leave that preparation in your capable hands, Mamma?"

Their mother inclined her head. "Of course. And perhaps the Scots should also be invited. It will be a show of great diplomatic strength to entertain two erstwhile enemies together within the walls of Fib-eviot."

"Excellent," Etain said. "While MacAlpin didn't send his dogs to ensnare Orabel— otherwise why have they not made that plan clear to us? —it will certainly give the Northumbrians pause. Without any of us," she gave Orabel a knowing glance, "needing to say a word on the matter."

THIS WAS INTOLERABLE.

Orabel exchanged a glance with Saoirse as they worked in her apothecary later that afternoon. The five young ladies, who were now in her service, had been thrilled by their promotion and were clearly eager to please. But their constant gasps as they examined her precious jars and pouches, and excited whispers and giggles, jarred on her frayed nerves.

Her apothecary was a place of calm. And while she'd brought the girls here before, to learn basic remedies, this experience was entirely different.

"Perhaps the young ladies *would* be better employed with their needles," Saoirse said under her breath and Orabel gave a heavy sigh. The queen had made it clear she expected her to embrace more traditional pursuits now she possessed a retinue of impressionable ladies, and embroidery was high on the list.

To be sure, she and Saoirse were more than adept at sewing, but compared to other noblewomen her gowns were plain. She didn't have time for the intricate needlework that adorned her sister and mother's gowns but then again, neither had she ever had half a dozen ladies at her bidding.

"Do you suppose they might be happier spending their days with threads of silk?"

"Not without supervision, I fear. Even if they joined the dowager queen's ladies, the princess or I would be expected to oversee their progress."

Saoirse was right, of course. She would not be able to rid herself of the girls' constant chatter quite so easily. But it was hard to think when she was constantly on alert to ensure they didn't touch something they shouldn't, and she desperately needed to think.

No, it was more than that. Panic at the impending visit from the Northumbrians was clouding her reason. What she needed to do was beseech Bride for guidance. Insight. *Anything.*

She would go to the sacred standing stones at dawn and beg her goddess for deliverance.

CHAPTER NINE

As dawn broke on the eastern horizon, turning the sky violet and streaking the mountain peaks an iridescent indigo, Ross left his tent and drew in a great lungful of the crisp, early morning air.

On his return from the village yesterday, he'd discovered the reason for Orabel's hasty departure. The Northumbrians were on their way.

He rolled his shoulders. Did they intend to finish what the bandits had started? Nothing would convince him the attack had been random. And if he discounted that the Picts were behind it, that only left the Northumbrians.

Unless they're in league together.

The possibility seemed only too probable. Especially since he and his men had been invited to the feast this eve, to welcome the arrival of the southern barbarians.

Brooding, he strode from the camp. Birdsong filled the air and the distant low of cattle gave a deceptive sense of familiarity. But he couldn't afford to lower his guard in a land where every glance proclaimed him as an enemy. They weren't wanted here.

Even if their princess had used her magical arts to save him from certain death.

He raked his fingers through his hair and expelled a harsh breath. Orabel had invaded his dreams last night, her raven black hair cocooning them in a scented haven as her fingers and lips had driven him to the edge. Even now, he was as hard as a damn rock, with no chance of relief in the foreseeable future.

Certainly, his coin would be welcome in the village. But he didn't want to seek out a willing wench, or even, if the opportunity arose this night, one of the queen's ladies. He wanted Orabel.

What mystical gifts did these princesses of Pictland possess that they could ensnare a man so easily? Yet it wasn't always so. While last year he'd been enchanted by the Princess of Circinn, she'd never haunted his thoughts the way Orabel did. And he'd wished Cameron MacNeill nothing but luck when the man had fallen utterly beneath her spell.

But Orabel. Savagely, he kicked a rock. The thought of her with Stuart MacGregor made something dark and ugly twist deep in his gut. There was no way in hell he'd wish the other man luck, should he end up winning her hand.

It had nothing to do with wanting to wed her himself, whatever warped ideas Rourke might harbor. He'd never marry. He had made that vow ten years ago, after Una had chosen his brother over him.

No. He desired the princess. What red blooded man wouldn't? She was exquisite. But her fascination would fade as soon as he left the Kingdom of Fib.

Just so long as they left her in Fib-eviot, too.

He tramped over a ridge, beyond which lay the church. But it wasn't the church that caught his attention as it came into view. Because standing before one of the ancient stones, her head bowed and hands pressed against its face, was Orabel.

As though he had conjured her from the tangle of his thoughts.

The lust he had awoken with, and that the early walk had yet to quench, roared through his blood like liquid fire. It was madness. He would skirt the stones and leave her in peace to continue whatever pagan rite she was invoking. It was not his concern it verged on sacrilege, being within a hefty stone-throw of the church.

Who was he trying to fool? He didn't give a damn who she worshipped or what Godly laws she defied. He would avoid her because in his current state he was likely to steal a kiss.

And have her warrior rip his head from his shoulders for the unforgiveable transgression.

His gaze sharpened. Where the hell was the Pict who always shadowed her? Or Lady Saoirse? Hell, was she *alone*?

Outrage at her vulnerability surged through him. Anything might happen to her. He swung on his heel and marched down the ridge.

She appeared completely unaware of his approach which only served to heighten the unnerving vise that gripped his chest. What if bandits had come upon her?

"My lady." His voice was harsher than he intended, and she sprung back from the stone as though it burned. He sucked in a sharp breath and tried not to notice how her hair was tied into a messy plait, so unlike the way she usually allowed her dark curls to tumble in unrestrained abandonment over her shoulders.

He swallowed. Not that it helped with the visceral image imprinted in his brain, of how she had taken him into her mouth during his lust filled nighttime fantasies.

"MacIntosh." She clutched her shawl more securely around her, as though it were a flimsy barrier against his unwelcome intrusion. "What are you doing here at this hour?"

He tore his gaze from her and swept a glare about them. "Are you unaccompanied, my lady?"

She straightened and slung him a regal look. Clearly, he had offended her. "I do not answer to a Scot."

What the fuck was wrong with him? He should have stuck to his plan and left her well alone. But he was here now, and there was nothing for it but to tell her the truth. "I was concerned for your safety. In Dal Riada, no highborn lady would wander alone. The world is full of danger."

"I do not *wander*." It was obvious his choice of words hadn't appeased her. "I seek the benevolence of the great goddess. No one who values their life would accost me here, while I commune with Bride."

"I meant no disrespect. But I saw you were alone and could not in good conscience pass by without offering you my protection. Surely even in Fib, not everyone respects such boundaries."

"Perhaps not in Dal Riada. But in Pictland the ancient gods protect our sacred places and those who worship there."

The early morning breeze caused a rosy blush to heat her cheeks. Or maybe it was merely indignation at his breach in etiquette for having questioned her. Either way, with her magnificent violet eyes flashing at him, and errant tendrils of black hair dancing around her face, he was entirely bewitched.

Yet he had to defend his actions. "It's true that in Dal Riada we don't worship in the old places. But our churches are just as sacred. Yet our royal ladies would never attend even a church by themselves."

And while his knowledge of the habits of the royal ladies in the House of Alpin was limited, he knew well enough that even noblewomen never went anywhere without at least one serving woman.

"Thankfully," Orabel said, "I am not a Scotswoman."

He sighed. "That you are not, my lady."

"I am unsure how to take that remark. I feel you mean it as a slight."

"Not at all. I have no wish for you to be a Scotswoman." Even if the unthinkable happened and she ended up wed to MacGregor, it wouldn't change who she was.

A Pict to her very soul.

She shook her head. "This is most unseemly. I thank you for your concern. I know it was kindly meant. But..." Her voice trailed away, and she cast a furtive glance at the standing stone beside her. "It seems my goddess, in her wisdom, chooses not to reveal the path before me."

"I'm sorry to hear that." He meant it, too. Orabel believed in her goddess, and he knew only too well how deep it cut when prayers were ignored.

"It's very hard to," she hesitated, before taking a deep breath. "It's hard to know what is expected of one, if clouds obscure the way."

He took another step closer before he even realized he'd moved. "Will it help to talk about whatever is troubling you?"

She gave a small, mirthless laugh, that cut deeper than it had any right to. And the overwhelming need to protect her, that had consumed him when he'd first seen her by the stone, washed through him once again.

"I doubt you would find it so very troubling. It is the fate of all women, after all."

Dull rage knotted deep in his gut. Their suspicions had been right. The royal house of Fib intended to make an alliance with the Northumbrians, with Orabel as the sacrifice.

"You are betrothed to the Northumbrian prince?" God only knew how he managed to push the words out without sounding completely rabid. But somehow he had, as Orabel didn't look at him as though he were mad.

"No." Her denial was swift and filled with loathing. "There is no understanding between us."

Something in her manner aroused his suspicions. "You know him?"

"I do. Prince Raedwulf is related to my late husband. Goddess." She pressed her hand to her mouth and horror filled her eyes. "I should not speak of such things to you."

Her words were muffled but he heard, and understood, them well enough.

"My lady, you have broken no confidences. Such rumors have reached Dunadd." Aye, and all he could do was rail against the repugnant possibility that Orabel would wed the Northumbrian warlord, instead of coldly assessing how this confirmation showed the truth of Fib-eviot's loyalties.

But he couldn't think about the political implications when the stark misery on Orabel's face tore through his chest.

Slowly she dropped her hand, and realization filled her beautiful eyes. "That is the real reason why you came to Fib-eviot. To confirm your suspicions. Isn't it?"

How could he deny it? He wasn't sure he could deny her anything when she looked at him with such despair.

"Aye," he admitted, and when she closed her eyes and inhaled a ragged breath, as though he had personally betrayed her, an impotent slash of anger against his king polluted his reason. He ached to pull her into his arms, to comfort her as best he could, but there was nothing he could say to ease her concerns. "But that doesn't mean I don't empathize with your situation."

"I wed one Northumbrian warlord for the sake of Fib. When I gained my freedom, I swore never to marry again. Yet my wishes are as insignificant as ants beneath our feet."

It was not his business. He had no right to ask. Yet he couldn't remain silent. "Your marriage was unhappy?"

She gave a dismissive shrug. "It was a political alliance, little more. But it deeply offended the great goddess and now I fear she may turn her back on me for good if I cannot find a way to escape this new imprisonment."

It had never occurred to him a woman might compare marriage to imprisonment. Although, in truth, he had never given it much thought. Even last year, while he'd despised his king's methods of entrapping the princesses of Pictland, his sympathy for a forced match and all it entailed had been with his fellow Scots' warriors, not their royal brides.

But now it affected Orabel, and he was anything but indifferent to that.

"If there's no official betrothal between you and the Northumbrian prince, this concern may be unfounded."

"I wish I could be so certain of that. I fear there is only one reason why he travels to Fib-eviot, and it's not merely to pay his respects."

Derision dripped from her last words. Was she including the Scots in her comment? If so, she wasn't wrong. Even if he wished she were.

And then something she'd said snagged in his mind. "Why would your goddess be against this marriage?" His God wasn't against marriage. In fact, it was a cornerstone of the civilized world. "Does your faith frown on such alliances?"

"No." She sounded reluctant to admit it. "Pictland is founded upon alliances between the seven kingdoms. But that was never the path Bride showed me." Suddenly, she flung back her head and her eyes flashed with a wild conviction. "Husbands and children are not my destiny." Passion heated her voice, burning away the despair that had clung to her like a spectral shroud, and white-hot lust speared through him, shredding his reason.

Before he could stop himself, he traced a finger along her heated cheek, and she gave a silent gasp at his presumption. It should have been enough for him to stop, to return to sanity, but if anything, that hushed inhalation of breath was the most seductive sound he'd ever heard.

"What is your destiny, Orabel?" His voice was raw with hunger and her name slipped out, unintentional, yet sounding so right on his tongue.

Her violet eyes darkened. God help him, a man could lose himself in those eyes and count himself fortunate.

"Whatever Bride decrees." Her words were husky and sank into his senses like a fabled aphrodisiac from the mystical east. "I am but her faithful servant."

His gaze roved over her face, from her dark lashes and high, aristocratic cheekbones, to her full, rose-tinted lips. The image of her belonging to a wild, southern barbarian was intolerable. "How will your goddess save you from Northumbria?"

She pressed her palms against his chest and the heat from her hands ignited an illicit blaze deep in his blood. Without thinking, he wrapped his arm around her and tugged her close.

"It is not for her to save me." Orabel's voice was a sensual caress against his lips. He barely prevented a tortured groan from escaping. "Her benevolence is the light that leads me. But the path is shadowed. I must find the way or risk her justified wrath."

The evocative scent of heather and arousal perfumed the air, sinking into his senses until all he could see, all he could feel, was Orabel.

There were so many reasons why this was wrong. He could not recall a single one of them. Not when her fingers grasped his shirt, and her erratic breath was warm against his jaw. Not when her body was so tantalizingly close to his that her breasts pressed against his chest.

The heavy thud of his heart echoed through his head, obliterating everything but the primitive need to taste, to possess.

His mouth met hers. There was no resistance, no gasp of outrage. She was soft and warm, and his fingers tangled in her hair, clasping her head, holding her still.

She moaned, a primal sound that vibrated inside his mouth with suppressed need. His arm tightened around her waist, pulling her so close he could feel every luscious curve of her body pressed against his. Her fingernails scraped along his jaw, a delicate whisper of forbidden pleasure, and ravenous craving spiked through his blood.

The soft material of her gown was a seductive impediment as his palm molded her hip and slid along the length of her thigh. Her mouth opened and he pushed inside, tasting her sweetness, exploring hidden temptations. *Possessing.*

Or maybe he was the one possessed.

He backed her up against the stone, and the sharp tugs of pain as her fingers tangled in his hair damn near drove him out of his mind. Her tongue stroked his, a duel of unimagined bliss and torture, sucking him into a vortex where time ceased to exist, and his only anchor was Orabel.

He grasped her grown, crushing the material in his fist, craving only to feel her naked flesh beneath his fingers. She hitched in a sharp gasp and broke their kiss, her hot breath caressing his lips with erotic abandonment.

"Ross." She breathed his name like a provocation to sin and God knew, he was willing to risk his neck for one more dangerous kiss. He captured her mouth once again and it was everything, more, and the sliver of sanity he retained drowned a silent death.

Her nails scored his head and down his face, digging into his jaw and with a muffled curse he pulled back. For endless moments their gazes clashed, and breaths mingled, as savage lust gripped his vitals in an unrelenting vise.

"This should not have happened." Her whisper held no condemnation, and he couldn't pull back. But neither could he deny the truth of her statement.

"No." His hot gaze roved over her flushed face and the desire that filled her eyes. "Do you regret it?"

"Regret isn't something I dwell upon. But still, you are the enemy of my people."

"I'm not your enemy, Orabel. I could never be your enemy."

She hitched in a ragged breath, and he tried, and failed, to ignore how her breasts strained against the fabric of her bodice.

"Your despicable king slaughtered my beloved father. We can never be anything but enemies."

He expelled a sigh and pressed his forehead against hers. "I have no defense for what happened in the past. My men and I traveled from Northumbria that night and I don't know what happened at Dunadd. Aye, our people have battled each other for generations, but does that mean we will always do so?"

"It doesn't matter, Ross. In a few days you will leave Fib with whatever information your king sent you here to discover. And I shall remain here, and no matter what treaties are made none of us shall think any differently than we did… a week ago."

"You're wrong." His lips brushed a kiss against her temple, and she gave a delicate shiver. "A week ago, I did not know you."

"That makes no difference to your king or his ambitions."

She was right. But he couldn't admit it.

Did not want to admit it.

But what he wanted was foolhardy. Yet he'd curse himself forever if he didn't even ask.

"We have five days, my lady. I'm willing to meet you anywhere, if we might be alone."

She cradled his jaw, and he pulled back just enough so their gazes meshed. "A clandestine affair?" Each smoky word was a sensual caress, and he barely swallowed the groan that razed his throat. "I cannot even imagine such a thing."

"There's no need to imagine. Let me show you."

"I should have your head for such impertinence." She made the accusation sound like a lover's embrace, and he offered her a feral grin.

"I'd offer you my head if I thought it would help my suit."

Her smile was entrancing. If she but knew it, he had already lost his head.

"A bold offer, indeed."

"My lady." Saoirse's shocked voice splintered through his mind, and he reeled back, as Orabel hastily straightened from the standing stone and turned to the other woman. Fuck. The last thing he wanted was to tarnish her reputation. Why had he been so careless?

Why the hell hadn't he been aware of Saoirse's approach? She might just as easily have been an enemy, intent on harming the princess.

Or him. But that possibility didn't concern him nearly as much as the other.

He dragged his fingers through his hair, and shot Orabel a glance, but she didn't appear horrified at having been caught in a compromising position and he drew in a steadying breath. Maybe Saoirse could be persuaded to say nothing of this, for the sake of her mistress' honor.

"Lady Saoirse." Orabel held out her hand for Saoirse. "I am just returning to the palace."

"Neilan accompanied me." Saoirse's meaning was plain and with a grimace Ross took a step back from the princess to show he meant no harm. Clearly, the Pict warrior was within calling distance, even if he couldn't see him.

"I had to commune with the great goddess," Orabel said, and Saoirse inclined her head in understanding. "MacIntosh entered the circle but there is no harm done."

"Indeed."

That was all she said, but Ross had the strangest conviction that something unspoken had passed between the two women. But then, it was easy to imagine fantastical things within this ancient circle, where Orabel worshipped a pagan goddess and where, for a few glorious moments, he had entirely lost his mind.

"I shall bid you farewell." Orabel's smile was enigmatic as she looked at him once again. "And see you again soon, I have no doubt."

He bowed his head and watched them leave the circle as her parting words echoed in his ears.

It was madness to pursue an assignation with the Princess of

Fib. Especially when the Northumbrians would be in the kingdom within hours. But the seed was planted, and her ambiguous farewell stoked the fire that licked through his veins like a relentless serpent.

He would have Orabel before he left Fib and quench this flame that burned between them.

CHAPTER TEN

Ross strode back to their camp but although the breeze cooled his skin, it did nothing to calm the pound of his heart, the anticipation that sizzled his blood or the conviction that he and Orabel would find a way, no matter how many obstacles were in their path.

He expelled a harsh breath. One thing was certain. He needed to find a nearby loch and plunge headfirst into its ice-cold depths. Maybe then he'd be able to function without his rock-hard erection dictating every thought in his head.

Aye. A dip in the loch was the first order of the day.

And then he saw MacAllister striding towards him. God damn it. He'd guessed MacAllister would arrive at Fib-eviot some time today but not this early. The sun had barely risen.

"Ross." There was an uncharacteristic note of concern in the older man's voice as they halted before each other. "We left as soon as the messenger told us what happened. You're fully recovered?"

"I am." He kept his voice brusque even though, in the back of his mind, relief surged. If he and Orabel had remained a few more moments within the circle, it was likely MacAllister would have come upon them. And unlike Lady Saoirse, Ross was sure MacAllister would certainly find a way to take advantage of the situation.

"Good." MacAllister eyed him and Ross returned the scrutiny. It was always best to show no emotion before the king's man. Even as a boy, before MacAllister had been his commanding officer, Ross had been wary of the man's uncanny ability to understand things he had no right in knowing. "Rourke tells me the evidence mysteriously vanished."

Careful.

The warning was lightning sharp through his mind, and he barely managed not to flinch. Where the fuck had that come from? And what was he warning himself against?

But since MacAllister required a response, he gave an abrupt nod. "Correct."

"Do you have suspicions?"

He had plenty of suspicions and it was his duty to report them all. But he also had no evidence to support his theories and reluctance to fan the flames of a fire that might not exist clawed deep.

"The bandits may simply have been random peasants who set upon the wrong travelers."

"You believe that?"

No. Not for a heartbeat. "They were no match for us, but they were trained. Possibly Northumbrians."

"Or Picts?"

"Unfortunately, there's no way of telling."

"Because the arrow is missing. Although even its recovery might not tell the truth." MacAllister gazed into the distance, in the direction of the standing stones, his eyes narrowed. "Tell me. Have you uncovered any indication that the royal house of Fib is planning an alliance with the Northumbrians?"

Orabel's impassioned confession burned through his mind. He would sooner rip out his tongue than betray her confidence to anyone, least of all MacAllister.

It was treachery, perhaps even treason, not to share his knowledge with his commanding officer. But for the sake of Orabel, he could live with that. Besides, as soon as the Northumbrians arrived at Fib-eviot their intentions would no longer be concealed.

Impotent rage at Orabel's possible fate blazed through him once again and managed to douse the lingering threads of lust. With difficulty, he kept his face impassive before MacAllister noticed and drew his own politically twisted conclusions.

"We've not been welcome in Fib-eviot. There have been no feasts and no opportunities to discuss such matters informally."

MacAllister would know what he meant. It had been a tactic, in other Pictish kingdoms, for warriors to extract information from their conquests. The practice had sickened him even though, as far as he was aware, nothing of great import had been discovered that way.

The noblewomen of Pictland had more integrity than MacAllister or their king gave them credit for.

"I understand we are welcomed this eve. When the Northumbrians arrive."

"Aye." There was little else he could say.

"A power play." Instead of cold anger at how the royal house of Fib flirted with treachery with the alliance between their people, MacAllister sounded oddly intrigued. "With the youngest Princess of Fib as the prize."

The admission of his suspicions was a punch to the gut but somehow Ross managed not to react. At least, not outwardly. Inside, denial howled like a rabid wolf at Orabel's fate.

"We were sent to Fib to secure the princess' hand for Dal Riada?" His voice was flat, but MacAllister shot him a shrewd glance before once again contemplating the distant standing stones.

"We came to Fib to pay our respects and discover if an alliance existed between the royal house and the Northumbrians.

You know as well as I that such a treaty cannot be allowed to flourish."

His usual caution crumbled under the knowledge of how Orabel was nothing but a pawn in the game between his king, the Northumbrian warlord, and her own sister, the queen.

She wasn't the first. God knew, she wouldn't be the last. But she was Orabel, and he couldn't remain silent.

"Who does our king decree worthy of requesting the princess' hand?"

"Aye." MacAllister shot him another indecipherable glance. "That's the question, is it not?"

No one was worthy of her hand. Knowing who MacAlpin had in mind would not make any difference to the outcome. Why the fuck was he torturing himself? It didn't help Orabel. And yet the need to know plagued him.

"Unless there are any other unrecognized princes of Dal Riada"— *Careful.* The warning clanged loudly in his head. He was perilously close to treason. Yet still he couldn't shut his mouth. "That leaves only Stuart MacGregor."

MacAllister grunted. In another man, it might be an indication of surprise, but MacAllister was not another man. He was the king's man and knew exactly what plans MacAlpin conspired.

"MacGregor possesses a trace of royal blood," MacAllister conceded, and it was all the confirmation Ross needed. They had been right. God damn it. "With the right incentive, it could work."

The right incentive? What did MacAllister mean to do, compromise Orabel's reputation so she had no choice but to surrender her freedom?

He wasn't making sense. He knew it. And he feared if he stayed any longer, he'd say something that could not be taken back, not misconstrued, something that wouldn't help Orabel but would certainly result in his own execution.

"I must return to the men." Although now MacAllister had

arrived, he was no longer officially the commanding officer. The knowledge poured oil onto the flames that ate through his gut.

"We shall speak later," MacAllister said, and for a second Ross could have sworn amusement flashed across the older man's face.

Ross clenched his fists and turned sharply away, before he sealed his fate by taking a swing at the king's man's smug expression.

A CLANDESTINE AFFAIR.

The evocative words spun through Orabel's mind as she returned to the palace with Saoirse and Neilan.

By rights, MacIntosh's presumptuous proposition should offend her deeply. For the sake of her father, if nothing else. Yet Ross had told her he hadn't been at Dunadd on the night of the massacre. Surely that counted in his favor?

And while guilt still flickered it was a tremulous thing, overshadowed by the memory of MacIntosh's fierce blue gaze, the passion in his voice, and the wanton fire that had flooded her veins at his touch.

And his kiss. She could still feel his lips pressed against hers. His tongue inside her mouth, exploring with flesh-tingling delight. Sharp darts of pleasure collided between her thighs and her breath shallowed in primitive response.

Great goddess. She was still aroused. And merely thinking of him aroused her further. But she couldn't push him from her mind. Or discard the scandalous notion of accepting his offer of an illicit assignation.

"My lady?" There was a concerned note in Saoirse's voice and with the greatest of difficulty, Orabel dragged her lust-drenched senses back to the present. It was disgraceful she had allowed her thoughts to wander so. Even more disgraceful that she didn't regret it. What had her friend just said?

She glanced over her shoulder at Neilan, who had a grim expression on his face and strode with purpose, although he kept his distance. She returned her attention to Saoirse, whose instant understanding of what had occurred in the sacred circle was a great relief to her, since she wasn't certain how to explain what had possessed her.

"I confess I'm tempted to indulge," she whispered, and even admitting that much caused heat to wash through her. "Truly, I am certain MacIntosh's arrival was a sign from Bride."

Although she wasn't entirely sure why the goddess didn't disapprove of the notion of a brief affair with the Scot, what other conclusion could she draw? Bride had given her no other sign as to her future path, despite how desperately she had begged for insight this morn.

"Perhaps," Saoirse hesitated. "Forgive me, but perhaps the goddess brought MacIntosh to Fib so the princess might experience true passion before Bride lights the path ahead?"

"Yes," she breathed. "I feel this, too. A healer should experience all she can, should she not?"

"Indeed. It makes perfect sense."

She understood the trials of a political marriage. But until now, passion had eluded her. Another ripple of white-hot desire coiled within her, deep and low, and goddess help her, dampness bloomed.

"Tonight, after the feast." She refrained from glancing over her shoulder again. Even if Neilan did overhear this conversation, he would never repeat it. And besides, if she intended to take Ross as her lover, she needed to confide in her loyal warrior so he could ensure they were not discovered. "During the entertainment we must slip away, unnoticed."

"We must first ensure the Northumbrians are well-plied with the finest wine."

"Perhaps I might add something special to Raedwulf's goblet to ensure he enjoys himself most pleasantly." There were a variety of sleeping droughts she could employ that would leave no lingering aftereffects. Droughts she had sometimes used on her late husband, especially during the early years of their marriage, when his attentions had become too obnoxious to bear. "I do not trust that wine alone will sufficiently dull his senses."

As they entered the courtyard, a servant rushed to their side. It seemed the queen had summoned her yet again. With a smothered sigh she returned to her chamber so Saoirse might make her presentable, but she'd forgotten about the five young noblewomen who were now under her care. And their eagerness to assist Saoirse turned a simple task into a monumental exercise.

Not that she really minded their overzealous enthusiasm or the possibility of annoying Etain with her tardiness. She was too entangled in the delightful possibilities of what this night would bring.

CHAPTER ELEVEN

he Northumbrians had arrived. Earlier than expected, but Orabel wasn't surprised. Unpredictability was, after all, one of their more consistent traits.

If only her sister hadn't decided to welcome them with such an outward show of camaraderie. It was in stark contrast to the chilly reception she had extended to the Scots.

Especially when it was all for the sake of appearances for the Dal Riadans, who had been invited to join the welcome reception in the great hall.

The great double doors were flung open as the Northumbrians entered the hall, where vibrant tapestries from the queen's own chambers had been hung upon the walls, as a temporary replacement for the faded ones that usually covered the stone. For the hundredth time since following the queen and king onto the dais mere moments ago, Orabel told herself not to glance at Ross MacIntosh, who stood in front of his men on the left side of the hall. And for the one hundredth time, she failed.

Goddess, he was magnificent. Her furtive glance admired his beautiful hair, tamed with a black ribbon, but her fingers tingled as she recalled how it felt beneath her touch. And how different his stern features were when he smiled.

When he kissed.

Her breath shortened and pulse raced, and heat flooded through her, pooling in all the most inconvenient places. She had not yet been able to speak with him again since she'd left him at the standing stones a good three hours ago. To inform him she was agreeable to a fleeting affair. Perhaps she wouldn't have the chance before the feast. But at least she had set things in motion, and sequestered a sleeping draught which was now safely in a pouch on her girdle.

The Northumbrians approached. Orabel tore her besotted attention from MacIntosh and focused on the warlord and his warriors. Despite the mild weather, Raedwulf wore his beloved wolf pelt slung over his shoulder, its polished black stone eyes glittering with eerie malevolence, the wolf he had killed at the age of nine and allowed no one to forget it.

He bowed low, before launching into a flattering speech on the bounty and wealth of Fib and its illustrious royal house.

"As a token of our continued loyalty to our neighboring kingdom," Raedwulf continued, as one of his men approached, "We present these fresh wolf pelts to my lord and my lady."

His man displayed the pelts on the dais and murmurs of appreciation rippled around the hall. The fur was luxuriant and when two of her sister's ladies picked one up so the queen might feel its texture, bile rose in Orabel's throat.

She was not against the culling of wolves. It was all part of the goddess' cycle of life. But to hunt pregnant she-wolves, when they were at their most vulnerable, simply for their rich fur, turned her stomach.

It was cruel. And Raedwulf, no doubt, had relished the hunt.

He turned to her and offered a half bow. Somehow, she managed not to let her disgust show on her face.

"Lady Orabel, what a pleasure it is to see you again."

He paused, clearly expecting an agreeable response but all she could summon up was a regal dip of her head. "You are too kind."

Did her voice sound too chilly? She scarcely cared. He was fortunate she did not call upon her goddess to wreck the havoc he so deserved upon his cursed head.

No. She could not think such thoughts, even in fleeting anger. The goddess, after all, heard everything.

If Raedwulf felt slighted, he chose not to show it. "It's been too long but the memory of your beauty and healing skills has remained with me always."

Goddess. Her face heated in silent outrage. How dare he attempt to flatter her in company, when she knew full well the only skill he admired in a woman was her ability to breed a dozen sons?

Etain glanced her way, clearly expecting her to give a complimentary rejoinder. In which case her sister could wait forever. She would not be a puppet to play to Raedwulf's vanity.

Especially with Ross MacIntosh bearing witness to this excruciating farce.

Raedwulf gave an imperious wave and another of his men approached, bearing a casket, which he handed to his prince. "Allow me to present you with a gift to capture your heart, my lady."

With that preposterous statement, he opened the lid and dared to step upon the dais to present it to her. Despite herself, curiosity stirred at what the warlord imagined could possibly cause her to look favorably on his suit.

She looked into the casket. And gasped in shock.

IT WAS HARD NOT to simply gaze at the vision of Orabel as she sat on a stool beside the queen, but for the sake of her reputation, Ross curbed his obsession. But even when he resolutely studied his boots, all he could see was her beautiful, raven hair tumbling over her shoulder in a fascinating, single curl, and admire how stunning it looked against the rich blue of her gown.

Stealthily, he shifted his weight from one foot to the other. It did little to ease his discomfit. Later, he would dance with her. And hope to God he hadn't misunderstood her enigmatic parting words by the standing stones earlier this day.

With grim stoicism he watched as the Northumbrian warlord presented his extravagant display of gifts before the king and queen. Maybe if MacAlpin had considered sending more than a contingent of warriors to Fib it would have helped the situation. But no. As far as his king was concerned, the alliance was everything and Fib should count itself lucky in being included in his coronation and able to call on Dal Riada in times of need.

Clearly, the Kingdom of Fib felt no such gratitude was required.

Raedwulf uttered slimy compliments to Orabel, but her glacial expression suggested she wasn't impressed. And this was the man her sister wanted her to wed. He gritted his teeth. Orabel's alternate future gave him no joy, but MacGregor was a better man than the Northumbrian. If MacAllister had orders from their king to offer for the princess, what was he waiting for?

Not that he wanted MacAllister to play his hand yet. For once Orabel was betrothed, she was beyond his reach.

The knowledge twisted his gut. And not simply because he wanted her in his bed. It was because she didn't want a husband, no matter his nationality.

The Northumbrian opened a casket which he then offered to Orabel. She gasped, obviously taken aback by the contents, and he frowned, unwillingly intrigued as to what the warlord had offered that she found of such interest.

She lifted something from the casket. It was a brown, whiskery ball. He'd never seen anything like it before in his life and even if he had, it would not have occurred to him to offer it as a gift fit for a princess.

"A coconut." The awe in her voice was palpable and Ross fisted his hands.

A fucking coconut. The one thing guaranteed to break down Orabel's defenses.

"My merchants have been searching this past year for such a treasure," Raedwulf proclaimed, so the entire hall could hear. "A gift so priceless it could have but one purpose." The Northumbrian's voice dropped, but Ross heard him well enough. "So the Princess of Fib might look kindly upon the giver."

The bastard had all but claimed Orabel's hand in front of scores of witnesses. Ross knew what magic she could extract from the exotic fruit. This gift meant more to her than furs or precious gems and the warlord knew it.

Futile rage at how she had been trapped surged through him but even one word of protest would ignite the simmering hostility that swirled in the hall. And it wouldn't stop there.

MacAllister's hand gripped his arm and Ross froze. Christ. He had stepped forward without even realizing it. The king's man didn't look at him or give any other indication that he had guessed Ross' deranged thoughts, but that one touch was enough.

War had been waged for lesser affronts upon an enemy's honor.

"This is most unexpected." Orabel finally tore her gaze from the coconut to give the Northumbrian a smile. The fact her smile was remote and chilly did nothing to appease Ross' seething injustice at the situation, merely fueled it. "I'm deeply appreciative of the lengths Lord Raedwulf went to secure such a rare treasure. But I can only accept this magnificent fruit if you allow me the honor to return its weight in jewels for your kindness."

Good God. Ross gazed at her in awe. She had refused to fall into Raedwulf's trap. Despite the lure he had set.

Raedwulf's jaw flexed. He was clearly furious and battling to hide it, and a dark certainty gripped Ross' soul.

Should Orabel end up wedded to the warlord, he would never forgive this slight.

"It is unthinkable," Raedwulf said, his expression once again showing nothing but a façade of high regard, "that the princess should feel the need to repay the royal house of Strathclyde, for this symbolic gesture of our mutual love and respect for the royal house of Fib."

"The gesture is most warmly received, my lord," the queen said, before Orabel could respond. "We look forward to continuing the most cordial of relations with our southern neighbors."

The gathering dispersed soon afterwards, without Orabel once glancing in his direction. Which was likely just as well. The Northumbrian had her in his sights and would doubtless have deliberately misconstrued any stray glance to strengthen his pursuit.

He and Rourke strode across the courtyard in silence, which suited Ross since he wasn't certain he'd be able to contain his contempt for the southern barbarian if he opened his mouth. Unfortunately, MacAllister joined them as they tramped towards their camp.

"It appears the house of Fib has shown their hand." For some reason the king's man sounded entirely too jovial and Ross battled the urge to sling him a black scowl. "Perhaps the king thinks to cower Dal Riada by such a display of neighborly fidelity with the Northumbrians."

Ross doubted it was the king. But MacAllister would never believe it was the queen who held the true power in Fib.

"Or Fib merely despises Dal Riada and doesn't care what we think of them." Rourke shrugged. "Historically, they've always been more powerful than the size of their kingdom would suggest."

"Times change," MacAllister said. "The Kingdom of Fib needs to look to the future instead of their past."

"And what is this kingdom of Strathclyde? I've never heard of it," Rourke said.

At least he knew the answer to that. "The kingdom emerged last year. Raedwulf and his kin claimed the throne, expanding their power in Northumbria."

"Aye." MacAllister still sounded far too satisfied with the way events were transpiring. "But the power that binds Northumbria is splintering under the warlords' very noses, while Dal Riada strengthens her borders with every new treaty. The southern barbarians will soon pay dearly for their arrogance."

War was coming. Ross only hoped Orabel wasn't caught in the middle of it.

CHAPTER TWELVE

It was just as well Orabel had prepared the sleeping draught first thing that morning, as the queen had scarcely allowed her out of her sight since the Northumbrians had arrived.

She had been denied permission to visit the village, or even her precious garden, and the five young noblewomen were constantly fluttering around her, even accompanying her to the garderobe, goddess save her.

It was late afternoon, and she, Saoirse, and her ladies were with the queen and her entourage in the queen's private chambers. Orabel was finding it increasingly hard to remain seated with her embroidery, when her stomach churned with a combination of excitement at seeing Ross again at the feast—and the clandestine plans they would make—and impotent affront at how blatantly Raedwulf had attempted to corner her with his unexpected gift.

The coconut which was now in her bedchamber.

"Raedwulf will be given no opportunity to come upon you unattended," Etain said, when Orabel once again asked if she might be allowed to work in her apothecary for an hour or so before they needed to ready themselves for the feast. More to the point, she wanted to ensure the coconut was safely secured. "And you are responsible for the wellbeing of your ladies. Their reputations must remain unsullied, and I do not trust either the Northumbrians or the Scots not to tempt them with their silken tongues."

Yet the Scots had been in Fib-eviot for days without her sister worrying about the young ladies' reputations, and she couldn't keep silent.

"Perhaps if Raedwulf had not been offered a chamber in the palace, we shouldn't need to worry about such things."

"We couldn't allow a prince of royal blood to camp with his men," their mamma said. "It would be seen as a snub."

"Indeed. One can only hope he doesn't believe Orabel snubbed his," Etain hesitated, before slowly enunciating the word. "Co-co-nut."

Orabel didn't care if he did. But she couldn't confess to such a thing aloud. "I shall not be coerced in such a manner. He's used to getting his way, but I am not a Northumbrian woman who sits at her master's feet."

Her mother shot her a startled look. "He would never expect such subservience from you, Orabel. Even if you do wed, the marriage contract will plainly state your rights."

Even if you do wed. Her mamma's words reminded her, forcefully, of how her beloved goddess hadn't answered her desperate prayers this morn. For as much as she longed to spend the night in Ross' arms, how could that ensure her freedom from Raedwulf?

To be sure, Bride worked in her own mysterious ways and didn't share everything with her faithful children. But it was clear the Northumbrian warlord had come to Fib with a single purpose, and he appeared not to care who knew of it.

"This is true," Etain confirmed. "We shall allow none of our royal house to be so degraded. Not by a Northumbrian, nor by a

Scot. How gladly we shall issue a refusal to attend MacAlpin's farce of a coronation. It is unthinkable."

Yes, it was unthinkable, even if her sister's last words had veered back to the contentious issue of the Fortriu coronation.

Tonight, after she and Ross had enjoyed a magical moment out of time, the answer would come to her. She was sure of it. Otherwise, why else had Bride allowed Ross to find her at the sacred stones?

It was all connected and once she had discovered the wonders that a true lover could provide, the path forward would be revealed.

And it did not include Raedwulf, Prince of his newly forged kingdom, Strathclyde.

When the feast ended the musicians tuned their instruments, but the tables were not pushed back to the stone walls. The queen had decreed there would be no dancing this night.

Silently fuming, Orabel, along with Saoirse and closely followed by the young noblewomen, made their way to the side of the great hall where servants stood ready with jugs of wine. Both Scots and Northumbrians remained standing beside their tables, waiting for a sign from their royal hosts that they, too, might partake of the additional refreshments.

"How am I to meet with Ross MacIntosh under these conditions?" She kept her voice low so only Saoirse could hear.

Her friend inclined her head and whispered in her ear. "The queen has given stern instructions to the young ladies that if they allow you out of their sight for even a moment, they will be dispatched back to their parents' strongholds in disgrace."

Orabel took a long sip of wine before she said something she might regret. But for the love of the great goddess, what was Etain doing? Did her sister not trust her?

A chill shot through her. Had Etain somehow guessed that she planned an illicit assignation, with the compelling Scots' warrior she had brought back from the brink of death?

"My lady." MacIntosh's bone-tingling accent broke through her moment of panic, and she smiled, for who could not smile when confronted by such a breathtaking sight?

"MacIntosh. How good it is to see you again."

He cast a glance at her ladies. Although Saoirse kept her gaze averted, as though she found the visiting Northumbrians of utmost fascination, her five young attendants were openly agog. It was somewhat off-putting.

If only she could speak to Ross alone, even for a moment. To explain she hadn't known what her sister planned for this eve. After all, who would expect to be invited to a royal feast and then not make merry afterwards?

"Princess Orabel." Raedwulf appeared by Ross' side like an ominous shadow. *Damn* him for interrupting. Somehow, she managed to keep a serene expression on her face, although it was sorely tempting to ignore his outstretched hand. But since there was no way around it, she allowed him to take hers and give her an extravagant kiss. "Your beauty outshines all in the hall this eve."

How rude of him to say so, when dear Saoirse stood next to her. She was in no mood to pander to his insincere compliments when there was only one thing he wanted from her, and it certainly wasn't her good opinion. "Lord Raedwulf, how remiss of me. May I introduce Ross MacIntosh from Dal Riada?"

Thankfully, he transferred his lecherous gaze from her to give Ross an inscrutable look. "MacIntosh."

Ross gave a brief bow. How irritating that Raedwulf outranked him. "My lord."

"I understand your contingent was attacked when you entered the Kingdom of Fib. How fortunate none of your men were injured."

Orabel tightened her grip on her goblet as the satisfying vision of throwing its contents into the Northumbrian's face swam through her mind. As far as she was concerned, there was no doubt Raedwulf was behind that attack. What nerve he possessed, to try and implicate Fib with a few well-chosen words.

"Most fortunate," Ross said. "I was the only casualty of a poisoned arrow. Thank God the princess with her skill was able to save my life."

She refrained from correcting him that they should thank Bride and gave a smile when he glanced her way. Why couldn't Raedwulf go and annoy someone else? But that was a foolish wish. She should excuse herself and spend the rest of the eve in deep mediation on how she could escape the dark fate that hovered over her.

But she couldn't. Because, even with Raedwulf casting a shadow, this might be the only opportunity she had to be close to Ross before he returned to his king.

"A poisoned arrow." Raedwulf's expression was inscrutable. "The princess is skilled, indeed. Was this arrow recovered?"

She couldn't bite her tongue any longer. She certainly had no compunction in hiding the truth from *him*. "Alas, it was not. And MacIntosh and his men dispatched the bandits who attacked their contingent. There is no way to discover who sent them on this mission."

What a pity none had survived who might have shed light on the matter. Not that she believed any in the warlord's employ would ever betray him through fear of reprisals. She had seen firsthand how Raedwulf treated those who displeased him.

"Bandits only have one mission. To steal whatever they can to extend their miserable existence."

Was that a thread of mockery in his tone? Before she could take issue with his remark, Ross spoke.

"These were no ordinary bandits, my lord. They were trained

in military maneuvers but despite that, were no match for my men."

It was obvious by the way Raedwulf flexed his jaw that Ross' comment had hit a nerve. It was a fleeting reaction, but it was enough. Nothing would now convince her that he hadn't ordered the ambush himself.

"Military maneuvers?" Cynicism dripped from each word. "What are you suggesting, MacIntosh? That your contingent was targeted for political purpose?"

"Without evidence, I should not care to speculate."

"A wise decision. But we should always be on our guard against our common enemy. The Vikings wouldn't hesitate to destabilize peace to help their agenda."

Neither would the Northumbrians. Or the Scots. But for now, her ire was focused on the southerners. Or, more accurately, on Raedwulf. "There are no Vikings this far south in Pictland."

"I've heard," Raedwulf said, "they have their eyes set on claiming Dunadd."

"And I," Ross countered, "have heard they seek to claim Northumbria. But the Norse are upfront in their attacks. They aren't known for subterfuge or for hiring others to do their dirty work for them."

Did Ross suspect the Northumbrians were behind the ambush? She hoped so. Perhaps they should have shared the existence of the arrow with him. He was not like other Scots.

Not like MacAllister, or their upstart king. But in the end, her decision had been taken from her by her own queen and king.

"My lady." She was torn from her tangled thoughts by one of her sister's ladies, who dropped a curtsey. "The queen requests your presence."

What? Orabel flashed an incredulous glance at her sister, but Etain was descending from the dais and speaking to their mother. Even though Raedwulf's presence was unwelcome, she didn't want to leave Ross. If her sister hadn't wished to entertain their foreign guests, why had she authorized this feast?

But she could scarcely disobey a direct order. She didn't always agree with her sister, but one thing was true. A united front from the royal house of Fib was essential when dealing with outsiders.

"I must take my leave." She directed her comment to Ross and was gratified to see disappointment flash over his face before he managed to hide it. "The queen requires my presence." She bestowed a brief glance at Raedwulf so he wouldn't feel slighted, although goddess knew, her inclusion of him in her farewell was for appearances sake only.

"I trust we shall speak together on the morrow." Raedwulf bowed, grabbed her unwilling hand, and once again kissed her. It was hard not to snatch her hand free, but she endured his touch for the sake of Fib. Especially since this touch was *all* she planned on suffering from him. Thankfully, he released her before her self-restraint unraveled.

"My lady." The merest hint of a smile touched Ross' lips as he bid her goodnight, and her heart gave the strangest flutter as their gazes meshed. Goddess, she wanted to kiss him again. The way they had kissed at the sacred stone, where she had forgotten who he was, and where they were, where, goddess help her, she had forgotten everything but the primitive desire that had consumed her reason.

Heat flooded her, burning her cheeks. She thrust her goblet at one of the young ladies before she dropped the cursed thing and clasped her fingers together in an effort to contain her rampaging libido.

It didn't work.

Every reckless sense she possessed craved to wrap her arms around his neck and lose herself in his seductive embrace. If she didn't leave directly, she feared she might do just that.

She could not disgrace Fib so. Mouth dry, she inclined her

head at him before turning away and following her sister from the hall.

Not that Etain wanted her. She merely wanted her to return to her chamber and not leave until sunrise.

Once in Orabel's chamber, with Neilan and another warrior posted outside the door, the young noblewomen gossiped in breathless whispers as they prepared her for bed. Except this wasn't what she had planned for tonight, and resentment against Etain seethed in her breast. Ostensibly, warriors guarded her door to keep Raedwulf from defiling her. But was it really to keep her from enjoying a thrilling assignation of her own?

"MacIntosh is quite dashing," sighed one, pressing her hand against her breast. "I fairly swooned when I glimpsed his incomparable blue eyes."

"He is most charming," agreed her friend. "Not at all like the savage Scots we've been led to believe inhabit the wastelands of Dal Riada."

Goddess help her. Orabel exchanged a glance with Saoirse who gave a faint smile. She wasn't sure if she should reprimand the girls. After all, as Etain had pointed out, she was now responsible for their welfare. But since she, also, thought Ross MacIntosh had incomparable blue eyes, and was the most charming man she'd ever met, she could scarcely fault another for coming to the same conclusion.

"He is handsome enough," said a third girl. "But great goddess, I was entirely overcome by the Northumbrian prince. Such black eyes and hair I have never encountered! Surely his magnificent features were crafted by the gods themselves."

And that was a step too far.

"One should never judge a man solely on his looks," she said, and instantly the five girls bowed their heads, and the one who had admired Raedwulf looked as though she was about to burst into tears. Curse the man. He distressed maids even when he wasn't in the same chamber as them. She gave the girl a gentle pat on her shoulder. "I'm not angry at any of you. I merely wish to warn you against any unthinking folly."

"Yes, my lady," they murmured, and continued their duties in a subdued silence. She hadn't meant to upset them, but even the mention of Raedwulf's name was enough to twist her insides with a combination of rancor at the fact he drew breath, and an insidiously growing fear that his noose was inexorably tightening around her.

Tonight was all wrong. She was certain Bride had given approval for her to take Ross as her lover. For just one night. That was all she wanted. All she expected.

Had she misunderstood the message at the standing stones this morn? But why else had he appeared so suddenly from the early mist, as though the goddess herself had delivered him there?

Thwarted dreams of spending a wondrous night with Ross kept Orabel awake long after Saoirse and the young noblewomen had fallen asleep. She stared up into the darkness, her mind racing, but no solutions presented themselves.

Except that Raedwulf might meet an untimely end.

She screwed her eyes shut and sent humble apologies to the goddess. But it was hard to feel contrite if that was the only light in this dark nightmare.

Finally, slumber beckoned, but there was no respite from her worries. The vision came upon her instantly as the metallic clang of swords clashing, hoofs pounding, and fierce battle cries rent the air. The acrid scent of blood scorched her senses and she gazed at the scene before her.

Countless yew trees stood stark against the piercing blue of the cloudless sky, a majestic avenue leading to the realm of the immortals. *I should not be here.*

Terror coiled through her. One could not simply enter the ancients' realm without invitation. And even though Bride had brought her here, to the gateway between their worlds, Orabel was not certain if the great goddess desired her to travel further.

She glanced over her shoulder and her terror coiled tighter. There was no summer visage. Only dark clouds and black shadows that shifted with menace between land and sky.

The message could not be clearer. Trepidation shivered through her as she stepped into the sacred avenue.

The yews enclosed her, and the fearful sound of battle faded. When she once again glanced over her shoulder, the entrance had vanished, consumed by a dozen or more tangled yews, their branches entrenched into the ground as though they had grown there for a thousand years or more.

It was too late to retreat. She moved forward, trying to ignore the strange blue-green lights that shimmered beyond the trees. The avenue stretched onward, endless, into a shimmering, iridescent blur.

Without warning, the path before her erupted and two massive serpents slithered from the ruins, twining around each other, their malevolent eyes glowing as they focused on her.

She froze. The serpent was a manifestation of the great goddess, but why were there two? What was Bride showing her?

Why did evil emanate from them?

Her nerve fled. This was not Bride. No matter how fearful the goddess' power was, she was not evil.

It was a test of her devotion. She had to pass through the gateway and then all would be revealed and her future secured.

She darted to the right, intending to weave through the trees until she safely passed the serpents. But the moment she stepped onto the tangled roots they wrapped around her, pulling her into the heart of the yew, squeezing the air from the lungs.

Do not stray from the path again.

The voice filled her mind. Condemning. Icily enraged. Her courage wilted but she could find no words of supplication for her transgression.

You must heal the rift—

She gasped and the vision splintered around her, into shards of glowing indigo, green and red. *Heal the rift.* Dismay streaked through her at how she had misunderstood Bride's previous message.

The goddess hadn't commanded she heal Ross MacIntosh, as she had so foolishly imagined. How could she have let herself believe Bride would care about such a thing?

It was the rift between Bride and herself that she had to find a way to heal. And until she did, her goddess would never look upon her with favor again.

The vision may not have given her the answer on how to avoid her fate. But it had reminded her that, unless she did, it was not merely a lifetime shackled to a ruthless Northumbrian warlord that awaited her. It was banishment from the benevolence of her goddess and, as such, the ability to call upon her bounty when treating her patients.

Sharp cramps gripped her womb and she curled into ball, gritting her teeth. Her moon time, never regular, was yet again a full five days early.

With a grimace she slid from the bed. Perhaps it was just as well she hadn't spent the night with Ross, if this was the spectacle he would have awoken to. But it didn't make her feel any better for what she had missed.

Her glazed eyes focused on the stained bedcover.

Blood.

And in that searing moment of clarity, she knew exactly how she could escape the clutches of the Northumbrian warlord.

CHAPTER THIRTEEN

Ross left the camp at dawn, needing to get away from his fellow warriors and clear his head. Fragmented dreams had haunted his night. Dreams where the Northumbrian warlord dragged Orabel back to his kingdom and a lifetime of suffering.

He shuddered and dragged in a harsh breath. This obsession with the princess, and her future, was madness. In the end, whether she was destined for Raedwulf or Stuart MacGregor made no difference. There was nothing he could do about either fate.

If only they had spent last night together, this unnatural need to ensure her happiness would have faded into something that he would always regret, but would learn, through necessity, to live with.

But they hadn't. And instead of acceptance of the way of the world, his lust for her burned hotter with every enraged beat of his heart.

As the standing stones came into sight, unwanted anticipation thrummed through his blood. It was too much to hope Orabel would be communing with her goddess two mornings in a row, but he hoped to God she was.

And that she wasn't surrounded by her retinue of young girls.

One last kiss within the circle of her heathen gods. Unless he could persuade her to escape her guards and meet him… somewhere. A cave? A derisive laugh razed his throat at the notion. There was nowhere for them to meet but God help him, he was willing to consider anything.

She wasn't in the circle. It had been foolish to imagine otherwise. Early morning mist wove among the stones, evoking an eerie ambience, where it was only too easy to imagine archaic, pagan deities might gather.

He ran his fingers across the face of the great stone where Orabel had been worshipping yesterday. Carvings covered its surface, worn faint by the passage of time, but they were clear enough to see.

A cauldron, with a serpent wrapped around it. There were many similar stones and carvings in Dal Riada, but their meaning had long been lost. He had the wild urge to ask Orabel what they signified, even though he was certain to even think such things was blasphemous.

With one last, searching glance around the circle, he swung about. But he didn't return to camp. Instead, he made his way to the stronghold of Fib-eviot, as though his presence might miraculously tempt Orabel from within those ancient walls.

The rising sun cast long shadows and as he approached the stronghold, he slowed at the sight of MacAllister and Rourke, and half of his contingent, all of whom led their horses. Grimly, he marched up to MacAllister. It hadn't taken the man long to wrest back the command.

"MacIntosh." MacAllister gave him an assessing look. "I'll take the men to where you were ambushed."

Rourke and his men had already thoroughly searched the area more than once, but MacAllister knew that.

"I'll fetch my horse." Nothing would induce him to remain behind today. Not with the king's man here.

Before MacAllister could respond, Raedwulf strolled from the stronghold as though he owned the damn place. From shadowed corners, five of his men materialized and followed their prince as he made his way over to them, his black gaze never leaving Ross.

This was all he fucking needed. The man made his flesh crawl but, Northumbrian or not, he was still of royal blood and to turn away would be a snub the warlord was unlikely to overlook.

"Leaving?" Raedwulf said in greeting, casting a disparaging eye over the Scots. "Good. It's never wise to outstay one's welcome."

Ross didn't wait for MacAllister to reply. Besides, Raedwulf addressed him, not the king's man.

"No, my lord." The honorific all but choked him. "My men and I seek evidence of who attacked us with the intent of assassination."

"Assassination now, is it." It wasn't a question. "You may be right. Scots are not respected in these parts. With good reason."

He could say the same about Northumbrians. Fortunately, he had not entirely lost his good sense.

"We may well be right, but that does not necessarily implicate the Picts. As no doubt you're aware, Lord Constantine, Prince of the House of Alpin, survived an assassination attempt last winter. At the hands of a rogue Northumbrian."

He wasn't convinced the assassin had been rogue, but he'd made his point. Even if it would have been diplomatic to keep his mouth shut.

Raedwulf's smile was as cold as his eyes. "So the Scots would have us believe. We are happy the prince is recovered but accept no responsibility for his injuries."

From the far side of the stronghold, the princess and her entourage emerged. It was hard to tear his gaze from her as she made her way across the courtyard, but he did, for the sake of her reputation. He didn't trust Raedwulf not to use any underhanded tactic to somehow compromise her, over an unwary glance, and force her hand.

Raedwulf glanced over his shoulder before returning his attention to Ross. Malice glinted in his eyes. "A fine specimen, is she not?" His voice was low, for Ross' ears only and it took all his self-control not to clench his fists in reaction to the warlord's disrespectful remark. "I intend to breed many strong sons with her. Sons who will be princes of Strathclyde and look to their northern neighbors with the contempt they deserve."

Disgust curdled his gut. In a small, sane, section of his mind, he understood Raedwulf was baiting him. That despite his efforts to hide the truth, the warlord knew of his interest in the princess. And that he goaded Ross for a reaction.

All this he knew. It made no difference. He prided himself on his diplomacy but for the life of him he would not stand silently by and allow Orabel to be spoken of in such a base manner.

"My lord presumes much. The princess is not betrothed to the Prince of Strathclyde."

For Christ's sake, he had to hold his tongue. Or risk the possibility of losing his damn head.

"She will be." Supreme confidence oozed from the Northumbrian. "The princess is mine to claim, and when we depart this kingdom, she will be by my side, regardless of any foolish protests she might harbor."

"The hell she will." Fuck. He had to retreat. But he was rooted to the spot, unable to move, because if he moved, he feared he would smash his fist in the warlord's arrogant face.

From the corner of his eye he saw Orabel approach, so close that surely she would soon overhear this conversation. Sweat slicked his brow, fire pumped through his veins, and still his damn mouth would not quit. "The princess is already spoken for."

Raedwulf grabbed his shirt and instinctively he grasped the

warlord's shirt, and they were locked together as Scot, Pict, and Northumbrian surged closer at this unthinkable breach of etiquette.

"You lie." Raedwulf spat the words in his face, but all he could see was Orabel, standing not an arm's length from them, shock etched across her beautiful face.

"My lord," she said, focusing on Raedwulf. "I must speak with you urgently."

"Be silent," he said, not even glancing her way. "This is man's business."

"Indeed. But I fear what I must impart to you may cause you to change your mind about—"

"You," Raedwulf said to him, ignoring Orabel, "will pay for your insolence."

This was how he treated the princess in public, when they were not even betrothed. He could well imagine how the bastard would treat her when she belonged to him, when no one else bore witness.

He tightened his grip on Raedwulf's shirt, before thrusting him back so suddenly the other man stumbled, ripping Ross's shirt in the process. "The princess is already betrothed," he snarled. Stuart MacGregor's name floated in his mind, gone in an instant as crimson rage flooded his reason. He would entrust Orabel's future with no one but himself. "To me."

ORABEL REELED BACK, as Ross's words reverberated around her head and Neilan marched from his usual position to stand in front of her. What madness possessed Ross? Surely, she had misheard. But the rumble of voices around her, and the way both the Scots and Northumbrians drew their swords, told another tale.

Goddess save them all. Her heart thundered in her ears and

for a horrifying moment the ground seemed to rise around her. Saoirse grasped her hand, pulled her from the brink, and she hitched in a sharp breath as the dizziness receded.

"You dare besmirch Lady Orabel's honor." Raedwulf's incensed roar echoed around the courtyard. "You will pay with your life, Dal Riadan. We will meet out yonder in one hour. The victor takes the princess."

With that outrageous claim he swung on his heel and marched off. She released Saoirse's hand, stepped around Neilan, and caught sight of Ross. He was breathing hard, his ripped shirt showing a glimpse of his chest, and the fact her body thrilled at his disheveled appearance utterly infuriated her.

He caught her gaze and slowly straightened. She ignored Neilan's warning growl and took two steps closer to MacIntosh.

"What in the name of the great goddess are you doing?" Even in her horror, she kept her voice low so no one else would overhear. In a section of her mind she found it strange, how everyone kept their distance, but it was a small concern when Ross MacIntosh had just claimed her hand in front of half the court of Fib-eviot.

"My lady." He ground the words between his teeth. "It was the only way to save you. If he believes you are already betrothed, he cannot stake his claim."

Stake his claim? Without quite meaning to, she took another step closer. "It was not your place to save me, MacIntosh. I can save myself from such an odious fate. But you—you have raised his ire and now he has challenged you."

Terror of another sort blazed through her, momentarily paralyzing her as vivid, grotesque images flooded her mind. Her hand hovered perilously close to his chest before she realized what she was doing and forced her arm back to her side. But the terror remained. "You could die."

"I will not die." He sounded so sure. How like a man, to believe they were invincible when honor was on their side.

Except she knew of Raedwulf's skill with a sword, and not merely through reputation. She had seen him dispatch more than one warrior who had displeased him.

"I will never forgive you for this," she hissed, and it wasn't his audacity she was thinking of, but the very real possibility that this was the final hour of his life. "I told you it was up to me to find the right path, and I had. There was no need for you to—to sacrifice yourself in this manner."

"You found the right path?" He sounded skeptical and it was the final indignity to this entire public humiliation. She would tell him, watch the disgust roll through him and settle in his features, and it would *serve him right* for daring to mortify her before the court of Fib-eviot.

"I did. This morn, I was to explain to the prince how I cannot wed because of my condition." The uncomprehending expression on MacIntosh's face fueled her acidic fear at his likely fate. How dare he cause her such distress when by rights she should feel nothing but disdain for his actions?

She flung him a regal glare. She had girded herself to recount this story to Raedwulf, for she did not care what he thought of her. But the galling truth was, she did care what Ross MacIntosh thought. But there was no help for it. He had forced her hand, and she would simply have to live with the disgust that was certain to twist his features before he managed to hide it.

Apprehension flashed across his face. "Does something ail you, my lady?"

Nothing ailed her. But he wanted to hear her plan, and so he would. "A man such as Raedwulf has no use for a woman who suffers continually from bloodied fluxes that her womb cannot contain. A womb that could nurture no seed, much less grow a prince."

"Christ, Orabel." His horrified whisper carried no further than her ears, but there was no trace of disgust on his face. Goddess help her, was that concern she detected? "Are you in pain? You're the greatest healer I have ever encountered. Is there nothing you can do to ease your"—he swallowed, clearly struggling to find the right word, and fascinated despite herself, she couldn't tear her gaze from him— "condition?"

He hadn't recoiled. He hadn't diminished her very existence by the fact she was unable to bear a child. Both reactions she'd expected from Raedwulf, along with the demand his own physicians provide him with a second diagnosis.

But all Ross wanted to know was if she was in pain.

It shouldn't make any difference. Yet it did. But she was still infuriated with him.

"I do not suffer from this malady," she whispered, when all she wanted to do was shout it in his face. How unimaginably undignified this man made her feel. "But if Raedwulf believes I do, he would rather wed a Viking barbarian."

Relief washed over Ross' face, which only enraged her further. Why did he have to be so understanding? "It's a bold plan," he said, and his eyes captivated her the way they had the first time she had seen him on that blood splattered meadow. "But the warlord would never simply take your word for it."

"That is of no consequence. I'm more than able to fabricate any evidence they require to substantiate my claim. So you see, there was no need for this… this…" She gave an exasperated gasp and glared at him again because what else was there to say?

"Orabel." His voice dropped to a bone tingling caress, no matter how she tried to ignore it. She wanted to tell him to flee, to preserve his life at all costs, but of course he never would. He was a warrior, and a warrior did not run from their fate.

"My lady." Saoirse's soft whisper by her side pulled her forcibly back to reality. A dozen warriors from the king's own guard marched towards them, clearly intent on escorting her back to the palace. And to her sister, no doubt, who even now was likely scheming on how she could twist these events to her own advantage.

She flung one last despairing glance Ross' way. He appeared inexplicably calm for one who had initiated his own death warrant. And as she retraced her steps to the palace, surrounded by her ladies and encircled by the guards, a terrible chill invaded her heart.

Although she had tried not to let the hope take form, there was no denying that, deep in hidden recesses of her soul, she had wanted Raedwulf's end. Had Bride heard her, after all, and this was her punishment?

An end was in sight. But would the blood spilled be the Northumbrian warlord's—or the Scot she had come to care for?

CHAPTER FOURTEEN

"*I* thought you weren't getting involved." Rourke's growl dragged Ross' attention from Orabel's departure. Not that he could see her since she was surrounded by Pict warriors. And now he could no longer see her, cold reality slithered along his spine.

No. He drew in a deep breath and turned to his friend. He regretted nothing. The warlord deserved to be slain for his disrespect.

MacAllister approached and Ross braced himself. He'd thought no further than saving Orabel from a vile fate, but the truth was, should he survive the challenge, it was very likely his king would order his execution regardless.

"Camp." That was all MacAllister uttered and in silence he and his men returned to their camp. Only when they reached Ross' tent did the other man round on him.

But he didn't speak straight away. Instead, he raked his expressionless gaze over him and several of the warriors shifted in palpable unease.

Finally, MacAllister inhaled a long breath. "The Prince of Strathclyde is reputed to be a remarkable swordsman."

The remark was unexpected. He'd thought the king's man would have roasted him for daring to claim the princess' hand and causing the warlord to issue his challenge. There was no point telling MacAllister neither he nor Orabel intended to honor his hasty pronouncement. They could deal with that once this challenge had been satisfied.

If I survive.

He would.

"Remarkable?" Rourke glowered at his sire before transferring it to him. "His reputation is fearsome and is well known even across the sea."

Irked by Rourke's apparent lack of faith in his own prowess, Ross shot him an equally dark glare. "My swordsmanship is also renowned."

"Aye. But you were close to death from wolfsbane barely five days ago."

Ross gritted his teeth. God damn it, he had all but forgotten that. A testament to the healing power that Orabel possessed.

He couldn't fail her. Couldn't let her be taken by the warlord. Orabel might believe her story of suffering from a malady would sway Raedwulf's hand, but Ross wasn't convinced. The only way to keep her from the Northumbrian's grasp was to slay him.

"This development," MacAllister said, "is entirely unexpected."

As was MacAllister's reaction to Ross' misconduct. He had the feeling he should keep his mouth shut, but that didn't stop him from responding. "I didn't plan this. But the princess deserves better than being shackled to another barbarous Northumbrian."

"Indeed." MacAllister's cold eyes bored into him. "In which case you had better ensure you win this challenge, MacIntosh."

THE HOUR WAS nigh as Ross, Rourke, and his men tramped to the stone circle where, only yesterday, he had kissed Orabel. But today he intended to win her freedom.

A crowd had gathered, the court of Fib-eviot and villagers alike, and anticipation and ale spiked the air. God only knew who the Picts would back in this fight. Treaties or not, the brutal truth was they were all enemies at their core.

The warlord arrived with his men, and they stood at the opposite side of the circle as Rourke and, surprisingly, MacAllister, gave a last check of the leather bracers that would, God willing, protect him from a lethal strike.

"Even if you inflict the killing blow," Rourke said, "I doubt his men will take it with honor. We should ready ourselves for battle."

"There will be no battle here this day," MacAllister responded. "Without their prince, they'll return to Northumbria. And make their plans."

While, doubtless, his own head adorned a spike for being the instigator of yet another battle between their people. Maybe, after all, Orabel hadn't managed to destroy all the wolfsbane that had poisoned his body, and his reckless actions now were a result of damage to his judgement?

It was possible. It would make a credible defense, should MacAlpin give him the chance to appeal for his life. But he didn't believe for a moment that the wolfsbane had anything to do with this.

It was because he couldn't shift the agonized expression on Orabel's face from his mind, as she had denounced the prospect of a future tethered to the brutal Northumbrian warlord.

An excited ripple among the crowd heralded the arrival of the royal family. Orabel stood behind the queen as the king and his warriors marched to the center of the circle, and imperiously beckoned him and Raedwulf to approach.

"God be with you," muttered Rourke, briefly clasping his shoulder. Ross took a deep breath and advanced to the Fib king who gave both him and the prince glares of contempt. At least it appeared the king didn't favor Northumbrian over Scot, for whatever that was worth.

"The Kingdom of Fib shall not be host to a blood feud," the king said, his voice loud enough for half the gathered crowd to hear. "There will be no death in this sacred circle. Honor shall prevail between the Kingdom of Strathclyde and Dal Riada by the spilling of first blood. This is our word, and it shall not be denied."

First blood? Ross tightened his grip on his sword and eyed the Northumbrian, who looked furious enough to run through the king for the proclamation. But they were both beholden to the King of Fib's command, here in his domain, and there was no chance of disputing the rules of combat.

But dissatisfaction gnawed through him. The only sure way to keep Orabel from Raedwulf's grasp was to kill him. He knew it as surely as he knew the sun would rise each morn in the east.

For as long as the warlord drew breath, Orabel was in danger.

ORABEL CLASPED her fingers together in the vain hope that would stop them twisting with agitation. But it didn't help quell her churning stomach nor the remnants of rage against Ross that still clawed through her breast.

After being summoned earlier, she'd hoped either her sister or the king would decide to prohibit this spectacle of masculine pride. But no. Indeed, Etain, after giving her a piece of her mind, despite how she had denied that any agreement existed between herself and Ross MacIntosh, had been most agreeable to a fight to the death.

It was Dugald who had decided on the spilling of first blood only.

Which meant Ross would not die. Which was, most surely, an

answer to her desperate prayer to Bride, but it did nothing to ease the fear that ate deep into her soul.

Neither warrior had known of the king's edict until a moment ago. She was in no doubt that Raedwulf was behind the ambush of the Scots which only proved the lengths he was prepared to go to further his own agenda. What if he had tipped his sword with wolfsbane? It was dishonorable, but she would put nothing past him.

Merciful Bride, I beg you. Do not let Ross die.

Ross and Raedwulf circled each other, weapons raised, each searching for a weakness in their enemy. The villagers jeered and whooped, and the nobles of the court joined in, urging them to engage, to draw blood.

It was clear if they were to be deprived of an exciting death, a great deal of first blood was demanded.

Their swords clashed, reverberating around the sacred stones like an ominous echo of battles past. Why had Etain not overruled Raedwulf's arrogant demand that the challenge be held here, within the sanctuary of the ancients?

It was wrong. Goddess save them, could no one else feel the fury of the gods rumble beneath their feet?

The two men were locked together, their animosity palpable in the late spring air. Their blades, too close to their opponent to cause injury, glinted in the sun, and for an endless heartbeat they were not swords at all as the metal melded, became liquid, and coiled around each other like living rivers of silver.

Serpents.

Terror clutched her throat and sent icy tentacles slithering along her spine. The serpents from her vision. Bride had been warning her of this challenge. The battle between Scot and Northumbrian. If she had understood the message, could she have prevented this?

How?

She had already formulated a plan to repel Raedwulf. What

more could she have done?

Deep inside, a treacherous flicker of denial stirred. While she was only too willing to believe one of the serpents was a manifestation of Raedwulf and his ilk, she couldn't paint Ross with the same sense of evil that had infiltrated her vision. Yet what other conclusion could she draw without further angering Bride?

The two warriors staggered back and their weapons, no longer snakelike, clashed once more. The hostile sound of the crowd throbbed in the air, a malignant wave that pounded against her skull, magnifying the certainty that, yet again, she had offended the great goddess by her actions—or inaction.

Storm clouds rolled across the sky and shadows raced across the land, bringing a chill to the breeze. Raedwulf swung his sword and thrust at Ross, but the Scot parried the blow, goddess only knew how, and followed it up with a maneuver that sent the Northumbrian reeling.

She was going to be sick. *I will not disgrace myself so.* How much longer would this challenge last?

It was risking the wrath of Bride to beg for her benevolence, when it was clear the goddess no longer looked favorably upon her, but she couldn't help it and the rash entreaty tumbled from her thoughts.

Show me a sign, great goddess. I will do anything to ensure the Scot's survival.

Thunder rumbled in the distance, rolling across the sky and a shudder rippled through her at this harbinger of Bride's wrath. As rain burst from the skies, the clouds split, and a shaft of sunlight glinted on the swords, momentarily blinding her.

A roar erupted from the crowd and crimson dripped to the sodden ground. *Whose blood?*

Heedless of the rain she staggered forward, only to be pulled to an inelegant halt by her mamma. Warriors surged to the center of the circle, Pict, Scot, and Northumbrian, obscuring who was the victor—and who was the vanquished.

"We should return to the palace." The dowager queen did not release her grip on Orabel's arm as they followed Etain and the king. Wildly, she glanced over her shoulder, but could see nothing to ease her pounding heart as the rain slashed down, and nobles and villagers alike hastened to reach shelter.

"Who drew first blood?" She raised her voice over the thunder of the storm and Etain deigned to glance over her shoulder.

"What does it matter?" The queen was drenched, despite how her ladies tried to shield her from the elements with flimsy shawls. "There is no turning back now."

Now the challenge was over, and the outcome assured, a new fear gripped her as she recalled her reckless plea. If Raedwulf had won, and had not coated his blade with poison, then Ross would live.

But that hadn't been what she'd meant.

I will do anything to ensure the Scot's survival.

Had she saved Ross MacIntosh's life by promising to wed the Northumbrian prince? Hadn't she learned that one should never bargain with the ancient ones? Not unless one was prepared for an unforeseen outcome.

"My lady." Saoirse came to her side as they entered the palace and Orabel gripped her hand as tendrils of panic wound through her breast. "Neilan has confirmed it was the Scot who drew first blood."

Relief scorched through her, causing her heart to skitter and the hall to momentarily spin before her eyes. Ross had won. Even if Raedwulf had cheated, it did not matter, for he had not struck the bloodied denouncement.

The king turned to her. "Lady Orabel." His voice was grim. "When you are dry, we shall convene in the war chamber."

Her relief scattered as reality intruded and with it the possibility that honor might not prevail. Raedwulf had issued the challenge. Surely he would abide by its outcome and not use it as an excuse to invade?

CHAPTER FIFTEEN

s Ross and Rourke dried off in their tent, Rourke sent him dark glances which he ignored. When the challenge had been satisfied, he'd looked for Orabel, but she had vanished, along with the sun.

Fucking weather. He didn't usually care about the sudden storms that could appear from seemingly nowhere, but he could've done without it now.

MacAllister entered the tent without waiting for permission and Ross faced his commanding officer. Now, doubtless, he would learn of his fate.

But at least Orabel was free of the Northumbrian, by his own imperious proclamation.

"We have been summoned to appear before the King of Fib in his war chamber." MacAllister sounded as though he was merely giving an opinion on the rain, rather than announcing an undoubted political conflict. "There are matters to discuss."

"Does Raedwulf not accept the terms he set?" He wouldn't put anything past that bastard.

MacAllister shrugged, apparently unconcerned by what the

Northumbrian might think. "He's leaving Fib, which is all that matters."

"Then the princess is released from his claim." And thank God for that.

"From his claim, aye. She is."

It took a heartbeat to understand MacAllister's meaning. But he had to be mistaken. Surely, the King of Fib would set no stock by words uttered by a Scot warrior in the heat of the moment?

He deliberately chose a different tack. "The Pict king wishes to punish my impertinence?"

"Aye. That is most likely the case." MacAllister appeared faintly amused by the prospect which was odd. It was up to MacAlpin to decide his fate, not a foreign king. But then, the king was Orabel's brother-through-marriage and Ross' interference had cost him a possible alliance with the Kingdom of Strathclyde.

He should likely tell MacAllister the truth. "There is no agreement between the Princess of Fib and myself, MacAllister. She is blameless in this deception. It was merely a means to ending Raedwulf's interest in her."

For a brief, shining moment he imagined how a future with Orabel could be, if things were different. But it was a fruitless dream, for he had pledged long ago never to wed, and the princess never wished to marry again. There was nothing to be gained from such a self-indulgent envisioning.

MacAllister eyed him but it was impossible to gauge his thoughts. It always was. Then he spoke. "I suggest you modify your defense, if you do not wish to be the cause of a bloody war between Dal Riada and Fib."

ORABEL ENTERED THE INNER SANCTUM—OR, rather, the war chamber since it had been the king who had summoned her. The numerous oil lamps cast forbidding shadows across the dozen advisors who flanked the walls, their faces grim; several warriors guarded the doors, spears clenched in their hands, and Etain sat beside the desk with the dowager queen, while the king stood in front of it. The fact that her sister was deferring to Dugald in this instance felt ominous.

"We have summoned the Scots to negotiate this political dilemma," the king said.

Alarm spiked. Had her suspicions proved true? "Dilemma, my lord? Does the Prince of Strathclyde dispute the outcome?"

"He accepts it, with ill grace. But you must understand, Lady Orabel, that terms were set."

Raedwulf's contemptuous voice filled her mind. *The victor takes the princess.*

How could Dugald take any account of Raedwulf's bitter words? They meant nothing and were certainly not binding. She had not escaped the Northumbrian's grasp merely to become another royal bride in MacAlpin's collection.

But I would be Ross MacIntosh's bride.

Illicit thrills chased over her as the memory of their kiss seared her. If she had to wed again, surely it would not be so very terrible to be with a man such as him. He did not scorn her word in public, nor had he recoiled when she'd shared her fabricated story with him. He was a Scot, to be sure, but he—

The king lifted a small dagger that he'd been holding, and its blade glinted in the oil lamps that illuminated the chamber. And once again she saw the serpents from her vision, their merciless eyes fixed upon her in silent condemnation.

Do not stray from the path again.

Twice, the great goddess had warned her. She knew her path. Knew what Bride expected from her. And marriage was not part of it.

Until she'd met Ross, it wasn't something she'd wanted again, either.

But this was the price the goddess demanded for his life. And she would have to fight for it, even if a small, despicable part of her craved to step from the path that had been her destiny from the moment of her birth.

Except that wasn't an option. Her vision had shown her that, only too clearly. Duty and desire collided in her breast, but she knew what she had to do.

"But, my lord," she said, "we cannot—"

She didn't get the chance to say anything more, as the door opened, and the Scots were announced. Hastily she stepped back, but it was too late for her to take her rightful place behind the queen and their mamma without being too conspicuous and so she stood by the edge of the desk and hoped Etain would not hold it against her.

Three Scots entered but she couldn't take her gaze from Ross. How splendid he looked in his foreign plaid and his still damp hair curled with wild abandon to his shoulders. Her fingers tingled with the need to rake through his dark blond hair once again, to feel the silken texture slide over her skin, the way it had during their magical, stolen kiss.

A moment out of time. She had known it then, despite her wistful hopes of a fleeting liaison, and nothing had changed.

The Scots bowed before the king and as they straightened Ross caught her gaze. For an unguarded heartbeat, molten lust burned in his eyes and ignited an answering flame deep within her soul. She drew in a ragged breath as he turned his attention to the king and resisted the urge to press her hand against her breast. It wouldn't help calm her erratic pulse, merely draw attention to how recklessly Ross MacIntosh managed to affect her.

And while none of the men in the room would notice, her mamma might.

And Etain certainly would.

"We face a grievous choice," the king said. "The Prince of Strathclyde will not allow this outcome to besmirch his honor."

Orabel pressed her lips together before unwary words escaped. Raedwulf had little honor left to besmirch, but alas, that was only her opinion.

"Sire," MacAllister responded. "Dal Riada would never wish to cause the prince any such discomfiture. Honor must prevail."

Goddess, how men loved to bandy about that word, when all they truly meant was their pride could not withstand a few well-deserved cracks.

The king turned his attention to Ross. "MacIntosh. What are your intentions towards our Princess of Fib?"

"I have the utmost respect for the princess, sire." Ross bowed his head, but once again his gaze caught hers and her breath tangled in her breast. Even when he looked back at her king, the burning blue of his eyes haunted her mind. "I deeply regret any distress my actions caused."

She would never forget the terror that had consumed her over the consequences of his rash words, but she could forgive him. Especially when such genuine regret threaded through every word he uttered.

"Indeed." The king sounded singularly unimpressed. "Your actions have far-reaching consequences, and we find it difficult to accept you were unaware of what they entailed."

She glanced at Dugald, oddly stung that he questioned Ross' word. Her brother-through-marriage was a fair man, but his imprisonment at the hands of MacAlpin last year had, inevitably she feared, hardened him.

"I can offer no defense, sire. The princess had no inkling of the events that transpired. My only wish is that she is not made to suffer any repercussions caused by my actions. Any retribution is mine to bear alone."

Ah, goddess. Liquid heat surged through her breast, enveloping her in an ethereal cocoon of wonder. Ross MacIntosh was a Scot, but he was truly a man of honor. A man willing to sacrifice his pride to ensure the truth was heard. It was not, after all, hard to see what was on offer here.

Another man would be only too eager to grab the opportunity to secure a royal bride and the prestige that went with such an alliance. Even a man who had no interest in matrimony.

But not Ross. He knew the real meaning of honor, and it had nothing to do with the bloodshed of enemies or the subjugation of those less powerful.

"Your wishes are noted and mirror ours." Dugald's voice was dry. "Alas, our wishes in this matter are scarcely relevant." He looked at her, and the sorrow in his eyes sent shards of alarm through her heart. "Raedwulf threatens war if he discovers the reason for the challenge was false."

Injustice surged through her that Raedwulf should have any say in this matter, let alone the final word. "He had no right to issue that challenge, nor dare offer me as the prize to the victor."

"We do not disagree." The king's voice was grim, and the terrible certainty rippled through her that it didn't matter what she said, for her fate had already been decided. "Nevertheless, the challenge was accepted, and Strathclyde has powerful connections throughout Northumbria." He turned and gave MacAllister a cold look. "Dal Riada will not escape his wrath."

MacAllister inclined his head. "Dal Riada is willing to align with the Kingdom of Fib against the Northumbrian threat."

Orabel stifled a gasp. The man almost looked smug about it. As if it had been planned.

Her gaze clashed with Ross and the fierce glow in his eyes reflected her own turbulent thoughts. They were trapped, together, in a web neither of them had foreseen, to prevent a bloodied battle over one man's wounded *honor*.

"We shall draw up the marriage treaty. The Princess of Fib shall be accorded all rights and privileges as befits her royal status."

Orabel sucked in a sharp breath and flung her brother-through-marriage an unwary glare. This was a side to him she had never seen before. That he could treat her with such disrespect, as though she were nothing more than a chattel to give away, a bargaining piece to use to his advantage, without so much as *discussing* it with her?

Even Etain would not sink so low.

It was intolerable. She would not stand silently by while he—

"Sire." Ross' voice penetrated her tangled thoughts, and she favored him with her glare although goddess knew, he did not deserve it. "May I request a moment alone with the Princess of Fib?"

Silence thundered around the chamber at his insolence, but a spark of pleasure ignited deep inside her at his nerve. For a commoner, and a foreigner at that, to request a favor of a king, without being invited, was courageous indeed.

She expected nothing less from Ross MacIntosh and the pleasure twisted into a sliver of pain. Why could there be no happy outcome to this conundrum?

Dugald looked at her. "What is your wish, my lady? Will you speak with MacIntosh alone?"

So now he was asking for her permission? When he'd already decided to throw her to the Scots to appease Raedwulf's sense of outrage? Somehow, she managed to contain her ire at her king and merely inclined her head. "I will speak with MacIntosh."

As the chamber emptied, her mamma briefly squeezed her hand in sympathy, but Orabel did not return the gesture. She knew she was being foolish. There was nothing the dowager queen could have done but the lack of support still hurt.

The last guards left the chamber, and she was alone with Ross. Heedless of the eyes that watched them through the open door, he came to her and took her hand. And unlike when her mamma had offered similar comfort, this time she responded and held him tight.

"Orabel." His husky whisper sent shivers of need coursing

through her blood, despite where they were or the predicament they found themselves in. "God, you must believe me. I didn't imagine for a moment your king would hold us to my unwary words."

"This is Raedwulf's doing." She squeezed his fingers to emphasize where the blame truly lay. "I know you were only trying to save me from his clutches." She shook her head, and couldn't stop herself from adding, "Even though my plan would have worked."

"I know how the prospect of another marriage repels you."

Marriage to another Northumbrian warlord had repelled her. But to wed MacIntosh? That was something else entirely, yet how could she admit that out loud? It was dangerous enough to keep it a deathly secret, deep in her soul, where, perhaps, Bride might never discover her treachery.

But she couldn't let Ross think she imagined a life as his wife so unendurable.

"I fear I overestimated my ability to sway my king's hand in these matters." Goddess, that was an understatement. She had been so sure Dugald would temper any possible marriage alliances Etain might put forward and yet, in the end, he had offered her up as a sacrifice with barely a murmur. "But if I must wed anyone to ensure the safety of Fib, I would choose you, Ross MacIntosh."

And, without a doubt, would spend the rest of her life paying the price for failing to follow the path Bride had laid before her.

His smile was sudden, unexpected, and the trepidation gnawing her at her goddess' certain anger with this situation, fled.

"That's good to know," he said. "The truth is, I never intended to marry nor sire bairns. There are… reasons, and I made this pledge many years ago. What woman would want marriage without the prospect of bairns? But you don't wish for them,

Orabel. I hope for that, at least, your goddess will continue to look kindly upon you."

The possibility of children hadn't crossed her mind. Because children were not a part of her future and whether she wed or not, she had vowed long ago to do everything within her power to remain immune to a man's seed. But that was women's knowledge, and not what Ross meant.

Heat crawled over her face at what he was implying. A passionless marriage? Was that what she wanted? Would that appease Bride, since there was no way out of this alliance without bringing bloodshed to her beloved land?

His roughened fingertips trailed over her hot cheek, an intimate touch, as though he had the right. Soon, by the laws of their land, he would possess that right. But in truth, she had already granted it to him the moment they had kissed in the sacred circle.

Now she had tasted a fleeting promise of what they could share, could she bear to be his wife in name only?

"You do not wish to consummate our union?" Her voice was hushed. She would likely die of mortification if anyone outside this chamber overheard her question.

"Is that what you think?" Was she imagining it, or did a thread of amusement heat his words? "After yesterday at the standing stones, do you believe I could share your bed without making you mine?"

She wasn't often lost for words. But the earthy image Ross evoked plundered her mind, stealing her breath. There was only one reason why a man shared his wife's bed, and it was not to sleep, as Ross had so plainly stated.

Desire curled between her thighs, needle-hot, spiraling through her blood like the finest wine and eliminating the cramps from her moon time more effectively than any of her potions.

It was heady, intoxicating. A phenomenon she understood from her years of study but had never experienced herself.

Because before she had met Ross MacIntosh, she'd endured the connubial bed with little more than distaste and had wanted only a life of celibacy. A life dedicated to healing, as commanded by her goddess.

But now she wanted so much more.

Do not let Bride discover that truth.

His hand cradled her face, as if they were already wed and the hostile glares from her kinsfolk and Pict warriors beyond the door meant nothing to him. But then, they meant little to her, either, for if she cared surely she would step back, severing this magical touch, and remind him they were not yet even formally betrothed.

He lowered his head and for one heart-stopping moment she fancied he was going to kiss her. And she couldn't summon the will to turn away.

But his lips didn't claim hers. Although his eyes held her captive deep within their mesmeric blue depths, as compelling as the caress of his fingers against her flesh. "I want you, Orabel. Never doubt that. And if we are to be wed, I shall be your husband in every way that matters. You need not fear I will ever give you cause to regret this alliance between us."

It was hard to think of anything but how her body thrilled at his touch and, she couldn't deny it, his words also. But she had to know what he meant, so there were no misunderstandings between them. While she'd had no compunction in doing all she could to prevent her first husband from impregnating her, she didn't want that kind of secret between her and Ross.

"You are certain you do not wish for children? It's unusual for a man who weds not to wish for sons, at least." *And how I would love a daughter to pass my knowledge onto.* The thought came from nowhere, gripping her mind with a primal longing she'd never experienced before, and another wave of mortified heat blasted through her.

That was not her path. She couldn't allow herself to think of such things, much less dwell upon them. She was already defying her goddess by agreeing to this alliance with Ross. She couldn't risk Bride's wrath further by imagining a future that by its very nature would distract her from the goddess' purpose.

"Siring sons is the last thing I want." There was a trace of bitterness in his voice, of something dark and hidden, and an uneasy shiver glided over her arms at things unsaid. "In this, at least, we are of one mind." And then he smiled, and it was oddly sad and sent a shaft of pain through her breast. "Will you find it very distasteful to share your healing skills with a village filled with Scots, rather than Picts?"

For a heartbeat she held her breath, but no wave of immortal fury assaulted her at the prospect of utilizing the goddess' gifts in such a way. Relieved, she returned his smile and hoped it did not seem as sorrowful as his. "I did everything I could for Northumbrians, and that was without my husband's blessing. Do you think I would do less for Scots, even if you disapproved?"

The intangible air of desolation faded, and his grin warmed her heart in a way that was most strange. "I'm glad to hear it even if I'm not surprised. Our villagers will be lucky to have you."

There was so much more she wanted to say but Neilan and Saoirse entered the chamber. Clearly, her allotted time alone with Ross was over.

She smothered the flare of irritation at the interruption. The order came from the king, she knew. And even if she wasn't as averse to this marriage as she should be, she would never again look at her sister's husband with the same respect. He had betrayed her trust in him, and she would not forget it.

Ross took her hand and brushed his lips across her knuckles before he bowed and left the chamber, and it was only with the greatest difficulty she managed to drag her gaze away from his retreating figure.

It was one thing to admit to herself she was inexcusably bedazzled by her future husband. But it would not do for anyone else to guess. The fewer people who knew that truth, the greater the chance that Bride would forgive her transgression.

She tried to cling onto that flimsy possibility, but doubt echoed in the shadowy corners of her mind.

It would take more than hiding her feelings from those around her if she truly wanted to convince her goddess that, despite this inconvenient marriage, her loyalty was, and would always remain, with her beloved Bride.

CHAPTER SIXTEEN

Ross left the stronghold, barely registering the malevolent glances from the Picts that followed his progress. Christ, he could scarcely register anything at all, but the fact Orabel was to be his bride.

It was surreal. He entered the courtyard and sucked in a deep breath, but the sense of unreality didn't fade. All he could see in his mind was the way she had looked at him, with such trust, as she had pledged, *I would choose you, Ross MacIntosh.*

To save her kingdom from bloodshed.

"What the fuck." Rourke growled as he clamped his hand on his shoulder and propelled him forwards. He hadn't even realized he'd halted. "You're betrothed to the Princess of Fib."

"Aye." What else was there to say? God knew, he had wanted her from the moment he'd first seen her, but marriage had never been in his sights. Yet the knowledge his reckless statement had led to this juncture didn't fill him with dread, the way he'd always imagined he'd feel should one day his king order him to wed.

But then, MacAlpin had no hand in this. And Orabel, unlike any other woman forced into a political alliance, had no wish to seal the pact with a bairn.

Rourke swung him about and gripped his biceps. "You don't look like a man who's just had his freedom snatched from him."

He acknowledged it made little sense, but the truth was he didn't feel his freedom had been snatched away. Since he had no idea how to explain that to Rourke, he shrugged. "It's far better than the alternative of my head on a spike for speaking out of turn."

Rourke released him but his glower remained on his face. "That's not it. You have the same bewitched gleam in your eye as Ewan did when he was ordered to wed the Princess of Fotla."

"Lady Orabel has not bewitched me." Hadn't she, though? Why else did the prospect of marrying her fill him with fierce delight, if she had not somehow stolen his good senses?

Except he didn't believe in witches or the casting of spells. Orabel offered him something he had never dared to dream of before. A bride he desired, who wanted nothing more from their union than he was prepared to give. Why the hell shouldn't he be happy with that?

"Then you allowed lust to cloud your judgement after all and put this alliance at risk."

Irked that his friend had thrown his own words in his face, he retorted, "What would you have me do? Stand by, and allow that Northumbrian bastard to invade Fib and take her by force?"

Rourke grunted. "It was too late the moment you opened your mouth to defend her."

"Lady Orabel is willing to make this work."

"Is she? And how will she like sharing your stronghold with your lady mother and your brother's widow?"

God help him. He'd been so entangled by the miraculous prospect of claiming Orabel as his bride, he'd given no thought to base practicalities.

"Shit." By the laws of Dal Riada, Dunmor was his. In the eyes of his countrymen, he was responsible for his brother's widow and bairns, but his own bride would take precedence, since Gordon had no son.

But he had no right to Dunmor. No right to oust Una from her role as the lady of the stronghold. How the hell would he explain that to Orabel, a royal princess, who would rightly expect him to at least provide her with a stronghold to call her own?

He wasn't so concerned about the presence of his lady mother. Orabel had a kind heart, and with her healing knowledge she would surely understand there was nothing to be done.

But Una. He didn't know how he was going to explain the mangled threads that tied him to his sister-through-marriage.

"Maybe MacAlpin will bestow a prestigious stronghold upon you, as a boon for capturing another Pictish princess." Rourke sounded grim but it didn't help ease the guilt that burned through Ross at the other man's prediction.

One thing was certain. "I'll accept nothing from MacAlpin."

"That's if he doesn't run you through first for thwarting his plans." Rourke paused. "Although aside from his great-grand-mother's unspoken claim to royal blood, you have far more to offer a royal bride than Stuart MacGregor."

Except he didn't. Because at least MacGregor had a legitimate claim to his family's stronghold.

MacAllister joined them as they reached their camp. "Rourke, you'll accompany me to the negotiations."

"As will I," Ross said.

MacAllister eyed him. "You will not. The negotiations require a cool head which you've plainly proved you don't possess when it involves the princess. We cannot afford to lose any ground in this alliance."

Irritation spiked. "We will lose no ground by ensuring the princess retains all rights to everything she brings into the marriage."

"And that stance," MacAllister said, "is why you will not be party to the settlement."

Fuck that. Ross clamped his jaw shut to keep the damning words from escaping. He was walking a dangerous enough path as it was without further antagonizing the king's man.

But there was no way on God's earth that he'd claim anything Orabel brought into their marriage.

Nothing but Orabel herself.

IT HAD BEEN a week since the hasty betrothal and Ross had scarcely spent an hour in Orabel's company. Not that she didn't appear willing to converse with him, whenever they met by chance, but she was always surrounded by her ladies and Neilan, and the few pleasantries they exchanged did nothing to ease the mounting frustration that gnawed through him.

He wanted time alone with her. To explain how things were at his stronghold. And reassure her that he had no intention of appropriating her dowry.

He and his men had just returned from a successful hunt, which they'd presented to the queen as an offering towards the great feast that was being prepared for the wedding. As he strode across the great hall, intending to return to their camp, he caught sight of Orabel and her ladies and savage hunger tore through him.

Two more days and she will be mine.

It was an effort to keep his expression impassive as he approached her, when all he wanted to do was pull her into his arms and feel her body melt against him. He swallowed a groan. Thank God this madness would soon be quenched in the marriage bed, and she would no longer haunt his mind at all odd hours of the day.

Knowing she was his wife, at the stronghold of Dunmor, could not come soon enough.

But as he bowed and took her hand to kiss, the unpalatable

truth hit him once again. He still had to tell her about Una.

"I am glad to see you," Orabel said, and from the corner of his eye he saw MacAllister and Rourke continue across the great hall, leaving him alone with the princess. "There's something I want to show you."

"I'm intrigued." By rights, he should release her hand and follow in her wake. But she didn't appear to mind when he threaded his fingers through hers and the touch of her arm along his was too delectable to forsake for mere propriety. And as for Neilan, he could glare all he liked but there was little he could do, now Ross was betrothed to his princess.

"I hope so. There's an ulterior motive, I assure you." Her smile caused his gut to tighten, and it wasn't unpleasant, and neither was it surprising, since he found every damn thing she did affected him in ways he'd never imagined before.

Two more days...

She led him through a passageway and the incongruity finally pierced his lustful fog. "We're going to the kitchens?"

"No. To my apothecary." This time, her smile appeared strained, and he frowned as she paused before a door and selected a key from her chatelaine. She opened the door, and he swept his gaze around the small chamber, its shelves packed with all manner of sealed pots and vials, before coming to an abrupt halt on a coconut, that sat on its own plinth in exotic splendor.

The coconut Raedwulf had presented her with.

It was madness to allow that fact to irritate him, yet it did. He only hoped Orabel did not guess. To that end, he injected a light note in his voice as he turned to face her.

"I am both intrigued and impressed. This collection is remarkable."

"I started it here, of course, while I was very young," she said. "And I continued to expand while in Northumbria. We brought everything back with me when I returned but the truth is, I never expected to move again from Fib-eviot."

Belatedly, he understood why she had brought him here. And if not for Una, he'd reassure her that she could have every spare chamber in the stronghold for her needs. But it wasn't his stronghold. And what of Una's needs?

The words stuck in his throat. Orabel took a deep breath, as though his silence was not unexpected.

"I ask only for a small chamber like this that I can utilize. It must have a lock, to prevent unwary accidents, but I—"

To hell with it. He couldn't stand here, mute, and let her believe he expected her to beg for such small favors. "You shall have the use of whichever chambers you need, my lady. I confess I'm not familiar with the kitchens at Dunmor, but I'm certain accommodations can be made."

Her smile of evident relief churned his gut. If only they were alone, and he could explain about Una. But Orabel was never alone and while Lady Saoirse had a quiet dignity he admired, he had no wish to spill secrets before the young girls who now shadowed Orabel's every move.

But when they were wed, she would not always be surrounded by her entourage. And he would tell her of Una, and how he was obligated to ensure she remained at Dunmor. That was all his bride needed to know for he sure as hell had no intention of sharing his sordid past with her.

"That is good news, indeed." Orabel cast a loving glance around her apothecary. "While you are in such an accommodating mood, may I request a corner of your estate for my medicinal gardens?"

God, did she really believe Scots were such barbarians?

"I hope you don't think Dal Riada is such a savage land that our strongholds do not possess their own medicinal gardens."

"Not at all. That is unthinkable, even for Scots." She accompanied her slight with a delightful smile, and he grinned back, even though he suspected she didn't entirely mean her words in jest. "But I've cultivated many uncommon plants over the years. Some

I acquired while in Northumbria when merchants passed through." She hesitated, and shadows clouded her beautiful eyes. "I fear some may not survive the Dal Riadan climate. Even here, in the southernmost corner of Fib, the winters are too harsh without specialized attention."

"I regret I have no power over the elements."

She sighed. "Doubtless I shall make the best of things."

He squeezed her fingers and lowered his head so his words would not be overheard. "I'll do all I can to ensure you have everything you need, Orabel."

Everything except the moral right to call herself mistress of Dunmor.

It was the morning of her wedding to Ross MacIntosh. Orabel stood in her bedchamber as the dowager queen dismissed their ladies and when they were alone, her mamma took her hands.

"We've not had the chance to speak candidly, Orabel, and Etain will doubtless soon join us. But I want you to know how deeply I admire your fortitude in this distasteful state of affairs."

It was true they hadn't had the chance to speak privately since that confrontation in the war chamber. But if her mamma had truly wanted such an audience, she could have arranged it.

Yet to what end? The stark truth was the king had decided Orabel's future and there was nothing the dowager queen could do about it. But the lack of protest from her mother still stung, even a week later.

"This fate is not as distasteful as marriage to Raedwulf would have been." She suppressed a shudder at how narrowly she'd escaped that dark future. It was clear her brother-through-marriage would not have hesitated to throw her at the feet of the Northumbrian warlord, had Ross not drawn first blood.

"Perhaps," her mother acknowledged, with evident reluctance.

"Yet the Scots are no allies of ours, despite their continual assurances to the contrary."

There was something she dearly wished to share with her mamma, but she wasn't certain how to say it. Especially since it was a nebulous thing, without any shred of proof to back it.

But she had to, even if it only served to assuage the guilt buried deep in her soul, guilt that she didn't loathe the prospect of this marriage to Ross with every fiber of her being.

"Unlike their upstart king, not all Scots lack integrity and honor, Mamma. Not every Dal Riadan warrior took part in the betrayal in Dunadd last spring."

Please let Ross have told me the truth of that night.

The plea was formless, trapped within her mind, an agonized wish she could never share. Not even with her beloved goddess. Because to do so would bring unwelcome attention to the illicit sentiments that tangled her good sense when it came to Ross MacIntosh.

Her mamma's gaze sharpened. "Has the great goddess bestowed her wisdom in this matter? Orabel, is this alliance between you and the Scot blessed by Bride?"

Heat scorched through her, burning her face. It was one thing to secretly believe Ross' word that he didn't carry the blood of her father on his hands. But it was quite another for her mother to believe such a declaration came from the goddess herself.

Her bedchamber door opened, and Etain and her ladies entered. It was one of the few times Orabel could recall being relieved to see her sister. Etain bid her ladies to leave them and then she came over to them, her face tightening as she cast a brief glance at their joined hands.

"We shall expect regular correspondence from you," Etain said, her glance now taking in the chests and caskets filled with Orabel's and her ladies' possessions that were waiting to be packed into the wagons the following day. "And since we have no intention of attending the farce of a coronation MacAlpin is planning, you shall be our representative."

She knew exactly what her sister was saying.

"I know my duty." Her voice was stiff. It might be inevitable, but she did not relish her role as a spy for her homeland. Yet it had always been this way. Even when the seven royal houses of Pictland intermarried it was an unspoken understanding that one's loyalty remained with the house of one's birth. "I served Fib well while in Northumbria, did I not?"

"Certainly." Their mamma shot Etain a quelling glance that the queen ignored. "Your commitment is not questioned, Orabel. Yet take care when you enter the upstart's lair. Doubtless every one of his minions is ordered to report your every move to their despicable master."

What a depressing prospect. But there was a sliver of hope her future would not be so bleak. "Ross MacIntosh's stronghold is some distance from the Kingdom of Fortriu." Where the upstart king now resided instead of his own domain, Dunadd. "I shall only be at Forteviot for the cursed coronation, nothing more."

"That does not serve our purpose." Etain cradled her belly before closing her hand into a fist. "Do everything within your power to remain at Forteviot. That's where you'll discover anything worth knowing. Not closeted away in a stronghold in some forsaken corner of Dal Riada."

This time she held her tongue, but it didn't stop the bubble of resentment that burned her chest. She intended to make the best of this new life, and Ross had assured her she could devote her time to her apothecary, to tending her gardens, and healing those in need. How could she follow that path if she remained at Forteviot, where she would be little more than a privileged hostage?

No. She would not do as her sister, her queen, commanded. Dunmor was to be her new home and she would ensure, in that corner of Dal Riada at least, the old ways would not be forgotten.

CHAPTER SEVENTEEN

The tables were pushed back to the walls of the great hall, the musicians tuned their instruments, and Ross led his bride from the high table to start the dancing. Orabel's jewels on her circlet, earrings, bracelets and around her throat glittered like fantastical stars in the flickering glow from the numerous candles, enhancing her enchanting indigo eyes, that her magnificent gown matched perfectly.

He couldn't drag his bewitched gaze from her.

In the back of his mind, a concern that had plagued him all week stirred from its wine-indued stupor. He had yet to present his bride with a wedding gift. Yet what could he bestow upon a princess who had jewels aplenty and personal wealth that ensured she could acquire anything she wished?

A coconut.

The distasteful image of the Northumbrian warlord presenting her with the exotic fruit slithered through his mind. Aye, Raedwulf had acquired the one thing she coveted, that her wealth had failed to provide.

She clasped his hands, as they took their place in the center of the hall, and a teasing smile lit her face. "You look quite ferocious, Ross. Are you still reeling from the ancient ceremony you were forced to endure for my hand?"

He grinned and tugged her closer. Fuck Raedwulf and fuck etiquette. Orabel was *his* bride, and if it was the last thing he did, he'd find her another damn coconut. "I would've walked through fire to claim your hand, my lady. We are wed in the eyes of your gods and you, and that is enough for me."

"Your king's man does not approve."

MacAllister could go to hell. "He approves of little. But it is done, and I'm certain God does not take as much interest in MacAllister's feelings as he imagines."

The music began, and he bowed as Orabel dipped into a graceful curtsy. "If it is not the ceremony that discomposes you, then why do you look so fierce?"

He held the tip of her fingers as she spun around him, the jewels a dazzling blur, but nothing could distract him from the mocking gleam in her mesmeric eyes. He tugged her closer than the dance prescribed, but all gazes were upon them, and he didn't want anyone to inadvertently guess his unwary words.

"Fierce, am I? Maybe it's because I cannot believe you are now truly mine, and if I glance away, you will vanish like morning mist upon the mountaintops."

Her breath caressed his jaw, a whisper of warmth that ignited a blaze across his flesh. "I won't vanish, Ross. I am made of firmer stuff than mountain mist."

"Aye." With deep reluctance, he released her and cast a frustrated glare at the other Picts and Scots who now joined them on the floor. All he wanted to do was sweep Orabel into his arms and carry her to her bedchamber, but even through the lust that fogged his reason, he knew that would be a breach too far. "But I shall be glad to get you alone."

"I shall summon my ladies shortly but," she hesitated and for a chilling moment he had the uncanny certainty her merriment was nothing but a flimsy façade.

Why would I think that?

His gaze sharpened, but then she smiled at him, and the unease melted. He was seeing shadows where there were none, because, God help him, his need to possess Orabel was tainting every good sense he owned. "It is a little early," she whispered, before she was swept up in the dance and beyond his reach.

He played his part and danced with the noblewomen of the court, and those who had traveled to attend the wedding. And then Lady Saoirse was in his arms, and her reserved manner was in stark contrast to the other ladies he'd danced with.

It was obvious Orabel's dearest friend wasn't happy about this match, however she tried to hide it from Orabel.

"I swear I'll never do anything to hurt the princess," he said.

Saoirse inclined her head. "I trust you may keep your promise. My lady deserves that, at least."

Aye. She deserved so much more than that. Once again, he searched for her in the crowd. She was dancing with Roarke, God help her, and he hid a grin at the other man's fierce concentration as he attempted to keep up with the prescribed steps.

The dancing continued for what seemed like hours and finally, he'd had enough. He strode over to his bride, and took her hand, and led her to the side of the hall where jugs of wine stood on the tables. But he didn't want more wine. All he wanted was here, in his arms, smiling up at him as if this marriage hadn't been thrust upon her by force of circumstances.

He leaned closer, breathed in her evocative scent of heather, and whispered in her ear. "Is it still too early to retire, my lady? I fear my restraint will not last another dance."

"Then I shall summon my ladies."

"You've no need of your ladies. You have me."

Her smile wavered. "It is our wedding night. I must be properly prepared, Ross. But if you wish, you may accompany us and wait in the antechamber until I'm ready."

All evening, he'd been fantasizing about slowly stripping Orabel of her magnificent jewels and gown, until she stood naked before him. A groan tore his throat, and he hastily disguised it with a cough, lest she thought him nothing but a savage.

This was not a regular marriage. His bride was a princess and clearly, this was how things were done in royal households.

He would play by her rules tonight. But he had no intention of this ritual becoming a regular nightly habit.

ORABEL STOOD in her bedchamber in front of the fire as Saoirse and the young noblewomen removed the heirlooms of Fib-eviot and placed them in their caskets.

Until she had met Ross, she hadn't experienced the thrill of an illicit touch, or a spellbinding kiss, and the knowledge that soon he would be sharing her bed was as intoxicating as though she'd consumed an entire jug of the finest wine.

And yet, she couldn't quite quell the insidious thread of apprehension that slithered through her blood. Which was entirely foolish. After all, she wasn't an untouched maid.

But it didn't matter how many times she reminded herself of that fact. And it wasn't as if tonight was simply a wondrous, stolen moment, that she had so longed for just days ago. Tonight was the beginning of the rest of her life.

"My lady." Saoirse dropped a curtsey before ushering the wide-eyed young girls from the bedchamber, and Orabel drew in a steadying breath.

She smoothed her hands over her pale blue under gown. How plain it was. But she had never found the time to embroider her undergarments, the way her mamma and sister did. Yet now, how she wished she had.

The door opened and Ross entered. Her heart thudded against her ribs as he shut the door before making his way to her.

Goddess, how magnificent he was, in the flickering light from the fire, which enhanced his blond hair with entrancing burnished streaks. He came to a halt before her and took her hands, his calloused fingers strangely comforting.

"You are a vision." His voice was hushed. "I can scarcely believe you're my bride."

"It's been an extraordinary two weeks, and that's for sure."

"It seems fitting I had to almost die before I could win such a treasure."

She laughed, and the tension coiling in her chest dissolved. "That's an extreme way to win any bride, and not one I can recommend. Although I confess, I'm intrigued you believe me to be such a treasure when you know how readily I share my opinions."

He grinned. "It's your candid opinions that makes you such a treasure."

She groaned. "Your honeyed tongue is becoming quite sticky, husband."

"A harsh accusation to level against your husband on your wedding night."

He pressed his lips against her knuckles, his gaze never leaving hers, and she smiled as sparks of fire ignited beneath her skin. How different tonight was from her first wedding night, when Edwin had barely said a word to her before claiming his rights.

"Thankfully," she said, and there was a husky note in her voice she scarcely recognized as her own, "my husband is not easily offended."

His teeth gazed her fingers as he smiled. "Aye, that is fortunate." He tugged her close, and his tantalizing scent of leather and woodlands ensnared her in a heady embrace as she sank against the granite hard strength of his body. "God, I want you, Orabel."

And I want you. How strange she couldn't say that out loud.

"I am glad," she whispered, instead. "It would be a poor marriage indeed if you did not."

His mouth met hers and stole whatever else she might have said, along with her breath. Her lips parted and his tongue teased, dipping and stroking, and leaving her gasping for more.

Her fingers clawed at his shirt, and his rumble of laughter vibrated through her in a delicious wave. His strong arms wrapped around her in a crushing embrace before he lifted her off her feet.

"Ross," she gasped, grasping his shoulders as he swung her around. "What are you doing?"

"Enjoying my bride." His teeth flashed in the firelight in an unmistakable smile of conquest. "Do you have any objections?"

"I can scarcely think straight, never mind formulate an objection."

"Good. My plan is working."

"I'm not certain how to take that remark."

He set her back on her feet and loosened the ties at her bodice. "Do you object to this?"

She swallowed as his knuckles brushed against her exposed flesh. "I do not."

He eased her under gown over her shoulders. "What about this?"

Who could imagine the lightest touch of his fingers against her shoulders could be so bone-meltingly arousing?

"I do not find this objectionable."

His lips twitched, as though he tried not to laugh. "And this?"

He slid her gown down her arms, exposing her breasts to his hungry gaze. Her mouth dried as he traced a lazy finger across her flesh and circled her nipple. Did he truly expect her to answer?

Before she could pull her scattered thoughts together, he wrapped her hair around his fist, and she gasped as his mouth blazed a trail along her throat. "I'm waiting."

A delicate shudder coursed through her. "I forget the question."

Ross gave a primitive growl that vibrated along her throat and over her breasts before he grasped her gown and tugged it down her body. His hot gaze devoured her, and then his eyes meshed with hers. "So have I."

"I have a question." She ran her fingers along his plaid, from his shoulder to his waist. "Why are you not naked for me?"

"That's easily remedied."

Fascinated, she watched him unwrap his plaid. She had never imagined such a sight could be so alluring. He kicked off his boots, and then tore his shirt over his head and flung it aside.

She had seen his chest once before. But that glimpse was nothing compared to the full delight of having him utterly exposed before her.

"You approve?" There was laughter in his voice, along with blatant lust. Her gaze roved over his splendid chest then dipped to his proud erection.

She had only ever been with Edwin, but she had seen many naked men due to her healing skills. None had come close to the impressive vision of her husband's manhood.

"I am quite overcome." Goddess, she could scarcely speak for how her heart thundered in her breast, making it hard to breathe let alone anything else. But how she loved this banter with Ross. "I may need to lay down."

"I have no issues with that." And then he cradled her face and his grin faded. "I want tonight to be everything you've ever dreamed of, and more."

She wound her arms around his neck and pressed her body against his. How good it felt. She shifted, and his thick erection was an unyielding rod against her flesh and dampness bloomed between her thighs.

"It already is," she whispered.

He claimed her lips, and the kiss wasn't gentle, or tender, but wild and exploring. She groaned into his mouth, needing more, and his hands roved over her back, his fingers leaving ribbons of fire in their wake.

He grasped her bottom, and she shuddered, as sparks ignited deep inside and sizzled through her blood. Then he swept her into his arms and strode to the bed before lowering her to the furs.

When he joined her, she hooked her legs around him, but he refused to bend to her unspoken demand and instead braced his weight on his fists. He lowered his head, and his burning kisses scorched her flesh as he explored her throat and breasts with leisurely disregard for her rising need.

"Goddess, Ross," she groaned, and his big body shook as though her curse had amused him. "Do you wish me to perish?"

"I wish you to fall apart in my arms."

"I *am*." She wriggled desperately, but he was impervious. Clearly, he wished to make her beg. But she was not finished with him yet. Her fingers found his hot erection and his choked groan as she teased his length spurred her on to inflict further torture.

"God damn," he muttered, raking his fingers through her hair, pinning her to the pillows, before he thrust inside her wet heat. She gasped, arching into him, the sensation of being filled so completely, shattering her reason.

He withdrew, almost entirely, before rocking into her once again, possessing her so thoroughly nothing else existed. His fingers caressed and teased, and when he stroked her swollen clit she clenched around him, mindlessly, as waves of exquisite pleasure claimed her.

He pulled out of her before she realized his intentions, and it took a scrambled moment to understand why. Goddess, she should have told him it was safe. It would always be safe, but she knew better than to share that womanly knowledge.

But tonight, oh, tonight she wanted it all. But her protests locked in her throat when he imprisoned her between his legs and pressed her hands either side of her breasts, creating a valley. Intrigued, she gazed at him, and he offered her a feral grin, his eyes glazed with lust.

"I need to make you mine." His voice was raw as he gripped his rod and pushed into the tight valley between her breasts. She gasped and renewed desire spiked through her as his hand covered hers, anchoring her where he wanted her, and his thumb caressed her sensitive nipple.

His engorged shaft, coated in her juices and entrapped between her breasts, was an erotic sensation she'd never imagined before, and his tortured growl filled her with a primal delight.

All she could hear was the sound of their erratic breath, and the thunder of her heart. Ross towered over her, taking her in a way she had never been taken before, and the fierce expression on his face was hypnotic.

"Orabel." He ground out her name, as though every syllable caused untold torment. And then he pinched her nipple, and she arched in shock, as unimaginable pleasure streaked through her, from nipple to clit, and with a primitive roar, he came.

Ross stirred, groaned and, still half asleep, his fingers tangled in a mass of silky soft hair. Orabel.

His bride.

Desire surged, as her naked body molded his, and her fingers trailed across his chest. *Lower.* Cradling his balls and instinctively he tightened his grip on her head.

She pushed herself upright, his hand still nestled within her hair, and her knee slid between his thighs.

"God, Orabel." He hardly knew he spoke at all, and in the dim glow from the embers from the fire, he saw her beautiful smile as she gazed down at him.

With a sensuous wriggle, she straddled him and shot him a look of triumph as she braced her hands on his shoulders. Greedily, he drank in the way her raven hair tumbled over her face, and how close to his mouth her tempting breasts were.

He released her head and cupped her breasts, reveling in how they filled his palms so perfectly. She arched her back and sighed as she provocatively teased her damp sex along his cock, as though she derived perverted pleasure from driving him out of his mind.

His growl echoed around the chamber as he pushed inside her wet heat. Christ, she was so tight, flexing her muscles around him until he damn near forgot everything but the need to utterly possess this woman who filled his world. He pinched her erect nipples, and she gasped, sinking down, taking all of him, up to the hilt, before rising above him like a pagan goddess from the dawn of time.

"Ride me." It was a hoarse command, and he abandoned her breasts to grip her delectable arse, the silken globes bucking as he urged her on.

Her breath shortened and her nails dug into him. She was so close. But so, God damnit, was he. He gritted his teeth, tried to slow down, but he was right on the edge with her.

Fuck. "Orabel." He needed to make her hear. To understand. Instead, she raked her fingers through his hair and leaned in close until their breath mingled.

"It's safe," she gasped. "You can come inside me, Ross. I want you to come inside me."

Her seductive invitation enflamed him more than he imagined could be possible and any fleeting question died a fiery death. She knew more of these things than he.

With a roar he feared was not contained within his head, he let go, gripping her arse in place as he rammed into her, his gaze fixed on her face as, God help him, she rode him as though their lives depended upon it.

And when her release consumed her, he followed her over the edge into sweet, eternal oblivion.

CHAPTER EIGHTEEN

The early morning light filtered through the shutters and Ross stirred, his arm instinctively tightening around Orabel. Her head nestled against his shoulder and her hand rested over his heart. He breathed in deep and the evocative scent of her hair, that teased his jaw with silken promise, ignited the embers glowing deep in his blood.

Mine.

It filtered through his mind, like a whispered caress, as though this moment had always been meant to be. A lazy smile tugged his lips. He wasn't used to such fanciful notions. But then, he'd never woken with his bride in his arms before.

He pressed his lips against her hair, and she sighed, her body melding against his with torturous delight. Aye, she was his. His bride. His cock thickened, which was expected, but a strange, unnamable constriction gripped his chest, sending spikes of obscure alarm through the warm sense of complacency and that—

That was not expected at all.

"Good morn, my husband."

Her throaty whisper splintered the formless thread of unease that plagued him, and he rolled onto his side, so they faced each other. Her tangled hair, sleepy eyes, and kiss-bruised lips were blatant reminders of the night they'd shared, and once again lust beat a heady tattoo through his senses. "Good morn, bride of mine."

"I don't believe I've ever experienced such a welcoming start to the day."

He laughed. "Nor I. But I can think of something to make this morning even better."

"Alas, we have a long journey ahead of us this day."

He grunted. It was true they were leaving for Dal Riada first thing this morning, but there was always time for a quick tumble. "When we are at Dunmor, there will be no such excuse to deny your husband."

She laughed. "I'm not denying you anything. But oh," she gave a long sigh. "Ross, it will be good indeed to be mistress of one's own stronghold again. It's true I never wished to remarry and would have been happy to remain at Fib-eviot for the rest of my days. But despite that, I must confess the prospect of not needing to defer to my sister or mother fills me with secret delight."

Well, shit.

And just like that, his lust vaporized.

"Orabel." This was hardly the time, and definitely not the place, but when would he ever feel the time was right? "I must warn you. My lady mother resides at Dunmor, and I fear—"

She sucked in a sharp breath. "Goddess. That's not what I meant. I look forward to meeting your lady mother, and of course I shall not usurp her position. I'm mortified you thought I would."

"What? No, that's not what I thought." He offered her a pained smile in the hope that might diffuse the situation. "She is…" How could he best describe his mother? Without warning, memories of when he was a boy, and how she'd lavished affection upon him, slashed through his mind, disorienting him.

He sucked in a deep breath. Those days had long gone. These days, she often didn't even know who he was. "She is very frail of mind. She hasn't been mistress of Dunmor for some time."

Not since Gordon had wed Una.

"I am grieved to hear it, Ross. I promise I shall do all within my power to help her if I can."

It was what he'd hoped she say, but now she had, he was inexplicably discomposed. "That's kind of you."

How stilted he sounded. How *guilty*. Because he knew damn well he should've explained the true situation that awaited her at Dunmor before they had wed. It was too late to regret that now. And he still hadn't told her of Una.

"My elder brother's widow also resides at Dunmor."

Orabel gazed at him, her expression giving nothing away. He had no idea what she thought of his revelation, and what was more, no clue what to say to improve the situation. But obviously, he needed to say something.

He cleared his throat. It didn't help and sweat prickled along the back of his neck. "Lady Una has two young daughters. I trust you won't find their presence too uncomfortable."

Inexplicably, she smiled, as though she understood, and another sliver of guilt twisted through him. Christ, what did she imagine she understood?

"I hope Lady Una and I may become good friends in time. It is the custom in Pictland, also, to protect vulnerable widows. I'm glad to see Scots also follow this practice."

She didn't understand at all. He racked his brains to come up with the words to explain, but they eluded him. Because the only way she'd understand was if he told her the truth of his origins, and nothing on God's earth would persuade him to share that with her.

The specter of seeing the admiration in her eyes, whenever she looked at him, turn to disgust, was something he'd never voluntarily risk.

Yet he couldn't let her believe she was to be mistress of Dunmor. It wasn't fair on her.

"Orabel." He hoped she didn't hear the note of desperation in his voice. "My brother Gordon was the rightful lord of Dunmor and as such the stronghold should pass through his bloodline. Yet the law doesn't recognize the rights of his daughters, and I—"

The words dried in his throat as Orabel cradled his jaw and stroked her thumb across his cheek. "Pray, don't distress yourself, Ross. Of course you must provide for your brother's daughters. I know the question of my dowry irks you, but I am more than able to support myself and my ladies, as well as my warriors who accompany us. The futures of Lady Una's daughters won't be impacted by my arrival. Their home shall always be Dunmor."

Irrationally, considering how accommodating she was being, Orabel's reminder of her extensive dowry rattled him.

"Dunmor is more than able to support my wife and all her needs. You need have no fear on that account." Of course she need have no fear. Orabel was impressively wealthy in her own right, far more so than he had imagined, until MacAllister had informed him of the outcome of the marriage negotiations. "You don't need your dowry to survive."

"That's good to know, but even so, it is there if needed." She drifted a featherlight kiss across his lips, and with a smothered groan he tugged her close. "Perhaps we do have time to indulge before we must arise."

"I'm already arisen." He offered her a leer and her smile, as she provocatively glided her palm across his erection, dispelled the last of his concerns. How graciously she accepted the situation at Dunmor. His bride truly was remarkable.

There was a knock on the door, and he couldn't prevent a savage curse from escaping as Lady Saoirse entered. At least the young girls didn't accompany her, for which he was marginally relieved, but it hardly improved his mood.

"My lady," Saoirse said, apparently unperturbed by the sight of his half naked body. Hastily he dragged a fur up to cover himself and Orabel. He wasn't accustomed to such interruptions, but his bride was a princess, and, like the way she was constantly surrounded by her ladies and guards, it seemed it was something he'd simply have to get used to. "It is time."

Orabel sighed. "Thank you, Lady Saoirse. Might you give me one moment longer?"

Lady Saoirse inclined her head and retreated to the antechamber. He pinned Orabel to the bed and growled in her face. She laughed and tugged her fingers through his hair.

"It was not my idea to leave for Dunmor the morning after our wedding."

No, it had been MacAllister's, and the Pict king had granted that concession since they had won the issue regarding holding the ceremony in Fib. "Nor mine."

Although he wouldn't be sorry to leave Fib.

"Well, there is nothing to be done about it now. And the sooner we arrive at Dunmor, the sooner my precious garden can be replanted."

Yesterday, he'd witnessed the wagons that were loaded with her plants. It had been quite the spectacle and like nothing he'd seen before when princesses of Pictland had left their homeland. But then, the other princesses were not his Orabel.

"I hope they survive the journey."

"We've done our best to protect them. Goddess willing, they will thrive in their new home."

A shadow flickered over her face, and he knew why. Tenderly, he brushed her hair from her cheek. "Your goddess surely understands you had no choice, Orabel. She would not want bloodshed simply so you can remain unwed and in Fib."

Even as he tried to comfort her, he doubted his own words. He knew little of her gods, but he had been taught enough of his own to know that, when it came to understanding what God wanted, bloodshed was often the only answer.

"I hope so, Ross." But her smile was pensive, as though she, like him, did not quite believe it was so.

It took almost three weeks before they arrived at Dunmor, and the early summer breeze was warm as Ross helped Orabel dismount from her mare. After their betrothal he'd sent a messenger to inform Una and his steward of his marriage, and it appeared the entire stronghold's inhabitants had congregated in the courtyard to greet their new royal mistress.

It was inevitable that was how Orabel would be seen as no one except Una and his lady mother knew the truth. And that was how it should be to the outside world. No one would question Orabel's authority. But within the walls of the stronghold his bride accepted Una's right as the true mistress of Dunmor, and that was all that mattered.

The thought of his lady mother dampened his good spirits, and a familiar knot of grief twisted his gut. There was no telling how she would react to Orabel, or if she'd react at all. But as soon as his bride had rested, he would take her to meet his mother. He could only hope today was one of her better days.

He held Orabel's hand as he led her over to where Una and her daughters stood. Despite having been wed for three weeks, the novelty of holding her hand in public, and defying every rule of etiquette in the process, hadn't yet worn off.

Neither had the fierce blaze of possessiveness that gripped his chest every time he looked at her. No one would guess she had been travelling for weeks. She looked as fresh and serene as if she had just emerged from her chamber.

"Lady Orabel, may I present Lady Una of Dunmor." It was an effort to drag his gaze from his smiling bride and address Una. "Lady Una, it's my honor to present my bride, Orabel, Princess Annag of Fib."

Orabel and Una said all the right things and Orabel spoke kindly to his two young nieces, Fia and Dona, who both appeared speechless at the sight of the exotic creature he had brought among them. When Orabel once again addressed Una, he winked at the girls and shot them a grin which broke their paralysis, and they flung their arms around his waist in their usual greeting.

With a laugh he released Orabel's hand and swung the girls into his arms. "Have you been good for your mamma while I was away?"

"Aye," they chimed in unison before they once again turned their gazes onto Orabel. Little Dona tugged on his hair. "My lady is a fae princess."

Orabel heard and smiled at the child. "You must share your tales of the fae with me, if your mamma has no objection."

"I have no objection, my lady." Una cast him a wary glance and he bit back a sigh. Naturally, she was concerned about her position. It wasn't something he'd been able to entrust to a messenger, but he needed to set her mind at rest as soon as possible. "If you would care to follow me, I'll show you to your chambers."

He set the children down and they clung onto his plaid as they went into the stronghold. It was only when Orabel glanced at them that it occurred to him how strange she might find it. But he'd always been close with his nieces.

Closer than their own father had ever been. Gordon had wanted sons and made no secret of his displeasure at siring only daughters.

Una led them across the great hall and while it couldn't compare to Fib-eviot, he hoped Orabel would not find it wanting. It was only as they made their way up the stairs that another thought occurred to him, and he silently cursed at the oversight.

He should have sent instructions that Orabel was to have his brother's chamber. It was the grandest in the stronghold with its own antechamber, and although it was now officially his upon Gordon's death, he hadn't moved into it.

Una paused outside her own chamber and opened the door. "I trust this is to your liking, my lady. I will ensure your trunks are brought up at once."

Orabel entered the antechamber and before Una could follow her, Ross grasped her hand. "Una, this is yours," he whispered. "We don't expect you to give up your own chamber."

Her smile didn't reach her eyes. "Your bride is a royal princess." Her voice was as low as his. "She cannot be expected to take any of the smaller chambers and besides your own, this is the only one that possesses its own antechamber. Truly, I have no regrets in relinquishing this for the princess. Besides, your new bedchamber is next to this one."

And that was one of the reasons why he'd been in no hurry to take over the master chamber. Even though the love he'd once borne for Una had long since withered, the thought of taking the bedchamber next to hers did not sit right with him.

But if it was Orabel sleeping here…

He shoved the enticing notion aside. "I'll keep my old bedchamber and the princess will have Gordon's." To hell with it, now was as good a time as any to tell her nothing had changed with regards to her position." Una, there's something I must reassure you of."

ORABEL MADE a great show of examining the beautiful tapestries that hung upon the wall of the antechamber, but every sense she possessed vibrated with indefinable disquiet.

Lady Una was charming. The stronghold, such as she'd seen of it, appeared sturdy, and although the village they'd passed through earlier had an air of neglect clinging to it, for all she knew that might be a legacy from Ross' brother's day.

How long ago had his brother died? She hadn't thought to ask him, and he hadn't offered the information. There wasn't an aura of grief around Lady Una and her daughters which would indicate a recent bereavement and yet…

There was something clouding Lady Una, but she could not fathom what.

Oddly, Ross hadn't followed her into the chamber, and surreptitiously she glanced at the door.

Her heart slammed in her chest. Ross held Una's hand, his focus on her entirely, and whatever he was saying to her was clearly filled with restrained passion. Indeed, they were both so engrossed with each other they had apparently forgotten her existence.

Mortification burned through her. No, she was seeing shadows where there were none. Just because Ross spoke so intimately with his sister-through-marriage did not mean there was anything untoward between them.

Why would she imagine such a thing? There were a thousand reasons why her husband and his brother's widow should converse in such an intense manner. They were not, after all, doing anything underhand. They were standing right in front of her.

Somehow, that was of little comfort. Goddess, what was *wrong* with her? Her late husband had done far more than merely hold hands with other women throughout their marriage and that knowledge hadn't discomforted her half as much as *this*.

"My lady." The childish voice pulled her sharply from her tangled thoughts and she forced a smile as she faced the two girls. Ribbons threaded through their blonde curls, so like their mother's sleek fair hair, and their matching blue eyes were beautiful. The elder, who looked to be about seven, held her younger sister's hand. "Your gown is very pretty."

"Thank you," she responded in Gaelic and crouched so she was not towering above them. "In Pictland, all the ladies wear gowns like this."

"The gowns of the fae," said the little one. "From the old country."

The elder one sighed. "They are just stories, Dona. Not real. And my lady is not from the old country, are you?" She addressed her question to Orabel.

"I am not," she confirmed. "My people have lived in Pictland since the beginning of time."

"Fia, Dona." Una hurried into the chamber, clearly flustered. *What did Ross say to you?* "Do not plague my lady with your questions. The princess must rest after her journey. I will have refreshments sent to you," she added, but her gaze did not meet Orabel's as she took her daughters' hands and ushered them from the chamber.

Ross came over to her, and Saoirse and the five young noblewomen remained in the antechamber as he led her into the bedchamber and shut the door. Sprays of purple heather had been placed around the hearth and strewn across the bed and its sweet, honey-tinged fragrance drifted in the air.

For the first time since she'd met him, she didn't know what to say. *Pull yourself together.* She and Ross had not known each other long, but she knew enough of him. He had honor, and she refused to believe he harbored anything more than brotherly concern for his sister-through-marriage.

"These chambers are most agreeable," she said.

He took her hands and kissed her fingers. Delightful tingles of awareness danced through her blood and the breath caught in her throat. It was always this way, whenever he touched her. And far from diminishing since their wedding night, the fever he ignited within her seemed only to heighten the longer they were together.

"These chambers are Una's." An undertone of agony ran through his statement, and she couldn't fathom why. Surely the possession or not of a chamber didn't warrant such an impassioned response?

"Lady Una's?" she promoted, when it became apparent he wasn't intending to elaborate.

"Aye." He heaved a great sigh which did nothing to calm her growing unease. "They belong to the lady of the stronghold. She insists they are rightfully yours."

Goddess, what did Ross expect her to say? To be sure, this situation wasn't one she had expected when she'd agreed to the betrothal, and the last thing she wanted to do was upset Una, but was Ross implying he believed his brother's widow should remain here?

The question was obvious. She wasn't certain she wanted to know the answer. "And you believe they are not?"

"You should have the master bedchamber next to this one, Orabel. There is more room for you and your ladies, but Una is adamant and there is no dissuading her."

"I confess this is most confusing, Ross. Are you suggesting you and I share the master chamber and Lady Una returns to this one?"

His sudden grin dispelled the shadows that had clouded his eyes, and despite the tendrils of apprehension that wound through her, she couldn't resist smiling back at him. Whatever this bizarre conversation was about, it had nothing to do with Ross wanting Una in the chamber next to his.

"I'm not adverse to that idea." Then he tugged her closer, his breath warm against her lips, and her nebulous sense of foreboding dissipated like mist before the sun. "It will save nightly treks from my bed to yours, that's for certain."

"It's a scandalous notion." But one she found utterly thrilling. "Although I must confess, I have no objections to sharing the same bed. I've become quite used to waking with you beside me, during our journey."

He wound his arms around her, pulling her close, and she breathed in deep, the fresh scent of leather and woodlands that clung to his plaid wrapping her in a cocoon of sensual anticipation. She rose onto her toes and gave him a lingering kiss, teasing him with the tip of her tongue, and his strangled groan caused shudders of need to pulse through her body.

"You bewitch me." His hot breath scorched her lips, and he trailed burning kisses along her jaw. His teeth grazed her throat, and she arched her back, pressing against him. If only they were naked. Liquid heat pooled between her thighs, and she raked her fingers through his hair, unheeding how her ladies were in the adjoining chamber and might enter at any moment.

"I cannot get enough of you." His voice was hoarse, as if the knowledge she tested his self-control razed him and it was a heady aphrodisiac. Feverishly, his hands roamed over her back before grasping her buttocks through her gown and a needy gasp escaped. Goddess, she wanted him. Needed him. But surely they could not…

Her thoughts scattered as he roughly hitched her gown up to her waist. Propriety reared a faint protest through the fog of desire. "Ross, should we be doing this?"

"Orabel, aye, we should. Or would you have me perish with want?"

"Never," she breathed. How could she deny him anything, when he gazed at her with those blue eyes filled with such fierce passion? "I ache for you."

His grin was feral and sharp arrows of lust pierced through her, igniting the flames that seared her blood. He dropped to his knees, still grasping her gown in his fists, and her fingers tangled in his hair as realization bloomed.

"Goddess, Ross," she gasped. "You cannot mean to—" She sucked in a sharp breath as he pressed an open-mouthed kiss against her damp slit, his tongue a tempting promise of decadent delight.

She clung onto his hair, her only anchor, as he licked her sensitized clitoris and delved inside her slick sheath. He released his grip on her gown, and the material draped over her hands, over his head, concealing him from her view, and somehow that merely enhanced the breath-stealing sensations he evoked.

Once again, his hands cupped her bottom, but this time there was no gown hindering his access. She moaned as his fingers explored her flesh, circling her buttocks, before sliding between her thighs.

Her legs trembled, and her erratic gasps filled the chamber. His fingers stroked her tender lips, increasing the pressure and she writhed helplessly beneath his relentless onslaught.

Spirals of need consumed her, and the world splintered. Her nails dug into his head as her body convulsed, his tongue claiming her as surely as his glorious cock ever had, and he held her, firm, steady, as she came with reckless abandon inside his plundering mouth.

Gasping, she sagged against him, unheeding of everything but this wondrous moment. Slowly, her galloping heart steadied, and hazy threads of reality fluttered through her mind. Yet she couldn't regret this hasty encounter. Ross was her husband, after all, the master of Dunmor, and if he wished to ravish his bride in the middle of the day, who would rebuke him for it?

The thought made her laugh and Ross rose to his feet, towering over her, a dangerous gleam in his eyes. "What is so amusing, my lady?"

"I'm not accustomed to daytime trysts, and find it all most engaging."

He grinned, but it was a feral thing, and fettered lust throbbed in the air surrounding them. "I'm gratified. For rest assured, I intend we shall enjoy a great many daytime trysts." His hands cradled her face. "And we are not yet done with this one."

"I should hope not." Goddess, was that husky, seductive whisper truly her voice? She scarcely recognized the person she had become since wedding Ross. The marriage bed was something she now craved, and graphic images of their lovemaking invaded her mind throughout the day, even at the most inopportune moments. "I should be a poor wife indeed if I allowed my husband to remain in such torment until night fell."

"The torment is real. I'll perish if I don't have immediate satisfaction."

She had the urge to laugh again. In the early days of her marriage to her first husband, Edwin had often demanded his rights *immediately*. But there had been no bantering between them, no sense of connection, no…

Anything. Just perfunctory exchanges. Being with Ross was a revelation on so many levels it was hard to fathom.

"Then I shall make haste." She threaded her fingers through his hair and pulled him close for a kiss. His tongue probed the seam of her lips, demanding entry, and she groaned as he pushed inside. He was hot, and he was ready, and goddess help her, he tasted of her.

The blood pounded in her head and in the far distance, a light tapping befuddled her senses.

Ross snarled, a savage sound that sent shivers of illicit delight over her flesh. Tension vibrated through his muscles as though he held back from tossing her onto the bed and taking her by only the slenderest of threads. It was thrilling, but she couldn't expect him to hold on for much longer. And she was determined to pleasure him, the way he had just pleasured her.

Something she had never done before. Never wanted to. But now, she could not wait.

"Orabel." Her name sounded like a curse as he forced it between his teeth. "I fear we are being summoned."

There was another gentle tap on the door and heat scorched her. How long had Saoirse—it could be no one else—been knocking on the door for her attention?

"Goddess." She straightened and patted ineffectually at her hair. It they were at Fib-eviot, she would not feel nearly so disconcerted. But, although Dunmor was now her home, and she its mistress, she had only just arrived. And there was no point lying to herself. Lady Una's presence disquieted her. She didn't want Ross' sister-through-marriage to see her as anything but utterly capable and above reproach. And if Lady Una had returned with the refreshments she'd promised, Orabel knew exactly what she would be thinking.

It shouldn't matter. She did not answer to Lady Una. And yet she felt wrong-footed, all the same.

Despite the circumstances, Ross managed a half-civilized grin.

"Don't fret, my lady. You look entirely composed. I shall merely burn with unrequited lust until we're alone again. But know this." He leaned in close, and his warm breath caressed her ear. "I shall expect full recompense for my suffering."

CHAPTER NINETEEN

$\mathcal{L}$ady Una and her daughters had, indeed, returned with the refreshments and as Orabel finished her third cup of herbal tea, she cast a sideways glance at Ross. He'd spent the entire time standing, hands clasped behind his back, and more than once she'd had the undignified urge to laugh at the pained expression on his face.

Truly, she wasn't sure why he stayed while she and her ladies discussed inconsequential pleasantries with Lady Una. She hadn't expected him to. Yet every time her glance strayed his way, she couldn't deny the frisson of delight that he had.

"My lady," said Lady Una, and she hastily returned her attention to the other woman. "Perhaps tomorrow, if it pleases you, I will show you around Dunmor?"

"I should like that very much."

Ross finally spoke. "I shall take Lady Orabel to meet my lady mother. How is she this day, Una?"

Lady Una's smile was strained. "The same as always. But I'm certain she will enjoy meeting the princess. Should I accompany you?"

Ross offered Orabel his hand, and she took it as she rose from her chair. She wanted to meet his lady mother but wasn't sure she wanted Una there, too. Why did she have this strange feeling that the other woman was hiding something? Una had been nothing but agreeable since the moment Orabel had arrived at Dunmor.

Yet the feeling persisted. If only she could make sense of it.

The image of Ross holding Una's hand flashed through her mind. Brutally, she crushed it. There was nothing going on between Ross and Una. She was sure of it.

Are you, though?

Ross sighed. "Orabel, it might be best if Una comes with us. My mother sees so few people now days I don't wish to unduly alarm her."

"Of course." What else could she say? It would be churlish to refuse.

"My lady." Una gripped her fingers together and Orabel resisted the urge to do the same. Why was Una so nervous? "Forgive me for speaking so freely, but might your ladies remain here? Lady Fia becomes overwhelmed so easily."

So Una's daughter had been named after her grandmamma. It was charming, and only right, so why did a sliver of apprehension rake along her spine?

She glanced at Saoirse. While she was only too happy to leave the young noblewomen in this antechamber, she rarely went anywhere without her dearest friend. On the other hand, it was unthinkable to leave the five young girls without supervision.

Saoirse inclined her head, understanding her dilemma without the need for words. With a smothered sigh, Orabel turned back to Una. "I should not wish to distress Lady Fia."

They left the chambers, and she acknowledged Neilan who stood guard outside the door before she and Ross followed Una and her daughters. Neilan brought up the rear, falling into step with Una's serving woman.

At the end of the passageway there was another staircase and trepidation snaked through her as she climbed the stairs. It seemed most odd that the dowager's chambers should be so awkwardly situated in a tower so far away from everyone.

At the top of the stairs was a large door. She couldn't shake the feeling this was more like a prison than a dowager's rightful chambers, and her unease magnified when Una selected a key from her chatelaine and unlocked it, before proceeding inside.

"Remain here," she whispered to Neilan, who gave a brief nod in response as she entered the chamber.

She released a relieved breath. The tower, far from resembling a stark dungeon as she'd feared, was luxurious in the extreme. Thick rugs covered the stone floor, faded tapestries hung upon the walls, and a small fire burned in the grate. And yet it was still only one small chamber, with a bed along one wall and there was not even a single window slit for fresh air or a glimpse of the outside world.

But there was something else. Something she could not explain. It was as though the rugs and the tapestries were merely a façade, hiding what should be plain, yet shrouded just out of sight.

A shiver trickled over her arms and again the question throbbed through her mind.

Why is the dowager kept here under lock and key?

A serving woman rose from a stool and dropped a curtsey before she went over to the bed and pulled back the hangings. "My lady, my lord Ross is here to see you."

After a moment, Lady Fia emerged. Her hair was faded and in need of combing, her gown was crumpled, but her eyes were a bright blue, so like Ross' that the breath caught in Orabel's throat.

"My lady mother." Ross went to her and kissed her hand, before embracing her. A vague smile touched the dowager's lips as Ross released her, but still held her hand. "It's good to see you looking so well. I have grand news to share. I'm recently wed to the Princess of Fib, and she is eager to meet you."

Ross made the introductions, but the dowager frowned and glanced from Orabel to Una.

"But your bride is Una," she said. "That is how it should be, Ross, now your brother is gone."

Orabel kept a smile on her face only through sheer force of will. It was painfully obvious the dowager was not in full possession of her senses, and yet, despite that, she heard the thread of truth ring through every word.

Agony flashed across Ross' face, and even though she struggled to contain herself in the face of her mother-through-marriage's apparent rejection, sympathy stabbed through her for Ross' obvious torment.

"No, my lady mother. My bride is Lady Orabel and I'm thankful for this. Will you greet her?"

There was a note of low desperation in his voice and Orabel crushed her foolish hurt feelings and joined him. "Lady Fia, it's an honor to meet you."

Lady Fia cocked her head and gazed at her as though it was the first time she'd noticed her. "You are not from here," she whispered. "I don't know who you are."

As she spoke, she reached out and Orabel took her hand. Instantly, a dark whirlpool blasted through her, chilling her blood, and she smothered a startled gasp.

Great goddess, save us.

A mighty vise pressed into her head, sending white-hot arrows of fire through her mind. The chamber blurred, became a maelstrom of fragmented images and memories, and terror gripped her.

No. No...

The dowager released her hand, and the connection severed. Orabel's heart pummeled with unnamed dread, but Lady Fia's face was serene as though she hadn't just experienced the same frightening confusion tearing through her soul.

A terrible comprehension dawned. Lady Fia hadn't reacted because she lived with it every day.

"…my wife," Ross said. He had obviously been explaining the situation to his mother again and hadn't noticed her own disorientation. Thank goddess for that.

"Mamma." Una took the dowager's arm and led her to a chair. "Please don't distress yourself. We are all very happy the Princess of Fib has wed Ross."

"But Gordon is dead," the dowager said. She still gazed at Orabel. "The wrong must now be righted."

Una's hand shook and she hastily grasped her fingers together, the way she had earlier, and cast a despairing glance at Ross.

Who returned it.

What was going on? It was dreadfully clear there was something more than she understood between her husband and Una.

After a gesture from their mother, Fia and Dona approached their grandmamma and the bond between the three of them was glowingly evident. Ross dragged his fingers through his hair and stepped back to her side. Una joined them.

"She knows of Gordon's death?" His voice was low.

"Aye. But I said nothing to her while you were away. This is the first time she's mentioned him. She obviously understood what you said to her at the time, Ross."

Ross turned to her. "Forgive me, Orabel. I would've given a lot to spare you from this. My lady mother scarcely remembers anything of her life, and what she does recall is often far from reality."

"There's nothing to forgive. Alas, your lady mother is not the first I've met who suffers from this cruel malady."

Yet even as she spoke, doubt lingered in her mind. Whatever malady Lady Fia suffered from, it was not merely constrained to her forgetting her previous life.

Although at least now she understood the reason for the

locked door. How easily a confused lady could trip upon the stairs and fall to her death.

He released a tortured breath. "We must find another chamber for her. This tower has served its purpose."

Orabel had no idea what he meant by it serving its purpose, but she heartily agreed with finding the dowager more suitable accommodation. "We shall surely find a better chamber tomorrow, when Lady Una shows me around the stronghold. A chamber that has easy access to the outside, so your lady mother does not need to navigate the treacherous stairs simply to breathe fresh air and take exercise."

Silence descended. In Northumbria, silence had often descended after she gave an impassioned declaration concerning a patient's welfare. But Lady Fia wasn't her patient. And with a ripple of dismay, she suddenly realized Ross had directed his comment not to her, but to Una.

Yet why wouldn't he discuss his mother's needs with his sister-through-marriage? Una was his brother's widow, which meant Fia was her mother-through marriage. Until this very day, Una had been mistress of Dunmor.

Yet Ross deferred to her as if she were still mistress of Dunmor.

"That is a wonderful notion, my lady." Una smiled, and for the first time since they had met, it appeared fully genuine. "I should be glad to assist you in this endeavor, if you wish."

"Thank you." Orabel inclined her head and tried to bite her tongue. But even though she understood why Ross had spoken to Una instead of herself in this matter, it still stung. And she refused to remain silent. "I confess, I don't understand why Lady Fia is in this tower at all. It's most inappropriate."

"Aye." Bitterness threaded through the word as Ross glanced at his mother. "Not to speak ill of the dead, but this was my father's doing, and my brother continued to keep her here after his death. Una and I ensured she was cared for but Gordon's threat of sending her to a nunnery in Eire, should her presence disturb him, forever hung over our heads."

How had she imagined, for even a fleeting moment, that Ross had been responsible for having his mother sequestered in this lonely tower? Part of her knew she should be ashamed of herself but the other part—the larger part—was still struggling to comprehend his true relationship with Una.

She wanted to condemn both his father and brother's actions. But she had not known either of them and it wasn't her place. As for Gordon, it seemed absurd to offer condolences for the loss of a man whose brother or widow didn't appear to mourn him and yet the event was recent. And her duty clear.

"Forgive me." She addressed Una. "I've been remiss in extending my condolences. If there's anything I can do, please let me know."

"You are too kind." Una dropped her gaze to the floor. "My husband died three weeks before Ross left Dunmor for the Kingdom of Fib. My daughters and I are—we have accepted his passing."

It was evident Una wasn't grief-stricken by her husband's untimely death. But it wasn't so very unusual. She hadn't been grief-struck by Edwin's death, either.

Guilty, perhaps. But there had been no love between them in life for her to miss upon his demise. She'd been too relieved by the prospect of her freedom to mourn a man who had shown her so little regard throughout their marriage.

Was Una relieved she was now free, or had she hoped for something more with her late husband's brother?

"The wrong must now be righted."

No. She would not go further down that dark path. The dowager did not know what she was saying.

If only she could believe that. Yet she didn't. Because somewhere in that terrifying vortex of memories and confusion she had glimpsed so briefly, there had been something else.

Something intangible, buried so deeply, she doubted if the dowager was even aware it existed.

But it was something she could not afford to ignore, and it was up to her to discover what truly ailed Lady Fia. Otherwise, why had Bride shown her?

CHAPTER TWENTY

Una had organized a grand feast that night to celebrate his wedding to Orabel, and although Ross appreciated her efforts, he wished there was no obligation to entertain the neighboring nobles who had descended upon Dunmor. It was obvious the main reason they were here was so they could meet the exotic Princess of Fib.

Truth was, he wanted his bride to himself for as long as he was able. After all, there was no telling when MacAlpin might order him on a new mission.

The tables had been pushed back to the walls, but as a concession to his brother's recent passing, no dancing was planned. Only a succession of nobles extending their condolences and congratulations on his recent turn in fortunes.

Orabel greeted each one graciously, but something wasn't right. She'd been unusually quiet since visiting his lady mother.

Not that he could blame her. Although his mother hadn't, thank God, been in one of her melancholy states where she didn't understand anything that occurred around her, deep in his heart he'd hoped she would welcome Orabel as her daughter-through-marriage.

He stole another glance at his bride, and a now familiar surge of pride and fierce protectiveness engulfed him. Despite his mother's reception, Orabel had been all kindness towards her. And adamant she should have another chamber as soon as possible.

But he'd been remiss not to realize she had taken his mother's reserved greeting to heart.

As the last of the nobles filed past, he took Orabel's hand. "Would you care for some wine, my lady? I confess I'm parched after acknowledging so many well-wishers."

He grinned at her, but she didn't respond with her usual smile. Instead, she merely inclined her head in agreement and allowed him to lead her to a table where jugs of wine stood. After handing her a goblet, she took a small sip as she glanced around the hall.

Then she looked at him. "How did your brother die, Ross?"

He shook his head. "I should have told you before now. It was a senseless accident. He broken his neck in a fall from his horse."

It was strange, how he'd simply believed she already knew. Yet sometimes he felt as though he had known Orabel forever, that she had always been a part of his life and, as such, knew all there was to know of his family.

All things, but one. And that one thing she would never learn of him.

"You were not close to him?"

As a small boy, he'd been in awe of his magnificent older brother who excelled in everything he attempted, and who was their father's undoubted favorite. Later, he'd understood why their father favored Gordon. And why his idolized brother treated his younger sibling with barely disguised contempt.

But none of that was fit for Orabel's ears.

"There was more than ten years between us. He had little time for a younger brother whose greatest talent was getting under his feet." He smiled at her, to prove he was merely jesting, but even now, after all these years, Gordon's rejection was still an unhealed scar he could do nothing to repair.

Orabel studied her wine as if it was the most fascinating thing she had ever encountered. "If your hand hadn't been forced in Fib, would you have returned to Dunmor and wed Lady Una?"

"What?" He stared at her, appalled. It hadn't occurred to him she would give such credence to his lady mother's confused comments. "Orabel, you must believe me. It's never been my intention to wed my brother's widow."

"I'm not accusing you of anything, Ross. But if there was an understanding between you and Lady Una, before you came to Fib, I would like to know the truth. There is no virtue in ignorance."

He took her goblet and put both on the table before taking her hands. To hell with what anyone thought. "There was no understanding between us. If I'd returned to Dunmor without you as my bride, I would not have wed Una. As God is my witness, that's the truth."

He willed her to believe him. But even as he did so, disquiet slithered through him at the prospect of a future without Orabel in it. It was madness. If he hadn't wed her, how would he miss her?

Yet the logic failed to register. Because the twist of fate that had made her his could so easily have ensured he lost her forever.

"I believe you." Her voice was low. "And yet I cannot help but see the special connection between you. Forgive me, but I feel there is more than you say."

Shit. Una was his past. He had no wish to rake over that part of his life, especially not with Orabel. Deniel thrummed in his mind. If he told her Una had never been any more than his sister-through-marriage, why would she not believe him? It was easier than the truth.

Yet he couldn't bring himself to do it. Orabel deserved that truth, at least.

"Una is the daughter of my mother's cousin. She came to live with us when she was but ten years old, and I eleven. We grew up together and aye, there was a time when we believed we might wed. But it was not to be, and it was long ago. Another lifetime. I have no regrets."

A strange lightness encased his chest, as though an intangible burden had lifted. Christ, it was true. He had no regrets when it came to Una. And although he had long ago grown past the love he'd once held for her, it was only now he realized a part of him had never quite been able to let go of what might have been.

Until now. When he gazed into Orabel's captivating violet eyes.

Her bottom lip trembled. Just once, but it was his undoing. "Thank you." Her voice was husky. "For honoring me with the truth. I'm glad you have no regrets."

"I'm grieved I gave you cause to doubt me." He pulled her closer and it was a battle not to claim her lips and show her, here and now, just how badly he wanted her. "I've a mind to forego the rest of this celebration and carry you to my bedchamber and give you many good reasons to never doubt my word again."

Finally, she smiled, and it seemed to illuminated the entire hall. He didn't even care that the fanciful notion drifted through his mind. If Orabel had enchanted him with her pagan magic, he had no complaints.

"Indeed, my husband, I believe it is I who shall be giving you many good reasons this night why I shall never doubt your word again."

Her implication was plain. His cock throbbed as graphic images of Orabel on her knees before him blazed through his mind. The lights from the lamps and candles that lit the hall shimmered and blurred, until all he could see was his beautiful wife, and the way she gazed at him as though no one else existed.

"You torture me with your promises." His voice was hoarse,

and he cradled her face, his thumb caressing her silken cheek. "Are you ready to escape this gathering?"

"If it's not too scandalous. I shouldn't wish our hasty departure to reflect badly on the new lord of Dunmor."

"No man here will blame me when I possess such a delectable bride." He threaded his fingers through hers. "Come. Before anyone else can accost us."

"Oh, but I must tell Lady Saoirse." She glanced around the hall, and he sighed. She was a princess, and used to being surrounded by her ladies, but he was her husband and surely some nights she didn't need her attendants' presence.

"Not tonight."

When she shot him a startled glance, he offered her an evil grin.

"It is most unorthodox." But she didn't protest as he led her from the hall. "My sister would strongly disapprove."

"Fortunately, your sister remains in Fib." He hastened her to the stairs, blood pounding in his ears. Had anticipation of slaking his lust ever entrapped his good sense so utterly? Yet the answer was by his side, holding his hand. Until Orabel, his good sense had never been so continually compromised.

"My bedchamber is so far away." She lifted her skirts as she went up the stairs and he grabbed the nearest torch from the wall, so they didn't fall to their deaths in the dark. "I confess, I had no idea marriage could be so enjoyable until we wed."

"Likewise," he growled, his hot gaze fixed on the delectable curve of her arse that her gown clung to so provocatively. "If I could arrange it, you would never leave my bed."

At the top of the stairs she turned, a teasing smile on her face. "It would be hard to undertake my duties if I never left your bed."

He wrapped his arm around her. "I disagree. You'd perform them most admirably; I have no doubt."

She laughed and rested her head against him, her hand pressing over his heart. "I do not consider the marital bed a duty."

"I'm glad to hear it." He swung open the door to his chamber before kicking it shut behind them. The fire in the hearth of the antechamber burned brightly, and he shoved his torch into the wall sconce. "I can think of nothing worse than an unwilling bride in my arms."

She twisted around and wound her arms around his neck. "Then do not think of it. It's not something you need concern yourself with me."

He groaned and raked his fingers through her glorious hair, dislodging her fragile veil in the process. He loved when she left it loose, instead of tied in braids like every other woman of his acquaintance. It reminded him of the first time he'd seen her, when he'd imagined she was a vision from heaven.

"I can scarcely think at all when you look at me with such desire."

For answer, she kissed him, the tip of her tongue teasing his lips as her fingers trailed a tantalizing path along his nape. He shuddered, his hands roaming over her back, before he clasped her backside. She filled his palms so perfectly. Damn her gown for being in the way.

"Let me finish what we started earlier this day." Her whisper was a seductive caress against his mouth as she glided her hands over his shoulders. "I hate to see you suffer so."

"Aye. My suffering has been great. It's a wonder I didn't haul you off to my chambers long before this."

"Your fortitude is admirable." She drifted kisses along his jaw before nibbling his throat. He let out a frustrated groan and instinctively tightened his grip on her behind. "Your restraint impressive, indeed."

"Yet still you inflict this suffering upon me." Despite the need that ravaged whatever good sense he retained, he couldn't help a savage grin. Orabel would drive him out of his mind before she was done with him. And he relished the notion. "Do you wish me to beg for mercy?"

He might even do it. For her.

"Another time, perhaps." Amusement threated through her voice. "I'm not so cruel to prolong your torment this night."

Was that a promise—or a threat? He had no idea, and cared even less, as she gracefully kneeled at his feet. The glow from the fire cast mystical shadows around her, but when she raised her head and looked at him, every delicate feature of her face burned into the fabric of his existence.

"Orabel." His hand shook as he raked his fingers through her beautiful midnight hair. "You couldn't be cruel if you tried."

The light flickered, distorting his vision, for there was no reason why guilt should flash across his sweet bride's face.

Her fingernails scored over his calves then higher, sliding beneath his plaid. Once again, she looked up at him and this time her smile of pure provocation caused his breath to lock in his throat. With slow deliberation, she inched up his plaid until it was above his knees.

"Wish me good fortune as I venture into unknown lands," she said, before dropping his plaid about her shoulders and vanishing from view.

"Christ." He choked on the word, torn between the need to succumb to the powerful lust that held him in its merciless grip, or laughing. No woman had ever come close to making him laugh the way Orabel did. And in the bedchamber, no less. Somehow, he managed to respond with a modicum of lucidity. "Good fortune."

She shook between his knees, clearly in silent laughter, and her erratic breath was warm and infinitely erotic against his naked thighs. Then she spoke.

"It's quite dark under here. I fear I cannot see a thing."

Did she know how desperately she tortured him? He was certain she did. Yet had the feeling that, maybe, she truly didn't.

Either way, his fate was the same. Willingly ensnared within the scented haven of her ministrations.

"We can move nearer to the fire if you wish." God, he hoped she didn't wish. He wasn't sure he was capable of walking. It took all his strength to remain upright, fists clenched, resisting the urge to grip her head and sink into her beckoning heat.

"No." Her voice was muffled, and her breath drifted against his erection with taunting disregard. He screwed his eyes shut, clawed desperately for control, but with every frenzied beat of his heart, control slipped farther from his reach. "I shall feel my way and hope I don't inadvertently damage you."

Fuck this. He had fantasized about Orabel taking him into her mouth and he'd be damned if he'd deny himself the added plea-sure of watching her while she did. With a harsh curse he unwound his plaid. Had it ever taken this long before? The mate-rial was endless and his hands uncommonly clumsy. And then her palm cradled his balls and he damn near lost his balance.

He flung his plaid onto the floor and tore his shirt over his head. Orabel kneeled at his feet, cupping his balls, and looked up at him with barely concealed mirth. "Is something amiss, my husband?"

He growled low in his throat. It appeared when it came to Orabel, his vocal capabilities frequently deserted him. "No. Not now I can see you."

She stroked his shift with the tips of her fingers and his mouth dried.

"And I can see you." There was a note of awe in her voice, which was as alluring as her touch. "You are quite magnificent."

His fingers tangled in her hair. God give him strength. "If your aim is to unman me, you are close to succeeding."

"Hmm." She wrapped her hand around him, and he squeezed his eyes shut, but it didn't help stem the fierce arousal flooding his blood and hammering against his temples. The wild imperative to take and conquer throbbed through his mind yet he was powerless to move beneath her gentle explo-ration. But when her warm breath caressed the head of his cock, he nearly damn well lost it. "Such a notion never crossed my mind."

She pressed her lips against his shaft, kissing his length, and the tip of her tongue was a tantalizing torture. He couldn't take his bewitched gaze from her, his bride, his princess, as she slowly sucked him into her mouth.

Her teeth scraped his rigid flesh, and her wet heat enslaved him in a cocoon of sensation. His vision glazed, and his chest burned with the effort of dragging air into his lungs, and the only sound that filled his head was the erratic thunder of his heart.

He wanted more. The need to possess his only coherent thought. Her fingers teased and explored, sending darts of agonizing pleasure wherever she touched, and still he couldn't get enough of her.

"Harder." It was a guttural command, and he gripped her head, showing her what he needed. She slid her hand to his root, and he took instant advantage, pushing further inside her addictive heat as she moved her head beneath his guiding hands.

It was as if this was the first time, the only time, a woman had been on her knees before him. Nothing had prepared him for this. For Orabel. For how she took him so completely.

He couldn't drag his mesmerized gaze from her. The sight of his cock in her mouth. The way her lips stretched around his girth as he thrust into her, taking her, making her his.

A raw groan razed his throat as the pressure spiraled and his balls tightened. *So fucking close.* He balanced on the precipice, desperate for release, yet not wanting this moment to ever end.

He gritted his teeth. Clawed frantically for control. Orabel's nails scraped his sac and her cheeks hollowed as she sucked him in, so deep, so hard, time lost meaning, the world ceased to exist, and she was his only lifeline to sanity.

The last thread unraveled, and his tenuous mastery combusted to ash. A harsh roar tore through him, echoed around the chamber, filled every particle of his being. Orabel, his Orabel, didn't pull back. She took him, took everything, and even when he had nothing left to give, her fingers and lips demanded more.

The thunder in his head eased, his fingers relaxed in her hair. The low crackle from the fire drifted through the air and Orabel rolled back on her knees. Her breath was uneven, her hair disarrayed, and he couldn't drag his gaze from her beautiful mouth.

His chest tightened, a strange sensation somewhere between the realms of pain and pleasure. "You bewitch me anew each day, Orabel."

"And you, I." Her voice was hoarse, and he instantly crouched before her, tenderly brushing back her hair that had fallen across her cheek.

"There's wine in the bedchamber." Thank God for his foresight earlier in ensuring a jug of wine and platter of fruits awaited them. "I shall personally see to it that you're thoroughly refreshed before our bed sport continues."

She laughed, and he grinned before he swept her into his arms and held her close as he strode to the bedchamber to fulfil his promise.

CHAPTER TWENTY-ONE

It had been seven days since Orabel had arrived at Dunmor. The days had flown by, and goddess help her, so had the nights, yet sometimes it seemed she had been wed to Ross forever.

As she and Saoirse entered the ground floor chamber that Lady Fia was soon to occupy, familiar warmth encased Orabel when she thought of her husband. How easy it was to forget he was a Scot, when he treated her with such esteem. Not at all the way she had been taught as a child, that all Scots were savages who treated their wives as little better than slaves.

As always when she daydreamed of Ross, she hastily tried to cover her errant musings. It was one thing to secretly delight in this new life. But quite another to allow it to consume her every waking thought, for Bride would surely not allow such disrespect to go unpunished.

She didn't wish to anger her goddess and risk another bone chilling vision. Yet all would be well, for the following day she intended to make her first visit to the village to make use of her healing skills, the way Bride intended.

The chamber allocated for the dowager's use wasn't large, but it did have a window and with the wooden shutters opened, a warm breeze fluttered through the chamber.

"I believe all is ready, my lady," Saoirse said.

"Yes. I'm certain once Lady Fia is away from the tower, her mind will ease." She hoped so, anyway. The terrifying chaos she'd glimpsed that one time had haunted her ever since. And she'd agonized whether she should share that experience with Ross. Yet what good could come of that? There was nothing more Ross could do to ease his mother's mind, and the knowledge of how she suffered would deeply trouble him. Perhaps, now she had sorted out her apothecary, she would find other ways to help calm the dowager's maladies.

Coira, the eldest of the young noblewomen, came into the chamber. "My lady, the dowager approaches."

The other young noblewomen all followed Coira inside and arranged themselves along the far wall, and Orabel took a deep breath as Ross and Una accompanied Lady Fia into the chamber. Although she had visited the dowager several times over the last few days, the older lady still didn't appear to understand who she was.

"My lady mother, you'll be far more comfortable here," Ross said, as he led her to a chair beside the hearth. "If there's anything you require, you must let me know."

She gave him a bemused look. "Where is Ross? He is such a bonny babe. Do not keep him from me."

Despair flashed across Ross' face, and Orabel's heart ached at the sight. "No, Mamma," he said, clasping her hand. "I am Ross. I grew up a long time ago."

The dowager became agitated, the way she always did when Ross or Una corrected her misunderstandings. Finally, Ross heaved a sigh and patted her hand before turning to Orabel.

"I must go, Orabel. I'm meeting Angus, and later going into the village to see what work and repairs need to be done." He took her hand and she smiled. Angus, the steward, was a good man and she was glad Ross, unlike his brother, showed such interest in ensuring the village should be well maintained. "I want to ensure everything is well before we leave for Forteviot."

Her smile grew strained but somehow she managed not to let it slip. She wasn't looking forward to the coronation next week but more than that, she feared that once they arrived, MacAlpin would command Ross to undertake another mission for him.

It was a warrior's life. She knew that. Her first husband had often been far from his stronghold. But then, Ross was not Edwin.

After Ross left, Una dipped a curtsey and also left with her serving woman. Orabel glanced at Lady Fia, who was distractedly threading the end of her shawl through her fingers.

There was so much she needed to do this day. Not least, check on how her precious plants were faring in their new gardens. But it did not feel right to leave the dowager when she was still clearly distressed. She went over to her and waited until the older lady looked at her.

"Lady Fia, my ladies and I are going for a walk in the gardens. Would you care to accompany us?"

"A walk?" She appeared startled by the question but did not protest when her serving woman brought over a thicker shawl and wrapped it around her shoulders. As they made their way across the great hall, Neilan joined them, and when they left the stronghold, half a dozen of her warriors fell into line behind him.

It was disconcerting to be shadowed so heavily whenever she left the stronghold. It reminded her of her years in Northumbria. But Neilan, when she'd questioned him on it, had been adamant. He did not trust the Scots any more than he'd trusted the Northumbrians; and would not allow her to wander as freely here as she had in Fib-eviot.

The early summer sun was warm as they trekked across the courtyard towards the generous portion of land that had been allocated for her medicinal gardens. Although at first, she hadn't been overly thrilled at the prospect of being so close to the Scot built church, Ross had assured her no monks had occupied the site since his father's time.

Which was a good thing, to be sure, but her main reservation was the fact whoever had constructed the building a hundred years ago or more had desecrated the old gods' original place of worship.

She could feel the ancient power in the earth beneath her feet. Were the gods angry? Or merely biding their time?

But the truth was, it was the perfect spot for her gardens. The church walls would give good protection for her less-hardy plants during the harsh winter months, and already Ross had instructed his men to construct an enclosed section where she'd eventually grow her hazardous remedies.

When they reached the gardens, she turned to the young noblewomen. Their education was ongoing and at least in this area she was proficient, unlike when she attempted to instruct them in the finer points of delicate embroidery. "Gather the herbs and plants you need should your household succumb to the bloody flux."

As the girls dutifully untied pouches from their girdles and proceeded to do as they were bid, Orabel led Lady Fia over to one of the raised beds she'd brought with her from Fib.

Tenderly, she traced her finger over the purple and blue flowers that nestled among their spiky leaves. Her rosemary had flourished in Ayr and Fib but would need more care during winter this far north.

She picked a few sprigs and rubbed the leaves, so their woody, aromatic scent drifted in the air, before handing them to the dowager. "Lady Saoirse and I are distilling an infusion of rose-mary to freshen your chamber, Lady Fia. Would you like that?"

Lady Fia sniffed the herb, and a soft smile lit her face. "Aye. That is most kind of you, my lady."

It was the first time the dowager had addressed her directly, and Orabel took hope from it. Perhaps, in time, her mother-through-marriage might accept her. "I'm happy to do it, Lady Fia. Working with herbs and plants is my passion."

"You are a healer?"

"Yes. It is the reason I was born."

"Ah." Lady Fia nodded her head sagely. "That is good, indeed. Ross and Una are fortunate you chose to come to Dunmor."

Her smile faltered but she forced herself not to show her dismay. For a moment she was tempted to remind the dowager of who she was, but it would only upset her, and to what end? Lady Fia believed her son and Una should be together. If that gave her any fragment of peace, who was Orabel to shatter it?

She quashed her hurt feelings They were foolish when Lady Fia did not mean to wound her.

"That is kind of you to say," she said and any misgivings she had harbored about not correcting the dowager faded, when the older lady bestowed another beautiful smile upon her.

"It is strange to welcome a princess of Pictland to Dunmor, but I'm happy you're here. Dear Una always takes so much upon herself. But perhaps now she can once more look to her own happiness."

Goddess, the dowager recalled she was a princess. But not that she was wed to her son. And, it appeared, knew Una's marriage to Gordon hadn't been happy.

The flashes of lucidity were illuminating. Perhaps, after all, there was hope for Lady Fia to recover her lost memories, now she was free of that terrible tower.

"I'm certain she will." *So long as she harbors no designs upon Ross.* Hastily, she crushed the thought. Ross had told her the truth about Una, and she wasn't going to fret about a youthful infatuation that had no bearing on the present.

"Once they are wed, the children will have the father they deserve."

Orabel caught Saoirse's concerned glance and she shook her

head. Maybe it hadn't been such a good idea to indulge Lady Fia. But she couldn't bring herself to correct the older lady, not now, after she'd recklessly encouraged her delusions. And if Lady Fia's fantasy world didn't hinge on the matter of Ross marrying Una, would she really mind so much?

No. Therefore, it was merely her own wounded feelings and not Lady Fia's damaged mind that really bothered her.

"The children are delightful," she said. And she meant it. Fia and Dona were enchanting, and she looked forward to the brief moments during the day that Una allowed her daughters to see her.

"Aye." Lady Fia clutched the rosemary as another beautiful smile wreathed her face. "They are the light of my life, my lady. I could not bear it if they were taken from me too."

ROSS STRODE TOWARDS THE CHURCH, Angus by his side. He had returned to Dunmor eleven days ago, and instead of the prospect of being known as the master of the stronghold weighing him down with guilt, he'd discovered he enjoyed the challenge of tackling Gordon's neglect.

And there was no mystery as to why. It was because of Orabel. Simply by being here, she somehow made everything feel right. Although Dunmor rightfully belonged to Una and her daughters, he wasn't working solely for them anymore. This was Orabel's home too, and he would ensure she had everything she wanted that was within his power to provide.

He and Angus halted by her gardens. They were impressive, laid out with paths for easy access to all the areas, and the wall she had requested, to protect her poisonous plants from the unwary, was almost complete.

But admiring her medicinal gardens wasn't the reason he had

come this way. He turned his attention to the church. "How go the repairs to the roof?"

"All but completed," Angus said. "The damage wasn't as bad as it looked."

They circled the church and Angus opened the large timber door and followed him inside. Ross cast a glance around the interior. As a child, he recalled the elderly monk who had intoned services for the family. But when a winter's storm damaged the roof, killing the old man in his bed, Ross' father had allowed the place to fall into disrepair.

Before he'd left for the Kingdom of Fib, he'd ordered works to begin on the restoration. Although Una had never complained about making the journey to the local village church, her position was such that she ought to have a functioning place of worship close to the stronghold.

But when he'd brought Orabel home, he had changed his mind. Una, after all, enjoyed taking her daughters to the village church. How many times had she mentioned that fact over the years? His change of plans didn't adversely affect her, but he was still thankful for his foresight in having the restoration begun.

It could take months, if not far longer, to procure an elusive coconut. But at least he would be able to present his bride with a secondary wedding gift that much sooner.

He went to the nearest window, that looked out over Orabel's gardens. "Are the shutters close to being finished?"

"Aye. All being well, by the end of the week."

"Good. Angus, I want you to ensure all is ready for the princess upon our return from Fortriu. God knows, the coronation will be an ordeal for her."

The words were unwary, but he and Angus had known each other their entire lives. One of the better things Gordon had done during his tenure as master of Dunmor was to have Angus take over his father's position as steward, when the older man grew too frail to continue.

The truth was, after Rourke, Connor and Ewan, he counted Angus among his closest friends.

"There's not much left to do. The structure is sound. What needs to be brought here from the stronghold?"

He had no idea. "My vision only stretches so far. I can't imagine how the princess wishes to arrange things. But at least she'll have her sanctuary and whatever she needs, we shall somehow provide."

A shadow fell across the floor, and he swung about. God damn it. Neilan stood in the doorway, his usual scowl twisting his features. Since it was obvious the man had overheard him, there was nothing to be done but to appeal to the Pict's honor.

"Neilan." He strode across the nave. Neilan folded his arms. Ross halted and scanned beyond the door, searching for Orabel, but it appeared the Pict was alone. Not that it made any difference, as if he couldn't convince her loyal warrior to keep his counsel, Ross' surprise would be ruined regardless.

"MacIntosh."

That was an improvement. Generally, the Pict didn't deign to acknowledge his existence by uttering his name.

"I'd be obliged if you said nothing of this to the princess."

"I do not keep secrets from my princess."

Ross doubted that was strictly true, but he understood the sentiment. "I'm glad to hear it. Your loyalty to Lady Orabel is unquestioned and although you may not believe me, I'm thankful. But in this matter, I ask for your confidence. I want her sanctuary to be entirely habitable before I settle the property upon her."

Neilan cast his unflinching glare around the nave. "You wish to give the princess this heathen dwelling for her sanctuary?"

"Aye. I think she'll appreciate the irony."

Neilan's mouth twitched. Good God, was that a smile he had almost cracked?

After a long moment, the Pict spoke. "I'll keep your counsel, MacIntosh. Beware you don't abuse my faith in this matter."

With that, he turned and marched away. Ross glanced at Angus, who raised his eyebrows. "I believe you won a small victory there."

He wasn't so sure about that. "A truce will do for now."

CHAPTER TWENTY-TWO

In two days, they were due to leave Dunmor and travel to Forteviot for the upstart king's coronation. It irked Orabel greatly whenever she thought of it, but there was no way around it. She was to represent the Kingdom of Fib, in her sister and brother-through-marriage's stead, and she wouldn't let her people down.

But she wouldn't let the prospect of that unpleasant duty mar today and as she and her ladies made their way to her gardens she smiled at Lady Fia, who had unexpectedly linked arms with her.

"The children," Lady Fia said, and Orabel followed her gaze to the church, where Fia and Dona, having caught sight of their grandmother, were now running towards them. Behind them, Una turned from where she'd been speaking to Angus, and followed her daughters.

Lady Fia released her arm and hugged the girls, before they pulled her into a somewhat undignified crouch to admire the five puppies the children took everywhere with them. Orabel's young noblewomen, after a glance to obtain her permission, followed the dowager's lead and the puppies were clearly ecstatic to be on the receiving end of such lavish attention.

"My lady," Una said, dropping a curtsey and Orabel smiled in return. Una was always respectful but there was an undercurrent of reserve as though she hid something. Orabel longed to tell her that she knew of her and Ross' infatuation when they were young, but it was scarcely her place to bring up such a private subject.

But it was a source of quiet sadness that she and her husband's sister-through-marriage might never become close friends because of it.

"Good morn, Lady Una. I trust all is well?"

For an unaccountable reason, Una blushed. "Indeed, everything is well, my lady. Angus was merely passing the time of day with us, nothing more."

"Of course." Goddess, she hadn't been trying to discover what Una and the steward of Dunmor had been discussing, although the other woman's strange reaction had now piqued her curiosity. "I was not trying to pry, Lady Una."

"Forgive me. I'm not quite myself this day."

"If there's anything I can do to help, please let me know. I would be more than happy to show you my apothecary, should you wish."

So far, Una had resisted the invitation and Orabel couldn't understand why. To be sure, not everyone was as invested in the magical properties of herbs and plants as she was, but every woman learned their most basic uses. The kitchen gardens at Dunmor were more than adequate, and she'd had to reassess her opinion that Scots were entirely ignorant of certain remedies, but nevertheless, it did not compare to the wealth of medicinal insights she'd learned over the years, due to Bride's benevolence.

But perhaps that was the reason? Did Una believe Orabel's methods would offend the new god she worshipped?

"It's very kind of you," Una said. "But I shouldn't wish to impinge on the princess' good nature."

Orabel smothered a sigh. She could scarcely force the other woman into friendship if she didn't want it. "Alas, it's not my good nature, but rather the fact I'm unable to find a new plant without undertaking to learn all I can about it. Is that not so, Lady Saoirse?"

"Quite so," Saoirse agreed. "Even since we were small children."

"It's a wonderful talent," Una said, before she glanced at Lady Fia, who was now hugging one of the puppies. A strange expression passed over Una's face. "I cannot fathom the change in my mamma-through-marriage." Her voice was hushed. "The rosemary you brought with you has wrought something I never imagined possible."

"It is a remarkable herb. But I think also, allowing Lady Fia to speak of the world she sees, rather than the world as it is, has somehow helped ease her mind."

Una shook her head and twisted her fingers together. "She wasn't always like this." Her voice was low, and pain laced every word. "Although she always suffered from melancholic days, it was not until I wed Gordon that she retreated so fully from us all. Not long after, my father-through-marriage banished her to the tower and forbade any of us to indulge her whims. We didn't agree with the tower but truly, I believed we were right to correct her fantasies. And yet..." Her voice trailed away, and she bit her lip.

It was the first time Una had spoken more than a few words to her, yet as much as Orabel wanted to take her hand and offer what comfort she could she resisted, in case it made Una retreat once more.

"You did the best you could."

"It was not enough. You are here for scarcely two weeks and Lady Fia is happier than I've seen her in many years."

"Even my precious rosemary cannot take all the credit for that. I believe simply moving from the tower helped Lady Fia greatly."

"Aye. It is foolish, I know, but something about that tower has always… disturbed me."

"It's not foolish." She hesitated, uncertain whether to continue. But Una, who had no connection to her beloved goddess, and therefore was unlikely to believe Bride might communicate with her chosen ones in such an obscure manner, had mentioned it first, so surely her confidence wouldn't upset her. "I felt a sense of great terror the first time I entered that chamber."

Una shot her an uncertain glance. "I always thought it was merely my guilt, a punishment because I was to blame for Lady Fia's decline."

"Goddess, no." Unthinking, she took Una's hand, and the other woman didn't recoil. "Whatever lingers in that tower has nothing to do with you, Lady Una." And then, despite how distressed the other woman was, her curiosity got the better of her. "Why would you feel such guilt? I cannot believe you capable of anything that might warrant such a harsh condemnation."

"It's generous of you to say, my lady, but if you knew…" Una glanced at the dowager and swallowed, before turning back to her and pulling her hand free. "I fear I greatly disappointed Lady Fia. She… she dearly wished for me to wed Ross, you see, but please do not think there was anything between us, I should not wish—"

Relief speared through her. At last, it was out in the open and they could truly put the past behind them. "It's quite all right. Ross has explained everything to me. There's no need to keep this an unspoken gulf between us anymore."

"What?"

It wasn't quite the response she'd expected, but clearly Una was shocked by her revelation. Perhaps she shouldn't be surprised. How many newly wed men would admit to a youthful infatuation with a girl he had grown up with?

"Ross told me everything," she said.

"God in heaven," Una whispered, and pressed her hand against her heart.

It seemed a little dramatic but perhaps, in Dal Riada, such openness between a man and his wife was unheard of? It didn't quite ring true, but she pushed the notion aside. The important thing here was she and Una had reached a new understanding. One that could now open the path to a genuine friendship.

"It is not so very shocking," she said. "I'm not upset by the knowledge, Lady Una."

Una let out a ragged breath. "I'm so glad he told you, my lady. This has eaten away at him for years, I know, and it has always grieved me greatly."

Unease slithered through her. A primal warning of something just beyond her grasp.

"Indeed," she said, since she clearly needed to respond and anything more intelligent was currently beyond her.

"It's the reason, of course, why he is so adamant that I remain mistress of Dunmor. But it's wrong, my lady, and I have told him so. But your forbearance in this matter is truly astonishing. I know, in time, he will see he must relinquish the past. For your sake, if not for his own."

Orabel's heart echoed in her ears, a hollow sound that reverberated throughout her body. She was aware that Saoirse drew closer, and took her hand, but she couldn't move. Could scarcely breathe.

She hadn't imagined it. Ross considered Una the rightful mistress of Dunmor. And there could be only one reason for that.

He'd confided that once he and Una had planned to wed and assured her that was all in the past. But it wasn't. How could it be, when Ross wished his brother's widow to remain mistress of his stronghold, rather than his own wife?

Why would a man do that, unless he still yearned for his first love?

Fia and Dona ran up to their mother, their faces alight with glee and their eyes filled with laughter.

Their beautiful blue eyes, that she had admired from the moment she'd met them. Eyes they had doubtless inherited from their paternal grandmother.

From their father.

A remorseless whisper slithered through her mind, despite how she tried to crush it before it could gain substance.

From Ross?

Deniel squeezed her breast. No, she would not believe it. Yet she had never asked him why he didn't want children. She'd simply accepted it because it fell in with her own plans.

But what if the reason he didn't want children with her was because he already had two daughters with Una?

"Once they are wed, the children will have the father they deserve."

Lady Fia's words rang in her mind, as Una and her daughters joined the dowager. Had she retreated into her own world when she realized the wrong son had fathered her grandchildren?

Was that why Una suffered from such guilt about the dowager's condition? What else could she mean?

Saoirse tightened her grip on her fingers, and Orabel slowly turned to look at her dearest friend.

"Things are not always as they seem," Saoirse whispered.

Orabel drew in a shaky breath. She didn't want to believe her suspicions. But she couldn't fathom what else Una could mean. No wonder she'd been so shocked, when Orabel had confided that Ross had told her everything.

He hadn't told her anything at all.

But he would. Even if the truth ripped out her heart.

CHAPTER TWENTY-THREE

It was late afternoon before Ross returned to the stronghold. He and Angus had been in the village and his head was filled with the improvements he planned. He'd been away from Dunmor so frequently during the last ten years he hadn't realized just how far both Gordon's father, and then Gordon himself, had allowed things to deteriorate.

In the courtyard, he grasped Angus' arm. "If not for you, I'm aware the cottages would be in a far worse state. Even so, it will be a challenge to have the works completed before winter falls."

"I'll ensure it's done."

Ross turned to leave when Angus gripped his shoulder. "I have a personal request."

"Aye?" He couldn't recall Angus ever making a personal request before.

"I want to build an addition onto the steward's accommodation."

"An addition?" The steward's cottage, some way beyond the church, was a substantial stone dwelling, as befit the indispensable position Angus and his forefathers had held for generations.

Angus' widowed father still lived there, but Angus had not yet taken a wife.

Realization dawned and he grinned. "You've finally found a lass willing to take you on, is that it?"

Angus didn't laugh in response. "No. I wouldn't presume to ask unless I had more to offer."

"More to offer? Any woman would be fortunate to be mistress of your dwelling." Good God, who the hell did Angus have his eye on for him to imagine she'd expect more than an established steward could offer her?

"If my request is presumptions, I apologize." Angus' voice was stiff. He was not only serious but had taken offense at Ross' response.

"Christ, man, don't get on your high horse after everything we've been through together. If you need an addition to the cottage, then you have my permission. The estate can well afford it and by God, you've certainly earned it. Draw up the plans and we'll work out the logistics."

"I'll pay for the works myself."

Ross would see about that, but he wasn't about to fall out with Angus over it.

"I look forward to meeting this elusive woman who has stolen your good sense," he said instead, before hiding his grin and striding into the stronghold. As he passed through the great hall, Lady Saoirse, with the young noblewomen following in her wake, approached him.

His senses went on full alert. Where was Orabel?

"All is well," Lady Saoirse said before he had the chance to demand to know the princess' whereabouts. Saoirse didn't smile and there was a distinct chill in her voice, reminiscent of how she'd addressed him when they'd first met, neither of which helped to allay his concerns over Orabel's absence. "The princess wishes to speak with you in her medicinal gardens."

"Alone?" He could scarcely believe it. Orabel never went anywhere without her entourage.

Saoirse inclined her head. "Neilan accompanied her. But she wishes privacy to speak with you."

Neilan was with her? The spike of alarm receded. "I'll go there directly. Thank you for informing me, my lady."

He strode across the courtyard and past the stables. In the distance, he could see the church. What the hell could Orabel wish to say to him that she couldn't in the stronghold? Even though her ladies were present, they weren't always within hearing distance of whispered confidences.

Not that he was complaining. He was looking forward to being alone with her, outside of their bedchamber. Even Neilan didn't glower so much whenever they encountered each other, since they had spoken of his plans for Orabel's sanctuary. And true to his word, Neilan hadn't told Orabel of it.

As he approached her gardens, he nodded at Neilan in greeting. The Pict's surly expression remained intact. So much for him thinking they'd made progress.

Orabel was in the walled section of her gardens, and he strolled along the paths that subdivided the various areas, until he reached the restricted section, and folded his arms across the gate post. She wore a wide brimmed straw hat and thick gloves as she handled her poisonous plants, and anything less fitting for a princess to occupy her time he couldn't imagine. And yet even kneeling in the dirt, she emanated an air of regality that was unmistakable.

"You summoned me, my lady." He grinned as he watched her rise to her feet and turn to face him. But she didn't greet him with an answering smile. Instead, there was a remote expression on her face and unaccountably a chill slid along his arms.

"I did." Her voice was quiet, and she concentrated on removing her gloves as though such a simple thing required all her attention. But since the gloves had been in contact with an untold number of poisons, maybe it did.

She placed them on the wall, smoothed her hands over her gown, and then clasped her fingers together before finally meeting his gaze.

But she still didn't speak.

He unlatched the gate. "Orabel, what is it? Is something amiss?"

She took a deep breath. "Yes."

Certainly, he had asked her the question. But he'd not expected her to confirm there was a problem. He pulled open the gate but didn't step inside the garden. "What's happened?"

She licked her lips. It was a nervous gesture and not one he'd witnessed from her before. Concern coiled deep in his gut. What the fuck had upset her?

"I had an illuminating conversation with Lady Una this day."

He stared at her blankly. "Did you?"

"I found it most… distressing."

He wracked his brains, certain he had missed a vital element of their exchange, but couldn't grasp what. "Does something ail Lady Una?" he ventured.

For a fleeing moment Orabel's lips thinned as though he had just insulted her. "Please do not make this more difficult than it already is. You know of what I speak."

"No, I don't. You're speaking in riddles. How am I meant to understand unless you tell me plainly?"

Her violet eyes flashed with what appeared very much like anger. What the hell was he missing?

"Very well. If you demand that the words must be said aloud. Why would you insist that Lady Una remains as mistress of Dunmor, in my stead?"

He frowned. "But we spoke of this already, Orabel. You were most gracious about it."

She drew in a deep breath, and it was clear to see that this time he had mortally offended her. "I assure you, Ross MacIntosh, we most certainly did not discuss this. Do you think it something I would so easily forget?"

Shit. Heat crawled through him as he cast his mind back to before their betrothal. He'd intended to tell her of Una, but they had scarcely spent any time together before their wedding. Yet when he'd explained the situation, she hadn't been upset.

Why was she so distraught now?

"I explained how my brother was the rightful master of Dunmor. How the stronghold should pass through his bloodline. You assured me Fia and Dona's futures wouldn't be impacted by your arrival."

She took a step closer but there was no softness in her expression. For a mad instant, he imagined she wanted to claw out his tongue.

"You told me your brother's widow and daughters resided at Dunmor on the morning after our wedding. While we were in bed. You said nothing of how you did not wish me to be mistress of your stronghold."

Fuck. He raked his fingers through his hair as that morning flashed through his mind. Had he truly not made the situation plain to her? Now he thought about it, he had the sinking feeling she was right.

"You are mistress in all but name," he said, and as soon the words were out, he realized what a grave error he'd made.

"Well." She straightened her already rigid spine. "It is the name that matters, is it not?"

Inwardly, he flinched, even though he was aware she had no way of knowing how keenly her barbed words flayed him.

Aye. The name was everything.

"This changes nothing, Orabel. To the outside world, you are the mistress. The truth is only between the three of us."

"The truth." Derision dripped from each word. "That is

exactly what I want to hear from you. The truth of Lady Una's status."

"You know her status. She's Gordon's widow."

Orabel made a dismissive gesture with her hand, as though his response irked her greatly. "Not her official status. Tell me what she is to you."

"Christ, Orabel, what is this about? I told you we once thought to wed, but that was long ago. Why are you upset about this now?"

"I'm not upset." She all but spat the denial at him. "Not about the past. But Lady Una isn't your past, is she? Why else would you insist she outrank me in your own stronghold, if you did not still love her?"

Well, fuck. He hadn't seen this coming, but he should have.

Rourke certainly had.

Orabel wasn't merely a noblewoman who might have accepted the unusual arrangement. She was a royal princess. The least she could expect from their marriage was authority over her own stronghold.

"You're wrong. I don't love Una."

"Very well. Then what of the children? Are they yours?"

"What?" He stared at her, disbelief thudding through his chest. How the hell had she jumped to that conclusion? "That's an outrageous accusation."

"But you do not deny it?"

"Of course I deny it."

"Yet you don't want children with your own wife. What other conclusion should I draw?"

He clenched his fists, lest he was tempted to grasp her shoulders and shake some sense into her. "You told me before we were even betrothed that children were not something you wished for. What's changed?"

She glared at him as if he were being deliberately obtuse. "Don't attempt to deflect my questions. It is not normal for a man to agree with such a thing. But you didn't agree with me, it was you, yourself, who did not wish for children from this marriage. I can only conclude it's because you already have two daughters, and you do not wish to jeopardize their positions."

"God damn it, Orabel. They are Gordon's daughters, and I refuse to discuss this any further."

"Why? Because you cannot justify your reasons to me?"

"I don't need to justify anything to you. It's the truth, and you should believe me."

Her lip curled in clear disdain, and something akin to the blade of a dagger stabbed through his heart. "Perhaps a meek Scotswoman would abide by your word, Ross MacIntosh. But let me tell you, your assurances mean nothing when you will not even honor me enough to explain the truth behind your actions."

His chest tightened and heart thudded remorselessly against his ribs. He gripped the gatepost, the wood biting into his fingers, but it didn't stop his muscles tensing or the alarming sensation that he was standing on the deck of a boat in the midst of a raging storm.

Una had left him when he'd shared the truth with her. Orabel was his wife. She could not leave. And if she did, he'd bring her back. But every time she looked at him, he'd see the disgust in her eyes. Feel the contempt in her glance. And he'd have to live with the knowledge that his bride, his princess, could not bear the very sight of him.

Orabel's gaze burned with scorn, and she didn't even know the truth. Would she ever look at him again the way she had before today?

"It has nothing," he forced out the words, despite how each erratic breath suffocated him from the inside out, "to do with your honor. We will speak no more of this, do you hear?"

Strangely, she didn't cast venom his way. Instead, concern flickered over her face, and she took another step closer.

"Ross." She didn't sound angry anymore. She sounded... uncertain. "What is it? Please tell me."

He shoved himself back from the gatepost, but with nothing to brace his weight upon, he swayed, as though he'd consumed a skinful of the strongest ale. Why did she look at him with such compassion glowing in her incomparable violet eyes? He could take her scorn, even if it lacerated the essence of his being.

But this gentle distress, on his behalf, he could not withstand.

"There's nothing to tell." God help him, he needed to get away before he spilled his guts. But before he could will his feet to move, she grasped his wrists, and he could no sooner pull free from her touch as he could erase his sordid past.

"I need to understand," she whispered. "I cannot live with this uncertainty, Ross."

A mirthless laugh tore from his throat. "If I tell you the truth, you couldn't live with me anyway."

"I believe you're wrong."

Every sane particle he possessed urged him to remain silent. But Orabel gazed at him with such understanding, he was powerless to resist.

No. That wasn't true. He could walk away, refuse to tell her, and maybe she'd accept it. But something he couldn't name would be lost, and nothing would be the same again.

Did he really have so much more to lose by telling her what she wanted to know?

You could lose everything.

Aye. But he risked losing it, anyway.

He pulled free of her touch and grasped her hands, so she couldn't retreat. For all the difference it made. If she didn't stay because she wanted to, what the hell was the point?

"Dunmor has belonged to Gordon's bloodline for generations. Should Fia or Dona have a son, the stronghold will pass to him."

"I understand." Her voice was still soft. So soothing. Because she had not yet grasped the truth. "It is admirable indeed of you to sacrifice having a child of your own for the sake of your nieces' future. And yet…" she hesitated, and a frown marred her brow. "There's something more, isn't there?"

Instinctively, his grip tightened on her hands, and his gaze roved over her face, drinking in every delicate feature, and committing it to memory. It might be the last time she'd look at him with any degree of favor.

He sucked in a tortured breath. "I have no claim to the name MacIntosh. My beloved lady mother—" The loathsome words choked him, but he forced them out, regardless. "Was brutally attacked, and I am the result."

A thick silence descended, filling his head, and blocking out the distant lowing of cattle. Orabel didn't recoil in horror, and revulsion didn't fill her eyes, but regardless, he braced himself for the inevitable.

"Merciful goddess." Her whisper was like an ethereal caress in the wind, and he let out a jagged breath. Waiting for her to fully comprehend the meaning of his words. "Ross, I'm so sorry. I did not mean to cause you such pain with my questions. I didn't realize… it did not occur to me this is the reason you're so protective of your nieces' future."

"Aye." There was little else he could say, after all.

"Please forgive me." She raised their joined hands and pressed a kiss against his knuckles.

"Forgive you?" Had he misheard? "For what? You've done nothing wrong."

"Perhaps," she said. "But you certainly have not. I'm grieved you feel that you have."

An odd compression gripped his chest, and he bowed his head, resting his forehead against hers. And before he could stop himself, his deepest, most despicable, guilt spilled from the depths of his soul. "I'm responsible for my lady mother's condition, don't you see? If not for me, her husband wouldn't have scorned her, and Gordon would not have followed his lead and treated her so badly. If not for me, her life would have been so much easier."

"You cannot know that." There was a catch in her voice that pierced him so deeply, he wondered how he could not bleed from it. "You're not to blame for what happened. None of it is your fault."

Slowly he straightened and their gazes meshed. There was no condemnation in her eyes. No glint of abhorrence. She wasn't pulling from his grasp and turning her back.

He released a jagged breath and the knot in his chest eased by the smallest degree. "It's why I vowed never to wed." His voice was hollow. "I knew one day my king might order it, and that was beyond my power. But I vowed I wouldn't allow my tarnished bloodline to take what was not rightfully mine."

"I understand." Her voice was soft, and once again she pressed her lips against his knuckles. Such a tender touch, he feared he might break from it. "You're an honorable man, Ross. Perhaps the most honorable man I've ever encountered." Then she gave him a small smile. "For all that you are a Scot."

Incredulous, he stared at her. Was she flirting? As though they were back in Fib, when her candid remarks had so intrigued him. Before she'd discovered his despicable past.

"Orabel." The word was tortured, but before he could say anything more, although God only knew what he could possibly say, she pressed a finger against his lips.

"There's no need to speak any more of this. I shall talk to Lady Una myself in the morning, and explain she has nothing to fear for her daughters' heritage from my presence. All will be well. You have my word."

CHAPTER TWENTY-FOUR

The following morning, Orabel managed to convince Lady Una to spare a few moments in her private chamber, while Saoirse occupied the young noblewomen and Una's daughters in the great hall. Unfortunately, the conversation with Lady Una wasn't progressing quite as Orabel had imagined.

After Ross' confession yesterday, so many things had fallen into place. Not just the way he treated his sister-through-marriage or his nieces.

But also with Lady Fia.

She'd rip out her tongue before admitting such to Ross, but deep in a hidden part of her soul, she had understood his heartrending conviction that he was to blame for his mother's condition. Except it wasn't Ross she blamed, not even a shred.

It was the act itself. And how Lady Fia had been treated so despicably afterwards by her husband.

And not only that. For surely the atrocity had been committed in that tower? The very same tower in which her husband had later imprisoned her, when her mind had splintered under the pressure.

What a cruel man Lady Fia's husband had been. And his son had been no better, to continue in his father's footsteps. It was as well they had both continued their journeys before she'd had the misfortune to meet either of them, and she hoped they were reaping what they unquestionably deserved.

It was wrong and she tried not to let the thoughts manifest, but they slithered in the back of her mind, regardless.

How hard it would have been, if she'd been forced to share this new life with them, not to wish the wrath of her goddess upon their worthless heads.

Stop…

She crushed the images, even though her errant thoughts could do no harm against those who had already passed through the veil. Yet her ire against the men had scarcely diminished overnight, and it seemed she hadn't managed to hide it from Lady Una as well as she'd hoped. Clearly the other woman was under the impression that Orabel was aggrieved with her. It was the only explanation for why Lady Una was obviously so uncomfortable.

"My lady, I cannot express my dismay in how I distressed you yesterday." Una twisted her fingers together and shot a desperate glance at the shut door, as though she longed to escape. "If I realized Ross hadn't explained about his past, I never would have breathed a word about it."

Orabel managed to keep a serene smile on her face, but it was an effort. "But you didn't breathe a word about it, Lady Una. You disclosed no confidences. Indeed, I had no idea of the truth until Ross explained it to me."

Certainly, she wasn't going to upset Una any more by confessing she'd suspected Fia and Dona had been fathered by Ross. But she was determined to clear the air between them so there were no more misunderstandings.

Una gave a ragged sigh. "Aye, well, my words still stand, my lady. I'm glad he told you. And I'm glad you are able to stand by him."

Stand by him? Of course she would stand by him. What a thing for Una to suggest. And yet...

If Ross' status had been known before they wed, would Dugald have considered the alliance worthwhile? Would he have ignored the outcome of the challenge, and instead ordered her to marry the Prince of Strathclyde?

She had the feeling her brother-through-marriage may very well have ordered such a thing.

An uncanny shiver inched along her spine as she gazed at Una's averted face. Why had Ross and Una not wed? It may have been a youthful infatuation, but that didn't necessarily preclude marriage. Especially since it was clear Lady Fia hadn't been against the match.

Was that the reason? Because Lady Fia had wanted it, and so her brute of a husband had forbidden it?

Torn, she wrestled with her conscience. This was not something she should ask Una. It was none of her concern. If she wanted to know, she should ask Ross. Except she wouldn't, because the last time she'd confronted him about his past, she had inadvertently opened a terrible wound.

Yet something gnawed at her, something she couldn't name yet inexplicably knew was intertwined with Ross as surely as his mistaken belief he was to blame for his lady mother's malady.

"Forgive me," she said, and with clear reluctance, Una once again looked her way. "Might you share what you mean?"

"It is nothing." Una glanced at the door before her shoulders suddenly drooped and she cast a despairing look her way. "Truly, it is nothing, my lady. I did once love Ross and wish to wed him more than anything. But I was a young girl then. I love him only as a brother now."

"I believe you." And she did. But Una hadn't answered her question. "Why didn't you marry him, Lady Una?"

The other woman shuddered and briefly closed her eyes before fixing Orabel with a piercing gaze. "You must swear never to tell him." There was an unexpectedly fierce note in Una's voice. Startled, Orabel inclined her head in agreement. "For all that Gordon possessed, he was jealous of Ross, of how he was their mother's favorite. When he discovered our unofficial betrothal, and that I knew of the terrible secret that clouds Dunmor, he threatened to spread the truth of Ross' origins unless I married him."

"Goddess." Orabel pressed her fingers against her lips as the horror of Una's words reverberated around her mind. "You married one brother to save the other."

"Ross would have survived. He is strong. But Lady Fia—how could I allow Gordon to blacken her name and ruin her reputation? She was always so kind to me. I couldn't tell Ross the truth. I feared he would challenge Gordon and what good would that do? So you see, my lady, why I'm so thankful that you can remain by his side."

Finally, realization struck. Ross believed Una had turned her back on him because he was the product of rape. That was why he had reacted so violently yesterday. Because he thought she would turn her back on him, too.

But Una never had.

And Ross had no idea.

She had grown up believing Scotswomen were weak-willed, at the mercy of their menfolk. Yet weren't even princesses of Pictland at the mercy of their kings' command?

And Lady Una, who seemed so meek, possessed the strength of character that Orabel had scarcely encountered before. Wordlessly, she held out her hand and after a moment, Una took it and Orabel embraced her, their foreheads touching, and implacable dread rolled through her soul.

She would keep Una's counsel, even though, deep in her heart, she knew Ross should be told. But if he knew the truth, that Una hadn't rejected him because of his past, would he want her back?

Could I let him go?

Her heartbeat echoed in her ears. What a foolish thought. They were husband and wife. She could not let him go, even if she wanted to. They were bound by the laws of her land, by the will of the old gods.

Yet this is not Bride's will...

There was a sharp rap on the door before it swung open, and Ross entered the chamber. He stopped dead and stared at them, as though he could not believe his eyes, and guilt spiked through her even though she had done nothing wrong.

Except it was wrong to keep this truth from him. Yet she would. And not only because Una had asked her to.

"Is something amiss?" His glance traveled to Una before returning to her. She and Una straightened, severing their embrace, but that was a superficial thing when during the last few moments an unbreakable bond had been forged between them.

"Everything is well," she said, going to him and taking his outstretched hand. *I will not let you go.* "Lady Una and I have come to a new understanding. You don't need to concern yourself, Ross."

"Aye." Una came to their side and without meaning to, Orabel tightened her grip on Ross' hand. "The princess was gracious to allow me to relinquish my position as mistress of Dunmor. All is as it should be."

To be sure, her intention had been to discuss that prickly matter with Una, but the subject had not arisen, and they certainly hadn't come to any such agreement. Not that she was going to dispute Una's word. After all, it wasn't as if anything fundamental was going to change.

Ross gave her a searching look. "I should have told you before we wed. I know that now."

"Think no more of it. I do not blame you for keeping your counsel, Ross."

From the corner of her eye, she saw Una leave the chamber and quietly close the door behind her. Ross heaved a sigh before brushing a kiss across her knuckles.

"I thought I was doing the right thing by Una."

"You were. You did." Goddess, this was hard. All she could think of was the sacrifice Una had made, to ensure Lady Fia's reputation remained intact, and so Ross wouldn't issue a challenge to his half-brother. "Nothing has changed save for the fact I now understand Lady Una's wishes. It is not as though you and I ever wanted children that might displace her daughters, after all."

A small pain twisted deep inside, and it wasn't easy to brush aside or ignore. She had never dreamed of having a babe or raising a family of her own. That was not her path. And yet here, with Ross, the prospect of never having his child caused a grief she had never imagined.

How foolish. She had already strayed from the path Bride had set before her at the moment of her birth. She couldn't afford to test the great goddess' benevolence any further by even thinking of such a thing.

And yet it lingered, all the same.

Ross was silent for so long, a whisper of unease fluttered through her mind. Had he somehow guessed her errant thoughts? But then he gave a crooked grin that for an unnamed reason caused her heart to squeeze in her breast.

"That's true enough." He cupped her face, the callused pad of his thumb caressing her cheek in a tender gesture. "God, Orabel. What would I do without you?"

LATER THAT DAY, Orabel left a thrilled Coira in charge of the other four young girls in her antechamber, with the task of packing the trunks for their journey to Fortriu, and she and Saoirse made their way to the tower. She hadn't been there since Lady Fia had relocated but, now she knew the truth of what had happened, she was compelled to return.

She wasn't even certain why. What else was there to learn?

Without the tapestries on the walls or rugs on the floor, the chamber was cold and stark, and she shivered, pulling her shawl more securely about her shoulders. Saoirse went to the far side, the oil lamp she held casting ominous shadows, and trailed her fingers along the stone wall before turning to face her.

How she longed to confide in her friend. But the secrets were not hers to share, and Saoirse was too canny to ask what had transpired.

"Even I can feel the evil that lingers in this chamber." Saoirse's voice was hushed, and another shudder assailed her as she crossed the floor to her friend.

"Something terrible happened here." And she was sure she knew what that terrible thing was, so why had she returned? What good could it do? She took the lamp from Saoirse and slowly circled the chamber, searching for... something.

Anything.

A dark shadow on the floor caught her eye and she crouched to get a better look. It was a large, dull stain, and had been covered by a rug the last time she'd been in the chamber. Wordlessly, she glanced at Saoirse, and the concerned look on her face confirmed her own suspicions.

Blood.

She handed the lamp back to Saoirse. Bride had brought her here for a reason and she wouldn't let her reluctance stop her. Her hand hovered over the stain before she braced herself, took a deep breath, and pressed her fingers on the floor.

Nothing.

No flash of insight or glimpse of the echoes that haunted this place. Even though she hadn't wanted to see the distressing truth of the bloodstain, disappointment slid through her, nevertheless. And so did something else.

Uncertainty.

Had she been wrong, believing Bride had led her here? Did the great goddess have no interest in this tower, and it was all merely her own need to understand the truth?

Hastily, she rose to her feet and rubbed her fingers against her gown. She had settled so easily into this new life she often forgot this was not the path her goddess wished for her. Why would Bride want her to discover, or even care, what had happened here so long ago?

Her goddess had made it very plain, in her last frightening vision, that Orabel needed to heal the rift between them. Yet the truth was, she had done nothing to do so. Instead, she'd focused on learning all she could of Ross during their intimate conversations, on the delights of the marital bed, and the intrigues of his family.

Trepidation slithered through her. She did care about his family. But it didn't affect the promise she'd made Bride, to use her healing skills on those in need. The villagers didn't trust her, not yet, but they would, in time, when they saw the results of her goddess' benevolence. And Bride would see that Orabel was following her path as best she could.

"Come." She took Saoirse's hand. "We should not be here."

Saoirse gave her a troubled look but said nothing before they left the tower and returned to her chambers.

THAT NIGHT, her vision returned.

The yew tree loomed before her, magnificent in its antiquity, a miniature forest in its own right. Heart pounding, Orabel glanced around, willing for there to be another way forward, but mountains crowded all around, and the grassy path she stood upon led directly into the tangled yew.

The gatekeeper between this world and the next.

Bride's command could not be clearer.

There was no impending sense of dread in this vision, as there had been in the last, but unease still swirled through her as she drew closer to the impenetrable yew. As she pushed her way through the thick branches, that had long ago embedded deep into the earth, the light faded, and a thick silence descended.

Great goddess, I am here.

But it seemed she was alone.

She reached out and pressed her fingertips against the furrowed bark. Instantly, the tree enveloped her, and she sucked in a panicked breath, but she wasn't crushed, or suffocated, even as the outside world, as it existed in this immortal realm, vanished.

Tiny pin pricks of blue-green lights danced in the darkness, revealing a small cave. It was oddly calming, and her panic faded as a warm glow bathed her soul. Bride might not deign to speak with her but there was no doubt in Orabel's heart.

This sacred place was Bride's domain, and her goddess had brought her here for a reason.

In the distance, the hypnotic splash of water—a waterfall, perhaps—was the only sound that disturbed the tranquility yet, if anything, it enhanced the bone deep sense of rightness.

Of peace.

A low rumble shook the ground beneath her feet, and she stumbled as rocks cascaded from the walls and cracks appeared in the earth. Two mighty serpents erupted from the crevices, their fangs dripping blood as they glared at her with dead, malevolent eyes.

Terror gripped her. *But I stayed on the path.*

Flames burst from the ground, licking along the walls of the cave, and engulfing the tiny blue-green lights with malicious intent. Once again, the serpents twined around each other, their thick bodies melding, a terrifying, two-headed monster intent on devouring everything it encountered.

The fire crackled. The serpents hissed. And the implacable voice of the great goddess echoed through every frenzied beat of Orabel's heart.

You must heal the rift that threatens our land.

CHAPTER TWENTY-FIVE

Ross drew his horse alongside Orabel, and her ladies, who had surrounded her after he'd galloped ahead to speak to his men, drew back to allow them privacy. She smiled at him, and he grinned back, for how could he not, when she looked at him so sweetly? But it didn't disguise the air of disquiet that had emanated from her for the last few days, since just before they'd left Dunmor.

It was because they traveled through Fortriu. The High Kingdom of Pictland, that had belonged to her blood kin for a thousand years or more, but which MacAlpin now possessed. How she must loathe this duty, but she hadn't uttered a word of censure throughout the journey.

Yet a stubborn shard buried deep within his soul couldn't dislodge the fear her hint of reticence was because she now knew the truth about him.

"We'll arrive at Forteviot shortly." He sighed. "If I could have spared you this farce, I would have."

She reached across the small space between them and grasped his wrist. "I know." Her voice was gentle and once again he lost himself in the magic of her eyes. Would he ever grow accustomed to their haunting beauty? Somehow, he thought not. "I'm here at the command of my queen. I shall suffer through this ordeal for the sake of my beloved Fib."

"Aye." He acknowledged the truth of her words, but it didn't change the way he saw things. "Yet I would still have saved you from it, if I could."

"Doubtless, I shall survive three days in the enemy's lair."

She had always been candid with him. It was just one of the many reasons why he treasured her.

Treasured her. The words echoed in his mind. It was the truth yet was it the whole story? A deeper truth stirred, fragile, unnamable, and brutally he pulled back before it could drag him under and shatter everything he had right now with Orabel.

Don't tempt fate.

"Not all Scots are your enemy." How hollow the words sounded. How he wished she could believe it.

"I know *you* are not." Briefly, she tightened her grip on his wrist and a corresponding pressure gripped his chest. He didn't even question it. Everything Orabel did affected him in the strangest manner. "You are the most honorable of men and I include the bravest Picts of my acquaintance in this number."

"It's good of you to say so." His voice was gruff, and he squinted ahead so she wouldn't see how much her words meant to him. "Considering what you know of my past."

"But it isn't your past, Ross. If you are speaking of the manner of your conception, that truly has nothing to do with you at all. You may be the consequence, but you are not the perpetrator."

He grunted. God damn it, the sudden ground mist was clouding his vision. "I thought, after you had time to consider the matter, your opinion had changed."

"Why would you think that?"

He risked glancing at her. Although for the journey she'd braided her hair, a few glorious strands of raven silk had escaped its bindings and caressed her flushed cheek. He had the wild impulse to snatch her from her mare, hold her close, and ride deep into the mountains. Just the two of them. To some place where no one would ever find them and the outside world, and all its politics, could go to hell.

He dragged in a ragged breath. Maybe, thank God, his suspicions had been wrong, but something troubled her. "Sometimes I catch you looking at me, as though there's something you wish to say. But then you look away and it's as if a gulf opens between us." He managed to offer her a sardonic grin, to lighten his words, even though he was more serious than she could ever imagine. "You cannot blame me for thinking the worst."

Inexplicably, guilt flashed across her face. No, he was mistaken. Orabel had nothing to be guilty about. It was the sun playing tricks.

"No." Her voice was hushed. "I'm grieved I caused you to think that. Nothing could be further from my mind. You must know, this isn't something that would cause anyone to look less favorably upon you."

"Sometimes they do." It had mattered to Una. But there was no heartache when he thought of that time. Hell, if anything, relief knotted his chest. If Una had married him ten years ago, he would not now be wed to Orabel. "You've been reserved since our talk in your gardens."

"It's true I've had much to think about." For a few moments she didn't speak and then she drew her mare closer as her hand once more tightened around his wrist. "I was going to say I'm sad for your lady mother. But it's more than that. I'm enraged by what she suffered. What women suffer for the fragile pride of men. And I feel this so deeply, but I cannot speak of it. And I do not mean to cast any shade on you, Ross, and I hope you don't believe I am."

"I don't." He gazed at her, secretly shaken by her impassioned speech. He'd asked her what had been on her mind and by God, she had told him. And now he wasn't certain how to respond. "I'm also enraged by what my gentle mother suffered."

"Ah." She shook her head. "Indeed. But you misunderstand me. I speak of how she was mistreated by her husband and eldest son for so many years."

Not for the first time when speaking with Orabel, his world slipped sideways. She'd never met his half-brother nor Gordon's father and yet she had the measure of them. And it seemed she hadn't finished.

"You must forgive me my forthright words, for I shall not apologize for them. It's as well I never met them, Ross. Diplomacy has never been my strongest suit."

"If they were still alive, I would never have taken you back to Dunmor." God knew, he'd amassed a sizable fortune during the last ten years. Not enough to acquire a prestigious stronghold like Dunmor, but certainly a substantial hillfort.

A princess cannot live in a hillfort.

"Sometimes," she hesitated before taking a deep breath. "Sometimes the strength of my contempt can be…" again, she hesitated, and he took her hand that had clasped his wrist and brushed his lips over her glove-clad fingers.

"Your contempt would be well-earned, I'm sure." And well deserved when it came to Gordon and his father. Even though remnants of his childhood hero-worship of Gordon lingered in the back of his mind, since bringing Orabel to Dunmor, and seeing how well his lady mother had improved in just a few short weeks, he'd been forced to face the ugly truth.

Gordon had treated their lady mother with the same cruel disregard as his father.

"That may be so," she said. "I won't pretend to deny it. And yet…" Her voice trailed away, and she stared into the distance, where, high on its magnificent hill, Forteviot had come into view.

"And yet?" he prompted, intrigued.

"Alas, I fear I'm too proud to risk seeing the kindness on your face turn to abhorrence."

He laughed at that. "I assure you, there's nothing you can tell me that would cause me to look at you with anything less than wonder."

"You mock me."

"I don't. Whatever your great secret is, it cannot possibly be as terrible as you assume."

"It's not a laughing matter." Her voice dropped to a whisper. "I do not jest when I say I'm relieved I didn't meet Lady Fia's husband or your half-brother. I fear what my contempt for them might have… unleashed."

Unleashed? His amusement died, although not his regard for her. "You speak of your powerful plants. Of poison?"

"Goddess, no." She appeared shocked by his remark. "I would never so misuse the goddess' benevolence."

"Then you need have no fear of sharing this terrible secret with me. When I thought you might poison those who displeased you, my esteem for you did not waver." He tried not to smile, since Orabel was clearly distressed, but for the life of him he couldn't imagine why. She was incapable of unkindness, and he'd challenge anyone who disputed it.

"That is," she hesitated, "alarming that you might imagine I would poison those who displeased me. But I fear the truth is far worse."

"I fail to see how anything could be worse."

She glanced over her shoulder, as though she wanted to ensure no one could overhear. He leaned closer, furrowing his brow so he wouldn't inadvertently smile.

"My first marriage was not happy." Her whisper was so low his frown became genuine as he strained to hear her words. "But this, I think, you already know. I endured it for the sake of Fib but towards the end…" Her voice trailed away, and she swallowed, and once again he pressed his lips against her fingers. The desire to smile had long since vanished, replaced by a cold anger.

"Did he mistreat you?" Even asking the question sickened him.

"He didn't dare to beat me, if that's what you mean. My status was too high. I didn't care that he bedded every woman who caught his eye, even though his behavior degraded me. But when he would come to me, so drunk he could scarcely stand, and spew obscenities he swore, when sober, he could never remember uttering… my contempt for him became a terrible thing."

"And as I've already said, your contempt was well-earned." He didn't want to think about the things she hadn't said, but his mind went there, anyway. A wife could not refuse her husband, no matter the provocation.

"During the final year of our marriage, whenever he filled me with a burning rage, I called upon Bride and allowed my disdain to consume me." She shuddered. It was clear she still suffered, and while he hated what she'd gone through with the Northumbrian, he didn't understand why she was so distraught that she'd shared her feelings with her goddess.

"Orabel," he said, but she flung him a despairing glance and shook her head.

"You do not understand, Ross. The great goddess allowed my contempt to become a malevolent entity, that cursed Edwin and led to his death."

"I'm certain that isn't what happened." His voice was firm. For a start, there was only one God and to Ross' knowledge, He rarely answered prayers and certainly not to such a personal degree. But then, Orabel didn't believe in his God. Who was he to suggest her faith was foundless?

Yet in the end, none of that mattered. Because Orabel believed she was responsible for the bastard's death.

"How did he die?"

"It was quite horrible. He had been particularly obnoxious and stormed from my chamber and I—I confess I silently raged about—about everything. Late that night, I was hastily summoned to the great hall. Edwin had been drinking with several of his warriors and choked on his own vomit before stumbling into the fire. I can smell the putrid stench that filled the hall to this day."

Christ. Not that he spared any false sympathy towards the other man, but what an ignoble way to go.

"I regret you witnessed such a thing. But Orabel, you must see, it had nothing to do with you. By your own admission the man was a drunkard and if anyone besides himself is to blame, it's the warriors he was with that night."

"Edwin was used to drinking. He had never choked on his vomit before. Or fallen into the fire and… and burned."

Inspiration struck. "Was that night the first time you'd shared your contempt with your goddess?" He knew it wasn't. She'd told him as much. But could she see that?

She shot him an uncertain glance. "No. But—"

"It could have happened at any time. You're not to blame, Orabel. It's not as if you were in the great hall, forcing him to drink, was it?" And even if she had, she would still be blameless in his eyes.

"If he had drunk the wine I offered him—but he threw the goblet against the wall. He was not impaired by anything but his ale, and why would merely doing something he had done for thirty years affect him so that night?"

He wasn't sure what she meant about the wine. She'd already told him she would never use poison to harm someone, and he believed her. But surely she could see the error in her thinking?

"You're a healer. You must have seen similar accidents, when something irregular occurs in the normal course of events." He recalled the time he'd watched her heal the eye of the blacksmith's apprentice. "What of the lad, Jed? How many times had he performed his tasks without injury? Do you think someone wished him ill, and that's why he was nearly blinded?"

"Of course I don't. That is quite different, Ross. I have a sacred connection to the great goddess and I… I fear…"

"I know what you fear. And I don't pretend to understand this connection you have but I do know this. Your late husband died in the manner he did because of his own actions. Not because you prayed to your goddess."

She was silent for a few moments. Up ahead, a party of warriors approached to escort them into Forteviot, and he needed to greet them, but he couldn't leave Orabel until he was certain she was at least considering his words.

Finally, she sighed. "I was so desperate to escape that marriage. And bereft without Bride's sacred presence. Edwin's death granted me the freedom I craved, the freedom to return to the path my goddess set before me. I cannot help but think I had some hand in it."

"You didn't plunge a dagger through his heart. And if your goddess decreed it was his time, that has nothing to do with you. Even though you are her faithful servant."

It was blasphemy to say such things. But if it helped Orabel, he would say a great deal more. God surely had more important matters to attend to than cause lightning to strike his head.

MacAlpin's coronation for one thing.

"You could be right." She sounded reluctant, but the very fact she'd conceded at all was a victory.

He smiled and briefly squeezed her hand. "I know I am. I will return to you shortly."

With that, he rode off.

CHAPTER TWENTY-SIX

Orabel had been a child on the one occasion she'd previously visited Forteviot, but the imposing palace was as grand as she recalled with its expansive forecourt and unparalleled views over the surrounding land.

But it wasn't just its prestigious position that had made it the jewel of Pictland. The finest craftsmen had always gravitated to the Supreme Kingdom, enriching its prosperity with their skilled jewelry work, pottery, and leathers.

Had they stayed, after the Scots upstart claimed the kingdom for his own?

Ross helped her dismount and remained by her side as Neilan approached. She had the strangest feeling that something fundamental had shifted between the two men before they'd left Dunmor. Neilan no longer glowered at Ross every time their paths crossed, and although she'd yet to hear the Pict utter a civil word to her husband, she was certainly grateful her faithful warrior appeared to have accepted the situation with reasonable grace.

"I've assigned four men to escort you at all times, my lady," he said. "As soon as I've ensured our warriors are accommodated nearby, I shall return to you."

"Very well." She glanced at the contingent of Picts who'd accompanied them from Dunmor. Every man looked ready to murder any Scot who looked sideways at them. Did MacAlpin have any idea just how hated he was? If not for the fact he kept hostage so many Pict nobles, this cursed coronation would end in a bloodbath.

But that, of course, was the weapon he wielded over all of Pictland. Their grudging acceptance, in return for the lives of their nobles.

Ross offered her his arm, and together they followed MacAllister into the great hall. MacAlpin, it seemed, was too busy to greet the royal representative from Fib. She pressed her lips together at the slight. But then, why should he care about propriety when he had already grasped his prize? The invitations to the seven kingdoms to attend this farce were for show only.

MacAllister hailed a servant to take them to their chamber and as they reached the stairs, Ross leaned in close and whispered in her ear.

"I greatly admire your restraint."

"You wouldn't say that if you could hear my thoughts."

"Your thoughts are written upon your face."

She shook her head. It felt wrong to be amused within the walls of Forteviot, now it had fallen to the enemy. "Then I need to learn to hide my true feelings while in the serpent's nest."

Ross smiled and squeezed her fingers, before she lifted her skirts and went up the stairs. But her mind gnawed on her last, unwary words.

Serpent.

Her last vision haunted her, and not only in the dark of night when she couldn't sleep. It clung in the back of her mind during the day, a malevolent shadow that would not fade.

She'd been so certain the serpents Bride had shown her in Fib were the manifestation of the challenge between Ross and Raedwulf. Even though Ross was not a serpent and never could be, in her goddess' eyes he likely was.

But if that was so, why had Bride once again led her to the twin serpents? What was Bride trying to tell her? That she needed to beware of MacAlpin?

She already knew that.

The servant opened a door and bowed as she entered. Although the chamber was small, a fire burned in the grate, tapestries hung upon the walls and a large, faded rug covered the floor.

She had expected worse.

Ross gave a disagreeable grunt. "This is scarcely adequate for your own use, never mind having to share with all your ladies. My apologies once again, my lady."

His use of the honorific was a clear sign of his irritation, and she took his hand and gave it a little shake.

"I do not care about the size of the chamber. We shall be here for only three nights, in any case."

Ross didn't appear mollified. "You're a royal princess."

How charming he was so insulted on her behalf. "You forget Lady Mairi, the true Princess of Fortriu, is also here and I hope she's been given the best chamber in the palace. I believe Lady Briana of Fotla was also persuaded to attend and let us not forget the Scots' princesses of Dunadd."

"You're being very reasonable."

"Indeed. I have my moments."

He laughed, as she had hoped. It was trial enough being in occupied Forteviot, without Ross being irked about things that scarcely mattered.

"Then I shall leave you with your ladies and your guards while I see to our men." He grinned, and she understood. Neilan would ensure the wellbeing of the Pict warriors, but it was highly doubtful he'd extend the same consideration to the Scots warriors who had also accompanied them from Dunmor.

After he left, and she and her ladies had washed away the dust from the journey and changed their gowns, there was a knock on the door and an elderly serving woman, along with two Pict noblewomen she recognized from when she'd visited Mairi earlier this year, entered the chamber.

"My lady," Lady Struana said, dipping a curtsey. "The Princess of Fortriu would be delighted if you and your ladies would join us for refreshments."

"We should be honored. Thank you, Lady Struana." As she and her ladies followed the other women, satisfaction glowed through her at how Struana had referred to Mairi. It had been deliberate, to show the Scots serving woman that no matter what her despicable master did, he would never be the true king of Forteviot.

The corridor was filled with Pict warriors, who had obviously accompanied Mairi and Briana into Fortriu. The palace was nothing less than a tinderbox, and if an errant spark ignited, everything would burn.

She suppressed a shiver and pushed the worrisome notion to the back of her mind.

The serving woman opened a door, and they entered a grand antechamber, filled with ladies. Mairi and Briana greeted her warmly, before Mairi held her hands.

"Orabel, there is a lady you must meet. Come." She led her to an older woman who sat beside the fire on a chair, a serene smile on her face, and unaccountably, an eerie shimmer of recognition danced on the edges of her consciousness. *Who is she?*

"Lady Catriona, may I present my dear cousin, Orabel, Princess Annag of Fib. Lady Orabel, I'm honored to present Lady Catriona of Duntorr, the Dowager Princess of Fortriu and grandmother-through-marriage of Briana, Princess Euphemia of Fotla."

Orabel's polite smile of greeting froze. Dowager Princess of Fortriu? She had never heard of such a title, far less of a princess who held it. She smothered her confusion and made the correct responses and only when that was all done did Lady Catriona rise to her feet.

"It's a pleasure to meet you at last, Lady Orabel," Lady Catriona said. "Lady Mairi is too generous. I have never been a Princess of Fortriu."

"You should have been acknowledged," Briana said. "Your blood is as royal as ours, after all."

Silence danced in the air between the four of them, of words unspoken, and realization struck.

Lady Catriona was also a chosen one of their goddess.

"Perhaps." Lady Catriona's voice was soft. Then she held out her hand to Orabel. The older lady's grip was firm, and sparks of lightning darted from her fingertips where they touched and raced through her blood. Awe spiked through her. How had she never heard of Lady Catriona before now?

"A long story," Lady Catriona said, as though she could read her mind. "My dear half-sister, Clodrah, was Kenneth MacAlpin's mother."

Orabel gasped. MacAlpin's mother, the treacherous Princess of Fortriu, whose name had been erased from the annals of Pictland until her son had laid claim to her birthright over a year ago.

Surreptitiously, she tried to withdraw her hand, but Lady Catriona didn't release her. "Not everything is as clear as they first appear," the older lady said, which scarcely made sense, since it was very clear Kenneth MacAlpin's mother had betrayed her own people. "Sometimes we must search deeper, Lady Orabel."

"Indeed," she responded, relieved the other lady had finally released her hand.

"This is true," Briana said, as they sat on stools beside Lady Catriona's chair, and their ladies brought over refreshments.

"Who could have imagined, a year ago, that the three of us would be wed to Scots' warriors?"

Over the rim of her cup, Orabel glanced between Briana and Mairi. She knew Mairi and Finn were devoted to each other. It had been plain to see when she had visited them in the early spring. It seemed Briana was well pleased with her match, too. What was intriguing was they both appeared to believe her marriage, also, was quite wonderful, without even asking her if it was.

To be sure, she was happy with Ross. But still, Briana's words stung. "Who, indeed," she said before she could stop herself. "When the Scots are responsible for the bloodied massacre at Dunadd that took the life of my beloved father."

A terrible silence descended, and she took a sip of her herbal tea, so she didn't have to catch her cousins' horrified gazes. Yet she didn't regret her words, even though they were hasty. Even though she was glad to be wed to Ross. Because none of that changed the facts.

MacAlpin was responsible for the death of her rightful king.

"Goddess." Briana leaned closer, clearly contrite. "Pray forgive me my unwary words, Orabel. It was most thoughtless of me. However, that's no excuse. And I'm deeply grieved for the loss of your esteemed father and king."

Orabel inclined her head. Her father had been massacred, and Briana's had been taken hostage. But the King of Fotla had been released earlier this year, thanks to MacAlpin's desire to claw superficial support for his upcoming coronation.

She was glad for Briana. But it didn't make her own loss any easier to bear.

"Orabel." Mairi's voice was hushed. "Finn and I were already at Duntorr, visiting Briana, before we heard of your betrothal. I know now it was wrong for me to presume, but I imagined this was something you wanted. Are you unhappy in your marriage to MacIntosh?"

Briana took her hand, and a sliver of guilt inched through Orabel. She hadn't meant to upset her cousins. She'd just been irked by their seeming acceptance of everything.

"I am not," she said. "Ross MacIntosh is an honorable man, for all that he is a Scot."

Mairi gave a relieved sigh, and Briana squeezed her fingers. It was clear her reply had eased their minds.

"I feel the same about Finn," Mairi confessed. "With respect, Lady Catriona," she added, glancing at the older lady. "He is nothing like his father."

Of course. Finn Braeson was MacAlpin's bastard. What a legacy for him to bear.

"I love the king," Lady Catriona said. "He is of my blood, after all. But I am not blind, my lady."

Great goddess. Should they be speaking so freely in front of someone whose loyalty was so compromised? Yet Briana looked upon the older woman with warmth, empathy, even, as though she trusted Lady Catriona with all her secrets.

Briana turned to her. "I love Ewan," she said. "Even though I vowed never to love again after my first marriage. And," she hesitated, and it seemed a silent message passed between her and Lady Catriona. Briana drew in a deep breath and a faint blush highlighted her cheeks. "It's very early, but I am with child."

"Oh, that's wonderful." Mairi rose from her stool and gave Briana a hug. "I cannot believe you didn't tell me while we were at Duntorr."

"I scarcely knew for sure myself until this day," Briana's fingers fluttered self-consciously over her belly. "I won't announce it yet, but I wanted you both to know."

"I'm delighted for you. May the great goddess Bride bless you with her benevolence." Orabel gave her a hug but couldn't stop the unease that wove through her. Why hadn't she known Briana was with child? It was one of her gifts to sense when a woman conceived, often before the woman even guessed herself.

But even now, after Briana had shared the news, that special *knowing* did not manifest. It was as though something hid that truth from her.

There was only one reason how this had happened. Bride had withdrawn from her.

"Dear Orabel," Briana said, once again taking her hand. "There's something I must share with you. Something I've known all my life, yet could not accept until recently. It was not Bride who chose me. I am a child of the great goddess, Cailleach."

Cailleach? The mighty Goddess of Winter, who was forever locked in a battle with Bride, the goddess of new life? Stunned, Orabel stared at her cousin. To be sure, there were ancient stories of how the powerful goddess had, long ago, blessed a chosen few. But those stories were whispered in the dark, for those chosen ones had been witches.

"I'm happy for you," she breathed, even though she could scarcely comprehend the revelation. But as Briana gave her another hug, another revelation revealed itself.

Bride had not turned her back. It was Cailleach herself who had hidden the truth from Orabel, protecting her chosen one, and relief tumbled through her.

"Thank you." Briana drew back and sniffed, clearly overcome. "Ewan is beside himself with excitement. I had to force a promise from him that he wouldn't share our news with a soul."

"The future is unfolding," Lady Catriona said softly. "Just as Bride foretold, so many years ago."

An eerie shiver trickled over Orabel's arms. "Bride foretold… this?" She waved her arm, encompassing herself and her cousins.

"The great goddess honored me with a glimpse of the tapestry that had yet to be woven. The threads are coming together, just as she promised."

Orabel wasn't sure what to make of that. Surely, if Bride had foreseen the terrible massacre at Dunadd, she would somehow have stopped it?

"Orabel," Mairi said. "I'm not certain if the messenger arrived at Dunmor before you left, but our dear cousin Elise was safely delivered of a daughter two weeks ago."

"That is wonderful, indeed." Elise, Princess of Circinn, had also wed a Scots warrior last year. "Have you heard how our cousin Aila and her son are faring?"

"I know Connor MacKenzie is here in Forteviot, and incandescent with fury that he could not remain with his lady wife instead." Mairi raised her eyebrows. "MacAlpin, on the other hand, is irked that Aila chose to remain in Ce-eviot rather than make the trek here. However, he can scarcely fault her reasoning."

"And so poor Mae bears the brunt of MacAlpin's ambition during this farce of a coronation," Briana added. "We minor princesses are scarcely worth his while."

"There is nothing minor about either Fotla or Fib," Lady Catriona said with a gentle smile. "But to unite the land, the people must believe the Princess of Fortriu is willing to work with Kenneth MacAlpin."

To unite the land, indeed. Orabel took another sip of her tea, to hide her disgust. If not for MacAlpin, their land wouldn't be fractured in the first place.

CHAPTER TWENTY-SEVEN

After Ross had spoken to his men and inspected the site they'd been allocated to make camp, he returned to the stronghold. He didn't want to leave Orabel alone in Forteviot for any longer than necessary. And he was still irked by the chamber she'd been given. To hell with however many other princesses were staying in the stronghold. She deserved better.

As he crossed the forecourt, he caught sight of Ewan MacKinnon and Connor MacKenzie emerging from the stables. It had been an age since he'd last spoken with Connor, and he hadn't seen Ewan since he'd last been at Duntorr earlier this year, and so he made his way over to them.

They grasped arms in greeting before Connor pulled back, a dark frown marring his brow. "It's good to see you're still alive, Ross."

"We heard rumors you were poisoned with wolfsbane," Ewan added with certain relish. "Clearly, not."

"It wasn't a rumor. Whoever attacked us, used wolfsbane in their arrow tips."

"Northumbrians?" There was no trace of amusement in Ewan's voice now.

"It seems likely, but we have no proof."

"The Northumbrians grow bolder by the year." Connor's voice was harsh. "They don't want this alliance between Scot and Pict to succeed."

"MacAlpin has them in his sights." Ewan glanced over his shoulder, as though to ensure they couldn't be overheard. "He won't forgive them for the attempted assassination of Constantine and this attack will merely add fuel to his fire."

"The arrow that felled Constantine wasn't poisoned." Connor frowned. "Wolfsbane, though. A man can't survive that, Ross. Are you certain?"

"Aye." There wasn't a glimmer of doubt that Orabel had correctly diagnosed him. "If not for the skill of the Princess of Fib, I would not be here now."

Connor folded his arms. "And now you are wed to the Princess of Fib."

It sounded like a challenge. Certainly, the tone wasn't congratulatory. But since the statement was certainly the truth, there was only one response. "I am."

Connor and Ewan exchanged looks. It was novel, and not in a good way, to feel excluded while in the company of two of his oldest friends.

"How did MacAlpin wrangle that?" Ewan sounded grim. "Don't tell me you have foreign royal blood in your veins also."

He had no idea what blood flowed in his veins, but for the first time that knowledge didn't twist knots inside his chest. "Unlike you," he said, "my grandmother isn't a secret Pict princess. And let me be clear. MacAlpin had nothing to do with the marriage between Lady Orabel and I."

"What?" Connor shot Ewan another glance before returning his attention to Ross. "You didn't go to Fib with orders to entrap the princess into matrimony?"

"Those weren't my orders." Although he and Rourke had certainly had their suspicions, which, as it transpired, had been baseless. "I'm fortunate the Princess of Fib consented to be my bride."

"Aye, aren't we all the fortunate ones." Ewan gave him a probing look. "So, MacIntosh. Do I offer my congratulations or commiserations?"

It was the same question Rourke had asked of Ewan, that day in Fotla, when he'd been ordered to wed Lady Briana. The same day Ross had asked him if he cared for the princess.

Christ. This was fucking surreal. Once again, a shimmer of how much Orabel meant to him threatened to flood his good sense and he swiftly shoved it to the back of his mind. But it wouldn't fade, and the truth was, he didn't want it to. But it was too raw to put into words. Especially with the men he'd known all his life.

Instead, he sidestepped the obvious intent behind Ewan's question. "How the hell did we all end up with royal brides?"

"We know how we did," Connor said. "And I thank God that Aila is my wife. But Finn was certain MacAlpin had plans to wed the Princess of Fib to Stuart MacGregor."

"Interesting choice," Ewan said.

"Only because he has a trace of royal blood." Connor rolled his shoulders as he eyed Ross. "Yet you knew nothing of that order. And your head is still attached to your neck."

Reluctantly, he conceded Connor was right. But then again, the man had said nothing that hadn't already crossed his own mind. "I would not stand silently by while that foul mouthed Northumbrian warlord disrespected the princess. Any man would do the same as I did."

"Aye," Ewan said, and this time there was a faint smirk on his face. "Any man would do that for the woman he loved."

"I—" He bit back the words that threatened to spill. Ewan would only take a denial as proof he was right.

Fuck it. Who was he trying to fool? Orabel meant more to

him than anyone he had ever known before. But he still couldn't face it. Not yet.

Not when facing the truth might cause this fragile peace he'd found with her to fall apart.

Connor grunted. "My lady wife will be greatly relieved to know both Lady Briana and Lady Orabel have devoted husbands. And the Princess of Fortriu, naturally. Discovering this truth was my prime objective in coming to Forteviot so I could report back to her."

"The only reason Lady Briana is here is so she can support Lady Mairi tomorrow." For some reason, dark worry clouded Ewan's eyes. "And she wouldn't hear of my lady grandmother traveling here without her. But I would far rather she was safely home at Duntorr."

"Lady Orabel attends only to represent the royal house of Fib." Ross eyed his friends as the incongruity of their conversation hit him. "Intriguing that none of us mention we're here because we wish to support our liege's ambition of finally being crowned King of Fortriu."

Silence greeted him. But it spoke volumes.

Finally, Connor spoke. "We are all wed to princesses who have suffered greatly from MacAlpin's actions. And I believe we all of us know where our loyalties lie."

Ross released a measured breath. Since that night in Dunadd, over a year ago, when the Picts had allegedly turned on their hosts, suspicions had seethed, unfettered.

The three of them, along with many others, had been at the border, pushing back the Northumbrians, and they'd returned to Dunadd to witness the bloodied aftermath of MacAlpin's men having slaughtered the Pict nobles in defense of their king.

They had never spoken of that night between them. They likely never would. But now he knew for certain.

He wasn't alone in his treacherous thoughts when it came to MacAlpin.

~

THE CORONATION BEGAN the following morning and was a lengthy affair. MacAlpin appeared determined for the lavish procession and ceremony to show every Scot present and, more importantly, every Pict, just who the new king of the Supreme Kingdom was.

From the stronghold, the procession wound its way to the nearby standing stones, and then onward to the church. Ross had expected to lead his men, along with all the other warrior contingents, in the show of strength MacAlpin had surrounded himself with, but instead he and Ewan had been relieved of their duty and instructed to remain with their royal wives.

So here he was, in the midst of Pict and Scot royalty, with a front seat view of the altar, where the ancient Stone of Destiny had been placed beneath the coronation throne.

Finn, as befit his new status, was in the thick of it, standing beside MacAlpin's legitimate sons in the chancel, and he looked damned aggravated by the so-called honor.

Connor stood beside MacAllister, a prestigious placement, doubtless because his wife was the Princess of Ce, but his expression remained forbidding.

Ross cast a sideways glance at Orabel. Her face was a mask. To hell with etiquette. He threaded his fingers through hers and gave her a comforting squeeze, as MacAlpin sat on the throne and the monks he'd brought with him from Dunadd commenced Latin liturgies.

Orabel met his gaze, but she didn't say anything. Not that she had to. Her violet eyes flashed with suppressed anger, and he sighed, before raising her hand to his lips and pressing a kiss on her fingers.

She exhaled a long-suffering breath, before returning her attention to the coronation, but he couldn't drag his bewitched gaze from her profile. How regal she was, in her splendid, vibrant gown, the peacock blue of her richly embroidered gown and the sparkling jewels she wore eclipsing every other woman in the church, even MacAlpin's own queen.

But there was so much more to Orabel than the wealth of the Kingdon of Fib she wore so proudly. She could wear the drabbest rag and she'd still dazzle him.

God, he couldn't wait until they were back in Dunmor. The renovations to the old church should be finished by now, and anticipation sizzled through his blood at her delight when he presented her with her sanctuary.

Two days hence, when they could leave the oppressive walls of Forteviot, could not come quickly enough.

The ceremony droned on but, finally, it ended, and they left the church. Outside, scores of peasants had gathered, their distrustful eyes taking in the opulent scene until MacAlpin's men tossed coins into the crowd, and any brewing antagonism vanished as the villagers scooped up their bounty.

Orabel's ladies, who had been relegated to seats further back in the church, joined them as they made their way back to the stronghold.

"At least it's not raining," he remarked.

Orabel sniffed. "A storm would be most fitting."

"Aye. But you would get drenched."

"There is a great sorrow in my heart, Ross."

"Your sorrow grieves me. When we return to Dunmor, I'll do all in my power to lighten your heart."

A faint smile lit her face. "Then I shall think of that, and not of the outrage MacAlpin has committed this day."

They entered Forteviot, and the great hall was swathed in green and scarlet, the colors of Dal Riada. MacAlpin sat at the high table on a dais, with the Princess of Fortriu by his side, Finn next to her, and flanked by MacAlpin's queen, their sons, and their wives.

The king launched into a speech of victory, of how a united

Dal Riada and Pictland would repel their mutual enemies, emphasizing the blessing bestowed upon him and their land by the gracious Princess of Fortriu.

He sounded so sincere. The curse of it was, deep in his heart, Ross knew the king was right. A united land was the only way to ensure both the Norse and Northumbrians thought twice before launching a full-scale invasion.

Not that he'd ever say as much to Orabel. She had lost too much at the altar of MacAlpin's ambitions.

He stole a sideways glance at her, and she gave him a faint smile. God, he couldn't wait until they were away from here, back home in Dunmor. It was torture, leaving her alone at night but the thought of sharing her bed, while her ladies slept in the same chamber, was not something he could bring himself to entertain.

Would it truly matter if they left a day earlier? MacAlpin would scarcely notice their absence. Decision made, he offered her a conspiratorial grin. He'd request permission from MacAllister first thing in the morning.

CHAPTER TWENTY-EIGHT

After the interminable coronation and subsequent feast, the musicians played and Orabel danced with Ross, as protocol demanded. But her heart wasn't in it. How could they celebrate this farce?

"Would you rather return to Lady Mairi and Lady Briana?" Ross whispered in her ear, and she nodded, grateful he understood without her needing to say anything. But at least she had been spared dancing with MacAlpin, unlike her beleaguered cousin, Mairi.

Ross led her to where her cousins stood with Lady Catriona before he bowed and made his way to his fellow warriors. How fine he looked in his foreign plaid and saffron shirt, that emphasized his broad shoulders to glorious advantage. Goddess, she had to stop gazing at him like a lovestruck maid and hastily she took a sip of wine to hide her besotted smile.

"It must feel strange," Briana said to Lady Catriona, "being back in Forteviot after so long. Has much changed?"

Lady Catriona sighed and glanced around the great hall. "Forteviot will never change. Whoever may come or go, the walls remain. And so do the memories."

"I'm grieved your name was erased from our histories, my lady." Mairi gently touched Lady Catriona's arm. "It was not right."

"But we shall rectify this." Briana sounded fierce. "Our children shall know of you, and how you saved our land from bloodshed."

Good goddess. What was Briana talking about? Lady Catriona loved MacAlpin, and he was the one spilling blood across their land.

"My dearest." Lady Catriona gave Briana a fond glance. "We all of us here are saving our beloved Pictland in our own ways."

"Indeed." Briana took the older lady's hand. "But if you hadn't saved Lord Tavish from the wrath of the Fortriu king, who knows what terrible conflict would have blighted our land? Forteviot may have fallen almost fifty years ago, if not for you."

Almost fifty years ago, the Princess of Fortriu had run away with her Scots prince, Alpin. For her treachery, her father, the King of Fortriu, had expunged her existence from the annals.

But he hadn't declared war on the Dal Riadans.

Mairi drew closer to her. "Lady Catriona's beloved husband, Lord Tavish, half-brother to the Prince of Dal Riada, returned to Forteviot, despite the danger, to tell the king the princess had left of her own free will. That is the reason the Picts did not declare war upon Dal Riada."

Orabel didn't wonder how her cousin had guessed her thoughts. It was always this way when they were together. And besides, she was certain her face had given away her confusion.

But if Lady Catriona's husband had been Alpin's half-brother, that meant Kenneth MacAlpin was her nephew twice over.

Goddess. What a tangle.

"That was brave, indeed," she said. There were, after all, honorable Scots. She had wed one herself.

"I did not greatly miss the palace," Lady Catriona said. "But how dearly I should love to visit the eastern glen again."

"The eastern glen?" Mairi sounded enthralled. "Do you mean the one with the sacred yew? I always loved going there as a girl, and climbing the branches, much to my ladies' distress. I always felt so close to the great goddess, there, wrapped in those timeless branches."

"Yes. The gatekeeper between this world and the next." And then Lady Catriona looked at Orabel. "If you find the gateway, my lady, I hope you discover its hidden truths, as I did."

A shiver raced over Orabel's arms as she recalled her dark vision. The twisting branches of the yew tree, spread out like a miniature forest.

The gatekeeper between this world and the next.

As Saoirse combed her hair early the following morning, Orabel forced her churning antagonism against MacAlpin to the back of her mind. She wouldn't let that odious man poison her thoughts. The deed had been done.

If Mairi could stomach the way her kingdom had been wrenched from her grasp, then the least Orabel could do was accept it, too.

But she would never forgive the Scots upstart for how he had betrayed her father.

Ross had left the bedchamber soon after sunrise that morning, and although he hadn't told her what he had planned, it was clear he had something in mind, since he hadn't tried to hide the air of intrigue that clung to him.

She smiled. It seemed whenever she thought of her husband, her heart lightened. It was quite extraordinary how the mere thought of him caused such a warm sensation to bathe her, but she wasn't about to question it. Or investigate it further.

It was enough that it simply existed.

If only they were returning home today. But she had no intention of spending endless hours within the walls of Forteviot. As Saoirse put her comb away, she stood and faced her ladies.

"Shall we enjoy an early morning ride?" They had been at Forteviot for only two days, but she longed to escape the oppressive cloud caused by MacAlpin's occupation.

"I shall inform Neilan to ready our guards," Saoirse said.

As Orabel and her ladies left the stables leading their horses, Neilan greeted her with the dozen warriors he had assigned for the excursion. It was only right, of course, but how she longed for the freedom to ride with only Saoirse for company.

In the distance were the standing stones they'd passed on their way to the church yesterday. Were the old gods still there, deep within the sacred stones and blessed earth, despite everything that had happened during the last year?

There were many Picts and Scots about, taking advantage of the fine day, but no one else were near the standing stones. She entered the circle, and Saoirse, the young noblewomen, and the warriors, remained at a respectful distance outside the perimeter.

She pressed her palm against the face of the greatest stone and bowed her head. But no insight washed through her nor great truth revealed itself. Birdsong floated on the warm breeze, and the distant lowing of cattle gave the comforting illusion that nothing had changed in Pictland for a thousand years.

She sighed and opened her eyes. Bride was not here. Her mare tossed her head and Orabel soothed her, but just as she was about to return to her ladies, a movement from the substantial coppice some distant ahead caught her eye.

The two men had their backs to her, but she'd recognize Ross anywhere. He hadn't seen her and was deeply engrossed in conversation with his companion.

For a moment she merely watched, as they marched onward,

apparently making their way to a strangely placed, partially ruined circular wall.

She glanced over her shoulder, and Saoirse hurried to her side.

"Stay here," she told her faithful friend. "I wish to speak with my husband."

Saoirse inclined her head. "Of course, my lady."

So long as Neilan could keep her in his sights, he would allow her this small freedom.

She followed Ross and sure enough, he and his companion—Rourke, she now recognized, disappeared behind the wall. What was he doing?

As she drew closer to the structure, the hair on her arms prickled, and her mare was clearly uneasy. The wall was ancient, older than the palace itself, and a dark and twisted power lingered in the stone and seeped into the surrounding air.

Anger. Blood. *Death.*

Orabel shuddered and glanced over her shoulder, half inclined to return to Saoirse. But that was foolish. Whatever had happened here, had happened long ago and all she could feel were echoes of a bygone time.

She took another step forward and then froze as a voice rang out. It was the one she'd suffered through yesterday. One she had no desire to hear again. So what was her husband doing here? Talking to the enemy.

To MacAlpin.

AFTER LEAVING Orabel in their bedchamber, Ross went to the camp to ensure all was well with his men. Unfortunately, there was no sign of MacAllister. Typical. From the camp he went to the stables and checked on his horse. The animals were well cared for, but the truth was, he trusted no one to look after the fine creature other than himself.

He was part way through a thorough grooming session when Rourke strode into the stables.

"You're wanted," the other man said.

Ross tossed him a glance. "Any idea where your father is?"

"Aye. With the king. Who is the one who wants to speak with you."

Well, fuck. He rubbed his horse's neck before making his way to Rourke. "What about?"

Although he could guess. His rash actions in the Kingdom of Fib were now likely to come back and bite him. And judging by the sideways glance Rourke threw him, his friend was of similar mind.

"I doubt he's going execute you. He's in too good a mood after yesterday."

They marched across the forecourt and beyond, to where the standing stones stood. They reminded him of the stone circle in Fib, where he and Orabel had shared their first kiss.

He smothered a groan and forced the image from his mind. It had been too long since they'd been together at night and his need to possess her once again was a constant gnaw that was starting to affect his reason.

He could only hope his king was as agreeable about the situation as MacAllister had been, and with luck, would allow him to leave Forteviot this day.

They walked through the outer edge of a sprawling coppice and Ross frowned at the structure ahead. "What the fuck is that?"

It looked like a tumbled down tower, except from this angle he could see the wall surrounded a massive pit.

"Some pagan place of worship." Rourke shrugged. "Not used anymore, by all accounts, but rest assured if MacAlpin throws you into the pit, Connor, Ewan and I will rescue you later."

"That's reassuring," he muttered, as they entered the enclosure through a wide gap.

MacAlpin and MacAllister were deep in discussion, and a handful of the king's most trusted warriors stood on the far side of the pit. Ross gave it a surreptitious glance. A man could break all his bones being flung into such a thing.

It was obvious MacAlpin knew he had arrived and just as obvious he intended to keep him waiting. Which did not bode well. But it wasn't as if he had any options.

Finally, MacAlpin turned and scrutinized him, as though assessing his worth. Was it his imagination or did an oppressive silence hang within this ancient structure?

He thrust the uneasy sensation aside as he and Rourke bowed low before their king.

"Ross MacIntosh." The king didn't sound angry. He sounded amused. "I'll be damned. You did it."

Ross didn't glance at Rourke, but it was clear by the way the other man shifted his stance that he was as much in the dark by MacAlpin's comment as himself.

"My liege," he said, since he had no idea what response his king required.

MacAlpin laughed. "Aye, you've proved your loyalty, Ross, as your father did before you. We confess we had our doubts when Conall," he glanced at MacAlister, "advised caution, but once again, he was right. Congratulations on winning the hand of the Princess of Fib in such an ingenious manner."

Heat crawled over Ross' neck at the king's implication.

"We don't know where you got the idea for the wolfsbane from. That was risky. When we said you were to do anything to prevent an alliance between the Kingdom of Fib and the Northumbrians, poisoning yourself so the princess might save you was not what we had in mind."

MacAlpin and MacAllister shared a knowing grin, as a band tightened around Ross' chest as the cryptic words MacAllister had uttered in Dunmor, before they'd left for Fib, echoed in his head.

"To eliminate the threat, by any means possible."

For fuck's sake. This was madness. Was MacAlpin actually insinuating he had expected Ross to entrap Orabel into marriage? That he'd *poisoned* himself so the princess would treat him? How in the name of God did that even make sense? Had MacAlpin known she was a gifted healer?

It was nothing less than a miracle that Orabel had not only found him but was possibly the only person on earth with the knowledge to save him.

Even a fool would not have gambled with those odds.

"Sire, we were attacked. We're still not certain who by, although I suspect it was the Northumbrians. However—"

"Whatever the truth of it," MacAlpin said, "your quick thinking is impressive. MacAllister has furnished me with a full report, and you may expect a substantial boon for bringing the Kingdom of Fib into our fold."

To hell with a boon. "My orders were to extend an invitation for the King of Fib to attend the coronation and discover if a treaty was in place between Northumbria and Fib."

"Which you did. We understand you are well pleased with your bride, MacIntosh. Is that not so?"

It was a trap. The whole thing. Stuart MacGregor had never been in MacAlpin's sights to wed the princess. It had always been him.

And he had fallen headfirst, oblivious.

It scarcely mattered that a thousand things could have easily prevented the outcome MacAlpin had wanted. Because none of them had.

But still, he had been an unwitting pawn in the game. Yet in the end, how could he rail against it?

Because Orabel was his bride and she more than pleased him. God, he could scarcely imagine life without—

A flash of forest green and the swish of a horse's tail caught his eye and he swung about.

Through the gap in the wall, he saw Orabel astride her mare, and for a fleeting moment, her incomparable violet eyes clashed with his.

God damn it, he couldn't risk her hearing anything MacAlpin was saying. Heedless of his king he marched towards her. "My lady."

But she didn't offer him a welcoming smile. Without a word, she turned her back and urged her mare into a gallop, away from the stronghold, heading God only knew where. Wildly, he glanced around and saw her entourage by the standing stones. Neilan started after her, followed by several warriors, and he broke into a run.

"Neilan," he yelled, and with obvious reluctance, the Pict came to a halt. "Give me one of your men's horses. I must find the princess."

Neilan jerked his head at one of his warriors who dismounted and thrust the reins at Ross.

As he drew alongside Neilan, only one thought pounded through his mind.

How much had she overheard?

CHAPTER TWENTY-NINE

The wind whipped against Orabel's cheeks, and it was no longer warm as befit a summer's morn, but chilled like ice. The ice that slid through her blood and clawed her heart.

Congratulations on winning the hand of the Princess of Fib in such an ingenious manner.

Her eyes stung and throat ached. There had been laughter in MacAlpin's voice, and admiration, too.

Admiration for how his faithful warrior had so easily trapped his foolish bride.

Grimly she glared ahead, uncaring how wild she must appear to the villagers she passed. What did she care what anyone thought?

Poisoning yourself so the princess might save you was not what we had in mind.

Shame scalded through her chest with every ragged breath she took, and her stomach churned in distress. The fleeting suspicions she'd harbored on the truth of that attack had been right. It had all been planned in meticulous detail so she would arrive at just the right time to miraculously save Ross MacIntosh.

The fragile new life she had so tenderly cherished was nothing but an illusory façade with a rotting core.

And she had no one but herself to blame.

The bitter knowledge didn't help. Ross MacIntosh had blinded her with his false charm but that was no excuse.

He was a Scot, and she should never have allowed herself to forget where his loyalty lay. How he must have laughed behind her back at her gullibility. At how she had told him, more than once, how honorable she believed he was.

The skies darkened, and an ominous crack of thunder echoed through the mountains. Shadows loomed across the land, the palace had vanished far behind, and there was no sign of Neilan or her ladies.

She had never been alone like this before. The knowledge she was unprotected, and in a land that was now hostile to her people, should alarm her. She should return. It was foolish to continue onwards, when she had no idea where she was or where she was heading.

Yet all that pounded through her mind was the need to escape.

To hide.

I cannot hide from myself.

The realization she had so terribly misunderstood her blessed goddess' warnings ate through her shredded heart like acid.

The serpents in her vision had been MacIntosh and Raedwulf. Bride had seen into his heart, where she had not, and because she'd so desperately wanted Ross to be the man of her dreams, she'd refused to see the truth. Had twisted it to her own ends, so she could justify the happiness she'd found in his arms.

This was the price she paid for her own arrogance. For ignoring Bride's command not to stray from the path chosen for her. If a secret part of her hadn't wanted to wed Ross, she could have challenged her king. Invoked the name of the goddess to retain her freedom.

But she hadn't fought hard enough, and Bride knew it.

A ragged sob tore her throat, and she tightened her grip on the reins. How could she face Ross again, knowing how little he regarded her? And yet she had to. To tell him she would no longer continue in this farce of a marriage. She'd return to Fib, pick up the tattered remnants of her life, and never stray from Bride's path again.

Etain would not be happy. Dugald would be furious. But this time she would not flinch. This time she would channel the wrath of her goddess and they would see…

Her fierce thoughts crumbled into worthless dust. What would they see? That Bride had deserted her?

As though to confirm she was utterly alone, the skies opened, and merciless rain pounded down. She slowed her mare and pushed her wet hair from her eyes, glancing around for shelter. A river cut through the glen and a cave beckoned in the mountainside.

It was an ideal refuge. But something made her continue along the riverbank. Something eerie, as though she was compelled, but how could that be when Bride had turned her back? She was clinging to flimsy hope and broken dreams.

It was time to face reality. To go back to Forteviot and confront the travesty that was her marriage.

But first, she had to let this storm pass.

She followed the flow of the river as it wound its way around a curve in the glen. And pulled up short as a shocked gasp escaped.

A massive yew stood in her path. The ancient guardian of the gateway between the world of mortals and the realm of gods.

The yew from her visions.

She dismounted and slowly made her way towards the sacred tree. It had surely grown here for a thousand years or more, its drooping branches long ago rooting deep into the earth and given rise to its own immortal avenue.

She reached out and tentatively pressed her hand against the nearest branch, half expecting the ground to crack open, and for two serpents to emerge. But the ground remained solid, and the branches did not wrap around her, and she pulled back her hand and pressed her fist against her breast.

This couldn't be a coincidence. She had ridden blindly, yet Bride had brought her here, to the very place Lady Catriona had told her of.

Her goddess had not forsaken her.

Once again, she wiped her wet hair from her eyes, and through the tangle of branches, glimpsed an opening in the rockface beyond the sacred tree.

The sign from her goddess couldn't be plainer. Yet instead of joy that Bride had not abandoned her, only grief filled her soul.

She darted to the rockface, but the opening was too narrow to lead her mare through. After a moment's hesitation, she took a deep breath and stepped inside.

The cave was small and unremarkable, and despair slithered through her. What had she expected? A miraculous solution to the travesty her marriage had turned out to be?

There was only one answer, and she already knew it. There was nothing left to salvage with the Scot who had deceived her. But she was being given the chance to beg forgiveness from her goddess.

She shivered and glanced around. A faint blue-green glow shimmered on the far wall, and she frowned, momentarily distracted. As she drew closer, she realized her mistake. The glow didn't emanate from the wall. It came from a narrow fissure in the rock.

The uneven passageway was so narrow, she had to stand sideways as she inched along its length. Elusive tendrils of panic wove through her at the specter of being crushed between the rocks, but she pressed onward, ignoring how her heart hammered in her breast.

It was Bride's will she follow this path.

She stepped into another cave, before gasping. Tiny, blue-green lights danced in the darkness, illuminating a waterfall that cascaded into a burbling stream. Frozen, she could only gaze in wonder at the mystical sight of Bride's hidden sanctuary.

The cave from my vision.

Bride's sacred place known only to her chosen few.

Lady Catriona had been here. Doubtless, too, had Mairi. But MacAlpin didn't know of it. No Scot could enter here, for they would only pollute and destroy it all, and that…

That was what Bride had been trying to tell her from the start.

She bowed her head and gripped her fingers together, accepting her goddess' word even though sorrow seared her heart making it all but impossible to draw breath.

Finally, she understood the warnings. Bride could only embrace her once she had repudiated Ross MacIntosh.

She was fortunate Bride had not deserted her entirely.

Why don't I feel grateful, then?

She squeezed her eyes shut, smothering the treacherous question. She couldn't think such things here, in the heart of Bride's realm, where the goddess could surely hear all her secret, innermost thoughts.

Focus.

She sank to her knees, concentrating on Bride, forcing Ross MacIntosh from her mind. Why would his image not leave? Would the cursed man haunt her for all time?

"Orabel."

The achingly familiar voice pierced through her head like a poisoned arrow, and she swiveled around, still on her knees, disbelief tumbling through her. How could Ross have found Bride's sanctuary? He shouldn't be here.

"Orabel, goddamn it, are you here?"

She scrambled to her feet. His voice was no guilty echo in her mind. He had followed her, despite the storm, and there could be only one reason.

Because he wasn't prepared to lose the boon from his king for ensnaring a royal Pict bride.

He was in the outer cave, but it wouldn't take him long to find the hidden passageway and she couldn't let him find this place. Couldn't be responsible for being the one to lead the Scots here. If they discovered this sanctuary, they would defile it.

The way Scots defiled everything they touched.

Stop.

She couldn't—*wouldn't*—allow MacIntosh to see how deeply his betrayal had cut. Let him think she cared as little as he about their alliance. Perhaps, if he believed it meant nothing to her, he wouldn't place obstacles in her way when she told him her plans to return to Fib.

It was a slender hope but all she had.

Ross and Neilan galloped side by side in the direction Orabel had taken. She was some way ahead, and he urged his horse on. Slowly, they were gaining on her, thank God.

Without warning, the skies opened, blinding him. Cursing, he dashed the rain from his eyes and glared ahead, but the dark clouds spread shadows across the land, and mist rose from the sodden ground.

Orabel had vanished.

The Pict did not falter. Above the howl of the wind he shouted in Ross' direction. "If she is harmed, I will see to it your upstart king doesn't live to see another sunrise."

Ross didn't answer. There was little he could say, since he agreed with Neilan's sentiment.

But Orabel was an accomplished rider. Despite the harsh turn in the weather, nothing would happen to her. He had to believe that.

He pulled ahead of the Pict as the wind became deafening, a roaring maelstrom that reminded him of a sea tempest. The terrain was treacherous, but his horse didn't falter.

As if the creature knew where it was going.

He huffed out a breath and pushed the fanciful thought aside. Yet he couldn't completely dislodge the eerie sensation that this path was preordained.

It was the kind of thing Orabel would say. Before he'd met her, such a notion would never have crossed his mind, but now not only did he think it, but he could also understand that belief. God, if anything happened to her…

A river cut through the glen, and he slowed his horse as shadows solidified ahead. A mare sheltered from the rain beside a yew tree and his heart slammed against his ribs. Was that Orabel's mare?

He pulled to a halt and dismounted, before making his way to the mare. Wildly he glanced around. Where the hell was she? Had she fallen, and he'd missed her?

No. He wouldn't accept that. He grabbed the mare's reins and looped them around a branch before securing his horse and peering through the lashing rain. A deep sense of certainty penetrated his heart.

She was here.

A dark slash in the rockface glimmered in the rain and he marched over, relief flooding him as he entered the small cave, bowing his head so he didn't crack his head on the low hanging rock.

"Orabel."

His voice echoed around the cave. From the dim light that penetrated through the small gap, he could see she wasn't here. And yet the conviction that filled his chest did not waver. She was close by.

"Orabel, goddamn it, are you here?"

A strange, shimmering light on the far wall caught his attention.

A cleft in the rock.

He sucked in his chest to give himself more room and inched along the narrow space. As he stepped from the constricting passage, he collided into Orabel who leaped back as though his touch burned.

He was too damned relieved to care.

"Thank God you're safe." He gripped her shoulders and searched her face. She glared back at him, her drenched veil plastered across her shoulders and her wet hair clinging to her cheeks but as far as he could tell, she appeared uninjured.

Instinctively, he bent his head but before he could claim her lips, she knocked his arms from her shoulders with her fists and stepped back.

"Don't touch me." Her voice was low, distaste lacing each word.

Shit. She'd heard. Fucking MacAlpin. He reeled in his need to ensure she was truly unharmed, the need to hold her close, to feel her heartbeat against his. Because first he had to defuse the damage his damn king had wrought.

"Listen to me," he said but she bared her teeth in what could be nothing less than a snarl, and the words died on his tongue.

"How dare you come in here?" She breathed the words—the accusation—at him, and somehow it was more potent than if she had yelled. "You should not be here. You should not have found this sacred place."

"I saw your mare by the cave entrance," he said, although he didn't know why he sounded so damned defensive. "It was a natural conclusion to draw that you were sheltering here from the storm."

She hitched in a breath as though his response had wounded her.

"This defilement is my fault," she whispered. "Bride will be driven from her sanctuary."

Orabel's face glowed a strange green-blue and for the first time the illumination within this cave registered. By rights, they were so deep within the cave system he should see nothing yet until now he hadn't questioned it. He'd been too thankful to have found her.

But now, as he tore his gaze from her face, he sucked in a sharp breath. On the far side of the cave a waterfall thundered into a fast-flowing stream, and blue-green lights hovered in the misty air.

He had never seen anything like it before. It was like being in a different world. One that held onto an ancient, pagan magic of its own.

"I would not wish your goddess to be driven from this sacred place." And somehow, in this mystical cave, his assurance didn't sound blasphemous. "No one shall know of this cave from me, Orabel."

"And I should take the word of a Scot?" Scorn dripped from each word, but it was the hurt in her eyes that caused a dull ache to compress his chest. "From *you*?"

"I don't know what you thought you overheard." Except he knew damn well what she'd overheard. Everything. "But you're wrong. It's not what you think."

"You have no idea what I think, and simply because you say I'm wrong, does not make it so."

He couldn't fault her logic, but the derision in her tone stung.

"You condemn me without first asking me for the truth?"

"Very well." She drew herself up and gave him a regal look. "Do you deny your orders were to do anything to prevent an alliance between the Kingdom of Fib and Northumbria?"

Silently, he cursed that she'd picked on the one thing he couldn't categorically deny. But that didn't mean her interpretation was correct.

"My orders were to discover if such an alliance existed between the Kingdom of Fib and Northumbria."

And to eliminate the threat, by any means possible.

He couldn't tell her MacAllister's exact words. Even to his own ears, when he knew the truth, they did nothing but condemn him.

"And did you discover that?"

Her scathing words scraped a nerve. How could she so easily believe MacAlpin, a man he knew she despised, yet question every action her own husband had ever made?

"Raedwulf certainly did his best to forge an alliance between the two kingdoms. It was scarcely a secret."

"Indeed. But at least he didn't use a poisoned arrow to inveigle himself into my good graces."

"For Christ's sake, Orabel. You can't imagine I contrived to all but die on the slender chance of a miraculous cure, surely?"

"I don't presume to know anything about you. But had the plan gone awry, I'm certain the fact it was a Pict made arrow would have served your king well in his ambition to crush all dissent."

Her words hammered through his head.

A Pict made arrow.

The evidence he and his men had searched for, in vain.

Because Orabel's people had already concealed it.

Yet he had to know for sure. "You found the arrow?"

"Of course we did." Her voice was scathing. "Did you think we would leave it there for your men to find, so you might use it as leverage against us?"

"But when we spoke of the arrow, you assured me..." His voice trailed into silence, for what had she assured him of, really?

"Had we Picts truly wished to assassinate MacAlpin's men, we wouldn't have made it so easy for you to lay the blame at our feet. But none of that matters. It was all trickery, to fool me into believing Scots possess honor when in truth they possess less than a Northumbrian warlord."

Her insult pierced deep, but she was wrong. Surely, she had to see she was wrong?

"I swear to God, my lady, I knew nothing of the ambush. Or who crafted the arrow. Or of MacAlpin's plans."

"You may swear to your God all you wish. But here, in the sacred sanctuary of my beloved goddess, my sister's belief that Forteviot is where I'd discover anything worth knowing has come true." She gave a bleak laugh that tore at him as keenly as her bitter accusations. "I never imagined it would be this."

Frustration tore through him that she refused to accept his word, but worse than that was the sliver of fear that stirred in the shadows.

Ruthlessly, he slammed the darkness into a far corner of his mind before it could manifest. Frustration at Orabel's stubbornness was something he could handle. But discovering what lurked in those black shadows, of acknowledging the fear that hovered at the prospect of losing everything he'd found with her, was something he had no desire to face.

"We'll return to Dunmor this day." To hell with it if MacAlpin didn't approve. He'd rather return home battling a storm than remain another night in Forteviot. "You'll see clearly once we're away from this place."

"I see clearly now. At least Raedwulf didn't hide behind pretty lies. I knew what I could expect from him. But you—how proud you must be, to have worn your façade so convincingly."

"I wear no façade." He glared at her, as the hollowness of his words reverberated around the cave. He knew she spoke of the time he'd been in Fib, but all he could think was the façade he'd presented to the world from the day he had discovered the origins of his conception.

It clawed at him now, sharper than a dagger. As if the cave itself was trying to punish him. Familiar guilt scalded him, guilt that he'd foolishly believed had retreated since sharing his shame with Orabel.

"Indeed." Pain vibrated through that one word as she looked at him as if he was MacAlpin himself. "Alas, I see through it now to the truth that is so plain in your eyes."

"Aye. And I see you, who knew there was no evidence to be found as to who my attacker might be, because your people had already hidden it."

A deathly silence echoed between them, that not even the cascade of the waterfall could breach. Finally, she drew in a deep breath and as she passed by him into the narrow cleft between this cave and the outer one, she cast him a withering glance.

"Once we are at your stronghold, I shall make plans to return to Fib-eviot."

Rage flared that she could even think such a thing, let alone voice it. But it was worse than rage as once again the crippling fear of losing her overwhelmed all else.

Of facing the rest of his life without her by his side.

He followed her along the stifling passageway, heart thundering, head pounding. And when they stood facing each other, with only the dim sunlight penetrating through from the outside world, he gripped her shoulders once again.

"No, Orabel. You won't return to Fib-eviot. You're my wife, and your place is at Dunmor."

With me.

"Is it?" Her voice was filled with bitterness. "Even now, you cannot honor me with the truth. Even when we both know it. You wish Dunmor for Lady Una, the woman you wanted as your bride, and always have."

Christ, did she not even believe him about Una?

"You know why that is. It's nothing to do with the past she and I once shared."

Indecision flickered over her face and for one delusional

moment he thought he had got through to her. But then she spoke.

"Unhand me." Her voice was low and filled with grief, and that, even more than any of the words she'd fired at him, pierced his heart with a thousand shards. Silently, he released her, and they left the cave.

Neilan and her warriors had arrived and were waiting beyond the yew. The rain had stopped, and weak rays from the sun pushed through the gray clouds, but a vise gripped his chest, growing tighter with every ragged breath he took.

Orabel could threaten whatever she wished. But there was no way on God's earth he would allow her to leave Dunmor.

CHAPTER THIRTY

When Orabel returned to Forteviot, Saoirse and the young noblewomen ushered her into her chamber where a fire burned in the hearth, and she stood mute as they dried her hair and changed her gown.

No one uttered a word.

How swiftly devastating news traveled.

Finally, her dear friend made her sit before the fire, and handed her a cup of hot herbal tea.

"Is there anything you need, my lady?" Saoirse whispered, so the girls could not overhear.

Orabel gripped Saoirse's hand. She would tell her everything, but not now. Not when the young girls hovered. But there was something they could do. Something that would help occupy her so she would not be driven mad by her colliding thoughts. "Have the ladies ensure our possessions are packed. We shall leave Forteviot as soon as Neilan has readied the men."

Saoirse inclined her head but before she could pass on the instructions there was a knock on the door. Orabel's stomach twisted with nerves. She couldn't face seeing Ross again. The confrontation in the sacred cave would haunt her forever and the journey back to the palace had been fraught with words unsaid.

Coira opened the door, and bobbed a curtsey as Mairi, Briana, and their ladies entered. But it wasn't her cousins her gaze fixed upon.

It was Lady Catriona.

"Thank the goddess you are unharmed." Briana took her hand, before sitting beside her. "When we heard you were lost in the storm…" her voice trailed away, and she glanced at Mairi.

Saoirse brought a chair for Lady Catriona, and the older woman sat on the opposite side of the hearth, a concerned expression on her face. Had she known all along how easily Ross MacIntosh had fooled her?

"I was not lost." She sounded hoarse and took another sip of tea. Not that it helped. It wasn't her throat that was raw.

It was her heart.

Mairi sat next to Briana, and Saoirse herded all the ladies to the far side of the chamber. It didn't give much privacy, but it was better than nothing. Orabel carefully placed her cup on a small table. "Bride guided me."

"To her sacred sanctuary." Lady Catriona's voice was hushed.

"But, my love," Mairi said softly. "What happened to make you flee from the ancient gateway of our ancestors? Finn saw you and Ross gallop away, before MacAlpin and MacAllister emerged from the gateway."

"MacAlpin is odious," Briana whispered, before casting an apologetic glance at Lady Catriona who merely gave a sad smile. "We know this, Orabel. But you cannot put yourself in danger because of his actions."

It would be easier to let her cousins imagine the Scots king had offended her by a barbarous remark. But she wasn't easily offended. And it wasn't the callous words she'd overheard him saying that wounded her so deeply. It was how Ross hadn't refuted them to his king.

It was because, when she'd confronted him in the cave, he hadn't denied he had been ordered to do anything to prevent an alliance between Fib and Northumbria.

Yet a part of her wanted to share, as if by sharing it might somehow ease the grief in her heart. If only Lady Catriona wasn't here.

"It was foolish of me." Briefly, she closed her eyes, and saw Ross' piercing blue eyes gazing at her in admiration. But it had all been a lie. She drew in a deep breath. Perhaps if she spoke the truth aloud, she could begin to believe it and stop wishing for a miraculous revelation that would prove she had not been so utterly deceived. "I truly believed MacIntosh had not been sent to Fib to entrap me. I fear I was wrong."

Goddess, she shouldn't have said anything. Sharing the truth hadn't helped. It seemed a great fist was lodged in her chest, squeezing her heart, and she wasn't sure how much longer she could bear to keep a false, serene smile on her face.

"I confess, it is a strange thing." Anxiety laced Mairi's words. "Finn and I were convinced MacAlpin would attempt an alliance between you and Stuart MacGregor. Yet Ross MacIntosh knew nothing of that order when Finn confronted him before he left for Fib-eviot."

Her smile cracked a little more. "It seems he is a master at concealing the truth."

"Indeed." Anger heated Briana's voice. "For just the other day he informed Ewan of the very same thing."

"Did he?" Mairi appeared distracted by that remark. "Why would he continue that fabrication with his oldest friend, when dear Orabel is already his wife?"

"I cannot fathom it." Briana patted Orabel's hand. If only she'd held her tongue. This dissection of her misfortune was tearing her apart. "Ewan has known MacIntosh all his life and was utterly convinced the only reason you wed was because he challenged the Northumbrian warlord."

Her cousins and Lady Catriona stared at her, as if expecting her to expose that outrageous remark as a lie.

She drew in a measured breath, but it was hard with the knot that filled her chest. "It's true there was a challenge. Raedwulf challenged Ross, after Ross told the entire court we were betrothed."

"Goddess." Mairi sounded scandalized. "He could have lost his head for such impertinence, even if he was acting on MacAlpin's orders."

Orabel studied her fingers, clasped upon her lap. Ross had been sent into Fib to ensnare her. Yet there had been no way of foreseeing that Raedwulf would also arrive in the kingdom, nor insult her in public, for Ross to then issue his foolhardy announcement.

"He did not mean it," she was compelled to say, even though she now knew differently. "It was meant to be a ruse, to prevent Raedwulf from claiming my hand."

"He told you that?" Briana asked.

Somehow, she managed a brittle smile. "He thought merely stating we were betrothed would be enough. But Raedwulf's honor demanded blood."

"The Northumbrian warlord is quite renowned for his swordsmanship. There was no guarantee MacIntosh would win." Briana sighed. "I'm grieved, Orabel, that he is clearly so devoted to his upstart king that he puts his life in danger so recklessly."

How tragic that, even now, she found it hard to believe Ross was that loyal to MacAlpin. Surely, if his orders were to entrap her into matrimony, it would have been easier to compromise her when they'd met by the sacred standing stones?

Yet even then, the outcome his king demanded might not have come to pass. The only reason it had was because Raedwulf had threatened war.

Unease slithered through her. If this was MacAlpin's idea of a strategic plan of action, it was riddled with flaws.

And yet Ross hadn't denied he had been ordered to *do anything* to prevent an alliance between her kingdom and Northumbria.

"Forgive me for asking, Orabel." There was an apologetic note in Mairi's voice. "But is it possible Ross MacIntosh was not poisoned by wolfsbane, but by something that merely mimicked the symptoms? Something that wouldn't kill him, if you hadn't found him in time?"

At least she was certain about that.

"It was wolfsbane. If we had not discovered him when we did, he would have died."

Silence greeted her. Perhaps she had sounded harsh, but even if a Scot had managed to blind her good sense with his beguiling charm and incomparable blue eyes, she always had her wits about her when it came to the healing arts.

"Oh." Briana frowned. "That is odd. If the attack was orchestrated, how could he possibly have known you would come across him before he perished? Or, that you would have the skill to save him?"

Unwillingly, she recalled that killing field. The truth was, even though she had thrown the accusation in Ross' face, she didn't believe he was behind the attack. No one in their right mind would agree to be poisoned with something as deadly as wolfsbane.

Ross might be many things, but he was not mad. Even revered healers were usually helpless in the face of such virulence. It was only through the benevolence of Bride that Orabel possessed the knowledge to counteract its effects.

But there was no way Ross could have known that.

"My lady," Lady Catriona said, and with a reluctance she did not quite understand, Orabel caught her steady gaze. "What does Bride say?"

She wanted to tell Lady Catriona that Bride was by her side in all things. But that was a lie, and the older woman, with her own powerful connection to their goddess, would instantly see through her flimsy deception.

There was no option but to admit the humiliating truth.

"Alas, the great goddess does not honor me with her guidance in this matter."

"Did she not invite you into her sanctuary?" Concern laced Lady Catriona's words and Orabel crushed the overwhelming urge to jump to her feet and flee from this chamber.

She would never disgrace her bloodline so. And, whether she liked it or not, Lady Catriona was also connected to her bloodline and somehow that made it even more imperative that she did not dishonor her foremothers.

"She did. For which I am grateful. But I was careless, and Ross followed me."

"Do you speak of the ancient yew?" Mairi enquired, glancing between her and Lady Catriona.

"Yes." Orabel gave a ragged sigh. "The great yew, guardian of Bride's sacred cave."

Only the sound of the fire crackling broke the silence. And then Mairi spoke. "What cave?"

Orabel stared at her cousin. Mairi did not know of the cave? But she had grown up in Forteviot. How could she not know of it?

"If Ross MacIntosh found his way into the sanctuary, it's because Bride willed it," Lady Catriona said. "You were not careless, my lady. There's a reason he could follow you. Just as there was a reason why my lord Tavish could follow me."

"But I do not know of this cave." Mairi's voice was hushed. "Orabel, the goddess has granted you a great honor. She is surely showing you something that has never been for my eyes."

How she wished she could believe Mairi. But she could no longer close her eyes to the truth. How foolish she had been to imagine she could keep how she really felt about her marriage to Ross hidden from her goddess.

Bride had always known. And like all immortals she did not forgive when she was slighted.

She had bided her time. Waited until Orabel had discovered the truth. And then, to ensure no misunderstanding lingered, she had allowed Orabel and Ross to enter her sacred sanctuary, to remind her of everything she had put at risk, because she had, instead, put her faith in a Scot.

Lady Catriona leaned forward, an intense gleam in her green eyes. "The great goddess has not forsaken you," she whispered. "Find the truth, my lady, and you will find the answer your heart craves."

CHAPTER THIRTY-ONE

As Dunmor came into view in the distance, Ross cast a glance at his silent bride. Orabel had scarcely uttered a word to him since their confrontation in the cave and he hadn't breached the widening gulf between them. Truth was, he had no idea how to.

But one thing was certain. If she believed, for even a moment, he would allow her to return to Fib-eviot, then she didn't know him at all.

I don't presume to know anything about you.

Her scathing words, as she had faced him in her goddess' sanctuary, burned through his chest like acid.

He'd confided his despicable secret to her. Something he hadn't even shared with Rourke. Yet she was right.

If she believed he'd lied and schemed against her from the start, then she truly didn't know him at all.

His grip tightened on the reins as he recalled MacAlpin's final words as they'd left Forteviot. The king had given his blessing to them, and Ross had half expected Orabel to tell him what she thought of him. Thankfully, she had merely stood by his side and gazed through his king as though he didn't exist.

"Allow us to present a wedding gift, MacIntosh," MacAlpin had said. "The stronghold of Duncnoc is yours. It is fitting that the Princess of Fib has her own household to run, after all."

Duncnoc, barely a day's ride from Dunmor, had long been coveted by Gordon and his father but despite it having no master for the last six years, MacAlpin had held onto its lands.

It had taken all his willpower not to tell his king what he could do with his fucking gift. It was obvious by the way Orabel had tilted her head as though a foul odor emanated from MacAlpin that she recalled the words she'd overheard.

The boon Ross deserved, for having entrapped another Princess of Pictland.

Morosely, he glowered ahead as they approached the old church. The church which should now be repaired and ready for Orabel to claim as her sanctuary. Except he doubted she'd accept anything from him, now.

As they drew closer, Angus emerged from the church, followed by Una. Fuck, he hoped there wasn't a problem. Orabel might well turn her nose up at his gift, but God damnit, he still wanted to offer it to her.

He pulled to a halt and dismounted before handing the reins to one of his men.

"I'll meet you back at the stronghold," he told Orabel, who merely gave him a glacial look before deigning to incline her head in acknowledgement. He clenched his jaw and watched her ride off, surrounded by her entourage.

Christ, what would he give to rewind time, and find a way for her not to have attended that cursed coronation?

"Sir." Angus sounded strangely guarded, which did nothing to improve his mood. Had the repairs fallen short of their expectations? "We didn't expect you back until the morrow."

"Aye. Change of plans." He nodded at Una and forced a smile to his face. "Good day, Una."

'Ross." Una smiled, but it appeared strained. Another reason as to why both Una and Angus seemed oddly ill at ease scraped through his brain, and he raked his fingers through his hair.

"Has something happened to my lady mother?"

"No, not at all," Una said hastily. "Our lady mother is… truly, the change in her since Lady Orabel's arrival is astonishing. You will find a great difference in her even in the short time you were at Forteviot."

He let out a relieved breath, yet it was tinged with regret. Aye, Orabel had made a great difference, and not only to his mother's life.

"Good." He transferred his gaze to the church. It appeared sound. "What's the problem, then?"

"There is no problem." Una stepped forward. "Come, I'll accompany you back to the stronghold."

"Una." There was a warning note in Angus' voice and Ross shot him a sharp look. To be sure, when they were alone, he and Angus abandoned the strictures of master and servant, but that didn't give him the right to address Una in such familiar terms.

"Not now." There was a firm note in her voice that he couldn't remember hearing before. What the fuck was going on?

Angus came to her side and looked Ross in the eyes. "Aye, now."

"One of you tell me to what you are referring."

Una let out a ragged sigh. "You are happy with the princess, are you not, Ross?"

He was so fucking happy that for the last two nights he'd been plagued with dreams of slitting his king's throat for the way he'd wounded Orabel.

He'd die before sharing that with a soul. The irony wasn't lost on him. If he did share it, and was overheard, the likelihood of him dying a traitor's death was highly possible.

"What does Lady Orabel have to do with this?"

"Well, everything." Una glanced at Angus, whose face

remained an impenetrable mask. "You must know, Ross, I wish only happiness for you."

The events of ten years ago, when she had rejected him, flickered through his mind. For all the difference it made to him, those long-ago days might have happened to someone else.

Another thing he had Orabel to thank for. Christ, how could he make her see that no matter what MacAlpin said, or how condemning it sounded, when it came to how he felt about her, none of it was the truth?

He forced his mind back to the present. "I do," he said, because, oddly, even in the early years of Una's marriage, she had always tried to be kind to him. Even when, during the first year or so, he'd been a cold bastard to her.

"I'm glad," she whispered. "And I beg of you, as the blood uncle of my beloved daughters, to be happy for me, too."

In the black shadows of his mind, a dull glow flickered. He transferred his gaze from her to Angus, but the other man gave no indication that he understood what Una was talking about.

He was clearly losing his mind. There was nothing between Una and Angus. Because that would be—

"I know I'm unworthy," Angus said, a stiff note in his voice. "Yet still I must ask you for the honor of Lady Una's hand in marriage."

Speechless, Ross stared at the man he'd been friends with all his life, the man he thought he knew so well.

Angus, who had just dared to ask for the hand of a gently bred noblewoman.

"You're more than worthy," Una responded fiercely, taking Angus' hand. "Do not ever say such a thing again."

He tore his condemning glare from Angus to focus on Una. "What happened in my absence?"

God help him. He couldn't believe Angus had taken advantage of Una. That wasn't in his nature. But something had happened.

Something that had convinced his sister-through-marriage that she had no option but to wed his steward.

It was Angus who answered his question.

"I've loved Lady Una for years. I never expected my love to be returned. But now she is free to finally live her own life and I'll do whatever it takes to ensure her happiness."

Thunder filled his head, and he turned on the other man. "Whatever it takes? You mean to tell me the lass you had your eye on, the reason you wanted to extend your cottage, is *Lady Una*?"

"I'll cherish her until my dying breath," Angus said, and it was almost as though he dared Ross to challenge his word. "She will want for nothing."

"Are you out of your mind, man? The villagers will ostracize her. A noblewoman can't live in a steward's cottage."

"Ross," Una began, but before she could continue, they were distracted by the arrival of Orabel and Lady Saoirse, who had obviously decided to leave the rest of the princess' entourage and the warriors and investigate what was happening here.

With a smothered curse he went to Orabel to help her, even though he knew full well she was more than capable of dismounting without his assistance, but it was the only damn time he touched her lately.

He helped Lady Saoirse, and she held the reins of both mares while Orabel made her way to Una. With a lowering sensation of impending doom, he followed her.

"Is something amiss?" she asked Una.

"No, my lady." Una twisted her fingers together and appeared on the verge of tears. God damn Angus for upsetting her. An unintentional growl escaped, and Orabel looked at him.

Would she ever look at him again with warmth and admiration in those beautiful violet eyes of hers?

"Am I interrupting?" Her voice was cool and while she certainly was interrupting, he'd rip out his tongue before admitting it to her.

"No," he said. "It's a misunderstanding, that's all."

"Please," Una said, a catch in her voice. "It's not a misunderstanding. I—I love Angus. I've loved him for three years, but I swear to you on my life that we've not brought dishonor upon Dunmor."

~

ORABEL BARELY KEPT a gasp from escaping as she gazed at Una. Of all the things she had imagined, when she'd glanced over her shoulder and seen the intense conversation between Ross, Una, and Angus, this had never crossed her mind.

And yet…

Hadn't she always believed Una was hiding a heartrending secret?

You feared she was still in love with Ross.

How wrong she had been. And how pitiful that the truth caused relief to wash through her.

"I regret you've been exposed to this tangle." Ross gave her a wary glance and she pretended not to notice the concern in his eyes. Despite his deception with her, she knew he genuinely cared for Una. What a tragedy that now, when her marriage lay in tatters at her feet, she finally saw he truly felt nothing but brotherly affection for Una.

"Life is an endless tangle," she said. "Even when we believe we have found the right path."

For a heartbeat, their gazes meshed, and she fancied she saw sorrow glinting in his eyes. But perhaps it was merely a reflection of the grief in her own.

"Aye." Resignation throbbed through the word and her heart squeezed at everything that could have been. He turned back to Una. "You know I cannot agree to this. Gordon's daughters cannot grow up in a cottage on the estate of their father's."

"Their father." Angus spat the words, fury vibrating from him.

But then he clenched his teeth, clearly biting back anything else he wanted to say. Did he know what Una had given up, ten years ago?

Perhaps he did. Perhaps he even knew of the circumstances of Ross' conception.

In the end, that scarcely mattered. Una had given up her chance of happiness, to protect Lady Fia and to prevent a challenge between Ross and his half-brother. She didn't deserve to lose another man she loved.

It wasn't her place to interfere. Yet despite everything that had happened between her and Ross, it didn't change how she felt about Una. She liked the other woman, and if there was any chance of her salvaging some happiness after all these years, she certainly deserved it.

If all was well between Ross and herself, maybe he'd want her opinion. And yet, even knowing that, she would not remain silent.

"It is unorthodox, to be sure. But the girls' can still be educated at Dunmor and see Lady Fia each day."

"That," Ross said, "is not the point."

Stung that he had not only interrupted her, but clearly wasn't inclined to even consider her words, she retorted, "The position of steward is highly regarded in Pictland."

"Aye, and in Dal Riada, too. Christ, Dunmor would have fallen into disrepair without Angus' steady hand these last years. But the villagers—"

"The villagers will take their cue from you." Her voice was sharp. "Why should a woman always give up everything, for the sake of a man's cursed honor?"

Silence greeted her. It was clear her outburst had shocked him, and from the corner of her eye she saw Una press her fingers against her lips in clear distress.

She was sorry she'd upset Una. But she wasn't sorry if she'd offended Ross' blinkered notions. Twice she had wed, against the wishes of her goddess, for the sake of her people and because her king had ordered her to do so. Certainly, she could blame only herself for having believed her marriage to Ross was so much more than it truly was, but that was a regret for another day. Today, she was simply infuriated at how Una's life had been torn apart.

And yes, she couldn't deny her fury at how the path that should have been hers had been shattered because of another man's self-conceit.

Except it wasn't fury at her own fate that shredded her heart. And it wasn't Ross who had twisted fate to save his face.

But fury was easier to deal with than the truth, and Raedwulf was back in the Kingdom of Strathclyde and beyond being subject to her ire.

If only it was merely ire she held for Ross.

"Lady Una would forfeit her birthright." Ross' voice was stiff. "She would no longer be welcomed by her fellow nobles and her daughters' statuses would be diminished. You can't tell me that would be condoned in the Kingdom of Fib."

Of course it wouldn't be condoned. It was unthinkable that a Pict noblewoman wed a steward, no matter how highly regarded the man was. But she wasn't going to give Ross the satisfaction of admitting to it.

"Perhaps one should ask Lady Una if she is prepared for the consequences of her actions."

Ross glared at her. "It doesn't matter, Orabel. It won't change the way of the world."

"Is a woman so insignificant in your world she is not deemed worthy enough to even seek her opinion of something that will affect the rest of her life?"

He ground his teeth, and she glared back at him, because how *dare* he pretend, in Fib, that he admired her forthright tongue, when it was nothing but a despicable plot to ensure she lowered her guard around him, and believe he possessed honor?

So that when the trap snapped shut, she didn't even blame him for it.

"I don't see that things are so very different between Dal Riada and Fib in that regard."

The injustice of his barbed words all but took her breath away. It didn't help that, deep inside, she feared he wasn't wrong. But even so, this was different. "I didn't wed to keep my status. I wed to prevent a war."

His jaw flexed, as though she'd struck a nerve, but she couldn't think why her retort would trouble him. They both knew it was the truth.

Even if, in her case, she had been secretly delighted by that turn of events.

"If there had been no threat of war, you know as well as I that a Princess of Fib would never have been permitted to wed a Scots commoner."

"Indeed." Her voice was icy. She had no idea how she managed it. "But here we are. Yet I still wish to see Lady Una happy with the man she loves."

"If Lady Una wishes to remarry, I shall find a suitable match."

Her head pounded at his careless arrogance. As though from a hundred miles away, she heard Angus growl something, but she could not make out the words. Ross glared at her, as though he, too, was oblivious to anyone else, and whatever caution she had clung onto, unraveled.

"You would force her to wed against her will?"

He bared his teeth as though she had just grievously insulted his honor. "I would force no woman to do anything she didn't want."

"You would force me to remain by your side."

"You're my wife," he shot back, as if he genuinely didn't see the hypocrisy of his statement. "And I'm responsible for Una and her daughters. There's nothing more to discuss."

"Ross," Una said faintly. "Please. I do not wish to be the cause of upset between you and the princess."

Shame burned through her as Una's words shook her back to the present. To the fact she and Ross were not alone.

It didn't matter how unjust this situation was. She had no right to display such coarse manners before anyone. Not even to her husband, but she refused to feel bad about that.

She turned to Una, where Angus had his arm around her shoulders in a protective gesture, a stony expression on his face.

"Forgive me, Lady Una. I did not mean to cause you distress. This is not your fault." She hesitated and glanced at Ross' grim face. Why was it that, even now, she had the despairing wish he could somehow convince her everything that had happened in Fib had not been a lie?

"There's no more to be said." The finality in Ross' voice was like a death knell, but the way Una's shoulders slumped, as though, after all these years, she could no longer bear the weight, was too much.

"There is more to be said." The words tumbled from her before she could stop herself and Ross swung around, anger simmering from him like a distant forest fire. But instead of flinging the truth in his face, she pressed her lips together. It was not her truth to tell. And she had already said too much.

"This is not your concern, my lady." His cold words sent shivers along her arms. "Lady Una is the widow of MacIntosh, the noble bloodline that has dwelled in Dunmor for three hundred years. We must all make sacrifices. I regret that this is Lady Una's."

She released a ragged breath. She understood the need for sacrifice. And if she didn't know the real reason why Una had wed Ross' half-brother, she would have agreed with him.

A noblewoman could not marry a steward.

Una deserved her chance of happiness. Yet if she refused to

break her silence on this matter, there was no more Orabel could do.

"I have made sacrifices." Una broke away from Angus' protective arm and straightened her spine as she gazed into Ross' frowning face. She took a deep breath and gripped her fingers together. "You asked me once, ten years ago, why I broke our betrothal. It was to prevent Gordon from besmirching our lady mother's reputation at court. It was no idle threat. I couldn't let that happen. The price for his silence was my hand in marriage."

Relief that Una had revealed the truth flowed through her, but at Ross' prolonged silence, trepidation slithered in its wake. With unnamable reluctance, she looked at him.

His fierce gaze was fixed on Una as though he'd never seen her before, but he still didn't utter a word. And a terrible ache consumed her heart, engulfing the trepidation, because it was starkly obvious that, despite Una's careful words, Ross understood what she hadn't said.

Abruptly, he swung about and marched off and she couldn't drag her eyes from his retreating back. Orabel knew Una would never have broken her silence if she hadn't behaved so unpardonably before her. Dread gripped her. Goddess, what had she done?

"I should not have told him." Grief threaded through Una's words.

"It was time." Angus took her hand and pressed a kiss against her fingers. Such a tender gesture, so filled with love, that Orabel had the absurd desire to weep. "He had to know, my love. There would've been no peace for you otherwise. He'll be all right, you'll see."

She turned and watched Ross, who stood some distance away, his hands gripping his knees. It was the stance of a man who had been cut to the core. It shouldn't affect her so profoundly. Didn't he deserve to suffer?

Yet there was no trace of satisfaction. Only a bone deep wretchedness that all the hopes she'd woven around this political marriage had been made with nothing more substantial than mist.

He may have tricked her into marriage. But he had never wanted Una to suffer on his behalf.

Why did he have to be so complex? Why couldn't he simply be a contemptible man she could easily despise?

She should return to the stronghold and prepare for her departure. There was nothing left to say to Ross, and nothing she wanted to hear from him.

And yet, knowing all this, she slowly made her way to his side.

CHAPTER THIRTY-TWO

*R*oss sucked in great lungfuls of air, but it didn't ease the constriction crushing his chest. Or drown out the knowledge thundering through his head.

Una had wed Gordon to save their lady mother more heartache.

Except that wasn't the full truth. If he'd known of Gordon's threat, he would've challenged him.

And that was why Una had broken the betrothal.

"Ross." Orabel's soft voice penetrated the storm raging through his head and he forced himself upright. Why had she followed him? He hadn't expected her to. But then, he hadn't intended to come to a halt within sight of her, either, but his damn legs had turned to stone.

"Aye." His voice was gruff, and he glowered ahead, seeing nothing. Except, in his mind, all he could see was scornful condemnation in Orabel's beautiful eyes.

When she didn't answer, he reluctantly turned to look at her. But there was no condemnation in her eyes, only sorrow, and somehow that was even worse.

He couldn't stand the silence. "What?"

She shook her head and dropped her gaze to his chest. "I don't know. I had to ensure you are all right, that's all."

He gave a mirthless laugh and dragged his fingers through his hair. "Always the heart of the healer. Even with your despised enemy."

"It's my gift and my burden."

For a delusional moment, he imagined a sad smile tilted her lips.

"Aye. Well, you have no need to waste your gifts on me for a second time. I'll survive."

The way he'd survived all his life. Except now he possessed the knowledge of why Una had wed Gordon, and it made him sick to his stomach.

"I just want to say," she hesitated, and plucked at the fingers of her gloves. He fought the urge to take her hand and pull her close. To bury his face in the scented haven of her hair. To fool himself she had followed him because she cared.

But he knew anything she'd felt for him had died when she'd overheard MacAlpin at Forteviot.

"I just want to say," she repeated, catching his gaze, and he was as lost in those violet depths as the very first time he'd seen her, on that cursed, blood-drenched field. "That whatever Lady Una endured was due solely to the actions of your half-brother. Not you."

How much easier it would be to do the right thing by her, the noble thing, if she flung insults at his head. But her quiet empathy, her insistence, even now, that he was not to blame for his mother's shame and Una's sacrifice, merely tightened the chains around his heart. The chains that linked him to her, irrevocably. Chains that, he feared, would destroy him should he ever set her free.

But as she continued to gaze at him, an eerie shudder inched along his spine. The last time they'd spoken of his tangled family ties had been on the way to Forteviot. When she'd reassured him that, even knowing of his past, her good opinion of him hadn't changed.

But something had caused her hidden anger. Something she hadn't shared with him. Unbidden, the words she'd said with such passion speared through his mind.

I'm enraged by... what women suffer for the fragile pride of men. And I feel this so deeply, but I cannot speak of it.

He'd thought she spoke of his lady mother. And she had. But was she also speaking of what Una had suffered?

"You knew." His voice was hoarse.

"Lady Una did not want you to know." Her voice was hushed. "I couldn't break her confidence. But perhaps you understand now, why it's a good thing I never met your half-brother."

"I would have killed him." His voice was strangely flat, despite the acid eating through him.

"And that's why women keep their counsel."

He exhaled a ragged breath, acknowledging her insight but he couldn't agree with it. Sometimes, the risk in defending the woman one loved was worth it.

It was why he'd defended her against Raedwulf.

Why was it only now, when it was too late, he could accept the truth of his feelings for her?

He dragged his bewitched gaze from her and fixed on the church in the distance behind her. How he'd looked forward to seeing her face when he presented it to her.

It would never happen now. The law might be on his side, but what would he gain by forcing her to stay?

She would only loathe him more with each passing day. Witnessing her growing contempt would be worse, far worse, than severing the chains that bound him to her. At least now she could still look at him and speak kindly, and his last memories of her wouldn't be drenched with bitterness.

It seemed a great fist squeezed inside his chest, cutting off the air, the very blood in his veins. The words to free her lodged in his throat. Unsayable. For once they were uttered, there was no turning back.

Yet he had no choice. He had failed Una. He would not fail Orabel.

But he still couldn't force the words out.

"You believe Una and Angus should be permitted to wed?" He kept his gaze fixed on the church. He wasn't sure that if he looked at her, he'd be able to keep her from seeing the anguish in his heart.

And that he could not bear.

"I believe Lady Una should be given the choice." Her voice was gentle, but he heard what she did not say.

Una should be given the choice that Orabel had been denied.

"Aye."

"I understand it's difficult, with respect to her daughters." Orabel sighed. "But unless you disinherit them, Dunmor will still go to their male heirs, in time. That alone will retain their status in the eyes of the nobles."

He would always see that Fia and Dona would want for nothing. But God. How he secretly craved a child of his own. A child of Orabel's.

But that had never been part of his future.

His gaze traveled from the church, past where Angus still stood with Una, to Dunmor. His childhood home. But without Orabel, what need did he have of his half-brother's ancestral stronghold?

He had no right to live there at all.

But Una did.

He exhaled a shuddering breath. Once Orabel returned to the Kingdom of Fib, there would be no need to continue with the masquerade he'd maintained since Gordon's death.

Una would retain her position as mistress of Dunmor, with Angus by her side. And as for himself…

"I'll live at Duncnoc." How fitting that the boon MacAlpin had bestowed upon him for ensnaring the Princess of Fib, should shelter him once she had left.

There was a long silence. Finally, he could stand it no longer, and reluctantly dragged his gaze back to Orabel. She wasn't looking at him. Instead, she appeared focused on Una and Angus, but then, as though aware of his scrutiny, she tilted her jaw in a regal manner.

"I must pay my respects to Lady Fia," she said. And with that she inclined her head and returned to Saoirse.

THE FOLLOWING DAY, as Orabel stood in the courtyard and watched Neilan swing about to carry out her orders, unease flickered through her. She'd expected her faithful warrior to show at least some satisfaction at the knowledge they were returning to Fib. Instead, he'd appeared oddly grim.

It had to be her imagination. She was simply seeing in Neilan the conflicting emotions that constantly plagued her. But she had made the decision to leave Dunmor, even if Ross expected her to accompany him to Duncnoc—without him even asking her—and once Neilan had dispatched a messenger to Fib, she'd inform Ross of her intentions.

He hadn't shared her bedchamber last night. She told herself she was glad, for she had no wish to endure his touch.

Except what was the point in lying to herself? She missed him dreadfully and despised herself for it. But the bed was empty without him. And she craved their shared banter like a flower craved the sun.

It didn't matter to her foolish heart that it had all been a charade to ensure her compliance in his king's plans.

Was it truly all a charade?

The insistent whisper of dissent gave her no peace. But it didn't matter how much she wished it were true. Just because she didn't want to see the evidence, did not mean it didn't exist.

Before the Scots had even arrived in Fib, her sister had assumed they came for one reason only. To capture another Princess of Pictland. And her king had never trusted any of the Scots. What had he said, when they were all gathered in his war chamber, when Ross had expressed regret for any distress his conduct had caused?

"Your actions have far-reaching consequences, and we find it difficult to accept you were unaware of what they entailed."

How proud she'd been when Ross hadn't immediately grabbed what Dugald had so shamelessly offered. For a man on a mission from his king to ensnare a princess, it was a daring gambit.

As she and Saoirse, followed by the young noblewomen, made their way to her medicinal gardens, she pulled her shawl more securely around her shoulders, even though the breeze was warm. The chill that caused her to shiver came from her heart.

Why *had* he pushed his luck that day? If Dugald had decided not to press the matter, he may have easily lost his chance. Or had he been so certain her king would brook no argument?

Yet the truth remained stark. If Raedwulf hadn't issued his ultimatum, the question of her marrying Ross MacIntosh would never have arisen. Without the warlord's interference, what was the Scots' strategy?

There was a missing piece. She was certain of it. Yet, in the end, what did it matter? It changed nothing.

How easily she'd believed Ross when he confided he had no wish to marry, since he didn't intend to sire children.

But he didn't lie about that.

Why did she find it so hard to condemn him, when he had

offered no defense of his king's words when she'd confronted him in Forteviot?

They reached the gardens that she'd tended so carefully since arriving at Dunmor.

"I'm not certain how many of the plants will survive another journey so soon," she said to Saoirse.

"We shall do the best we can," her friend assured her, but it was clear Saoirse had her doubts, too.

Maybe she would leave some of them here for Una to tend. Those that had helped Lady Fia. She gave a ragged sigh. She would miss both women. How had she become so entangled in the lives of her husband's kin?

Lady Fia had not only remembered her, when she'd paid her respects yesterday. She'd appeared delighted to see her and had conversed quite eloquently about her granddaughters and the fine weather. Orabel wasn't certain the older lady had yet connected she was wed to her son, but that didn't really matter, since she was soon leaving Dunmor.

The prospect of returning to Fib-eviot was dispiriting. Etain would never allow her to forget how she had failed at her task. And since she wasn't a widow, she could not be married off again for another advantageous alliance.

Perhaps, after all, she had returned to the path Bride had set before her. One where she could dedicate her life to her goddess and her healing arts, without the distracting danger of a husband or unwanted betrothal.

And before meeting Ross, how dearly she would have welcomed such a future.

Her gaze traveled from her precious herbs to the adjoining church. She had never been inside. Had never wanted to. Like many of the churches in Pictland, it had been constructed on sacred ground that the ancient ones had claimed countless years ago, but despite that, she had never felt her goddess' displeasure whenever she worked in her gardens.

In fact, except for the one vision she'd had after finding that bloodstain in Lady Fia's tower, she hadn't felt her goddess' displeasure at all since moving to Dunmor.

How different from when she'd lived in Northumbria, when distressing dreams had plagued her nightly.

She went over to the large arched door, but it suddenly swung open, revealing Ross.

Hastily, she stepped back, lest they accidentally touched, and he guessed how easily he could discompose her. Goddess, why didn't he say something, instead of staring at her as though she were an unwelcome shade?

Since it was very possible he did consider her presence unwelcome, she forced a smile to her face. She would not apologize for deciding to investigate the Christian church. Such a thing was not forbidden.

"My lady." He gave a formal bow of his head which sent a pain lancing through her breast. But this distance between them was for the best. And soon, the distance would be far greater.

She inclined her head. "I thought to explore the church, before—" she bit off her words. She hadn't yet told him her plans for returning to Fib-eviot and for a reason she didn't want to probe, she didn't want to spoil this moment with such a fraught discussion.

The silence hung between them, like a battle-ax waiting to fall.

It was excruciating. She should turn and walk away but her feet were rooted to the spot and her tongue refused to articulate intelligible words.

Finally, he stood back, allowing her entry, and she stepped inside.

There was no screen separating the chancel from the rest of the church, and no altar, either. Fresh straw covered the floor, the scent of heather permeated the air, and a freshly scrubbed aura emanated from the stone walls.

It wasn't what she'd expected. Were Scots' churches so different from the ones that had been constructed in Pictland?

Ross folded his arms and glared at a spot on the far wall. "I know it isn't as convenient or portable as a coconut." He practically spat the word and she stared at him, quite unnerved. A coconut? Had she misheard? Where was the connection between a coconut and a Christian church?

He cast her a dark, sideways glance, before returning his attention to the wall. A ferocious frown carved his brow. "When we spoke in Fib, your wish for a sanctuary to heal those in need touched me. I wanted to give you a worthy wedding gift."

He snapped his jaw shut, as though he'd been about to say more but thought better of it.

Great goddess. Surely, he was not suggesting...

She licked her lips. "A sanctuary?" Her voice sounded hoarse, but if he was suggesting what she thought he was, it was a miracle she could say anything at all.

"Aye. It seemed like a good idea. Situated next to your medicinal gardens. I know nothing of sanctuaries. But I hoped you might be able to make something of this."

"You would have given me a Christian church for a sanctuary in my goddess' name?"

Finally, he looked at her. "I trust the irony isn't lost on you. Neilan found it drily amusing, I'm sure."

"Neilan knew of this?" She could scarcely believe her faithful warrior hadn't said a word about it.

"I asked him to keep his counsel. He magnanimously said he'd consider it."

She let out a shaky breath. "This is... I do not know what to think. I've always longed to set up a sanctuary for those in need."

"I know." He gave a half smile that hurt her heart so profoundly, she could barely breathe. "I wasn't going to tell you. No point. But then you were at the door and..." he gave a heavy sigh and ran his hand through his hair in a gesture so heartbreakingly familiar she wondered how she could live the rest of her life without witnessing it again.

"It is the perfect gift," she said softly, and then, swirling through the confusion in her mind, the reason for his odd comment about the coconut came to her.

Whatever the truth of their marriage, he had taken exception to Raedwulf. And although she should keep silent, for why should she wish to comfort a man who had so easily deceived her, a contrary part of her wanted to know how deeply this gift touched her. "More thoughtful than even a coconut."

He grunted and focused on his boots. "A pity you'll never have the chance to use it."

Well, that was true. But not because she intended to accompany him to his newly acquired stronghold. Yet she still couldn't find it within herself to shatter this fragile peace between them.

"Nevertheless, I appreciate the thought."

"Christ, Orabel." He squeezed his eyes shut for a heart wrenching moment, before shaking his head and fixing his fierce blue gaze on her. "If I could go back in time to Fib and save you from this heartache, I would. Even if it killed me. You were right, what you said in your goddess' cave. I've worn my façade so convincingly, for so long, I scarcely know how to function without it. But that's no excuse for how I misled you. I should have explained why I had no right to Dunmor, so you understood what awaited you here. God knows, if I'd shared the truth, your king would never have approved our union."

Stunned, she stared at him as the condemning words she'd flung at him in the sacred cave echoed through her mind.

How proud you must be, to have worn your façade so convincingly.

She'd been so sure he'd lied to her from the moment they had met. And Ross' reaction at her condemnation had merely reinforced her certainty.

But the façade he wore was not the one she'd accused him of.

"You deserve more than to be a prestigious hostage in MacAlpin's game. I can't give you back the freedom you possessed before we wed. But I free you from the chains of this marriage, in all but name, so you can return to your homeland and continue the work your goddess commands of you."

She clutched the edges of her shawl, as his words thundered through her mind.

He was setting her free. Without her even having to raise the subject with him.

And most assuredly, against the wishes of his king.

Once, she'd feared banishment from Bride's benevolence should she wed again against her goddess' command. But, just as when she'd lived in Northumbria, Bride hadn't withheld her knowledge when Orabel had treated the local villagers.

Have I been wrong about what my goddess wants of me?

Her tangled thoughts and half-formed questions pounded in her head, threaded through with the mocking words she'd overheard MacAlpin say.

"Ross," she whispered, but before she could even formulate a coherent response, a shadow darkened the door, and she swung around.

Rourke stood there, with his customary glower upon his face, and frustration tore through her. Why had he come here, now?

"Roake." Ross sounded as irked as she felt. "What the hell?"

The other man grunted, and a chill slithered along her spine. *Please don't let him have overheard our conversation.*

"MacAlpin sends word. He did not wish to entrust the news to a messenger."

Curse the man, and his messenger, too. She had the feeling she and Ross would never have the chance again to speak so freely. And she so dearly wanted to ask him *why* he chose to go against the wishes of his king.

At Rourke's prolonged silence, Ross exhaled an impatient

sigh. "What is it, man? You may speak freely in front of the princess. She is more than aware of our political situation."

Indeed, she was. But would a man who was prepared to risk deliberately poisoning himself, or dying in a challenge with a warlord for his king, extend her such a courtesy?

Rourke grunted. "I doubt any princess of Pictland is unaware of MacAlpin's strategy by now."

"God damnit, Rourke." Ross sounded furious. "Watch your mouth."

"Doubtless there are many reasons why the princess might despise you," Rourke said, clearly oblivious to Ross' ire, or her own disbelief in his candidness. "But I will have her know we did not have orders to trap her when we entered the Kingdom of Fib."

"Is that all?" Ross glared at the other Scot as if he'd like to throttle him.

Rourke was silent as though considering the matter. Finally, he spoke. "Aye."

"In that case," Ross said, but Rourke interrupted him.

"MacAlpin is transferring Columba's relics from Iona to Fortriu."

She had heard of Columba, the monk from Eire, who had brought his new religion to Pictland nearly three hundred years ago. The treasures buried with him was one of the reasons why the cursed Vikings persisted in attacking the Isle of Iona.

"Are the Norse attacking again?" Ross sounded grim.

"No," Rourke said. "It appears since the king secured Forteviot, he's been negotiating with the Norse. In exchange for the hand of MacAlpin's youngest princess and a dozen of the Southern Inner Isles to the jarls' king, Eric Anundsson, they will turn their eyes from Dal Riada."

"I doubt a daughter of Dunadd will satisfy the Norsemen's thirst to conquer the land."

"Agreed. But MacAlpin has the alliance with Pictland on his side to stop the snakes…"

The sound of Rourke's voice faded, and a great roaring filled the church as the ground split asunder. Two mighty serpents erupted from the breach, their dark eyes gleaming with malice and crimson blood dripping from their fangs.

The sound of battle echoed around the walls and then the stone church vanished, replaced by the sacred cave of Bride, and once again she could only watch, paralyzed, as flames engulfed the dancing lights and smoke choked the waterfall.

You must heal the rift that threatens our land.

She gasped and stumbled back as lightning flashed through her brain and a shudder wracked her body.

The twin serpents that threatened Pictland were Viking and Northumbrian. And if the alliance between Pict and Scot should fracture, the serpents would claim their land.

The sacred places would be lost. The knowledge of the old ways buried forever.

And the ancient ones would fall.

Strong arms wrapped around her, pulling her close to a familiar, rock-hard body. Through the turmoil, she heard Ross calling her name, pulling her back from the brink, anchoring her in the realm of mortals.

Her breath stuttered, heart raced, and through the constriction in her throat she managed to gasp, "To survive we must unite, or perish."

Lady Catriona had been right. The great goddess herself had invited Ross into her sacred sanctuary, to show Orabel she was, indeed, on the right path. That it was only with Ross by her side that Pictland stood any chance of healing the rift that threatened their land.

That Pict and Scot stood together, against their mutual enemies.

Just as Lady Catriona had seen in Forteviot, Bride had never forsaken her. It was she who had been blind to the truth. And she had so very nearly strayed from the path her goddess had set before her.

"Find the truth, my lady, and you will find the answer your heart craves."

oss crushed Orabel against his chest, his heart hammering in unnamed terror. Her eyes had gone blank, as though she saw something beyond man's comprehension, and her whispered words had struck dread through his soul.

"Orabel." His voice was harsh and only when she dragged in a great breath and her rigid body relaxed against his, did the fear gripping him ebb. "I'll take you back to the stronghold."

By rights, he should allow Lady Saoirse and the young noblewomen to accompany her, but if this was the last time he'd ever hold her in his arms, he intended to make the most of it.

"I'm quite well, Ross," she said, as they left the church, but she didn't attempt to pull away from him. "But we need to speak in private."

She was right. They did. There was much to discuss and arrange, but if he could delay the inevitable by even a few wretched hours, he would.

"We will. But not until I'm certain you're all right."

"I finally understand the visions my beloved goddess has shared with me," she whispered, and eerie shudders prickled along his arms. He wasn't certain he wanted to hear about her visions, but if that was the price of her remaining within his embrace, it was a small one to pay.

"That's good," he said, as they crossed the courtyard and entered the stronghold, Rourke following some distance behind them, with Orabel's ladies. Thank God for small mercies. He didn't want Rourke overhearing anything Orabel might share.

"Bride has been guiding me all along. I didn't make the wrong choice, Ross."

If only she meant what he wished she meant. But even though that was too much to hope for he couldn't stop himself. "You made the right choice in wedding me?"

She gazed at him, and even though they weren't alone in the great hall, she may as well have been the only woman in the world.

Because, God help him, as far as he was concerned, she was.

"I—"

"Ross." His lady mother's agitated voice cut through whatever Orabel had been going to say, and he clamped down hard on the frustration that roared through him. With anyone else, he would've told them to leave. But he would never treat his beloved mother with such disrespect.

"Lady Fia." Orabel sounded alarmed. "Is something amiss?"

Despair gripped his heart. Yesterday, it had been hard to fathom she was the same woman from three months ago. But now, there was a wild look in her eyes as her frantic glance darted between him and Orabel.

"Let me find your serving woman," he said, but she grasped his arm, and shook her head.

"Una tries so hard to hide it, but she is sorely distressed."

Fuck. He didn't want to have this conversation now. Or face the truth that, whatever miracle had enriched his mother's life for the last few weeks had now died.

"Una will be all right," he assured his mother. At least, she would be, once he told her she had his blessing to wed Angus.

"But if she leaves—"

"She won't leave." Where had his mother got that idea from him? He cast a despairing glance at Orabel, and the compassion in her eyes was almost his undoing. "Una will always be mistress of Dunmor. You have my word."

"But that is not right. Lady Orabel… the Princess of Fib, is your wife. She is the mistress of Dunmor."

Of all the times for her to finally understand that Orabel was his wife, why now?

"The princess must return to the Kingdom of Fib." Somehow, he managed to keep his voice even although God knew how. "Una will continue here, as she always has."

"I've just come from Una's chamber, and I do not believe she wishes to stay."

He forced what he hoped was a reassuring smile to his face. "I shall speak with her."

"I was grieved when Gordon wed Una in your stead." She clutched Orabel's hand, her gaze still fixed on him. "Alas, he grew into a cruel man, like his father. I could not bear to see your suffering, Ross, but now I understand. It was because you are destined for Lady Orabel."

Aye. For one shining moment, he'd believed that, too. "We cannot rewrite the past."

"What do you understand, Lady Fia?" Orabel's voice was hushed, as though his mother had just revealed something he had missed.

"Confined to the tower, where my beloved died, my mind filled with fog and confusion as I tried to deny what had happened. But I feel… at last, the sun is shining through the clouds again and I understand Una was never meant for Ross."

Guilt twisted through him at all she had suffered. But even if

Orabel took his heart with her back to Fib, at least she'd freed his lady mother from the prison of her mind.

"Your beloved died in the tower?"

Ross shot Orabel a sharp look. What the hell?

"Aye," his lady mother said, and such sadness vibrated through that one word, a shiver crawled over his arms. "It was wrong of me to break my vows to my husband, even if we had lived as strangers for years. I loved Duncan with all my heart, but we didn't betray his lady wife, the sweet Athdara. Duncan had been widowed for two years before I sinned."

His mother's quiet words echoed in his head, growing louder with every heavy beat of his heart.

I loved Duncan with all my heart.

That was not the whispered confession of a woman who had been...

His mind clamped down on the word, but it squeezed through his brain, regardless.

Violated.

God help him, he couldn't ask her. Even now.

"Lady Fia, you did not sin."

"My sin was great." His mother's voice dropped so low, he could scarcely hear her over the thunder that filled his head. "I accepted I would be punished for my transgressions, but God forgive me, I did not imagine Duncan would pay the price."

His palms were sweaty, and he fisted his hands, but it didn't stop the unnatural echoes that collided around the stone walls of the hall. Or help ease the tight band that wrapped around his chest like a vise.

Duncan. Long dormant memories stirred in the deepest corners of his mind. He knew that name. God help him.

"The price?" It didn't sound like his voice. Orabel took his hand, loosened his death grip, and threaded her fingers through his as though, impossibly, she had guessed his outrageous thoughts. But that could not be, for he didn't even understand the scrambled fragments that slashed through his mind like shards of glass.

His mother pressed her palm against his chest. "Your father," she whispered. "The true master of Dunmor, until his younger brother, my husband, slayed him in the tower while I begged for mercy. You were my only light during those dark times, Ross, and I deeply regret I was not strong enough to withstand the punishment my husband inflicted."

Orabel drew in a sharp breath. "He forced you to live in the tower, where he had murdered his own brother in front of you. That's what Bride tried to show me the first day I arrived here."

Ross tore his gaze from his mother to Orabel. Her comment made little sense, but right now, nothing made sense. Except he wasn't the product of rape. His lady mother had not been violated by an unknown vagabond. And his conception and birth were not the reason why her mind had retreated from the real world.

"My husband accepted you as his own, so he would not be disgraced at court." His mother drew in a ragged breath, pain etched on her face. "But of course, he didn't accept you in his heart. And I… I'm so sorry I failed to protect you the way I should have."

"Lady Fia," Orabel said, in that gentle tone he'd learned disguised a formidable strength of will. "You're not to blame for how your mind tried to heal from what you witnessed. We must be thankful that the goddess—" She cut herself off, and a fleeting expression of discordance flashed over her face. "Or, perhaps, your God, has allowed the light to once again enter your soul."

He should say something. Anything. His throat ached and head pounded, but somehow, he pushed out a single word.

"Christ."

Fuck. He couldn't even summon up a coherent sentence. He sucked in a harsh breath and, disjointedly, saw how Orabel held both his hand, and his lady mother's hand, and how his mother still had her palm pressed against his chest.

"My lady mother." Una hurried across the hall to their side. Her face was pale, and it looked as though she had been weeping, and she avoided looking at him. "I apologize, my lady," she added, glancing at Orabel. "I fear I inadvertently upset Lady Fia."

His world had been turned inside out but there was one thing he was clear on. "Una, you and Angus have my blessing to wed. We'll discuss the details later."

Her face transformed, as though she had been living in shadows for untold years and the sun had suddenly appeared. "Ross, do you mean it? Oh, God. Thank you." She swung around and gazed at Orabel. "Thank you, my lady, from the bottom of my heart."

She took his mother's arm, and they walked off together, and for the first time he noticed that he and Orabel were alone in the hall. He had no recollection of when it had emptied, but he was profoundly grateful for it.

Silence stretched between them, filled with a thousand unsaid things. But at least she still held his hand.

And as the maelstrom in his head slowed its frenzied roar, a faint echo wound its way through the chaos.

Your father. The true master of Dunmor.

"Ross," Orabel whispered. "You need never wear your façade again. You are the rightful master of Dunmor."

It was like she could peel back the layers of his mind and read his innermost thoughts. But then, he supposed it wasn't that hard to guess where his thoughts dwelled. He bowed his head and drank in the sight of their entwined fingers. What did he care if he was the rightful master or not, if she wasn't by his side?

He wanted to ask her to stay. To tell her everything she meant to him. But it was easier to speak of other things. "You'll never know how grateful I am that your wisdom gave my lady mother her life back."

"It was the goddess," she said quietly. "I didn't know what ailed Lady Fia. I only knew what might ease her trouble. It was Bride who understood what must be done."

There was no point arguing with her. She'd said the same when he'd thanked her for saving his own life in Fib.

"I feel we've had this discussion before." He gave her a rueful smile. "Do you never accept your patients' gratitude?"

She didn't smile in response, and instinctively, his fingers tightened around hers, as if that could in any way prevent her from pulling free if she wished to.

"I feel I owe you an explanation." Her gaze dropped to his chest. "I ordered my men to find the arrow that injured you, to try and determine what had happened. It's true, it was Pict made, and that's the reason my king commanded it be kept from you." She glanced up at him, and their gazes meshed. "But it wasn't the royal house behind the ambush. We believed it to be a plot of the Northumbrians, to drive a wedge between the alliance and compromise Fib. If you had died, and your king had sought retribution, we would have had no choice but to embrace Raed-wulf as our ally, with a political marriage."

"Aye. It seems the Northumbrians will go to any lengths to destabilize the alliance. There was a fatal flaw in their plan though. They didn't account for your healing skill."

"I can only believe the goddess led me to you that day, Ross. If we hadn't found you when we did, it would have been too late to save you."

"Orabel." He knew he risked this fragile peace if he spoke his mind, but he had to clear the air. Even if she left Dunmor, he wanted her to know the truth. "I didn't tell you everything, in your goddess' sacred cave. When we were ordered to go to Fib-eviot, MacAlpin's man, MacAllister, told me that if we discovered a treaty between Fib and Northumbria, to eliminate that threat by any means possible. I know how MacAlpin's words must have sounded to you when you overheard him at Forteviot. But I swear to you, entrapping you into matrimony was not the order given to me."

"Yet it appears clear that your king's plan all along was for us to wed. How could he be so sure it would succeed when he kept you in the dark?"

He'd hoped, by confessing the truth, she would instantly forgive him for everything she had endured. But still he took hope from her words. Because at least she no longer believed he had traveled to Fib with the sole purpose of misleading her into marriage.

"That I cannot tell you." He sighed, and unbidden, a memory surfaced. Of how MacAllister had reacted to the fallout of Ross' rash proclamation that he and Orabel were betrothed.

By rights, the king's man should have had his head for such impudence. Instead, MacAllister had appeared bizarrely amused.

As though the development, although unexpected, did not entirely surprise him.

His king's words in Forteviot echoed through his mind. *"We confess we had our doubts when Conall advised caution, but once again, he was right."*

He was right? Right about what?

"Ross?" Uncertainty threaded through the word. "What is it?"

He gazed into her eyes. They were no longer filled with contempt. But if he told her the truth, would she think he was lying? In the end, he had no choice, since the truth was all he could share with her. "I don't know. But MacAllister has always had this uncanny ability to understand things others do not."

She didn't mock him. Then again, why would she? She understood many things that were beyond the grasp of everyone else he knew.

"It's possible your king knew of the Northumbrians intention to visit Fib," she said. "Spies are everywhere. But since you were not under orders to wed me at any cost, I don't understand why you put yourself in such jeopardy when you confronted Raedwulf."

The surge of anger that had consumed him that day burned through him once again. "No man, prince or not, shall dare disrespect you without facing my wrath."

"But it wasn't your place to defend my honor. Raedwulf is a prince of Strathclyde and would never tolerate such temerity. You knew—you must have known—what the consequences could have been. I shall tell you now, Ross, I'm not certain I will ever forget the fear that clutched my heart when he challenged you."

Warmth seeped through him at her confession, even if condemnation threaded through her words, for at least she cared that much for him.

"I'm sorry for that. It was never my intention to hurt you."

She gave a brief nod but didn't say anything. As though she was waiting for him to continue.

His chest tightened, and a strange churning sensation assailed his gut. It had taken him far too long to face the simple truth of why he'd risked his neck that day. Yet the thought of sharing that with her, of pushing out a few tortured words, damn near paralyzed him.

He couldn't do it. But God help him. He didn't want to let her go. "Stay with me."

Her bottom lip trembled. Just once. She might just as well have thrust his own sword through his heart.

"Why should I?" she whispered, and he pressed his forehead against hers, so he wouldn't see her face if his confession was the last thing she wanted to hear.

"You asked me why I confronted Raedwulf." His voice was hoarse and briefly, he squeezed his eyes shut. "It was reckless. My king or yours could have demanded my head for my actions. But I wasn't thinking of the consequences, Orabel. I saw only a man who wanted you for political gain. A man who showed you not even a glimmer of the respect you deserve. A prince, aye, and I am merely a foreign commoner, but I couldn't remain silent."

She drew in a shaky breath, and he wrapped his arm around her shoulders. But he still couldn't risk looking into her eyes. Because he still hadn't said all that needed to be said.

"All these weeks, I've avoided the truth. The reason why I risked my neck for a beautiful princess who did not even want my help. I never wanted to love again. But you stole my heart the first time I saw you, and I believe I knew, even then, that a fleeting liaison could never be enough."

She raised her head, forcing him to look at her. "Ross," she whispered. "You were the missing piece."

He didn't know what she meant, and he couldn't risk asking her now. Because even if he no longer had the flimsy protection of not seeing her face as he spilled his heart at her feet, he couldn't stop now. He knew, if he did, he might never say what she needed to hear.

"I love you, Orabel, Princess Annag of Fib. I love you for how you work miracles with your magical herbs, and your kind heart that sees paths where others cannot. You showed me I was worthy of respect when I'd lived all my life burdened by shadows. I love your laugh, and when you frown, and as God's my witness, had I known I was sent to Fib with the intention to entrap you, I'd have done all in my power to secure your continued freedom instead."

Her fingers traced along the line of his jaw. A tender touch and one that forcefully reminded him of everything he could so easily lose if Orabel turned her back on him. Grimly, he braced himself for her response.

"It's as well you did not know then." Her voice was husky and the hint of tears shimmered in her beautiful violet eyes. "How lonely my existence would be, without you in my life."

She isn't turning her back. Relief flooded through him, so visceral, he damn near swayed where he stood, like a drunken fool. But he could do nothing to prevent his grin.

"You'll stay?" He needed to hear her say the words, to promise she would never leave.

"Yes. I'll stay. How could I leave the only man I've ever loved, when he sees me more clearly than I see myself?"

A wild, raw protectiveness seared him, unlike anything he'd experienced before. "I shall build you another sanctuary at Duncnoc. One to your specifications, so it has everything the way you wish."

"I love the one you gave me here, Ross. Do you truly wish to leave Dunmor, now you know the truth?"

He hadn't thought about it. But now he did. In truth, he'd prefer to stay, for the sake of his lady mother and for the father he had never known.

"My home is wherever you are," he said. "Yet I cannot tell Una to leave the only home she's known since she was a child. And her daughters—"

"I believe," Orabel said softly. "You may find Lady Una is happy to leave Dunmor to start her new life with Angus. Without the memories of her first husband clinging to every stone."

Aye, he had to acknowledge Orabel was likely right. What was more, Duncnoc wasn't far from Dunmor, so his lady mother would still often see her beloved granddaughters. Maybe he'd bequeath Duncnoc to any future son Una and Angus had, and in the meantime, Angus could be the custodian. He was certain MacAlpin would disapprove of his bestowal being used in such a manner, and what could be more fitting?

"Are you happy to live here?" He drew in a shuddering breath. The truth would take some time to sink in. "In the stronghold of my forefathers?"

"I am. And there's something we should discuss, Ross."

"Aye. We should discuss how devoted you are to your husband."

"I've no objection to that. But I am thinking of something else."

His smile faded at the thread of concern in her voice. "What is it?"

"It is just, over the last few days, I've realized I misunderstood some of my beloved goddess' wishes. Things I thought she did not wish for me but now I see… I was wrong. And it makes me wonder if, now you know Dunmor is your legacy through the blood of your father, whether, perhaps, you might one day change your mind about siring a babe with me?"

"Is this something you want?" His voice was hushed, and it didn't escape him that, until he'd given his heart to Orabel, such a question would never even have entered his head.

"With you?' She gave a soft laugh and pressed her hand against his heart. "Yes, it is."

He cradled her face, his sweet wife, his reason for living. On their wedding night, she'd told him she was made of firmer stuff than mountain mist, but he hadn't believed her. In his eyes, she had been a fragile princess entrusted into his protection.

But she had been right, as, he had learned, she invariably was.

"You'll never vanish like the mountain mist in the morning, Orabel. You're more than that. You are of the mountains of Pictland herself."

With a smile that cast out for all time the lingering fragments of darkness from his soul, she wound her arms around his waist and her kiss held every promise of forever.

ABOUT THE AUTHOR

Christina Phillips is an ex-pat Brit who now lives in sunny Western Australia with her high school sweetheart and their family. She enjoys writing historical fantasy romance, paranormal romance and contemporary romance, where the stories sizzle and the heroine brings her hero to his knees.

She is addicted to good coffee, expensive chocolate, and bad boy heroes. She is also owned by three gorgeous cats who are convinced the universe revolves around their needs. They are not wrong.

Book 6 in **The Highland Warrior Chronicles** coming soon!

Join my newsletter to keep up to date with my release schedule (After my welcome emails, I only send one newsletter a month)

Visit Christina's store: ChristinaPhillips.com and sign up for her newsletter here:
ChristinaPhillips.com/pages/newsletter

AUTHOR'S NOTE

The origin of the Stone of Destiny, aka the Stone of Scone, is shrouded in mystery. Legend has it this sandstone rock was used as a pillow by the biblical figure, Jacob, more than three thousand years ago, although this is unlikely.

What is known for sure is that the Stone was used as a crowning seat in Scone Palace, Perthshire, for Scottish monarchs between the 9th and 13th centuries. In 1276, King Edward I of England stole the Stone and took it to Westminster Abbey, London, where it's since been used in the coronation of every English monarch.

In 1996 the Stone was finally returned to Scotland, and now resides in Edinburgh Castle.